HUMMINGBIRD BROKEN WINGS

SPENCER K. PRESCOTT

First paperback edition October 2020

Book Cover Design by ebooklaunch.com

ISBN 978-0-578-74323-3 (paperback)
ISBN 978-0-578-74324-0 (ebook)

www.spencerkprescott.com

To my husband for giving me the love story only found in fairy tales. This was achievable because of you.

To my three children, who I adore deeply. I dream for you.

To my parents for allowing me to watch all those wonderfully scary movies from a young age. I am inspired by you.

To my only sibling, who has always had my back. I am fearless because of you.

To those who believe in the unknown. I write for you.

Spencer

The physical body begins the process of dying at birth;
it's the soul that thrives.

TABLE OF CONTENTS

CHAPTER 1

TABS & BLANKS

I made my last walk to Allison Creek High, staring up the front steps one last time. Was one piece of paper worth the swirling sensation building inside of me? When school let out in the spring, I had made what I thought was my last walk away. I was the first-ever in the Creeks' history to graduate a whole year early. Despite all the positive attention, some lazy administrative assistant forgot to add my name to the print list for diplomas. Thankfully, I didn't attend the graduation ceremony, so there was no awkward, embarrassing moment of silence waiting on stage for a piece of paper that had yet to exist.

My stomach churned. Today was the last day I could retrieve my diploma without navigating my way through a body of students I didn't care to see. With each stride up the old stone steps, I stomped out all the things I wanted to forget. I tugged on the door handle, my throat tightened. Had my old counselor, Mrs. Pickett, forgotten I was coming? With a few more strong yanks, it opened. The smell of all things school, mixed with profound silence, sent a wave of chills through my limbs. My steps echoed through the centuries-old building. Classroom doors stood propped open in preparation for the next day's events. *Welcome back* signs, mixed with fall athletic posters, covered the once-bare walls.

Heavy taps from Mrs. Pickett's loafers approached. She owned a pair in black, brown, and maroon. They were the only shoes she ever wore, and at 5 feet tall, she never cared to add a few more inches.

"Abby, hi there! So good to see you," she said.

Mrs. Pickett was a third-generation Creeker. She knew every family and all the latest in scandalous gossip. Unfortunately for me, my family name was often included. Even still, she liked me. She worked hard to find opportunities I couldn't explore.

She moved in with a squeeze and all the intensity you would expect from a high school guidance counselor.

"Come to my office. I have it in there, all ready for you," she said. Her fingertips bounced off one another in a clapping motion as she hurried me along the multicolor blocked-tile floor.

I moved with her, preparing for the one-sided conversation coming with my arrival. Her round stature never slowed as she maneuvered up the stairs and to the right.

"How was your summer?" she asked.

I offered the vaguest and most hated response ever, "Fine." It was an appropriate answer, and the one meant to deter further questions. Still, Mrs. Pickett wasn't interested in ending our conversation so soon.

"You had to have done something fun?" she asked, and with her pent-up energy, she fluffed her bob, periodically looking over her shoulder at me. With every instance of eye contact, I gave a quick smile that digressed into a frown and a sigh as she turned away.

"Sure, I went on a few antiquing trips with my aunt and laughed, on occasion," I said, just wanting to get my diploma and leave. The emptiness of the school started drawing my attention away from her. I had never seen it so still or heard it so quiet other than the occasional swooshing sound of a mop brushing across the floor by another new janitor. But she was quick to shift my focus back, front, and center.

"What about your friends? Have you connected with any of them?" she went on.

"No, they're all still connected to Ben," I grunted.

She sighed, even louder, "I was hoping you would make a few new friends this summer and maybe even find a better suitor?"

"Suitor, no. Friends, well if you count all the women over fifty who shop at our store, then I'm doing just fine," I replied. Mrs. Pickett was used to my sarcasm and the one person least affected by it.

We rounded one last corner into her office on the right. Bookcases sat side-by-side around the boxy room, and bright posters with bold phrases meant to motivate covered the walls. The sweet aroma of brewed coffee filled the tiny space. I chuckled under my breath. Mrs. Pickett needed no encouragement or caffeine.

She began typing on her computer, focusing on the screen as she moved and clicked her mouse. "As much as I would like to press on about what you actually did this summer, I don't want to lose sight of why you're here. The school already failed you once."

Ha! Once, I thought, optimism at its best. I gave her credit for all the concern and decided to patiently wait for my diploma. Then the sound of music blared out of her computer speakers. I cringed. It was the graduation march. She spoke over it, clapping loudly.

"The first-ever in our history to graduate early and with honors; I am so proud of you," she said.

"This really isn't necessary," I replied.

She was pleased with her mock ceremony. I fidgeted with my clothes and avoided any awkward eye contact, thankful I didn't do this on a day with a full student body meandering around in the hall. She hummed along until it finally finished.

"Now tell me; what are you doing—what's your big plan?"

She stood behind her desk perfectly poised, pressing her lips together, holding back as much of her giant smile as she could, while she waited for my response. I hated disappointing someone who put forth so much faith and energy into my success, but she would see me around town, so lying wasn't an option.

"I'm taking this semester to figure things out. My mom needs help at our store, so I need to be responsible and do the right thing. I have time," I told her.

Her smile drooped with every word I spoke.

"Yes, you do. But don't you waste it," she said. "Few get the chance to gain an entire year in their lives. Make this year count for you." Her shoulders slouched forward as she opened the top drawer of her desk to retrieve my diploma. I wanted to grab it, run, and avoid any more discussion.

"I love our store, it counts for something," I said, but she ignored me.

"Did you get into any of the schools you applied to?" She fanned herself with my diploma.

"Yes, but I can't go spending money my mom doesn't have while trying to figure it all out. It seems like an expensive way to do things." I didn't want to be rude, but the truth was I never sent in my applications or even finished them. College was not an option this year, and I didn't want to defend my decisions to someone who didn't want to understand.

"Sure, but the scholarships?" she asked quietly. It didn't matter my excuse, she found an answer to any obstacle I threw her way. Copies of scholarship opportunities landed in my locker every week last fall. For nine months, she tried her best to give me the guidance I lacked; not going to college was not only unacceptable to her but incomprehensible.

"They didn't pan out. Look, thank you so much for getting this printed. It means a great deal to have it, but I have to get back to the store and help my mom close up for the day." I reached forward, placing my right hand on the maroon diploma case tracing the gold letters embossed in the leather, *Allison Creek High.* Mrs. Pickett released her hand, allowing me to open and fixate on my name, Abigail K. Anderson. Images of what my mom and dad would've looked like standing proudly in the audience ran through my head. I fought back tears. I clutched my diploma, hoping, wherever my dad's spirit was, he could see it and send a positive sign. Nothing.

"Are you okay?" Mrs. Pickett asked, her right hand reaching for mine.

I closed the case before she made contact and widened my eyes so the tears wouldn't spill.

"Thank you again for this. I appreciate everything you've ever done for me. Have a great year," I said, trying to withdraw from her space.

But Mrs. Pickett grabbed my left hand and cradled it in hers. "Please come back and see me. At the very least, keep me posted on your plans. If not, I will come find you at your store," she said. She smiled wide and gave another giant squeeze before I retreated down the steps to the main hall. I stopped and listened. She was playing the processional again. I shook my head and moved on.

I walked past the glass cases that ran along both sides of the hall with my diploma under my arm. They held a variety of trophies in all sizes from the different sports programs. The mirrored wall made the cases look expansive and deep. They were full of accolades and there were far more awards for groups like the Debate Club and the Science Olympiad, but they were tucked back into the corners and behind the pictures of star athletes.

The school had dedicated an entire section to the Allison High Wrestling Team, with decades of pictures filling every square inch.

"Benjamin Reyes State Runner Up 1999, 130 lb. Weight Division; Benjamin Reyes State Champion, 130 lb. Weight Division." My teeth gritted. Ben.

Pictures and newspaper articles with Ben, our Athletic Director, and even Mayor Quartano flagged the trophies and plaques. In the largest picture, and after his latest win, he stood side by side with his coach, who held his arm high with his hand forming the number one. Memories of how my life with Ben would change after that moment crept back in. I hated being so right about my intuitions. It only prolonged the misery.

Catching a glimpse of a shadow reflecting off the mirror, I froze. *Was it Mrs. Pickett again? Or maybe even the janitor lurking around with his bucket?* I spun around, but no one was there. It was me, an icy chill in the air and another case of very dated pictures. I chalked up my heightened senses to an environment that brought a mix of emotions and decided to view the next glass cabinet.

History was one of my favorite subjects, but after three years of running in and out of this school, I realized I paid no attention to the school's backstory. Black and white photos of the town sat on wooden plaques, with dates etched in from the early 1800s. The original schoolhouse, which now sat behind the high school, was a one-room brick house with a large chimney billowing with smoke from the wood burner. The original town hall, now the library, showcased three men dressed in their Sunday best on a wintery day. Sidestepping toward the front of the school, I viewed each case like a child witnessing the beauty of a giant aquarium for the first time.

Wrinkled pictures of families with their little girls in dresses and bonnets and young boys in pants with suspenders wading their way through the dusty roads sat protected and entombed within small glass frames. Outlines of townsfolk stood erect in their period dress on the dirt roads. A woman in a long black dress with a black ponytail sat at the forefront of one picture. She appeared larger than anyone in the other photos and was in mid-motion, flipping a coin into the air. Behind her, the stone buildings and landscape faded into an array of sepia tones. I touched the glass with my right hand and moved in closer. I didn't sense happiness. Life looked hard, contrary to the life of the people who inhabit the Creek today.

Chills spread along my back as my own reflection startled me. The color of my eyes darkened to almost black. I blinked. It was time to leave this building one last time. I removed my hand from the glass, straightened up, and walked out. As I pushed open the door, a gust of wind blew in some leaves and a small folded-up paper. I quirked an eyebrow. I had found one of these before with two straight sides and rounded third. Three tabs protruded outward like a puzzle piece. The words "Yule" and "Imbolc" curved around the outer edge with wolf-like creatures in between. Various triangles with symbols were drawn in the middle, with a half-moon located on the bottom left corner. I squeezed it in my palm, looking in all directions for the person who left this for me. I folded the paper, placed in it in my back pocket, and glanced back at the school; then, I trotted down the steps to the sidewalk that meandered its way back to Main Street.

A twenty-something-year-old blew by me on a scooter while a young couple lovingly sat together on a bench in the school's courtyard. I followed the path toward Main, walking past them. They both glanced at me with their somber eyes. The man offered a morning greeting, which I graciously returned. I had seen them around town before. She often wore a silk scarf that covered her long, light red hair and porcelain skin. He was pale as well with long brown hair, which he always tucked behind his ears. She squeezed his arm and rested her head on his shoulder.

I moved past with my eyes toward the ground, thinking about the paper. What did the symbols mean, and why were they directed at me? A muffled and broken whistle surrounded me. I glanced around but couldn't identify the source. Its chilling melody drifted away on the breeze.

The closer I stepped to the center of town, the busier the foot traffic became. Families headed out to dinner before the chaos of school began. In the mix, an unorganized few ran in and out of stores for those last-minute supplies. The rest of the town locked up and closed its doors in the usual manner for a late Sunday afternoon.

I politely weaved my way around people until I bumped into Jack Cicerello just outside our storefront. Jack managed an auto body shop on the edge of town—he was in his early forties and stocky with broad shoulders, an intentional baldhead, and a goatee. He wore one of his famous ball caps with a flat brim. He had an impressive hat collection, which always displayed some detail about one of his newest toys. Today, it paid homage to a bright red custom motorcycle.

"Hi, Abby. How are you? Heading in to see your mom?" he asked.

"Yeah, I just came from the high school, so I thought I would see if she needed any help closing. What about you?"

"I stopped in to pick up a gift from your shop," Jack lifted up a small, paisley print cloth bag cinched tight at the top with a gold ribbon.

"Oh, for who?" I asked, moving out of the way of passersby.

He stuttered. I placed my nose too far into his business, so I shifted my focus to what was in the bag.

"Sorry; may I see what you bought, though?"

"Of course," he said, loosening the ribbon revealing a modest, maroon velvet box. His thick fingers pried it open. Resting inside was a vintage opal ring with a diamond halo. The iridescent blue and green hues danced together in the oval-shaped stone.

I rubbed the stone with my fingers. Decades of love, affection and loss flowed through me, "It's beautiful," I whispered.

Who was the lucky recipient? Jack was quiet and kind. He helped neighbors, attended charity events, and even suited up as Santa at Christmas to deliver presents to kids. He was a hot ticket in town for anyone wanting a perfect mix of a gentleman and a bad boy. The list of potential partners was long, and if he had a new one, the town would know.

His coy smile and pink cheeks said it all.

"Your mom helped me pick it out," he said.

"Did she tell you the story behind it?" I asked.

"No, no story," he replied.

"It was an heirloom brought in by an elderly man who had no surviving family. The piece sat buried in a drawer for a year after his wife passed," I paused, "He was dying and wanted the ring to rest on the hand of another deserving soul." I returned.

He closed the box and placed it back in the sack, "How do you know all this?"

I shook the heartbreak from my hand and tied it closed for him, perfecting the bow. "Sometimes stories get passed along to us, occasionally it's a feeling."

Jack raised one eyebrow. I forgot most people never thought or cared much about an items past. They all had stories to tell, the average person couldn't hear it though. I simplified it, "My mom shared the tale with me. The ring will bring much love." I grinned.

"Thanks, Abby."

Jack's warm smile reappeared, "So, what do you have there?" he asked, changing the topic and pointing toward the leather binder tucked under my arm.

"Oh, nothing," I said, shoving my diploma back so far that it almost fell behind me.

Jack wasn't one to press, so he let me go with a quick goodbye and his signature fist bump.

"Have a great night," he said, moving past me and hopping onto his flat black motorcycle. With one turn of the key, the man who often melted into the background loudly waited for a break in traffic.

I stopped and looked into the front window of our store. The roar of Jack's engine caught my mom's attention. She lifted her head from the cashier drawer and watched Jack pull away. I stepped back when the last customer walked out. The tall, husky woman shoved the door so hard it stayed propped open. She waddled out with her bags and never stopped to close it.

The sound of the bike faded away. I contemplated whether to go in. She had matters under control and, was I ready to have an uncomfortable discussion about my diploma? I stepped toward the threshold of the door. It wasn't hard to think of reasons to leave, but still, I moved forward. I was about to walk in, but I stopped as the store phone rang. I slid back into the brick entryway and waited.

My mom's voice rose, and her tone changed after saying, "Hello."

"Can't we wait until after the holidays; give it one more season?" I heard her ask.

A lengthy pause followed as my mom listened. I peeked around the corner. She rubbed her forehead with one hand while holding the phone out in front of her with the other. An authoritative, low voice shouted through the phone. It was Mason. He halted after his rant, giving my mom a moment to respond.

"Fine, you're right. I know. Can you consider how difficult this is for me and how devastated Abby will be?" she asked into the phone.

My heart sank. Mason had been trying to close our store since the day he moved into our house. After rummaging through my dad's belongings at home and tossing out everything my mom didn't hide, he focused on the store. It was an ongoing battle that had laid dormant over the summer. I hoped he had moved on for good, but it was number one on his to-do list again, and it was the only subject that would have my mom so distraught. With a scowl, I turned away and headed for home.

I was less polite, weaving my way through the town toward Oak. I wanted to smash my diploma against one of the stonewalls and punch the next person who dared give me the look of disgust over my lack of manners. I kicked loose stones and didn't stop to apologize to anyone whose shoes they ricocheted off. How could Mason be so cruel? If he loved my mother and cared at all for me, then he would respect our desire to cling to whatever pieces of my dad we still had. He didn't. I was over Mason, over my mom, and over this town. But I was not over our family store, and I desperately needed to figure out how to save it.

CHAPTER 2

MIDDLE GROUND

I was on autopilot as I headed back home, which sat on the south side of Oak Street. I focused on the uneven sidewalk to keep my mind clear of all my negative thoughts. The cry of an overhead hawk caught my attention. It circled above and followed an oval-like pattern over the houses on both sides of the street. Its caw attracted two others that glided with it in the same fashion. I moved toward my doorstep. My neighbor, Mr. Kennicot, was taking out his trash.

"They must have spotted some prey," he said as he saw me walking with my head held up, looking toward the clouds.

"Yeah, a mouse or something," I muttered. It was common to see a hawk or two sitting on an overhead line near the rural part of town, but it'd been some time since I'd seen any around here. I quickly waved, disappearing inside to avoid one of Mr. Kennicot's lengthy conversations.

Thankfully, Mason wasn't home, so I grabbed bottled water, a leftover turkey sub from lunch, and a jar of rock salt from the cabinet. Upstairs, I removed a bowl of old salt from my dresser, dumped it down the toilet, flushed it, and closed the lid. Back in my room, I refilled the bowl with fresh pink salt, opened my crank window, and kept it on the windowsill. With a big inhale of fresh air, my mind as clear as could be, I exhaled it out over the salt and into the backyard. I propped my diploma on my dresser near the mirror but opted to stuff it in the top drawer instead. The stress of the day overcame me as I collapsed in my wooden chair and watched as the day turned to night.

Pulling open my top right drawer, I grabbed an old wooden art box I had received as a kid. It was heavy cardboard with a flip-open top. Two young girls in dresses pranced under a giant tree with multi-colored butterflies flying through the falling leaves. On the side was a place for my name, which I had written in a bright orange marker. In the bottom corner, a tiny red heart sat next to the smallest of letters that read, "Dad." It was fading after years of rubbing it with my fingers. I opened it.

Inside rested the other small piece of paper I'd found weeks earlier. The same two straight sides with blanks and corresponding tabs fit together and created a half-circle. Near the top were the words "Mabon, Samhain, Yule, and Imbolc". In between were the same small wolf-like creatures. Below it were parts of triangles placed intricately together. My fingertips held them up in the light, while I twisted them between my pointer, middle, and thumb. Deciding against the sandwich and moving to my nearby beanbag, large enough for two of me, I fell into the plush outer shell and let the papers roll between my fingers.

My gaze bounced between the water stains on my ceiling and the two puzzle pieces in my hands. My muscles relaxed from fatigue, though my brain was ramping up for endless hours of nightmares that had plagued me since childhood. With each new dream, I found myself either running away from hell or fighting my way into heaven. As I drifted off into the darkness, a red flash of light jolted upward. My dreams so vivid for so many years I had the luxury of knowing when I entered another realm. I had been to this same space before and cringed at the thought of being back. Some nights, I remained merely a spectator of the images that left me with the daunting task of piecing it all together the next day. But many nights, I became an active participant. As it cast me into another world, I wondered if any part of it could be real, the lines between the two often blurring. With all my might, I strained but failed to open my eyes. Once here, in this middle ground between dreams and reality, I was trapped.

Not moving my physical body, I attempted to calm myself with a series of deep breaths. The suffocating feeling of temporary paralysis intensified my heartbeat. I fought to squirm, rolling and slithering out of my chair and onto the floor. My weak legs buckled under the weight of my body. I used my arms to push up from the floor. I couldn't stand—I could barely crawl. There was no need to strain my eyes and focus on the same room with a wooden floor, large deep red curtains, and a blurry doorway waiting to draw me in. The smell of the air and the sheer force of wind dragged my body, smashing it through an old wood railing in the hall. Falling fast to the foyer below, I braced for the pain, collapsing to my knees, my limbs searing.

In a matter of minutes, images, smells, and noises overwhelmed me. A grandfather clock ticked fast with a horrific screech of metal hands scraping around the clock face. The tolling sounds of hundreds more deafened my ears. Suddenly, I was outside. Birds sang lullabies that strengthened into horrific shrieks. The sun appeared then disintegrated into dust. Silhouettes gathered around my curled-up frame. They clamored over me and spoke in a loud and distorted tone. I covered my ears and looked up. They parted, and a shadow resembling a female's shape sauntered away with her right arm raised, flipping small rounded objects up in the air. My body was forcefully bent and arched. I was hurled back up over the rail. I was thrown back into the bed; heat seared my flesh as I writhed in pain.

A wicked energy force crushed me from overhead with intense pressure. The smell of rotting skin turned my stomach while I struggled to escape back into the mortal world. Squirming, I dug my fingers into my eyes, trying to pry them open. My vocal cords strained and sought to create a sound as my neck flexed, begging for air. The invisible beast's grip didn't let go, growing tighter every second.

This was the closest it had ever brought me to death. My lungs gasped for air, and my heart pounded against my chest. Contorting my limbs, I fought, but the force I felt from above, I now felt from below. Bony fingers with sharpened nails scratched at my ribcage as I cried out in pain. The sting of the monster's fingers sank deep in my ribs, piercing the cartilage between my bones.

Both eyelids heavy, I worked to open them, only to catch sight of a dark form at the base of my bed. One evil force clawed at my skin from below while a tall, feminine shape with white skin and somber eyes, bleeding black, levitated in my room. She floated slowly up over my body. Her fiery breath brushed against me, the closer it drew to my face. A stench of burnt flesh consumed my senses. Her eyes turned yellow with snake-like pupils. The right eye marked with a large, black "X". She was straight from Hell, and I had to face her to separate from the grip below. With one last scream and one final push, I woke with such intensity that I flew out of my beanbag chair and onto the floor.

My eyes opened as the cold wood planks smacked into my body. Hands stinging from the fall and arms trembling, I strained to lift myself. Gasping for air, I looked around the bedroom, half-lit by the early sunrise. I glanced under my bed like a frightened toddler, lifting the bed-skirt only to see dust particles floating up into the light. My heart pounded through my chest as I sat, stunned and exhausted. It was a dread I could never overcome, and while I longed for more sleep, I couldn't close my eyes. Going to sleep too soon was the equivalent of walking back through the gateway where evil waited.

I shuddered. My therapists described a dream as random, mis-matched images or thoughts. Nothing about the images that plagued my mind were accidental. My dreams were gateways to a world I had yet to understand nor wanted any part of.

I dragged myself up and massaged my ribcage. In front of my dresser mirror, I lifted my shirt to reveal a trail of scratches inflamed on both sides of my chest wall. I dabbed each line, breathing deeply, allowing the blood vessels in my temples to shrink and slow the blood that fed my headache. I must have scratched myself when trying to wake. Any other explanation was horrifying.

Disgusted by my image and the night's events, I turned to the old crank window for air, squeezing myself through its opening. I bumped the salt bowl into the backyard and almost knocked out a chipmunk.

"Sorry, little buddy."

The sunlight struck my eyes like a batch of needles. The smell of the old sandwich still sitting on my desk triggered my gag reflex. I cranked the window open wider and, with a few more rotations, felt the cool breeze I needed. A fuzzy vision of birds flew overhead, chirping and chasing the squirrels that played in the yard. Tall, century-old maples lined the landscape preparing for the winter ahead. Leaves shook in the gentle breeze, trying to pull away and fall to the earth. They fell, joining the other foliage, each delicate piece covering the lawn like a blanket. The aroma cleared my senses and my head. Peaceful energy flowed again, pushing negative vibes out and away. It was a frightening contrast to the world I experienced most nights in my sleep. In fact, there were days when I pondered over which existence was reality. The lines between the two worlds ran thin, and I wasn't sure which one I was meant to thrive in.

My room lay still as I dragged out the old wooden chair from under my desk. My body sank onto the frame like that of a seventy-year-old man with arthritis, each joint popping and cracking while I stretched away a night's worth of tension. Once relaxed, I drew my attention to a photograph of my dad, which stood framed on my desk. There was one of him and my mom, one of him and me, and one of all three of us. I was five years old in all the pictures. We were playing out on the swing set that still sat rotting in my backyard. I had come down the slide when my dad picked me up and squeezed his face tight against mine. Nearby stood mom taking snapshots like an excitable first-time parent, laughing and barking orders at us to smile. The clicking sound of the shutter button embedded itself in my memory. For months, I had the picture sitting unprotected under my pillow. Now, it sat wrinkled beneath the glass of a wood frame my mom bought me years ago. I kept him as close as I could, but it meant beginning and ending each day with a pain I had yet to get over.

I tucked the two small pieces of paper back into my art box and hid it back in my drawer. I hastily tapped a pen on my antique writing desk, counting each tap. It helped me focus. From the lower left-side drawer, I grabbed my leather-bound journal. I began writing and drawing anything I could recall from my dream, taking breaks to shake out the tingling sensation still present in my arms.

My old therapist, Dr. Prudence Freidman, encouraged me to write it all down within minutes of waking. She would analyze my drawings during sessions and dig deep to find a rational reason for all of it. In my case, I needed to confront what my subconscious had been fighting with for over a decade. Each voyage ended the same, with me breaking free from a grip that came from two different worlds.

Prudence believed the demons represented some hidden conflict I had. I went along with it on most days. If I didn't, it'd be a quick way to land myself hospitalized and on a 24-hour watch. Trouble was, after all these years, neither of us had gotten any closer to an answer. But at one hundred and fifty bucks an hour, she never seemed in a hurry.

On bleak winter days, I would read back through hundreds of pages, never finding an answer to all the darkness, to the hauntings. I was reading a B-grade horror story, with me as the central character. The book flourished with sketches of dark spirits, demons, wild animals, half animals-half humans, and birds. Horrific looking females with charred skin and long fingers were a common theme. Some days, I would just sit as my pen dug in circles around their eyes, trying to make sense of anything. There were days I wanted to prove to myself I wasn't crazy. Still, the marks left behind on my skin contradicted anything my therapist ever taught me. Maybe being nuts was easier to accept than reality.

My left hand continued moving in a circular pattern, jarring my memory of the female-shaped spirit flipping something into the air. It mimicked the images of the young woman in a black dress I saw at school yesterday. I slammed the journal shut. The little hairs on my arms stood upright. Who were these evil women, and why were they stalking me?

My anxiety surged. I needed to get out of my room and the house. But I had to make my way to the bathroom for a quick cleanup and a change of clothes. Once my mom's boyfriend moved in two years ago, gone were the days of loafing around in my tee-shirt, socks, or lounging without a bra. Life was like living away in a dorm. I retreated to this tiny room at night and headed out for as much of the day as possible. I made my way to my bathroom, closing the door and yanking it in far enough to lock it. It was just the mirror and me. It took a few minutes of staring, but I started my routine. Staring deep in my own eyes, I searched for anything within me that might house some answers. My soul quieted; I reached for my brush.

My natural light auburn hair needed just a quick combing to smooth out the blond highlights that framed my pale face. I twirled a handful of bright blue strands I had since childhood and then positioned a few auburn pieces over it to hide them. After all these years, I still didn't understand the gene that created such an unnatural color and one immune from change.

My fingers pulled at the skin beneath my lids, showcasing the red lines in the whites of my eyes. I wasn't one of those lucky girls with glowing skin. I needed foundation to conceal the faint lines on my face and waterproof mascara to prevent smudges when my eyes filled with tears.

I dug through my hamper, trying to find a decent pair of jeans. As I pulled one out, a few dollars and some change fell out of my back pocket, ricocheting off the tile floor. I dropped to my knees and slapped my hands down upon a handful of quarters, nickels, and dimes. Images of the woman from the picture flashed before me. I picked up a coin, held it between my thumb and pointer, and began flipping it into the air.

CHAPTER 3

ONE MAN'S TREASURE

With a clean tee and all of my coins moved to the back pocket of my jeans, I was ready. I began my daily ritual of creeping downstairs to steal a coffee cup before rushing out for the day. The steps in this aged home were not forgiving and creaked louder the slower I walked. It was a gamble, and I never knew what days Mason would be home or which days he would leave early. He kept his schedule to himself so exiting the house without running into him was a game I played daily.

The steps leading to the first floor ended in a small foyer with a front door. To the right, a hall led to a half bath and Mason's office. It was always locked. His room of secrets sparked my curiosity but also angered me. It was my dad's old space and Mason didn't belong.

I should've kept moving out to the porch. Still, I went through the front room and back toward the kitchen, where Mason sat reading his newspaper and sipping espresso in the four-season room just off the kitchen. He saw me before I could escape.

"Good morning. You're up early," Mason said, never looking up from the morning news. "Store doesn't open until twelve today, right?"

A wall of windows with a cathedral ceiling formed the four-season room. To the left, sat a small oak table and chairs, to the right, an aged buffet was flanked by two brown, leather tufted chaise loungers. Small plants sat on the buffet surrounding a desktop waterfall filled with small rose quartz stones. The tiny but loud motor prevented the calming effect intended when I'd bought it for my mom.

I nodded to Mason while making a cup of coffee with cream and mostly sugar. He drank gross espresso from a ridiculous little cup that also gave him the worst breath ever. It was just another of many things I hated about him.

I was doing my best to move fast and leave, but Mason didn't take well to a cold shoulder.

"Why in such a rush this morning?" he said again, not moving his eyes from the words he was reading. He sat smug in his dark grey suit and multicolor tie. "Going in early or just can't sleep?" He sipped his espresso and then dabbed the leftover sludge off his lips with a napkin.

"Both," I said. Mason's attempt at rational conversation sickened me, even more so knowing about his call to my mom last night. I choked on the taste of his expensive cologne. I turned to get away from him, witnessing my mom now staggering into the kitchen. Mason was on the move now as his big, flat feet slapped across the wood floor in her direction.

"Good morning, Lauren," he said, kissing her on the cheek. Then, he commented on her black short sleeve sweater, khaki ankle pants, and black patent leather flats. Compliments spilled from his lips this morning. He ignored her pale skin and pink eyes.

"Mom, have you been crying?" I whispered to her.

"No, these baby blues are just not as pretty as yours," she whispered to me.

My mom had been commenting on my eyes since I was a child. It was the one thing she could fall back on when searching for something positive to say. My clear-as-glass eyes changed color throughout the day. They could be any solid color of the rainbow or a mix of many. My eyes were a mood ring to my soul and separated me from all of humanity, not just my mom. At birth, the color so unusual I endured needle pokes and genetic tests to determine what was wrong with me. Healthy, at least physically, there was no need to continue digging through my DNA to explain something modern medicine couldn't understand. I loved the vibrant difference, but the eyes and the streak of blue hair deviated from the norm in this stuffy town.

Mason slithered his way between us and kissed my mom for a second time on her forehead. It was an unusual display of affection so early in the day.

"I was just having a lovely conversation with Abby." He patted me on the shoulder before I shuffled away.

"You were?" she asked.

"We were?" I hated his lies, even his little ones.

"Yes, she's going into work early. I want you to talk to her first, though," he said, looking pointedly in my mom's direction, tilting his head forward. If I didn't know about last night, I would have thought his expressions strange. Still, understanding his intent, I realized he was desperate for my mom to begin the conversation.

I wanted to bolt to work at the store my parents built together. My mom ran it while my dad took care of the family through his remodeling business. He had quite a reputation in a town of century homes that always needed fixing or updating. But his love was traveling and picking up treasures for the store with her. Their romance grew like a cliché from a storybook, and it became housed in the only place Mason had yet to get his slimy hands-on, even though he was putting forth quite the effort.

"I'm just going to go; see you later, Mom."

"Lauren," Mason said to my mom. He spoke to her like a toddler, prompting her again to speak.

Mornings were not her favorite part of the day; she traded in a wine glass for a morning mug. The robust energy she once shared with the world disappeared years ago. Now, she was just a broken vase for Mason to put back together. He did so with lavish jewelry to cover the cracks and expensive clothes to conceal her scars. I saw the wreck of a widow passed out behind closed doors, and all of this was just a curtain. She didn't want to speak, and based on the conversation I heard a day earlier, I didn't need her to.

But she responded as if she owed him.

"Aunt Kate is coming in today," was all she could muster, but Mason wasn't having any of it.

"Lauren!"

My mom pretended she didn't hear Mason, but he was too loud. She continued on with her head down.

"Kate picked up a truckload of antiques from the Trail Tour and believes some items could sell fast. I'm heading in soon, after I eat something." She moved with purpose from the refrigerator, to the cabinet, to the utensil drawer. She pulled hard on the drawer that always stuck. Mason spun in circles, tracking her. His agitation moved up his neck with a red rash. I was quick to respond, not wanting to give him room to speak.

"Sure," I said. I never missed seeing Aunt Kate, my mom's younger sister by fourteen years. Dated a lot, married once, and a little on the crazy fun side. She was the sibling I never had.

Mason's demeanor only got worse the more my mom and I spoke.

"I think I'll just head out now and prep the store." My choice of words was intentional as each one stabbed Mason's side in a verbal assault.

"Sure thing," she said with a weak attempt at a smile and a slight pat on my right shoulder. It was her version of a hug after my dad passed. There was love in it, though, despite how small the gesture.

"Any more thoughts on going off to college?" Mason awkwardly asked, maneuvering back to his seat at the table.

"Yes; every day, it's all I think about," I replied. Like most, he didn't appreciate the sarcasm.

"Everyone should go to college, learn life skills, and spread their wings," he continued with an inappropriate chuckle. "You're wasting your brain trying to sell junk."

"I enjoy what I do. In fact, some people care more about being happy than being rich," I said.

"Oh, please, Abby. Save your soapbox speech. You're not happy or rich. You're stuck," he said.

"I'm stuck? I'd say you are. You've long overstayed your welcome!" I retorted.

"Don't use that tone with me!" His hands clenched the newspaper as he was losing control over his emotions. He stood again as I gathered my bag and keys to leave. He was preparing for a big speech, as he stood tall, stretching himself from 6'2" to 6'3".

"*You* are a nuisance," he said, pointing at me with his right hand. "I am tired of the disrespect, and I am tired of tiptoeing around your fragile feelings." His lanky frame moved around the table. "Speak, Lauren—tell your brat of a daughter what she needs to know." His words were crisp and quick.

My mom didn't speak. She squeezed a butter knife she held in her left hand, while her right hand strangled a plastic jar of jelly, her face now matching the pink hue of her eyes.

"Oh, I will handle it just like everything else, Lauren." He directed his attention back to me. "It's time to shut down the store, Abby. And your mom is following through this time."

I stood frozen, my eyelids heavy. We'd been down this road too many times before, but this time felt different. This time, Mason's intent was strong, and my mom's will weak, as she stood not speaking. I had to defend us and our family name alone.

"It's our store, Mason. It is not yours to close. We don't need to keep having this discussion with you when you are not an integral part of the equation," I said.

His arms dropped in displeasure. His head low, his eyes direct.

"I got a promotion and will travel every week starting in October. I refuse to be away from Lauren for any length of time. The store will close, and your mom is coming with me. And for the record, it's your mom's store, and it's hers to close." He looked in her direction, waiting for a crumb of support, which he didn't get. He continued an attack on me.

"We both know you can't run the business by yourself, and I will not have your mom running out here every weekend to help you. It's time for you to grow up and take on real responsibility," he added.

Heat flared in my cheeks. "This conversation is over, Mason. My life, my decisions, and my responsibilities are separate from your twisted relationship with my mother. You have no say in my life."

We both fought for her attention, waiting for her to pick a side, but my mom's focus stayed on nervously tidying up anything that didn't belong on the counter.

"Mom, say something, please," I begged.

"Abby, we need to talk, but maybe ... not right now," she said, but I could barely hear her, as she refused to look at either of us.

Mason slammed his mug down onto the table, shattering the ceramic. "Listen, your mom and I have plans, and the plans don't include my bank account supporting a failing hobby. So unless you can come up with a way to—"

I interrupted him, "Mom, talk, please. Don't let him run this conversation." I stared at my mother, who now peered over her shoulder toward Mason.

The sugar from my coffee had not yet reached my bloodstream as a nervous shake took over. I waited.

Her voice broke through her lips. "Mason, we agreed not to talk yet."

Mason's hands flew up in the air. "We did? I don't remember that part of the discussion. In fact, it was just the opposite!"

"There's no reason to discuss the store right now; we don't have all the answers yet," she said, trying to dodge as much as she could, which only infuriated both of us. She wanted to appease us with half-lies and distractions, but neither Mason nor I were ready for defeat.

"Lauren, we are leaving in two weeks to meet with an antique dealer. At what point do you plan on telling her? She's your daughter; you need to give her a heads up. She is not adaptable. Abby needs time to process this and have a plan," he carried on. Mason then pushed on the table, knocking the chair out behind him. The force launched the carafe onto the floor. The dark liquid spilled to the ground like a dam bursting, dripping everywhere. He jumped back to protect his suit and shoes while my mom rushed for a dishrag, frantically wiping each drop that fell to his feet. On her knees, she begged him to stop.

Mason looked at me with a smile the devil himself would be proud of.

"It's time. Besides, we will give you some of the money we get from selling all that garbage. You can use it to start a responsible life," he said, his fists clenching and pressing into the tabletop.

I braced myself against the counter. All of my negative feelings and emotions churned inside, waiting to explode with a force I wasn't sure I could manage. I closed my eyes tight, took a deep breath, and straightened up for a fight. I wasn't running from him anymore. My mom must have seen the intensity building from within as she cried out my name.

"Abby!"

Teeth clenched, I stepped toward him.

"I will see you in hell before I sell that store," I screamed.

"See me in hell? Oh, Abby! Watch what you wish for," he said and laughed boisterously, buttoning up his suit jacket and closing up his briefcase.

I turned to my mom, still trying to control the rage building inside.

"Is it true?" I asked her.

My mother stood silent. "Why is Kate coming in today with more stuff? She doesn't know yet, does she?" I watched her weakened soul giving in and giving up.

"So, it's true?" I asked one more time.

"Yes, Abby," she said.

"How could you do this? How could you betray dad?" I cried.

Tears ran down her face.

"The store has struggled for the last few years. It's a fun hobby but not a great living. You need more than what the store can provide for you. Your father would want me to do what's best for you," my mom said as she stood over the sink, rinsing and wringing out the hand towel full of Mason's mess.

I walked up close behind her. "You think Dad wants you to move away with Mason and close our family store? Really? You think that's what he wants?" My pain poured out in my tears as the salt stung my lips.

Mason stood, shaking his head, looking down at his feet. "Stop talking about your dad like he's still here. He is gone, Abby, which means he can't care about the store. And since he is never coming back, it is not a concern of mine."

With rage in my bones, I reached over Mom and grabbed a glass vase from the small bay window over the sink. I wanted to launch it at his head, but I didn't want to spend the next ten years in a jail cell, so I chucked it toward his shins and watched him lunge back just before the glass splintered. My strength surprised me as the shards shot through the air like arrows. Mason ducked, but I was not as fast, and a few fragments of glass cut into my right cheek.

Standing still, a slow trickle of blood ran down my face. Tears sped up the flow down to my chin. I had never felt so much anger and then acted on it, and I knew the backlash that was coming. Mason stumbled around while he and my mom screamed back and forth at one another. He was yelling so loud and fast. For a moment, I was just a witness as the hate whirled around me. So much evil flowed from his eyes. His intentions were obvious, and his motives grew from a place of insecurity and jealousy that my mom had yet to see.

Mason brushed past me toward the front of the home. "Your mom and I leave in two weeks. I expect you gone when we get back," he said.

He picked up his briefcase and stomped to the front of the house. I heard his key ring tapping against the glass on the locked french doors to his office. My mom knelt back down with some damp towels and an old grocery bag to clean up the glass. She stopped speaking. My violent outburst embarrassed both of us. I had become the type of person I despised.

"It was an ugly vase anyway," I said, but my attempt to lighten the mood fell flat, and my words only made her cry while she cleaned, wiping the tears away with her sleeve as they dripped off her nose.

"Mom, this is when you tell me not to worry, that Mason doesn't understand and that he'll change his mind in time. C'mon, Mom, give me hope you're not changing sides," I begged.

"You're bleeding," she said and stood up, opened our medicine cabinet, and handed me a box of bandages.

"You're the only one who can stop the bleeding," I said, shoving the box of bandages back into the cabinet and slamming the door.

"You're making life impossible for everyone," my mom said, dabbing my cut with a tissue she had pulled out of her front pocket. "My job is to guide you in the right direction. I've thought long and hard about this. I'm not changing sides. I've always been on yours, as difficult as it is for you to understand right now."

"I know you don't want this; he is evil, Mom. How is that good for any of us?" I pleaded with her.

"Oh, evil, please, Abby! You act as if the earth is crawling with demons and saints. He's good for us. He can provide us with everything we need," she said. The bag of glass she held in her hands now rattled with each move she made.

"Do you love him?" I asked.

"Do you?" I demanded.

"Yes," she said, looking at the floor.

My shoulders dropped, and my head fell forward in grief. She had never been able to look me in the eyes and lie.

CHAPTER 4

OLD MAN STUDDARD

In the upstairs bathroom, I swabbed my open cut with alcohol. It burned as I wiped away the blood, revealing a narrow slice across my cheek. My eyes glowed purple with a ring of red around the pupil. I exhaled with pursed lips while the wound oozed. I dabbed it with concealer, allowing the makeup and yuck to dry together. Fortunately, no one under the age of forty ever shopped in our store, so at least for the next twelve hours, it didn't matter all that much how old and worn I appeared.

Not wishing to stand and stare at myself any longer, I slouched onto the cold tile. I couldn't endure the walk past either of them. What would I do? Against the wall, curling my knees up to my chest, I rocked, distracted by my father's images. I reveled in what our mornings would be like if he were here, awaiting comfort that never came. Trapped in my bathroom, I waited for the sound of the front door to close, signaling that Mason had left. What was the delay?

His banging downstairs echoed off the walls and penetrated the floors. It was a tantrum that would give any three-year-old a run for their money. The war we waged against each other climaxed to this breaking point. I had graduated early from school and was now being pushed out, all while my mom sat and watched.

I tapped the back of my head against the rough wood of my door when a slight tremble of the walls grabbed my attention. I stood and the entire house violently shook. The mirror crashed down onto the sink, knocking the soap dispenser and toothbrush holder onto the floor. Great, I thought to myself, thirteen more years of bad luck. I didn't have time to sulk though as the house shook so forcefully the doorknob rattled itself loose, opening up to the hall.

I grabbed my bag and darted out of the bathroom, only to lose my balance from the fierce movement. Bracing myself against the wall, I inched my way down the long, narrow hallway when I noticed Mason standing at the top of the steps, staring in my direction. I stopped. Black spots flooded my field of vision as I stared up toward the ceiling. The pain traveled across my forehead and made its home in my temples. The stench of sulfur sent my stomach whirling. My legs buckled, and I collapsed to the floor.

I sat until the movement had ceased, and the spots in my vision cleared. The pain in my temples melted away as my mom's face appeared close to mine. Mason's frame over her shoulder disappeared, and his weight vibrated the floor as he headed down the steps.

My mom propped me up against the wall.

"What was that? Did you feel it?" I asked her.

"I think it was an earthquake," my mom replied, looking around and assessing the damage. All my school pictures that hung on the wall had crashed to the floor.

The last confirmed earthquake occurred when I was in the fifth grade, and it had lasted about ten seconds. I was in school when it shook the window frames so hard it knocked the blinds off, hitting one girl in the head and sending her to the ER. The school then instituted safety precautions and drills that we ran through for weeks. Never had another one since.

I doubted this was an act of Mother Nature. The timing was too coincidental. I dragged my short nails over the wood floor and then heard the slightest whispers from fading voices.

"What," I yelled out, startling my mom.

"Is it happening again? Who are you talking to? Abby, talk to me!"

"No," I said. "It's not happening again. I … I didn't sleep well."

"Are you sure? Please tell me if you're hearing them again?" she said.

My life wasn't just a series of awful nightmares. It included voices of people not present, shadows that hung out in corners of rooms, and images of people not from this century. But my mom had enough of her own problems.

Looking down at the floor, I responded. "Yes, I'm sure."

We sat silent for a moment, suffering, on the cold wood floor in the hallway. Sweet memories flooded in and played out like a movie. I blocked out the voices.

"Why are you doing this?" I asked, touching her hand still gripping my arm.

"I told you. He can take care of us." Her forehead leaned into mine then we fell back, resting our backs to the wall.

"Does he need to? We're okay, aren't we?"

"I'm doing you a disservice by keeping the store. It's holding you back. You've graduated a whole year early with honors. You should be at orientation, in an Ivy League school pursuing a dream, your own dream. Antiquing is all I know, but you still have a chance for something new," she continued.

I couldn't believe what I was hearing. She wasn't allowing me to choose my future. Managing the store someday was my dream, no matter how dumb it seemed to everyone else. I wasn't shortchanging myself, but somehow being super smart was actually preventing me from being happy and having what I wanted.

I reached for my purse and, in my haste, dumped it out onto the floor. My wallet, some stones, and a pill bottle rolled out. I shoved everything back in my bag.

I stood to leave. "You're using me as an excuse, Mom, to give Mason exactly what he wants. Control. Control of you. And once you give it to him, you won't get your life back."

"What are you basing this on?" she quipped back.

"My sixth sense."

Mom rested her head in her hands and rubbed her temples, disgusted. "You can't live your life making decisions off a sixth sense. Sixth senses don't exist." She pushed herself up off the floor and then dismissed me with her hand, "Abby, nothing else exists! We are born, we will die and in between, we survive until we succumb to the darkness."

My arms dropped to my side. She was dying. Her soul wanted out. I shook my head, "Of course you believe that." I threw my purse strap over my head and onto my shoulder.

"There is more beyond our existence and whatever it is, whatever it looks like, it will bring me back to Dad." I retreated downstairs and out the front door, slamming it behind me. The door wavered before clicking closed. Outside, I found some peace as I raised my arms up to take in a breath of fresh air. Jack roared by on his motorcycle while I stood stomping my feet and all the negative energy that consumed my soul. I felt another presence near. The girl next door now awkwardly stared from her front drive.

"Hi," she said with a half-smile, frozen eyes and a brief wave.

It was Cici Kennicot. She had the most beautiful light brown skin and a head of magnificent curls and natural highlights that everyone envied. But she was shy and never took well to the attention. We grew up together and even took some of the same advanced classes in school. She had one more year to finish.

"Are you okay?" she asked quietly.

"Yes, sorry. Just a bad morning," I replied.

"Are you excited you don't have to go back to school at least?" she said, standing with her backpack and her lunch bag, in no big rush to leave.

"Yes, I am," and walked down the porch toward her. We were on and off friends over the years. Nothing terrible ever happened, just life.

She contorted her torso, trying to pull her cardigan sweater closed over her D-sized chest and tight tee.

"What does your shirt say?" I asked, noticing the gold letters peeking through.

"Oh, don't ask," she blushed, hiding behind her curls.

"I'm intrigued; do tell," I said, smiling and remembering how we shared some good laughs.

"It's my brother." Her eyes rolled in many directions. "He set up a screen print shop in our basement. It's his answer to my dad's request to get a job." She opened her sweater and then laughed loudly.

"Irrational," I said, laughing along with her. "What's the meaning?"

"Nothing, but he thinks he will brand the next catchphrase. I am quietly supporting his efforts," Cici said as she buttoned back up her sweater, bit her lip, and let out a sigh of a very annoyed sibling.

"You're a good sister, but keep your sweater closed today, or you'll have a new unwanted nickname." It was nice engaging in some meaningless chit-chat after the last twenty-four hours, but I needed to move on, and so did she. "I'll let you get to class; you don't want to be late the first day," I said.

She gave me a crooked smile that spoke of the same dismay I felt for high school. She needed to suck it up for nine more months, and then she would be free. I could've walked with her, but I needed the time to gather my thoughts. I didn't want her to realize I was avoiding her, so I stayed back and walked toward my garage, waiting for her to get much farther ahead. It was a twenty-minute walk to the store, so I lingered for ten before heading back up to the sidewalk.

On the move, I paid extra attention to the surrounding beauty of the town. I loved the variety of colors that came with the changing season. Allison Creek was particularly beautiful this time of year. Every century building had its own tale rich in history. The town started out as a settlement of craftsmen and carpenters who moved from the east coast in the mid-1800s. Somewhere along the way, the entire town officially became the Village of Allison Creek. Families who lived nearest the center of town still referenced themselves as Villagers while everyone else called themselves the Creekers. Creekers believed their homes sat on the founding land in the city and prided themselves in its rich history. Villagers used the term as mostly a status thing since the houses were more significant and more costly the closer you lived to town. The entire city was only 2.4 square miles, and no one knew for sure where the cut-off lay between being a Villager or a Creeker. To this day, I still didn't know what I was.

I kicked the pebbles along the uneven pavement and inhaled the crisp air. It soothed my headache as I processed the beauty of the tree-lined streets and well-manicured lawns. Occasionally, a small dog would push the limits of their electric fence before the collar chimed, calling for a retreat. Kids darted out of their century homes that lined Oak Hill and meandered into town toward school. I slowed as much as I could, not wishing to catch up with any of them. I walked this route my entire life and looking around, it amazed me how much never changed. Every home stood tall and proud, displaying their shades of paint that only covered the beauty of the decaying wood beneath. The landscaping was well-groomed, with flowers and shrubs that bloomed in every season, and wind chimes rang in harmony with one another. And like every morning for the last seventeen years, I could hear the sounds of a chair rocking in tempo as I approached Main Street.

"Good morning, young miss," said the man in the rocking chair.

"Good morning, Mr. Studdard," I yelled while giving a quick smile and a short wave.

The flowers stood out, particularly vibrant around his house today. He meticulously doted over his landscaping daily, giving the rest of the town a standard to live up to. The bright purple, pink, and red hues attracted a variety of birds and butterflies alike.

"This is quite the day, isn't it?" he said. "Always enjoy it."

Old Man Studdard moved in twelve years ago and repeated the same phrase every time I passed by. Tall and gaunt, he kept a glowing tan all year. His large white teeth shone brightly through a wide-open, smiling mouth. I often wondered how he stayed so positive. He had outlived his wife, and his children lived out west. He was always alone. Early on, I stopped out of pity, always giving him a few minutes of my time, but eventually, I grew to enjoy our discussions.

"You look tired," he said as he rocked himself up and out of his chair. He used an old wooden walking stick, glossy and curved like a vine wrapping up around his right hand.

"I am," I replied.

"A little melancholy, too?" he asked.

"Yeah, that too," I said, fidgeting with my purse for my phone to check the time.

"You're also in a hurry," he said as he tapped the stick on the painted whiteboards of the wide porch wrapped around his house.

"No, no hurry." I slid my phone back into the purse. He was polite, but he was also quick to casually point out when someone was rude. He wanted the full attention of anyone who stopped to say hello.

"It's a big day. Kids running back to school and every stay at home sharing details of their summer vacations, one-upping each other," the old man said laughing and clearing his throat. He crinkled his nose and twisted his face, causing white lines to emerge from beneath his sunbaked skin.

"Well, I'm hoping to avoid all of them," I said. I wanted to hang out in the store, alone, in my safe place.

"You can't avoid the world forever," he responded. The old man and I had many conversations over the years. He had a big heart and a burning desire to dig deep into my subconscious with a series of well-thought-out statements and questions. It always left me in a state of reflection after walking away.

"It's not always the world I am trying to avoid," I mumbled.

He squinted and titled his head back. Then, he paused until it was awkward. He wanted clarification. So I asked the type of question he appreciated, the kind that garnered deep thought.

"Do you think there is a line between the world we live in and the space we occupy after we die?" Our experience with losing a loved one was something we shared, so discussions about life, death, and the afterworld were not off-limit topics. I yearned to learn more about what happens to our souls after death.

"Hmm," he said, his one brow dipped low. "I believe that while we are here, we should work hard to master our understanding of life, and once we do, we'll figure out the rest when it's time."

How could I work hard to master this life when the other side reached out so much? I never told him outright that I heard voices or saw glimpses of human forms in the corners of dark rooms. I admitted that only to a couple of people. I wanted to meet someone else who could see and hear what I did or at least believe in its validity.

"So, do you think spirits exist?" I asked.

He leaned over the railing and stroked the top of the delicate flowering bushes that lined his front steps.

"Ahh, a Papilio," he simply stated.

"What?" I responded, noticing a large, dark green butterfly glide in, sweep across his hand and perch itself upon a leaf.

"It's Latin for butterfly, a swallowtail, to be exact."

Had the old man digressed, or was this part of my daily lesson?

He requested that I move in closer, "Come, take a look," then pointed to her wings.

"The upper side has bright, green bands of color," the beauty flit through the air around us," the underside is grey with specks of green and blue. It's a chameleon of sorts. And the colors can change depending on the angle from which you view, but the two sides will always be different."

She was an exquisite sight with a myriad of iridescent colors painted elegantly on her scales, "Why the different sides?"

"It's believed the design protects her from both predators above and predators below."

"I'm sorry, but I still don't understand what this has to do with what you believe?"

"The body is a shell protecting the inner soul. While the body may go through physical changes, the soul, your spirit, is forever yours to keep. The swallowtail understands she needs the two sides to survive."

"So, you believe even butterflies have souls?"

He looked at me poignantly, "Anything with life energy has a soul, and that energy can dance around and mingle with us."

His comments had me thinking more in-depth, "What about the creatures who adapt and evolve? What happens with their soul?"

"I suppose it might change too. I guess we just have to hope the change is always for the better," he stood, leaving his walking stick on the porch rail and sidestepping over to the stairs where he slid down slowly to sit. He grimaced while both of his knees popped until he was in a more comfortable sitting position, "and we just have to trust that the soul will provide everything our mortal body will need."

I wanted to share my stories. I wanted to tell him about the evil commingling in the Creek, but I didn't know where to start. I had two pieces of paper with mysterious symbols, recent dreams of a woman in a long black dress flipping coins, and scratches on my ribcage from the night before. I was sure of the spiritual presence surrounding me, but I still didn't understand why. How would I track what was haunting me? My silence alluded to my inner thoughts. It was like he was listening to the words spinning in my head. He pointed towards town, "You should check out the archives on the second floor of the community library," he said.

"The archives?" I asked, straightening up, pondering how it would help. I let him finish.

"You're seeking many answers, and I while I love my conversations with you, I sense you need more. If truth is what you desire, then digging through history is an ideal place to start. You might find answers to questions that plague you, clues to what you may experience, or others like you. Either way, it makes for an eventful Sunday on a rainy Creek afternoon." With a cheeky smile and wide eyes, he waited for a response, tapping his feet against the cement steps in a rhythmic fashion. He grinned large and full as we both watched the butterflies fly up and disappear around back.

Others like me? Was his choice of words merely coincidental? Either way, given my lack of recent social engagements, I was open to anything that might bring me some peace of mind. A trip to the library was now on my list.

"Thank you, as always, for all the pearls," I said as I nodded and backed away to leave.

"Wait," he said, waving for me to come closer.

"What is it?" I softly replied.

"I don't believe there's a line. The space beyond is all around us," he said.

CHAPTER 5

WILD CHERRY

Crossing the street, I took the sharp right turn about the same time I stopped hearing the rocking from his chair. I thought about his last statement while I walked past all of the aged, stone, two-story buildings lining Main Street, which shaped the town center. The bottom level of each housed a store or an upscale boutique where some rich twenty-something hoped to jumpstart their fashion career before leaving for a big city.

Family-run restaurants and diners filled in the space and provided a place for meals, coffee, and ice cream in a social setting. Main Street was also where you shopped, bought groceries, or tools. The second levels of each space were apartments either used by the owners or rented to newbies moving into town who could not afford a home. Some were rented as offices for local lawyers or accountants, and some, like ours, were nothing more than storage units. One corner unit on the opposite side of the street sat empty. Its ample square footage and wall of windows covered in newspaper from the inside was prime real estate for the next big thing to come to town. Like everyone else, I waited and watched for any hint of movement or a clue as to what might go in next. As of today, nothing.

The library, the elementary, middle, and high schools were located in a campus setting at the end of Main. A small park sat smack in the heart of the Village, with a walkway that led to the actual falls. It was an ecosphere from which people who lived here never needed to leave.

Hearing the screech from a young hawk again, I paused and glanced up to an extraordinary sky. Thin, wispy clouds moved across a dark blue backdrop with crimson hues melting into the horizon.

"Excuse me," said a young mom, who jogged from behind me with her stroller while others converged to meet up for their daily dose of gossip and coffee. As I ducked over to the left and out of the way, another small piece of paper sitting untouched on the curb drew my attention.

I kneeled down and opened it. Its edges were cut the same with tabs and blanks where puzzle pieces would fit together. The words "Mabon and Lugnasadh" were displayed on the rounded edge. More triangles and a circle were depicted along with a triquetra, and a crescent moon. I remembered seeing the triple spiral on a notebook this girl carried around in high school. I had a study hall with her one semester and she told me it represented some Goddess. Kids in school called her a witch because she wore black and had unusual markings on everything she owned. I thought she was depressed and needed a friend.

The paper was white and smooth to the touch. Unfortunately, it was too smooth; my thumb smeared some of the charcoal, leaving residue on my fingers. Holding it to my nose, I inhaled, noticing a faint aroma of lemongrass. Folding it carefully to not disrupt the drawing, I placed it in my purse and walked toward my store. This was the third piece in two months. Why was I being targeted, and what did it mean?

Over the growing herd of humans, I saw the antique store sign dangling off the ornamental metal scroll that extended from the building out past the entrance. The words "North Main Antique" stretched across the light blue sign with a broad pink italic "A" in the background. Most people believed the fancy A stood for antique, but in actuality, it stood for Anderson. The color pink was in celebration of me.

I was almost at my destination when Manshaw Wu from the neighboring bookstore waddled out to the sidewalk. Manshaw was a portly fellow, standing in one of his signature suit jackets with a mandarin collar. He had one in just about every color. Today, he'd chosen a dark, navy blue silk situated over khaki ankle pants and a pair of matching cloth slippers.

"Good morning," he said, pulling a cart outside with a variety of bonsai and ferns that were not only for sale but likely in need of some extra light after a Sunday inside. His store space was small, so he was particular about the items he carried. Thankfully, he was my local source for sage, crystals, stones, and salt.

"Good morning," I replied, watching him fight with the cart's wheels and the threshold while trying to keep the plants from falling to the ground. I jumped in to help, staring at the greenery and remembering the front cover of a book he'd once sold. The hardback cover showcased a depiction of a forest at night, with a title that referenced the occult. I dug back into my bag and pulled out the small paper I had found.

"Mr. Wu, do you know what this is?" I asked, handing him the paper. He opened it and turned it 360 degrees, dropping his reading glasses from his forehead down to the tip of his nose.

He pointed to a figure that was cut in half. "That appears to be part of a waxing crescent and that's a witches knot," he said, looking to each as he spoke. Then he pointed to two of the smaller triangles with a line in each. "This one represents *water,* and this one represents *earth.*"

"What do you think it all means?" I asked.

"The triquetra are an ancient symbol representing the mind, the body, and the spirit. The waxing moon could mean several things," he replied.

"I have two other pieces at home, which I believe is making part of a circle. Does that help to decipher anything?" I continued.

He pushed his glasses back up, and his eyes crossed for a moment before straightening back out in my direction. His brows furrowed as he looked even closer, pointing out the two unfamiliar words with the wolf-like creature in between.

"Separately, they are harmless ancient symbols, but together, they suggest witchcraft. These words here represent two of the eight pagan sabbats."

"Pagan sabbats?" I inquired.

"Yes, as in witch holidays. Where did you get these?" he asked me as he pulled a small plant mister out from under his jacket and began spritzing the plants and me at the same time. I wiped my face, careful not to smudge the makeup over my cut.

"I've found a few pieces like this around town, and I am trying to understand the meaning," I replied.

"Around town? Oh boy. It's probably some dumb kids experimenting with powers they don't understand. You're better off ignoring, throwing away. This kind of stuff is dangerous. Don't get involved," he sputtered, leaving out words. I tried to throw a few more questions his way, but my curiosity only worried him.

"Give it to me. I will burn it," he said, reaching for it, but I pulled back.

"It's okay. I will take care of it," I said.

"Promise me," he said, holding out the bottle and threatening to respray me.

"I promise; no more water, either. Thank you for your help," I replied.

Manshaw dropped the water bottle on the cart and did not say another word. With a straight lip line and an expressionless face, he placed his fingertips together and slightly bowed. It was his version of hello, goodbye, thank you, and welcome, all wrapped up in one gesture.

I backed away into the front doorway of our store after giving him a slight bow back. The old lock always stuck, and I jerked the door forward just enough to get it unlatched with the small paper tucked between my knees. The sun gleamed off the window glass and created such a glare it hurt my tired eyes. With two shakes, I knew I was in when the bell above the door rang before slowing to a halt.

I held the door open and turned my back to the store, allowing the built-up energy to stream out through the opening, releasing anything negative out and into the atmosphere. I headed inside with a deep breath, letting the door close behind me and relishing the antique aroma. With one flip of the light switch, a room full of memories illuminated and awoke—generations of history and wisdom floating through the air waiting for someone to just listen. On occasion, some artifacts would emanate nothing but darkness and despair. Those vessels of evil would be sent straight to the dumpster, when my mom wasn't around, of course.

While I had work to do, Mr. Wu's comments had my brain working overdrive, and my stomach turning as fast. His presence and his remarks were my sign to smudge today. I removed a bundle of sage from under the register and lit the leaves of the bunch. In a clockwise motion, I moved around the store, allowing the sage to billow into the air, concentrating on the corners. The flame burned low today, and the smoke trail was thin as it danced and disappeared into a faint breeze. Its presence left telltale smells behind.

Kate hated the stench, and so did many of the customers, so I had to follow up with a few spritzes of spray I'd made with eucalyptus, camphor, and tea tree oil. I opened the door to allow fresh wind to swirl through the store like a blender replacing remaining stagnant air with the sweet smells of earth. My ritual for today was complete as I circled around, scanning the 1,500 square feet of space and wondering where we would place everything Kate was bringing in today.

Our busiest time of year was between Halloween and Christmas. Finding a spot for everything over the next month while blending in changing holiday décor had always been a challenge. Facing this season, knowing we had an enemy trying to take it all away, placed even more pressure on me to sell, and sell whatever we could. The thoughts were bittersweet as I visually took in all the effort we had put into this livelihood.

The light gray walls and bright white trim flanked the dark walnut wood floors. Three large wrought iron and glass chandeliers hung across the width of the store. Various antique buffets, hutches and tables framed the walls housing ceramic pitchers, lamps, books, vases, and creepy dolls. No antique store was complete without them. The silence made the creepy dolls uglier, so I always wound up the Victrola near the back and played whatever old album sat under it. An instrumental foxtrot rang out. My feet tapped as I moved around, not worried about my lack of coordination. A renewed sense of energy rushed through my soul.

I danced forward and back, turning on all the floor lamps illuminating the wall art and frames that consumed every square inch of wall space then took it all in. "*A new mirror.*" I retrieved a small step stool from the back, climbed up, and found a classic walnut-colored oval mirror with medallion ornaments. This would be a perfect replacement for the one smashed in my bathroom. I took it down and placed it on a shelf under the register.

Last, I turned on the Tiffany lamp with a blue and green glass shade. It sat on the corner of the showcase near the back. The case housed our jewelry, watches, and anything of significant value behind locked glass.

My fingers danced along the case while I hummed, when suddenly a pounding at the front door disrupted my peace. The bell slammed against the wood frame with each hard knock. Startled, I walked to the front only to see my boyfriend, or rather, my ex-boyfriend of 3 weeks, 2 days, 17 hours, and 8 minutes.

"It's unlocked!" I yelled as I opened the door. "What's your problem?"

Ben flew in and past me, slamming the door shut while the bell struggled to hold on.

He ran his fingers up through his medium-length, sandy blonde hair. He hated keeping it short during the wrestling season, so once it was over, the weekly haircut stopped and his soft, natural waves grew.

"Wow," I said. "Drinking already this morning or still recovering from last night?"

He ignored me, though I didn't need a response. I could see he hadn't been to bed yet. He was paler than usual, the whites of his eyes pink with tiny, red veins running in an outward direction. Even his thin lips lacked color.

"You need to stay away from her," he demanded.

Disgusted, I turned away to shield myself from the stale stench of alcohol.

"Stay away from whom?" I said, my heartbreak and sadness replaced with anger, frustration, and a hint of my infamous sarcasm.

"Riley," he replied.

My rolling eyes had become a natural response to her name. That pretentious, private school girl with the perfect blond girl name churned the acid in my stomach. The only negative about her was her long skinny nose and bony face. Everything else was perfection.

"Did you say Riley as in Riley Quartano? Really, you have come here first thing on a Monday to talk about her?" I knew exactly who he was referring to. Still, I didn't understand why he showed up suddenly wanting to talk about the one topic he'd been avoiding for weeks. And while I had been on the other end, demanding he acknowledge their relationship, I now regretted it.

"It was sick and twisted. What were you thinking?" he said, pacing behind me as I glanced over my shoulder, wrinkled my face, and mocked his movements.

"What?" I barked back. "Did you take some type of hallucinogenic?"

"Listen, I dropped her off late last night. When we were pulling up in the driveway, we saw something in the backyard, a shadow," he said and dug into his back pocket and pulled out his phone, scrolling to something while he spoke.

"Well, I thought I saw a shadow, but then, this," he handed his phone over to me. It was open to a picture of a large tree sitting in the moonlight and a white sac of something dangling from a branch.

"What is that?" I asked, zooming in as far as I could without it becoming blurry.

"It's a giant stuffed doll," he spoke slowly.

I scrunched my face, attempting to make out what it was. It resembled a life-size doll version of Riley. I giggled. It was funny and weird. I couldn't see the face from under the long blond hair. But its head, arms, and legs dangled from a large oak tree.

"You think I put that there?" I asked, looking up from his phone with the best annoyed expression I could muster.

"It's creepy," he said. "Creepy, in an Abby kind of way."

"So you imagine it was dark … creepy me. That's what I am to you now?" I asked back.

Why the accusation? There was not one creative bone in my body, and I couldn't have made anything that resembled a human, let alone a human Riley. And I wasn't known for my athleticism either, so the thought that I crept into her backyard, climbed a tree, and hung this thing, without injuring myself, was laughable.

"Look," he said. "Let's just hope her parents don't learn it was you. They'll come after you and your mom. You won't win. It's just better to stay away from her, and I'll see what I can do," Ben said. His movement and rage were slowing.

"What you can do? Why don't you have her parents check the video? I'm sure they have their compound surrounded by cameras," I said. All of my negative emotions whirled inside, causing me to move frantically about the store. I walked over and knocked the needle off the Victrola. Ben grabbed his ears as the needle scratched at the record.

"It wasn't me! You both are so quick to blame and too stupid to check the obvious," I said, thinking about the sage I just burned. I wondered if I burned the sage in the wrong direction. Maybe my mind was not clear enough when I did it, or I didn't leave the door open long enough, or perhaps this stuff wasn't working anymore. Whatever it was, Ben had walked in and with a barrel of negative energy. Oh, and I had Old Man Studdard's voice stuck in my head. Sure, this was turning out to be quite a day, quite an awful one. My flight of ideas led me to one quick decision. I wanted him out of my sight.

"Get out. Go home; go to the Quartano's. And don't come back. Not even to tell me you're sorry!" I threw my bag at him, hitting him in the right shoulder. I am not sure why I did it, but I seemed to be in the bad habit of launching things. It had zero impact, though.

"Abby," he said, stepping toward me and placing my bag in my hands. He looked into my eyes, "You're angry, I'm sorry." He touched my face and noticed the cut. He tried to calm the discussion after his embarrassing rant.

"It's nothing; I cut it ... climbing their tree," I said and clutched my purse to my chest and turned away.

"This is not a joke," he said. "They're furious, and they know your history. They think you're a threat." His pace slowed.

"I'm not the only enemy Riley has," I said. Walking in circles and moving away from him, I needed something, anything, to shake. I found and focused on the ugliest doll we had. Her scratched-up face and turned-in eye distracted my thoughts as I tapped at the side of her head, trying to get the one eye to go midline.

"You're the only one with ... well ... they're just not sure what you're capable of," he said.

"But you know, right? I'm the girl with time in the mental bin, and that makes me insane and even vicious?" I whirled my finger in a small circle around my temple. "You think I'm out to hang her? Believe me, I would like to hang someone right now, but reality dictates I wouldn't." I lifted the doll up in the air and mimicked hanging her by her bonnet string. I wanted to defend myself, but I also wanted to piss him off, too.

"Stop being a brat," he shouted.

I slammed the doll down. Her face shattered on the floor while the one marble eye rolled under a table. "I DIDN'T HANG THE DOLL!"

Ben grabbed my hand and headed over to one of the few areas of bare wall space.

Just then, the terrible sound of that damn bell rang out again. I thought for certain it would be Riley, and I braced myself for her entrance. But it wasn't. In walked a young woman near my age with long dark hair with chunky purple highlights. Her bangs framed her light skin and blue eyes. She wore a short black dress with ankle boots.

"She didn't go hanging any dummies from any trees last night. She was with me," she said.

I stepped back towards Ben and looked fixedly at this girl strolling around the store as if I was expecting her arrival.

"Who is she?" Ben whispered.

Her spot-on hearing left no room for me to provide an answer, which I didn't have anyway.

"Her new BFF, and you?" she said, shrugging her shoulders.

I had no recollection of ever meeting her before today. I pondered on for a moment wondering if she was even human. But Ben could see her.

"I don't know who you are or where you barged in from," Ben squeezed his temples in his right hand, "but you weren't invited."

"Oh, well, it doesn't sound like you were either," she said, as she found an old antique chair to sit down on. She crossed her legs and leaned into the both of us like a therapist at a couples retreat.

"How long were you listening to us?" I quipped back.

She cleared her throat and shook her head. "Doesn't matter."

Ben was angered by her presence and her crass comments.

"I need sleep, not this," he said, sighing and turning me around to face him.

"What do you want, Ben?" I asked, ignoring the girl sitting and peering around me, chomping and popping her gum.

"I don't know, Abby. What do you want?" he said, his hands cupping the sides of my face.

I had no response. I never did. I suppose that always frustrated him. I could never think past the day I was in. I loved him. I needed him in my life. But everything changed when he met Riley. There were things he could never take back, some things I couldn't let go.

"I'm not surprised," he said, pulling away and dropping his arms to his sides. "Stay away from Riley and her family. They are looking to blame someone, and you're first on their list." He glared at the girl. "Have a great day," he said, backing his way up to the door and waving slowly at the unknown gal, who was making herself at home in my store.

With that, he retreated, slamming the door hard enough to carry out a dramatic exit. Staring out the front window, I dealt with the grief of his departure once again. My life had turned into a vicious cycle of anger and sadness.

"You should go after him. Why are you giving up so easily?" she said. Her gum popped again.

"Do I know you?" I swung back around, annoyed with her intrusion of my personal space.

"I'm Agatha Pruitt, Aggie for short," she said.

She drifted back to the seat behind the counter and noticed the glass bowl full of hard candy. She unfolded a piece, spit her gum in the trash, and tossed a round, red ball into her mouth.

"I love cherry. It's my favorite," she said. Drool spilled out as she spoke. Her expression was genuine delight as she fumbled back through the bowl looking for more.

"I'm Abigail, Abby for short, and there is a bag of just cherry under the display case," I said, pointing down and around to the drawer that held the snacks.

I retrieved the broom and headed over to the damaged doll on the floor.

"She's sad," said Aggie, now rifling through the drawer full of candy, taking moments to peek up back over the counter.

"Who?" I asked, spinning around with my broom.

"The doll; you smashed her and ended her journey just like that." She clapped her hands together twice, leaving them up in the air long enough for me to see, then went back to her digging.

It sounded ridiculous, but I respected every piece in our store and suddenly felt guilty with her words.

"You'll get over it though; I don't think she had much to share anyway," she said.

She puzzled and intrigued me all at once. I wanted her to leave, but that trusted gut of mine told me to let her stay.

"I need your help, and maybe I can help you?" she said, and leaned back, tossing the candy up into the air like popcorn.

"And what kind of help do you need exactly, other than the Heimlich, which I will have to perform once that candy goes down the wrong pipe?"

She sat up, dropped her face into her hands, and rolled the candy to the side of her mouth, puffing out her one cheek. "I need a job. You own this place?"

"Uh, it's my parents', our family business."

"So you can hire me, or do I need to meet with someone else?" she asked.

"Yes, I can," I stuttered slowly, "but why should I?"

"Is that an interview question?" she asked in reply.

I peered around as if somebody else might burst in. Here she sat, as comfortable as an old friend. Still, she was a stranger, an edgy drifter who I needed to kick out five minutes ago. Yet I allowed her presence, contemplating the unthinkable while she sat behind our register, chomping on hard candy.

"Where are you from?" I asked as my eyes followed her over to the Victrola, where she flipped through the records beneath. The music returned after she situated the seven-inch on the turntable, cranked the arm, and placed the needle on the record. Opening the doors, she let the sound out as loud as it could go. There she stood her head tilted to one side with her eyes closed, tapping her right boot on the floor.

"You have ADD," I recanted, shaking my head.

"What's ADD? I'll stop playing this, sorry," she said and quickly pulled the needle off, dropped the lid, and closed the volume doors.

"It's okay. You can listen to it. It beats the silence," I said.

She didn't seem interested anymore, which had me convinced there were definitely some undiagnosed attention issues. She ambled from table to table, infatuated with touching everything and ignoring my questions.

"Did you mention where you are from?" I asked, continuing to sweep at nothing with my broom while I tried anticipating how this would all end.

"East Coast ... Battles, Massachusetts," she replied. "My grand-mother lives here in the Creek and is a snowbird this year. I'm house sitting and leaving in the spring. I only need something temporarily— you know, for some extra money."

"You should know my mom may sell the place, so even if I say yes, it may be very temporary."

"Really," she said. In fact, Aggie seemed very curious. "Why is your mom going to sell it?" Leaning back up on the counter, she tossed two more pieces of hard candy in her mouth. The cracking of the candy between her teeth echoed through the store.

"You can take some home," I said and reached around the cabinet and grabbed a bag, holding it up toward her face.

"Sorry; no, it's okay. I am being rude." She went to spit out what was in her mouth into her hand.

"No, no, it's alright. Please. Keep what's in your mouth." I left the bag on the counter if she changed her mind and handed her a roll of paper towels so she could wipe the spit off her chin. I then politely requested she answer my questions. I didn't feel the need to explain any more of hers. She agreed and allowed me to fire them off as fast I could.

"Have you visited here before? I don't remember seeing you, and it's a small town," I said.

"Nope, first time, too occupied with school," she replied.

"High school?"

"No, college; well, some college. I tried a few out, wasn't doing so well. Figured it was a perfect time to leave and get away."

"Was it your plan to come in here this morning and ask for an application?" I asked her then.

"No," she replied.

"So, how?" I paused. There were too many questions to ask. The more she spoke, the more puzzled I became.

"I heard you two arguing from the street, and I picked up on enough that I thought I could come in and help a girl out. You were mad as hops; my walking in was mutually beneficial," she said.

"How so, exactly?"

"I have a knack for antiques. See that candelabra," she walked over to a table with silver and picked one up. "This piece is from the 1850s. You could add a few hundred more dollars to this price tag. You're getting ripped off if you're not selling stuff for the right price. I helped you, and you can help me with a job in a field I know something about. Actually, if you hire me, I am helping you twice." She shook her head in such confidence that I started to shake mine too.

I put aside the remaining questions for a later date. If the store was one of my top priorities, then she was a viable solution. She tore off the price tag and handed the silver piece over to me. I rubbed the cold silver with my hands and made her an offer.

"You can start tomorrow, at 9:30 a.m. We have a big shipment coming in today, and I am getting organized. If you come tomorrow, I can show you around, get you acclimated. Let's start with ten to fifteen hours per week, ten dollars an hour?"

"You mean a week?"

"No, an hour," I drawled. "Ten to fifteen hours per week, ten dollars per hour."

She walked over and shook my hand. "Deal, and how about dinner tonight? Not like a date or anything, just a way for us to become friends and not just colleagues," she said.

It was turning out to be a decent day after a shaky start. First, I added a trip to the local library to my calendar, and now I had an offer to do something fun in the evening with a person I found intriguing. This was the busiest I had been in weeks, so I politely accepted and asked her to meet at the 1816 Tavern at 6 p.m.

With plans confirmed, I ushered her to the door, flipped the closed sign to open and felt grateful and hopeful for the hours left in this day.

CHAPTER 6

SIBLING RIVALRY

One hour had passed. Without looking at a clock, it was easy for me to tell time. I listened for the ticks when all else was silent. It was 1:05 pm and a slow start to this Monday. I was bored and wondering where my Mom was when a light floral scent drifted in on a gust of wind from the now open front door.

Aunt Kate walked in, looking beautiful as always—her five foot, ten inch frame and long legs were covered in cream slacks. Her blond hair cascaded over her signature $400 sunglasses, delicate features, and a mango-colored top. Her stilettos clicked across the floor as she carried a bulky box until the weight of it threatened to snap her heels. I helped her set it down and then waited for the usual greeting. Leaning in, she kissed me on the cheek.

"You look great," she said. "I love your color, especially this time of year. It matches everything."

My color was likely her natural one as well, but years of dyeing fogged her memory. She stopped carefully separating the single blond highlights that framed my face, not before noticing the fresh cut.

I didn't let the question roll off her lips.

"It's nothing," was becoming my go-to response.

"I don't believe that, but well enough for now," Kate said and lifted my chin, trying to catch a closer look. "How have you been feeling otherwise?"

Kate always shifted between being my aunt and being a sister. She was closer in age to me than she was to Mom, which had always been awesome being an only child. But my mom also expected her to be a good role model too, so she watched over me when she could.

"Fine," I mumbled, opening up the box to see what treasures she had inside.

"I mean, how are you dealing with Ben? I just saw him outside."

Her head tilted forward so her eyes could connect with mine. Kate understood heartbreak, too, and was the queen of burying the pain deep below the surface. She had spent her late teens dating some IT business mogul who was much older than any of us. She stunned us all when she married him at twenty-one, and with two "I Do's," he became the closest male figure to an uncle I ever had. His name, Fabrizio Dirossa, was the only handsome thing about him. But he had wit and charm and was kind despite how wealthy he was. I'm not sure what ended their marriage, but she was divorced at twenty-four. And moments after the ink on the papers dried, she was back in the Creek without him. She bought a modest Victorian that she decorated with high-end decor and a sports car. He was gone, but the money and his last name stayed with her.

"I'm not dealing with him at all. He has Riley, and I have to move on," I quipped, then turned my back and walked away from the conversation. The drama this morning had me exhausted. I sensed another hug coming as she followed close behind. Her trip had her absent for the last two weeks and desperate for gossip and attention. These were the times I appreciated my mom's shoulder pat so much more.

"Okay, well, make sure you are taking care of yourself. First love heartbreak hurts badly, and healing is a long process, but it will come. Don't give up on your happiness," she said.

Then she sliced open one of the boxes and leaned in, carefully pulling out paper and bubble wrap. She had a few more things to say, but the cardboard surrounding her torso muffled her words. Returning to a stance, she handed me a small figurine.

"Here, for you," she said and wiped off the dust from a small brass elephant.

I cupped it in my hands, drawing it to my face. A blanket covered the elephant with a hint of green patina. "I love it. It's adorable," I said, rubbing its back and trunk, deciding on a place to keep it safe and away from any customers. But thoughts of Fabrizio and Ben still clouded my mind.

"How did you do it?" I asked her while locating a small trinket box behind the register. I tucked the lucky little fellow into a bed of foam.

"Do what?" Kate clapped her hands together to remove the dust from her fingertips.

I hesitated. "Get over Fabrizio?" I didn't want to talk about Ben anymore, but I welcomed any opportunity to get more details about how her relationship ended and why.

Kate's fingertips danced along her thumbs one at a time. She let the air around her settle in after a big inhale and an even larger exhale. Her eyes moved in an up and down pattern as if she was trying to follow each bustling thought around in her head, the silence becoming more awkward with each second.

"I've healed," she said and pressed her fingertips against her lips.

"How?"

"First love feelings die tragically to prepare you for more heart-break ahead. I got over it, knowing it wouldn't be the last time I loved nor the last time I cried," she said.

Her lack of emotion had me wondering if she just spat out something her therapist talked her into believing. She wasn't lying, but she wasn't honest either. Out of mutual respect, I let the conversation go so we could go back to work.

Kate walked around, fumbling through objects and marveling at others while shaking off my most recent question. She quickly changed the subject back to her journey, taking breaks only to show me pictures on her phone. She usually took them with the people she bought or bartered with. Their faces had as much of a story to tell as the pieces they sold. And this time, her travels took her down through Kentucky and Tennessee before looping back up to Ohio. It was an annual event, an antique trail that was a combination of standalone stores mixed with roadside flea type markets. Every trip, no matter where, resulted in something unique. It was rare for her to come home empty-handed. She loved the travel and the hunt. She could spend days searching through a lot of junk to find one piece she could sell to the right person. She rarely kept anything she found; even the stuff she loved would leave with new families if the smile on a customer's face was large enough. And nothing was better to her than to help someone find an item they never knew they needed.

Each antique wanted a new home, and, like a puppy finding their person, she sensed when the match was spot-on. I, like my mom, wanted to keep so much. We were both only one more tragedy away from becoming hoarders, which was never good for sales or for our bottom line. I connected with pieces by touch and had visions with every personal story Kate told. So, when I had to see something go, I shared whatever story I had, to pass it along and keep its history alive. It would give me peace when letting it go. Thankfully, we had Kate too. She nudged the selling along and would dig out items from the back, which we would hide. The more I thought about how she balanced out our obsessive behaviors, the more I realized how much better we could be doing.

Seeing her was the best part of any day, but seeing the white box truck outside our front window made me wince. Not only did we not have space, I wondered if Mason would sell it for pennies on the dollars she'd just spent. All my thoughts were quickly coming to an end as my mom appeared through the front door. She walked right past the truck without giving it a second look. Kate hugged her immediately, as she always did. She was the younger, more outgoing, more affectionate, more everything sister.

My mom resisted her squeeze but gave a polite, "Hello, Katie."

"You look pale this morning," Kate said, as she held Lauren's chin with her two fingers.

"I need to have someone come look at our well. Our first floor smells like eggs again. It just comes and goes, and when it arrives, it's gross." Mom was quick on her feet with a false explanation, routing Kate off in another direction. I shook my head at my mom, but she never noticed.

"Call Jack," Kate said, looking at her truck out by the curb.

Unfortunately, Jack couldn't fix the cause of the stench. I waited and watched as my mom actively avoided any more conversation *and* the truck of goods altogether. The locals hated when Kate pulled up front and parked it, despite the hazard lights blinking. Main Street was narrow, and the truck's size caused a disruption in the traffic flow, making my mom uncomfortable. Usually, the two would end up in a brief disagreement about whether it was legal to unload. Kate would stall long enough for an officer to arrive who, while politely asking her to move it to the back, would end up helping her unload it from the front. Kate just had that way with people.

Still on a high from the stories she shared, she didn't notice my mom avoiding her. Her energy level kept her moving at a fast pace while my mom got the abbreviated version of her travels.

"I'm so excited for the holidays this year," said Kate. "Wait till you see what I found. I know we still have some space to create, but some of these items will fit nicely in the front window. It will be the best holiday season we've ever had."

Kate disappeared out front only to return quickly with a medium-sized box. She placed it on the jewelry showcase and pulled out a large copper bowl. Retreating to the back and returning with a sprinkling can full of water; she poured it into the bowl, filling it three-quarters of the way and then plugged it in. Water flowed up from the center of the bowl, swirling three floating brass bells around six fixed bells. The random chime created a soft rhythmic song, immediately calming the energy in the space.

"What do you think, Lauren? Isn't it beautiful? And the sound, so gentle. This will make a great gift for someone," she said excitedly.

But Mom kept her head low fidgeting with the register, glancing up for a brief second only to turn away again.

"Okay, why are you both acting so strange?" Kate's frame spun in my direction.

I didn't answer.

"Lauren?" she said, looking back at my mom.

"Someone talk. My neck is getting a kink from all this turning," she added.

Still, more silence as I puffed out my upper lip. It was a weird habit I had when I couldn't speak. Unfortunately, it was also my tell.

"Abby! Seriously!" Kate tucked hair behind her ears then crossed her arms.

I didn't want to do it. I opened my eyes wide in my mom's direction, but she ignored me and left me with no choice but to speak. "Mason and my mom are meeting with an antique dealer in two weeks. They want to sell the store," I said quickly.

It was like the beginning of a purge after a binge. I was sick from the information layered in my gut. But now, bits and pieces were working their way out, burning my throat as I let them out.

Kate didn't respond. She stood quietly and patiently.

"It's Mason," I said. "He's forcing Mom to sell the store, and whatever's in it. I'm not sure it will even be open for the holidays." I grabbed my elephant, rubbed it between my fingers, and walked away toward the front window.

"Explain," said an angry Kate, now glaring at my mom and tapping her index finger on the side of her own cheek. I counted her taps, looking for a pattern, but only noticed the hollow sound as her finger bounced off her skin.

The sound agitated me for no apparent reason other than the need to keep purging. The flow of words poured out of me. I rambled on about the events of the morning, Mason's paper, the coffee, the job, the earthquake, and the headaches, while never turning around.

"What headaches?" The sound of Kate's shoes clicked up behind me as I turned to look over my shoulder.

My mom's eyes grew wide, but I routed the conversation back to the store.

"It's okay, Kate. I'll keep the store. I'll save it and run it on my own," I said, while turning back toward the windowpane watching all the adults drifting around outside. I didn't want to see either of their expressions, or lack thereof, for that matter. I focused on life outside when a dark bird slammed into the window and fell. I gasped. Kate and my mom paused. I caught my breath and peered out the window but didn't see the bird. Kate dove back into the conversation.

"Wait. Are we selling the store or keeping it? Someone needs to get this straight," Kate said, her voice bouncing off each wall and every object, creating a million little echoes. She marched back toward my mom.

I continued searching for the body of the bird but it was gone.

"Don't look at me like that," I could hear my mom clamor.

"How would you like me to look? Just answer the question," Kate replied.

"Thanks, Abby," said my Mom.

I looked back at her with a weak attempt to apologize with my eyes. But then I snapped back into this reality and the mess that she alone created.

"You couldn't keep this from Kate," I quietly responded.

"Don't be mad at her; somebody had to tell me. I have a box-truck full of stuff outside," Kate said as she pointed toward the front of the store and stomped her right foot on the floor several times.

"And it had to be Abby. She would choose you over me any day," my mom said, and slammed objects on the counter, then paced behind it in small circles. She believed it, too. She wanted Kate to always be an authoritative figure in my life, but Kate spent more time trying to be my friend. My mom was jealous of that relationship and hurled it in Kate's face whenever she had the chance.

"Have you lost your mind? Choose me? I am her aunt; you're her mom. There is no choice. This is just another example of your insecurities. It gets old," Kate said. It was rare for Kate to call out any of my mom's traits negatively, but when she got mad, it was difficult for her to hold back.

"You get to be the rich, young, well-traveled aunt. I get to be the mom who has to make tough choices. This has nothing to do with me being insecure and everything to do with you always looking like the hero," my mom said and returned to the space behind the register, pressing down on the keys with both of her pointer fingers.

"Don't change the subject," said Kate, who pushed my mom out of the way to log onto the register. Her typing ended with a successful chime, indicating it was ready for the first sale of the day.

Lauren let out a loud sigh and then a garbled roar. They were both manic and awkward. Kate handled the confrontation head-on while my mom desperately tried to avoid it. Kate followed her around, barking out question after question. The faster my mom walked, the quicker Kate caught up to her. My head spun, watching them maneuverer around the small store.

"Stop, Kate; please stop chasing me," said my mom, as she twisted, looking for an escape.

"Well, then, you stop. Stop and tell me what is going on," Kate replied.

My mom halted, rolled her eyes, and then gave her the same explanation she had given me a few hours earlier. With my elephant in hand, I watched the people outside our window, wondering if the smiles on all their faces were sincere. Could it be that everyone around was happy and stress-free every minute of every day? Had they peered in and listened to the fights? Was this why they talked behind their hands when we were near?

"Are you crazy?" said Kate. "Did he talk you into this again?"

"Yes. No!" Lauren said.

"Did you think for a moment about discussing this with me? I have just as much invested in the place as you, if not more," Kate said.

I wanted to tune back out, but there was no end in sight of the argument. They were both too emotionally charged, and I had to end it. I closed my eyes to the beautiful world outside and headed back into the thick of the conversation.

"We all know how much you have invested, your ex-husband made sure of that," yelled Lauren before retreating to the backroom and avoiding Kate's looming response.

I glanced over at Kate and placed my hand up in a stopping motion. Lauren had taken a turn down an entirely different road lined with guilt, hate, and sadness. Kate's comeback would be equally devastating. But Kate blew past me and kept talking.

"My ex-husband is the reason you still have this place. We're all grateful, remember," Kate retorted.

My mom's tiny frame reappeared in the doorway to the back room. Her shoulder-length hair was a mess from her fingers digging into her skull. Her face and chest were covered in blotchy, red spots that she rubbed fiercely with her hands. Kate had dug the knife in deep. All I could do was look at Kate in heartache. Years after my dad died, our financial state took a downward turn during an awful recession. We struggled to keep the store and our home, but Mom managed to take out a loan from the bank she could never pay back. After Kate got married, she surprised my mom and paid off the balance. Kate stepped in and gave her money without ever asking for it back. In return, Kate became Lauren's business partner. My mom was always appreciative that she could keep our lives as normal as much as possible, but Kate's financial assistance hurt her pride.

"Real nice," responded my mom.

"You don't get to make this decision without me. It's our store," Kate said.

"This was my store, remember? My store with James, long before it was ever yours," Mom replied.

Hurrying around the store, my mom pointed at anything and everything that had been there for the last seventeen years. The store's sign out front, the curtain rod above the front windows, the cash register, the table linens, and the walls sconces, everything that had been there since the day they opened.

It was sad. She was a young child, laying claim over what was hers. The tears welled up over her bottom lids and streamed down her face. Her voice cracked as she tried to gain control of the muscles around her mouth, which went all crazy when she wanted to sob. She was failing.

Kate walked toward and wrapped her arms around her sister, but my mom pulled away.

"Why do you want to do this? You are not ready," said Kate. "If you were ready, I would help, but you're not."

Kate wiped away a few of her own tears and then tried regaining some hint of composure. She smoothed out her hair, fixed her shirt, and clenched her hands. She was angry, hurt, and sad for my mom all at the same time, but she felt as blindsided as I did.

"I don't want your help anymore! And this is what's best for Abby. It's been twelve years, and twelve years of struggle. Abby needs to move on and find something to do with her life. There is no future selling antiques. If I don't do this, she will rot here. It's time," Mom said.

"Rot? You call doing something you love 'rotting'?" I asked, still trying to keep the volume and tone down. People outside were starting to stare.

"You love it for the wrong reasons. You are holding on to your father. You need to find what you, Abigail Anderson, loves, not what your dad and I loved together," she said and dropped her body into a wooden rocker in the store's corner.

"It shouldn't matter why I am holding on to. If I love it, then I get a say in keeping it," I replied.

"Abby, look at your life. How many trips have I made over the years to the psychiatrists and counselors? How much money spent on prescription after prescription? How many sleepless nights? I know more than anyone how this has affected you. If you don't set yourself free from all of this, nothing will get better for you. It's this place that's holding you back," she returned.

Then, she stopped rocking and allowed the chair to propel her upward, and retreated to the back office, slamming the door behind her. Kate closed her mouth, bit her lower lip, and folded her arms tight across her body. I made eye contact and shrugged my shoulders.

"Now what?" I asked.

"Why don't you head home and take a break?" Kate said, walking over, picking up my bag and tossing it into my arms. "Your mom and I will get through the day just fine. Let's meet back up here tomorrow and make a plan."

Suddenly, a sharp pain entered my left temple and traveled across my forehead to the other side. My knees buckled as the room became gray.

"Are you okay?" Kate grabbed my left forearm.

"Yeah," I said, but I could only mutter a few words. "Going home is a good idea."

I grabbed my new mirror and walked to the front door, and pulled it open slowly to avoid disrupting the clapper in the hollow cup of the bell. I snuck out under it and closed it shut behind me. The pain in my head already subsiding, I took in a deep breath of fresh air and relief to be out of what would be a toxic environment for the rest of the day. The calm lasted only a second though before a blow to my left shoulder jarred me.

"Sorry," said a man with a low, hoarse voice.

He spun around to my front and center, revealing his identity. It was Mayor Quartano, trying to stop the inertia from his round, short body from carrying himself into our front window. His right hand held a tall Styrofoam cup that spewed hot liquid as he slowed his steps.

"Pardon me," he said in the most insincere way. Once he regained his clumsy footing, he started moving toward the town hall. He was obnoxious and rude unless he was posing for a picture or being interviewed for TV.

I responded with the same lack of empathy and a harsh squint. "No worries." I stepped back, rethinking my rude response. He was Riley's dad. Did he come here to accuse me of hanging a Riley look-alike in their tree? Was this the beginning of the threat Ben warned me about?

I watched for a moment, holding my breath when he dug his left hand into his suit pocket and pulled something out. I braced myself. Then, he lifted a small shiny object high into the air and watched as rays of sun bounced off and into the passersby's eyes. He flipped it up with his thumb, just like the gal from my dream and the photo. It spun and turned gracefully before falling back into his hand. Over and over, he tossed and whistled until he finally disappeared out of sight.

CHAPTER 7

BREAKING AND ENTERING

My afternoon flew by. I hung my new mirror and cleaned up the shreds of glass that still covered my bathroom floor. With an empty house I then chose to spend the remaining hours of my day in the hearth room off the kitchen. Our cozy space was one of my favorite places to chill when Mason wasn't around. A few odd and end pieces of furniture and décor we had accumulated over the years made it feel eclectic and inviting. We had an old stone fireplace and hearth, with all the wood-burning fireplace tools and an old puffer that hung from the mantle. White built-in shelves wrapped around and housed all of our trinkets. Though it wasn't cold enough for a fire, I built one anyway— an easy task for someone who had been building fires since they were little. The sound of the crackling wood echoed in the small space.

I dropped back into the best chair we owned and lounged with my legs up over the side and my head dangling, taking in the view. Mason had eliminated most of the photos that rested between candles and books, but I kept one slightly out of sight on the middle, right shelf toward the back corner. Every year, giant hot air balloons appeared from all over the state for the annual Allison Creek Blossom Festival. On the first night of the celebration, the balloons ascended into the atmosphere after the sun fell. The soft light from each balloon cast a glow over the town. I remember feeling like it was right out of a fairy tale. The balloons were enormous and lit up the night sky, and at age four, it seemed magical. My father held me, pointing up at the sky as the glorious backdrop took shape. I exhaled a feeling of security wrapped around the room and flowed with the heat radiating from the fire. It was comforting to remember the day without crying.

It was 3:33 p.m., and I began to regret agreeing to meet Aggie. I enjoyed the silence and the peace that dodged me all morning. I sat hidden from the outside world, my phone screen clear of calls, texts, and new emails, and the only sound in the house was that of our grandfather clock. Thoughts of Ben and my fake friends clouded my mind. I devoted most of high school to Ben, his friends, and their girlfriends. Not long after Ben disappeared, everyone else did too. I should've kept Cici closer to me. I regretted letting that friendship fade.

The doorbell chimed, forcing me to move. I had no stamina for Ben or anyone else. But outside our screen door stood Jack.

"Hi! Are you looking for my mom?" I asked, unable to think of any other reason he would be there.

"Yeah; she asked me to stop by when I had a moment. She mentioned some damage done this morning to a few of your kitchen cupboards and one of your door jambs," Jack said. He stood on the front porch in another signature ball cap with a patch displaying a racecar. In his right hand, he carried a small shiny black toolbox.

Jack was an all-around handyman, whether he was in his shop or working on something at home. He knew the names of every tool and loved the chance to use them. He lived only three doors down and had developed a solid friendship with my mom over the years. Fortunately, he was always around if a pilot light blew out on the furnace, or if the garage door got jammed, he was close and happy to be.

"Yeah, come on in. She's not here, but you're welcome to look," I said and led the way, turning on lights as we walked.

"You hibernating today?" he asked as he grabbed his shirt and pulled it away from his chest to move some air. "Wow, it's warm in here. Should I check your thermostat, too?"

"No," I giggled. "I built a fire, that's all."

"A fire? Today?" he asked, sounding puzzled.

"I know; I was in the mood for one," I said. I always ran cold, so the heat never bothered me much, but for Jack, who ran hot, this was torture.

"You know there is a cable channel with a fake fire you could look at too, without all the added heat," he went on. Poor Jack had already started to sweat, wiping his head with his forearm.

"I'll open some windows and turn on the ceiling fans. It was only two small logs. Should be out soon." I did my best to sell it, but Jack was not buying.

"Not soon enough."

Jack set his toolbox on the kitchen counter and took a paper towel to wipe his head off. I opened all the windows in the four-season room and then the front door, which ushered in a cool breeze that flowed through the house. Jack welcomed the air with outstretched arms.

"Your mom mentioned an earthquake this morning," he said, still cooling himself.

"Yes, it shook the whole house, pretty violently," I replied.

"So you were here?" he asked, opening his toolbox and throwing a few hand tools in his belt that sat low on his waist.

"Yeah, up in the bathroom. When I tried to make it down the hall, I fell, everything was shaking. It lasted a few seconds," I replied.

"Strange; they felt nothing at the shop and I was on my bike so I didn't notice. I haven't been home yet, but hopefully, what few dishes I have are not broken on the floor," he said, smiling.

"Maybe it's a sign you need more dishes," I winked.

"Or more company," he laughed.

Watching Jack move through the kitchen and remembering that Mason would be gone all day, I wondered if it was finally my chance to get into that locked office of his.

"Jack, since you're here, maybe you could also fix Mason's office door? It's jammed. Is there something you could use to unjam it?" I asked, raising my eyebrows, waiting for his response.

Jack looked over his shoulder. "I guess I could. Is he scheduled back anytime soon?"

"No, not likely till six, his usual return time," I said, speaking fast. The truth was, I wasn't sure when he'd return, but I wanted to get Jack moving while I had any time to spare.

"Well, let's head over and look at the door before I get started in here." He grabbed a few more tools and fumbled around in his back pocket.

"Perfect," I said and moved toward the front of the house and past the stairway where a short hall sat. To the right was a half bath, to the left, Mason's front office. Jack pulled up on both handles of two french leaded-glass doors that were heavily frosted.

"They seem jammed alright," he said, jiggling the knobs.

Or locked, I thought to myself. Jack was a smart man and played along. He liked my mom; probably a little more than he ever wanted to admit, and I knew he didn't like Mason either. He tolerated him for the sake of his friendship with my mom, but his facial expressions when Mason was around gave away his innermost thoughts.

"My most trusted tool," he said, pulling out something from his back pocket.

"What's that?" I asked, not be able to see what he cupped in his hand.

Jack pulled out a credit card from his wallet and waved it in a circle.

"Never leave home without it," he said.

Jack then placed a tiny flathead screwdriver in the right keyhole while sliding the card in between the two doors just above the lock. A few turns with a quick slide of the card, and Jack pushed the right door open.

"I would say it's fixed," he said, fanning his right arm outward, ushering me into the office space.

"Perfect! Thank you," I whispered, walking by him, my adrenaline surging.

"No problem. I'll finish up the rest of my duties in the kitchen. Leave this how Mason would like to find it, though." He half smiled and disappeared back toward the kitchen.

Pushing the door open, I stepped into space I had not seen in over a year. Mason's stench mixed with his signature cologne hovered over the room like a black cloud. I glanced around. Tall red curtains blanketed the front windows. A modest desk, a chair, and two giant mahogany bookcases sat, separated by a large, round mirror. A Victorian, rectangular area rug covered the early twentieth-century wood floors. Ambling, I tried not to make too much noise. Jack was the only other person in the house, but being quiet felt necessary when trespassing into someone's space. I was honoring what I thought would be breaking and entering 101. The shelves, mostly empty, held a few motivational books with similar titles about winning, succeeding, and being your best. I ran my fingers along each shelf; feeling nothing, not even dust on my skin. It lacked all things personal, no pictures of my mom or family, no old black-and-whites of him playing football in high school. Zero. For someone so caught up in his own personal accolades, there were no diplomas or awards hanging behind frames. The room was unwelcoming and mostly empty.

I walked behind the desk and sat in the black leather chair, taking a moment to enjoy just how mad he would be if he saw me sitting in his space. While it brought a sense of power, it reminded me of just how risky this was. I spun around and pulled the shades tighter, overlapping them to prevent any view from the street.

The computer monitor sat dark, and only a pad of paper and pen rested on the glass-protected desk. I opened the bottom left drawer filled with typical office supplies. I moved to the small upper left drawer. On top was a folded-up packet of blueprints. Pulling them out, I was careful to open them onto the desk paying attention to each fold. The entire time I wondered why Mason would have blueprints. They were definitely not in his line of work.

I unfolded the large packet of paper by its crease, saving the steps to memory so I could fold them back up in the same manner. Flattening it out with my right hand and noticing the architectural front of the neighboring town's church. The bottom right corner was labeled: "A1 of 15, Hunting Valley Memorial Church, Santos Quartano Architects LLC, June 1, 1998."

"Quaratano?" The mayor often spoke about his wife and daughter, but I had never heard of Santos. I turned the pages carefully. The first few pages were a floor plan of a church. The last few contained images of an intricate tunnel system that branched from underneath. It was all underground. There were stores, homes, schools, and farmlands all resting above this elaborate system. I scanned the last page, A7. In the upper left corner of the page in red cursive, were the words: "To find the witch is to find your way." A8–A15 was missing.

A puff of cold air swirled around the back of my neck, traveling down my spine to my limbs. My core muscles tightened. Dragging my fingers over the ink, I listened and remembered Manshaw's earlier warning about witchcraft. I continued to move my hand across the paper and up toward the top right corner.

"Meet with Santos, Monday at 10 a.m. Lunch with Lauren, noon." My stomach dropped.

It was my dad's handwriting, and these were his blueprints in the top left drawer of Mason's desk. But why? Mason threw out anything that belonged to my father. Why were these so important? I bit down hard, clenching my teeth until a noise from a car door outside startled me. I closed up the prints and placed them back in the drawer, but in my haste, my right hand hit the mouse on the computer. The black screen turned to a bright blue hue then a page began loading. I shook the mouse wanting to minimize, but it didn't. Instead, dark chords and sinister-sounding music blared out through the speakers.

I fell back into the desk chair, staring at a screen full of symbols and italic print. The cursor hovered over the domain name, "The Darkest Witches in History."

I heard more noise out front and rolled back to peek out the curtain.

"*No, no, no,*" I cried to myself. It was Mason.

I wildly shook the mouse and tapped at the keyboard, trying anything to make it stop.

"Oh God," I said out loud, as I heard the front door screen close.

"Mason," Jack said, extra loud.

"Hey there, how are you, buddy? It's been a while," Mason's voice pierced my ears.

The page minimized, and the sound stopped. I ran over to the doors and squeezed myself back through the glass, waiting for Jack to speak. When his voice was loud, I pulled up on the handle to close it. My body melted into the wall, waiting for Mason's footsteps to carry him past the hall. My breath quickening, I leaped over to the half bath, flushed the toilet, turned the faucet on for three seconds, shut it off, and then walked out into the front room. Mason turned around as the sound of the flushing toilet was fading away.

"Hi," was all I could muster.

"Hello," Mason said before he coughed a few times into his clenched hand.

"Just taking a potty break," I said, pointing back to the bathroom, and rushed past him to head upstairs, scolding myself over my poor choice of words. *Nothing odd here,* I thought. At the top of the stairs and now out of Mason's view, I stopped to listen.

Mason coughed some more, grossly clearing phlegm from his throat. Of all days for him to come home early and sick.

"Lauren has me fixing a few cabinets that came unhinged. Is there anything you need fixing while I am here?" said Jack, attracting Mason's full attention.

I leaned over the rail catching the slightest view of both of them.

"No, I don't think so; all is good," Mason spoke slowly as Jack walked over, patted him on the right shoulder, and guided him back toward the kitchen. But not before looking up the stairs at me with a nervous smile.

Instead of walking to my room, I waited and listened to the rest of their conversation.

"You do some good work, Jack; you'll be missed," Mason said.

"Missed, am I going somewhere?" Jack asked.

Mason gave his usual chuckle, the one he shared when feeling socially superior to someone else.

"No, we're going somewhere. I was promoted to National Accounts, which will require an extensive travel schedule that will have me away all month. Lauren will travel with me, so we are selling the store," said Mason, who was now obnoxiously blowing his nose.

Mason made my teeth hurt. Every time he spoke, my jaw clenched tighter and for a more extended period. I couldn't see Jack's reaction, but given the long pause, I knew he was struggling to respond with the congratulatory remark Mason was waiting for.

"Lauren wants to close the store?" Jack's voice transitioned from loud and boisterous to quiet and solemn with each word.

"Yep. And Abby is on board, too," said Mason.

My nails dug into the wood rail. My teeth chomped into the side of my cheek. I curled forward with the nauseating taste of blood, slapping my thigh as I waited for the sting to subside.

The raucous sound of a hammer hitting metal meant Jack went back to work without comment. Mason requested his help at the store in the breaks between swings, going on about how awful the place would look once we moved everything out. He wanted the walls painted and the floors redone, so the landlord wouldn't give us any trouble. Jack didn't say another word, not one I could hear anyway, so I moved back down the steps to join him. I passed Mason along the way. He loosened his tie, and despite clearly being sick, he tried his best to maintain his display of confidence. He sputtered a weak goodbye to Jack and ascended upstairs.

Jack still pounded away with his hammer while I stood and waited for him to feel my presence. He stopped and moved in closer to speak.

"Is your mom really closing the store?" he asked.

"I hope not, but he has her convinced it's the best thing for everyone," I said. My shoulders shrugged. Like me, Jack was curious for answers, but all I could offer was support.

"Is she moving away with him?" he asked.

"I don't know. They haven't talked about it with me. I'm sure selling this house is next on his list, though," I replied.

"Wow, I didn't think your mom would ever leave."

"Me neither, but I am not letting her or the store go without a fight," I said. I made eye contact with Jack, offering reassurance. I had nothing to be all that sure, but we needed to be there for each other.

"Well, if you need anything, you let me know," Jack said and tipped the front of his hat forward.

"I will, Jack. Thank you."

"You're welcome, and I hope you found what you were looking for," said Jack as he turned, beating on the cabinets once again.

CHAPTER 8

1816 TAVERN

I spent the rest of the afternoon pretending to read in the front room. Jack finished up his work and left, while Mason never returned from their upstairs bedroom. The house was almost silent when the chime of our grandfather clock rang out five times. I stretched and closed up the book, all my thoughts focused on getting ready and going out for a much-needed break. Escaping to my bathroom, I locked the door. I decided on a long shower where the slow cascade of warm water and the floral scent of soap would replace my anxiety with calm and the smell of cardboard and dust with flowers. I showered until the hot water was almost gone.

Fortunately, the rest of my routine was not time-consuming. I straightened my locks, made up my face, and spritzed a hint of perfume on my neck that Ben had bought me for Christmas last year. I hated the hint of jasmine and musk that he loved so much, but it was all I had. The upstairs quiet of footsteps was my cue to dash to my room and complete my look of skinny jeans, a vintage rock tee, a long black cardigan sweater, and short black boots.

Mason was likely passed out from cold medicine, which allowed me to sneak down the hallway and stairs without disturbing him. Outside, I stood in my driveway for a moment, staring at our garage that housed a dated, olive green SUV. I pondered whether to drive or walk when I remembered all of the high schoolers and their families out this evening. Sixteen-year-olds here drove miniature versions of their parents Audi's and Mercedes, nothing American-made. Parking was a hassle too and trying to valet the old tank was not an option. It would remain parked.

My walk into town got me there seven minutes later than antici-pated. Packs of people were all tripping over one another, talking about the first day back. I recognized a few kids from school and many people who shopped at our store. Cici was out too with her family, including her brother, flaunting one of his new tee-shirt masterpieces. "Your Cookies Suck" was boldly displayed across his chest. His mortified sister stood nearby, still hiding her support beneath a sweater. I smiled and gave a wave from across the room, thinking about the hordes of moms all competing for the best cookie recipe at every school fundraiser since kindergarten. His shirts were making more sense.

I kept my head low, closing in on the hostess stand when a voice caught me from behind.

"I thought you were standing me up?"

Turning to the side, I saw Aggie walking toward me.

"Sorry; remind me to get your phone number before I leave," I said. "Next time, I'll call you."

Aggie grabbed my hand and guided me back toward the dining room. Toasts were yelled out, ushering in the start of a new school year as wine glasses clinked together. Men tipped back their bottled beer while their wives snickered behind closed hands. It was a fantastic turn-out for the official kick-off to another nine months of social climbing for the Creeks' finest.

"Is this acceptable?" she said as she pointed to a table near the back next to a show window. The windows along the left side of the restaurant overlooked the natural waterfall the Creek was known for. The massive windows trimmed in black metal allowed for full viewing of the water cascading over, before plummeting down and disappearing west into the woods. It was a space more suitable for a couple but farther away from the discord upfront.

"It's good," I said, pulling out a chair and dropping my bag on the table.

I noticed she had changed from a black dress to a dark gray one with black tights. She had a black leather jacket with gray sleeves and an attached gray hoodie. A black choker sat snug against her pale skin.

Her hair was pulled up in a loose pony with evenly spread purple streaks along the sides. Her dramatic style attracted the attention of some nearby tables.

"Is my dress okay?" she asked, noticing the unwanted scrutiny.

"I really like what you're wearing. It's different from anything you see around here, as long as you don't mind being noticed," I said, making eye contact with a nearby mom who quickly turned away when caught.

"Doesn't bother me," she said, fumbling with the napkin. Our twenty-something male waiter slid in, grabbing her napkin and shaking it out before draping it across her lap.

"Oh, thank you!" Aggie said, blushing at the tall man in a white button-down with a tightly wrapped black apron over his jeans. His mane was combed perfectly, and his short beard was groomed and oiled without a hair out of place.

"Drinks?" he asked.

"I will have water with lemon," I said, looking over the one-page menu while I waited for Aggie.

Aggie thought for a minute before replying. "How about a Mary Pickford?"

He tugged at his beard and politely asked, "A what?" then looked at me, but I was just as confused.

"How about a Shirley Temple then?" she responded.

"Okay, well, for starters, I at least know what that is. Rarely get a request for one, but sure." He nodded in acceptance and moved along to other tables taking breaks to smile back in her direction.

"What the heck is a Mary Pickford?" I asked.

"Never mind, the Shirley Temple works. It has lemon-lime soda, ginger-ale, and cherries," she said.

"Well, cherries make more sense."

"Should I order something different?" she asked.

"No, if they can make it, enjoy it. I've just never heard of it," I said. I really didn't care—I was just curious. I chalked it up to another one of her unusual traits that I welcomed after growing up in a town where everything was the same. I didn't want to spend the evening talking about drinks, so it was an excellent time to transition to another topic.

"Why don't we exchange numbers?" I asked as I pulled out my phone.

"Sure; let me get your number now." Aggie dug in her black leather bag and pulled out her phone with the charging cord still attached. She tugged at it, finally releasing it from her bag then proceeded to tap at the buttons manically.

"New phone?" I inquired.

"Oh, yes," she said, still madly typing.

"Tell me your number, and I will call you. You can add me that way," I told her.

"Um, I don't know my number," she said.

"You don't?" I asked, amused.

"This is my first phone," she said, putting down her phone forcefully, the cord dangling off the table. "I don't come from a lot of money, okay? I didn't always get things when everyone else did."

"It's okay. I don't come from money, either. I'm not judging you, but let me help," I said. Then I reached out and politely took the phone out of her hand and pulled out the cord, handing the cord back to her. Why was she acting so weird? I was not sure which puzzled me more: her inability to use it or her reaction.

It was not password-protected either, so I scrolled through the functions and loaded my number in an empty contact list.

"Do you have your grandmother's number or your parents? I can add those, too," I offered.

"No, that's okay," she said, staring at me with a half-smile.

As I was handing her phone back to her, another hand reached in, covered in rose-gold rings and bangle bracelets. It was Avery Greene, behind her Casey Flynn, and coming up from the rear, Riley Quartano, her signature locks replaced with a short layered cut and bangs. I looked twice to confirm it was her. To my dismay, it was.

All three graduated from Berkshire Private Academy this past spring, an all-girl school for families with tons of disposable income. Intelligence was not a prerequisite, only a bank account capable of handling thirty thousand dollar per year tuition.

"So, who do we have here?" said Avery. "Looks like a new 023." She was the shortest and thickest of the three. She had medium-length dark brown hair, which she tried to sway with every exaggerated motion she made. Laughing, she showed the other girls Aggie's phone. Aggie tried to swipe it back, but Avery quickly turned. Aggie groaned. Her face turned red.

"What's an 023?" Aggie asked flatly.

While the three of them obnoxiously giggled, I leaned in and whispered a quick review. "023 is the ending of the zip code here in the Creek. The Berkshire girls all live in a city north of here. They refer to themselves as the 022s. It's dumb."

Avery didn't like my comment.

"One contact? And it's Abby, the weird girl from the old folk's store. Where did you wash up from? And where did you get those clothes? Gross," Avery said, glancing at me, and then focusing back on Aggie. Aggie was faster this time and ripped her phone from Avery's hand.

"That's a mighty big sentence for you, don't you think?" Aggie said, stretching her torso upward with her face only inches from Avery's.

Avery's eyes crossed, and then she leaned back and opened her lids wide to readjust. I giggled at the very image of her but braced myself. No one ever talked back to them. Ever.

"What?" said Avery, "It doesn't even make sense?" Riley and Casey pushed her closer to Aggie. They were nose to nose. Aggie didn't shy away.

"Really, I heard you failed every grade in high school and that your parents paid for your diploma. Care to spell disgusting? How about despicable, deplorable, and oh, here is an easy one … dumb?" she went on.

Riley laughed out loud, stunning all of us. She covered her mouth as Avery now glared at her with her hands up in the air. Riley dropped her hand and got back into character.

"Peasants," Riley said, fluttering her eyelashes and turning to walk away.

"Watch your back," added Casey, who was too busy checking out her outfit in the reflection of the window and straightening her long blonde locks.

"Okay," said Aggie. "Thanks for the trip back to the 1980s. I'll be sure to watch my back, but your ass is grass next time I see you." Then Aggie laughed emphatically.

A strange shriek exited my throat, stunning me and the tables nearby. Aggie was fierce, funny, and eccentric. Riley was the leader, though, and at that moment, she turned back to finish us.

Her finely manicured nails stroked the tablecloth while she spoke to Aggie then me.

"You picked the right loser to hang with," she turned, "and you better hope to God I don't find out it was you who hung that doll. I'll send you back to the trailer from which you came," she said.

I rubbed my brow. God! She was stupid. "I'm from here, Riley, the Creek; there are no trailers." Aggie and I shared a mutual eye roll and then waved them off. I smugly grinned. I don't know if I could've had the last word without Aggie's support. It was empowering and awesome.

Her cheeks flushed as she backed away snickering. The three tripped over one another as they tried dodging patrons and staff.

"Wow! Were they frosted?" said Aggie.

"Frosted?" I chuckled.

"Yeah, like angry," she explained.

Her choice of words baffled me, but I was more interested in her statement about Avery. "Where did you hear that about her?" I asked Aggie.

"Hear what?"

"That Avery's parents paid for her diploma?" I went on.

"I didn't; just an educated guess. It sounds like I hit a nerve, though," she replied.

"That's some guess," I said.

"I've always been good at reading people," Aggie said and stretched up. Then, she continued watching them until they sat at a table upfront.

"I'll say. It would make sense, though. She definitely functions on an inner dimmer switch," I responded.

Aggie laughed so hard she snorted.

"I think we're going to be good friends," I said. Aggie sat back then shot a piercing glance toward a nearby table of women, struggling to mind their own business. "Get used to it," I said. "It's a nosey town."

Despite running into the three halfwits, it was turning out to be a fun night. Thankfully, my back was to Riley as Aggie and I talked over two salads and a plate of mozzarella sticks. We were probably too loud, but crowds of people filled in the later it got and drowned out our cackling. It was going well until I caught a change in Aggie's demeanor. Turning around, I saw Ben with his two friends, Luke and Kyle. They confidently walked into the diner and found the three open seats at Riley's table. Ben never looked up, but Luke saw me and gave a quick wave.

"Ugh," I said out loud.

"So what's the story?" asked Aggie, who chewed apart every piece of ice in her drink. Occasionally, shrapnel from a once whole cube shot out toward me, melting as it hit my face.

"Long version or short?" I questioned while wiping my skin with a napkin.

"How about the authentic version?" she quipped.

Again, strange, but perhaps she wanted only the facts.

"I met Ben when I was in ninth grade. He was in the tenth. We were friends for a year when he surprised me with an invitation to the homecoming dance. We were inseparable from that point until about six weeks ago when we broke up," I told her.

"What happened?" she asked.

"Ben, Luke, and Kyle," I motioned upfront, "all wrestled for the high school team. Last year, Ben won States, first wrestler ever from the Creek. It brought a lot of attention to this small town, including attention from the Berkshire girls."

"And who are they?" Aggie asked.

I pointed back up toward Riley and her crew. "A bunch of rich kids who frequently hang out in the Creek."

"So how did Ben and Riley meet?" she went on.

"Riley's dad is also the mayor of the Creek."

"Mayor Quartano?" asked Aggie, who was now kicked back in her chair, glass tilted high, trying for that last chunk of frozen water.

"Yes, he was a wrestler back in the day, too. You wouldn't know it seeing him today, but he came in second at some point in our history here. At least that's what he claims anyway. He was pretty excited when Ben won," I told her.

"So, the mayor introduced Ben to Riley?"

"Yes, pretty much," I said.

"So Ben just left you?" she persisted.

"Not at first. It was bad timing, and I had a lot going on. Her attention was more than he could resist."

Our waiter was back now with two Shirley Temples this time.

"I had this gut feeling you wanted to try one, too. It's on the house," he said, placing it next to my empty glass of water. Aggie and I saw it as an opportunity to toast to our evening and raised our glasses high. We failed to come up with anything of substance and erupted in laughter instead.

"Wait, wait. You can't drink until you give a proper toast, otherwise you toast to nothingness and that's a waste," he said and cleared his throat while the table of ladies next to us rolled their eyes and tapped their fingers on the table, waiting for him to deliver their check.

"One minute," he said, looking back at them. "This is serious stuff."

Oh, he was not getting a tip from the table full of inpatient moms. I sat back and waited for the solo performance.

He raised his hand as if holding a glass.

"Cheers to the lovely gals not afraid to rock the norm in this stuffy town where all the cougars swarm. Cheers to my new friends who throw healthy foods to the wind and enjoy their fried cheese wide-eyed with a grin. And cheers to lovely Aggie who I hope will come again real soon, and I will have her Shirley Temple waiting under the moon," he said.

Aggie and I clanked our glasses with his imaginary one and then I slapped my hand on the table. "You're no poet, but excellent attempt!"

He blushed and bowed, backing away as his manager took notice.

"He likes you; the first night in town and you already have a date," I said and smiled. "Not bad."

"It doesn't matter. What were we talking about?" Aggie said.

"What do you mean, 'It doesn't matter'? He likes you, and he's cute," I insisted.

"I'm only here until spring. This is not the time for a love interest."

"Who says it has to be love? Just have fun," I took a big gulp of the Temple. Its sweetness had my mouth twitching as if I just ate a whole bowl of fresh cherries. No wonder she loved it.

"Oh my! No. I would expect to be courted," she replied.

"Courted? What?" I wrinkled my nose and squinted. "What era are you living in?"

Our friendly waiter inserted himself back into the conversation, placing our leather binder with the bill inside. Aggie was fidgeting while zipping up her hoodie, backing out her chair, and standing to leave.

"You ready to get out of here?" she asked. Aggie politely thanked the waiter, but excused herself from the evening, walking past me toward the front. I grabbed the bill, gathered my items, and apologized for her hasty getaway. What was the sudden rush?

I pushed my chair back under the table. "We'll visit again," I told him.

As I backed away from the table something outside the window caught my attention. Deep in the dark woods I noticed movement. Human like forms danced in and out from behind the trees.

"Are you ok?" asked the waiter as he started clearing our table.

I blinked, turned from the window and focused on him, "Yes, I'm fine," I remarked, then panned for Aggie.

Aggie and her confidence moved fast toward the one area of the restaurant I didn't want to be. She was drawing attention from everyone, and I was concerned about her sudden increase in pace. What was she up to? The closer I got to Ben's table, the more I heard Riley, Avery, and Casey chattering. Ben was equally obnoxious, which only added fuel to their malicious banter. I wanted out the front door before another encounter.

"How did you ever date her? I heard she spent time in a hospital for crazy people." I overheard Casey say.

"Shut up, Casey," barked Luke.

Luke was a country kid whose parents moved into the outskirts of the Creek. They bought a small farmhouse on thirty acres and farmed most of it. They had a barn of dairy cows and a little shack of alpacas. He was the only one still nice to me after the breakup and never cared much about what the others thought. So Casey shut up just like he asked.

I caught up with Aggie when she suddenly made a sharp turn back and straight to their table. I didn't turn around. I couldn't. I heard her yelling at them, scolding them like kids, ranting about what jerks they all were. They laughed and fought to talk over one another before a waitress grabbed Aggie and escorted her out past me. They all erupted into laughter. I put my head down and pushed my way out the front door.

Aggie walked up to me, giggling, lightly punching my arm like a fraternity brother.

I kept my head low and walked fast away from her, but she kept coming up next to me, punching at my arm, begging for accolades. I was starting to sweat.

"Stop!" I yelled, stomping my feet, "What were you thinking?"

"What? They deserved that. You can't let people sit and talk shit about you in front of everyone, especially Ben," she said, leaning into her right hip.

"You don't know me. You don't Ben. You don't know the Berkshire girls. I look so desperate and pathetic. This town has enough stories to ridicule my family and me about. You just gave them one more. You want to live here and be my friend, then you need to learn your place. Goodbye," I said. My chest and neck began to itch as the same nervous rash that plagued my mom now spread across my front like a tree with a million little branches. The skin on my ears burned hot with anger.

"But you didn't mind when I defended you earlier. What's the difference?" she demanded.

I hesitated, "You went too far; go home," I said and threw a twenty-dollar bill on the pavement, "You have to pay. I'm not going back in there."

She bent over to pick up the cash. "Abby, wait. I'm sorry," she said.

I ignored her apologies and raced south down Main and over to Oak, trying not to trip on the uneven pavement. Using my sleeves, I wiped the teardrops that poured down my cheeks. I hated being anywhere other than the store. With this damn town so small, I could never be free of Ben. And while I tried to get over my love for him, it was still there. But so were the dreams, and the shadows, and scrapes on my body. I was different, and Ben left me because of it. I yanked at my hair, feeling trapped in a world I couldn't understand.

I made my turn from a well-lit Main Street to a gloomy Oak. After the first few homes, street lamps were traded for individual house lamps. Neighbors kept them on until 11 p.m., but on occasion, you always had a few who forgot.

Unfortunately, it was going to be one of those dimly lit evenings. A dense fog weaved its way between the twenty-two houses I would have to walk past. Numbing gusts of wind laced the air with every step. The distinct sound of wind chimes mixed with an occasional cat's meow lingered along my path. Suddenly, a disembodied growl rushed up behind me.

I turned in various directions, scanning for the source of the horrific sound. I started to run, counting down the houses, thirteen, twelve, eleven, ten, nine, taking glances over my shoulder for any sign of what was chasing me. My momentum forward was stopped by a firm grip. A gray fog in the shape of two arms and hands with long bony fingers dug deep in my ribcage with so much force it paralyzed me. I could only move my eyes and panned the houses for any sign of help. Trying desperately to scream, I strained to move, but the fog continued to slither around me like a rope from my feet up to my neck. As it ran up around from under my chin, it crossed over my face to my left ear. It sniffed up and down my neck toward my shoulder.

"It's mine; you protect it, or I will come back for you," the wispy voice said, moving from one ear to the other.

The surrounding tightness immediately released all at once. The air flowed back into my lungs as I gasped. My knees buckled as I fell to the sidewalk. I was on all fours as if I was a tired dog, too scared to gaze in any direction. My home was still eight houses away. A moving light from behind approached me, causing me to leap to my feet. A pickup truck screeched to a halt with the lights blinding my eyes as I turned.

"Abby, it's me, Luke," he yelled before jumping out of his truck. "Are you okay?"

Luke approached me, his body blocking the light from his head-lights.

My head hurt and I couldn't speak.

Luke wrapped his arm around me and ushered me over to the passenger side of his truck and helped me in. Then he ran around back into the driver's seat.

"What happened?" he said, throwing it into gear and making the six-second drive to my home.

"I don't know," I said, rubbing my ears, trying to erase the sound of her voice.

"I came around down Oak, and I saw something moving on the road. As I got closer, I realized it was you," he said as he slowed and pulled up my driveway.

"You want to go home, right?" he asked.

"Yes, of course," I replied.

"What happened?" he calmly asked again.

"I don't know. One minute I was walking and the next thing I was thrown off my feet," I looked over at him, still mouth-breathing and shaking.

"You can sit here as long as you need," he said as he put his car in park and cut the headlights.

I moved around, looking out each of his windows then circling back for a second look.

"I should get inside. But thank you." I opened up the door slowly to step out. Luke got back out of the truck and came around to my side.

"I will walk you up," he said and held his arm out and walked me back up my front porch in the same protective manner as he'd helped me into the car. "You sure you're okay? I hate to leave you alone."

"I'm okay," I stuttered.

Luke waited until I opened the screen door before returning to his truck and saying goodbye. He turned his truck and headlamps back on, illuminating a small piece of paper fluttering around my ankles. I grabbed it off my boot but didn't want to stand outside to look at it. I crumpled it in my left hand, opened the door with my right, and went inside.

CHAPTER 9

PREPARATION

My mom and Mason sat in the front room watching TV as I rushed, passed them, and headed up the staircase. My mom tried to say a few words, but I didn't stop to listen. I ran to my room, flipped on the lights, and locked the door behind me. Over at my writing desk, I dropped the piece of paper from my hand. I opened the top drawer and removed a batch of sage and arranged it in a seashell. I lit the bundle. The once-cream shell, now gray and ashen from the burning leaves, billowed smoke. I cupped it in my hands before placing it on the floor in the center of my room.

Digging through my drawers, I grabbed a collection of old pictures of Ben and me. I rested them in a bowl and placed them in my window box outside. I lit each corner, watching the glossy three-by-fives curl inward. I watched as they burst into flames, the smoke carrying away everything that was us. The sage smoke streamed behind the memories and forced each one out into the atmosphere.

I spun, still needing some color, some security, and light. At the end of my bed on the floor, were two large baskets with brightly colored bohemian blankets. I tossed a multicolored one up on my bed. I wrapped another bluish-purple ombré around my body before shuffling over to my faux ficus tree, plugging it in. I waited for a half-second for the warm glow of its lights to turn on. I inhaled.

I pulled out my desk chair and watched the wind carry away my fears and then shifted my focus to the crumpled up paper on my desk. I flicked at it a few times, still terrified about the recent encounter on the street, contemplating whether I was ready for anything else.

I grabbed it and carefully spread it open, smoothing out the creases. It had two straight sides with a rounded third revealing the words "Ostara and Beltane", the symbol for female and ankh and a sword. I pulled out my art box and placed the four pieces together. They fit perfectly, creating a circle with the words "Samhain, Yule, Imbolc, Ostara, Beltane, Litha, Lughnasadh, and Mabon". The words curved around the outer edges, with wolf-life creatures in the spaces between each word. A large, six-pointed star hexagram covered the surface area of the circle, and in the middle of each overlapping triangle sat a symbol. One had a witch's knot, another, a triquetra. The remaining seven symbols were a mystery. In the middle of the Hexagram were a full moon and a waxing crescent to each side. While I didn't understand what I was viewing, my sixth sense told me that Manshaw's claims about witchcraft were suddenly more credible. I dropped my head into my hands then angrily brushed the pieces onto the floor. My heart pounded in my chest.

I dug through my drawers and pulled out an expired bottle of Ativan. *These should still work.*

I swallowed one pill and waited for the quiet to come. I fixated on the flames, which continued burning my memories. The smoke ballooned outward in a variety of colors before twisting into an onyx cloud. I slouched further down under the emotional weight of my life. My lids fell heavy and then opened on the other side.

She was back. The lady with the bleeding black eyes spun my chair away from the window and toward her. I squirmed as she crawled up over me, her hot breath searing the skin on my neck. My body shook as I tried to wake myself. She taunted me with her sinister laugh and her unnatural movements. I turned from her, but she slapped my face back center. In her dark eyes, I observed a naked female figure. Blood was smeared on her thighs down to her feet. She gurgled, and blood spilled from her mouth. I closed my eyes to the horror, but her touch sent a tremor of terror through my soul.

"What do you want from me?" I screamed out but she was gone. The room darkened and closed in on me. A hint of light shone down from high above. Grey mist swirled and surrounded me. I cowered into a fetal position, closed my eyes, and covered my ears and rocked.

Seconds turned to minutes and minutes to hours when I was startled and shaken back to my room.

"What in the hell is going on here? Abby, wake up!"

I gasped for oxygen.

"My God, Abby, your whole body is shaking. Are you okay?" Kate asked, peering over me, already dressed for work today.

Sitting up, I realized that it was morning. The sage had burned all night, and despite the open window, most of the smoke circled my room with a thick haze. She reached over me and cranked the window as far as it could go.

"What are you doing?" she demanded. Kate coughed incessantly and dramatically waved her arms in front of her face.

I couldn't answer. I waited for fresh air from the outside to enter into my lungs.

Sage smoke flowed out like a swarm of bees. My eyes hurt, and my head throbbed from the bitter odor, and I was fatigued from the sedative's hangover effect. Kate moved the shell out into the window box but not before grabbing the bowl full of charcoaled pictures. A couple of photos had not burned entirely, and she held them up to the light enough to make out Ben's profile in one of the three by fives.

"Make certain you don't intentionally put the sage out," I said, sitting up and cracking the kink in my neck.

"I was with you when you bought it, remember? Though I would say based on the quantity of sage you burned, the universe would give you a pass on dropping some water on it," Kate said with a partial smile. "May I also remind you, only a few leaves are necessary for a space this small?"

I was still contorting my aching bones, hoping for any relief from the stiffness, when Kate noticed the papers scattered across on the floor. She picked up one and held it out in front of her before picking up a second, third, then a fourth. Holding them like playing cards, she asked where I'd found them.

"I didn't. They found me," I said, exhaling slowly, closing my eyes, and pulling the blanket up over my face. I was achy from a night of sleep in an uncomfortable desk chair.

"Do you know what this is?" Kate asked, turning my chair toward her.

The motion sent a shiver down my spine, but I collected myself and answered. "Manshaw told me the symbols might have something to do with witchcraft."

My cocoon of Egyptian cotton and acrylic allowed the heat from my breath to warm my temples. I peeked out through a split in the blanket and watched Kate maneuverer the pieces in various ways. She slid them around fast, turning each piece as she moved.

"Here," I dropped the blanket off my head and placed them together.

I gave her a minute and walked to the bathroom to get a cup of water.

"When did Manshaw see these?" Kate asked, walking behind me and watching as I gulped down the water.

"Yesterday," I replied.

Manshaw's remarks had startled me some, but today, I realized anything was possible. Kate walked around the perimeter of my room, looking at each piece carefully.

"You're concerned," I pointed out.

She glanced back over her shoulder and said, "Manshaw's right."

"How do you know?"

"I've seen the symbols," Kate sank into my bed before continuing and pointing at the different pieces. "The words around the edge represent the eight pagan holidays or sabbats. And these symbols—they all relate to the practice of witchcraft."

"Manshaw mentioned the sabbats and some of the symbols. But why me? Why am I getting these? I don't practice!" I said.

Kate rubbed her lips. "Well, someone in town does."

Her words were not comforting. It was bad enough I saw and heard and seen things most couldn't, but now I was being targeted by someone practicing a craft I knew nothing about.

I bit my lip when the stinging pain jogged my memory.

"Damn, Agatha!" I blurted out.

Kate acknowledged. "The girl you hired?"

"You heard?"

"She showed up at nine this morning. Your mom didn't believe her first about the job, but then she mentioned having dinner with you last night."

"Ugh, it's after nine?" I couldn't believe it. I rarely slept past seven, and I'd promised Aggie I would meet her this morning. Well, I'm sure at this point, she thought my absence was intentional. While mad at her, yes, I still wanted to introduce her to my mom.

"She came in looking for a job and seems to know a lot about antiques. Hiring Aggie was like my Hail Mary." I turned back to open two dresser drawers, grabbed a tee, a tank, and another pair of jeans.

"No need to hurry now. Your mom has it under control, and while I think it will take more than Agatha to save the place, I applaud your commitment." Kate stretched herself out on my bed and lay staring at the ceiling with her arms crossed over her chest, and her legs crossed at the ankles.

"You look comfortable, given all the disturbing topics of conversation this morning," I said, moving over to my closet and locating my only pair of sneakers. She didn't respond initially.

"What happened last night?" she then asked, pressing her body further into my bed.

"Why do you think something happened?" I said, moving back to my desk, I closed the window from the air, which was now too cold for my liking. I rested myself in the chair to begin the labor-intensive process of putting on the narrowest of tennis shoes.

"Well, first, you almost overdosed on sage. Second, your mom said you rushed into the house last night noticeably upset. Third, Agatha told us about the run-in with Riley and her mean girl mafia," Kate spewed out her comments in a logical order, but there was more. Her fidgeting and frequent stares off into nowhere told me I wasn't going anywhere fast, even after my shoes were on. I set the story in motion.

"Last night, it all started with Avery just being, well, a bitch. They were all at the diner where we were eating. Ben showed up drunk. It was ugly. But it was not until I walked home that it appeared." My right heel slid down into my shoe, taking a top layer of skin from my thumb.

"What appeared?" Kate's head turned in my direction.

I lifted my arms to first shake out the sting from my hand then to rub my forehead. I opened my mouth, and out came the muck of madness in which I had been living. Kate pulled herself back out of bed, walked over to me, and reached for my elbows.

"Damn, what happened?" she asked, placing her hands under my elbows, holding them upright.

I pulled my arms away from my face and turned them. Fingerprint impressions embedded in a bright red bruise wrapped around each arm. A constant chill repeatedly spread down my back. I sunk into my chair and grimaced.

"Something grabbed me last night on my way home. Two hands held tight onto my arms, but I couldn't see it, it wasn't human. What lasted only a few seconds seemed like hours until I fell to the ground. Luke drove by, found me, and drove me home." My neck rested yet again on the rounded curve of my desk chair.

"Are you sure it wasn't Avery or one of the other girls?" Kate leaned over me to see my face.

I squeezed my eyes shut and shook my head, saying no. I paused as I considered what else to say. "No, they were still at the Tavern. Luke left shortly after me because he was sick of their banter. It wasn't them."

My stomach burned in pain, but I shared more.

"It was the same spirit from so many of my nightmares. She's here and now showing up in my wakefulness. I'm not crazy; it's real, and these marks are real and more painful than any other. I couldn't make this up, and I wouldn't harm myself," I said, manically moving my hands along my arms.

We sat in silence for a few minutes while Kate combed through all the details. The best thing: she wasn't judging me. She never did. She was thinking of the right thing to say to a person who experienced the most unbelievable things. It was Kate who somehow managed to give me strength when I needed it most.

"Have you thought of what this thing may want from you?" she asked.

"I have no clue. If I did, I would've given it to her a long time ago," I said, and forced my left foot into my other shoe, scraping even more skin off my right thumb.

Kate's face changed. "Why do you say that?"

"Because this is the first time this thing has fully shown itself in our world. She is not hiding in my head anymore. Something is drawing her out and into our world. If she wants something, she can have it, especially if it means she won't come back."

Kate and I traded places as I stood to pace, and she sat to reflect. Digging in her purse, she pulled out a piece of white copy paper and handed it over to me.

"What is this?" I asked.

"Just look at it," she said.

The folded up pieces of copy paper, while harmless to the rest of the world, conjured up nothing but anxiety in me.

On the 8?11 copy paper, WWW.CERULEANSOUL.COM was displayed across the top. Underneath, was an image of a human form with various blue colors radiating from the center and melting outward into a dark forest of blackened trees. The roots wrapped around branches in an intricate pattern, creating a canopy of black moss-like strands hanging down over the human shape. The paper drowning in ink was flimsy and difficult to hold. I walked with smaller steps while reading the hazy print near the bottom. In bright blue, the words read:

"Your child is never alone. Spirits from another realm are always near watching, influencing, guiding, and communicating. Click here to learn how we can help."

A hand icon sat with fingers spread out and colored in shades of a rainbow at the bottom edge of the paper.

"Where did you get this?" I asked, rubbing the excess ink between my thumb and forefingers.

"It was on the floor in our store's backroom this morning," Kate said, turning back around to fumble with the four pieces of artwork on my desk.

"Funny how paper keeps making its way to us," I half-laughed, sick of the fear, and wanting to chuckle about something, as inappropriate as it might seem. It sounded ridiculous, witchcraft, and spirits …. *Cerulean? What the hell did it mean anyway*, I wondered as I dug into my hair and pulled out my blue hues twisting them until my scalp hurt. "Maybe it fell out of one of the boxes you brought yesterday?"

"Maybe," she whispered.

"What are you thinking?" I asked her. Most people would've dismissed this, thrown it away, but Kate brought it here for a reason.

"Would you like to go on a road trip?" Kate inquired.

It was an unusual question and an even more bizarre time to take a trip. I stared at her with one raised eyebrow.

"Bear with me," she requested, "I went online at the store and looked up the website. I clicked on the icon, which led me to another page with contact information for a lady named Nora. So I took a chance and called. A young girl answered the phone, and while I stumbled over what to say, the girl asked me to hold. She called for her mom, elated that they contacted another."

She spun in my desk chair as she spoke.

"The woman on the other end answered, and with a loud tone, she introduced herself as Nora Owens. 'You're calling from Ohio, I see. Who are you calling regarding? Do you think you are Cerulean? Do you know someone who might be?'"

Kate said the woman was speaking so fast, she struggled to keep up.

I wanted to hear more, but the heaviness in my room was weighing on me. "Can we go outside for air?" I asked.

She politely acknowledged my request and waited for me to gather my things. I grabbed my burned up picture of Ben and dropped it in the garbage can, but as Kate turned towards the door, I tossed it back in the top drawer of my desk, slammed it shut, and then headed downstairs. Kate's shoes clicked behind me. I moved outside and sat on the cold steps of my front porch. Kate stood for a minute, contemplating on whether to sit in her light gray slacks. It was only a moment before her patent leather heels moved down so her butt could be right next to mine.

"Can I go on?" she asked.

"Yes; sure," I hesitantly responded.

"You know how we have always talked about gut instinct?" she asked then.

"Yep," I said, bending over and using a small stick from a nearby maple to scratch into the stone.

"The conversation was rough at first, but something told me to stay on the phone. This woman went on about how kids are born with an ability to communicate with the other side. Some lose the gift with time, but a select few retain. And this is where it gets crazy. She asked me if I had the signature glass-like eyes and a streak of blue hair," Kate was going on.

I stopped moving the stick and turned my head up toward Kate. "You're joking," I said.

"I wouldn't," she responded, "My silence answered Nora's question. She told me that there were others. The eyes and hair come packaged with headaches, nightmares, visions, and all things unexplained. She referred to the kids as Cerulean and created the website to find others."

My tongue curled up under my upper lip as my eyes fixated on the front lawn and my brain dissected what she'd just said. "She thinks we can *communicate* with the other side? Well, they're surely not listening to me."

"Or they communicate with you, and you haven't figured how to communicate back," Kate offered.

"Perfect, so you think we should go to meet them?" I asked sarcastically.

"I think we should go to Connecticut in four weeks and see for ourselves. Nora mentioned a few of the others would be there early in October. We could stay and learn or leave if we want," she said.

The line of traffic slowly trickled in toward town and backed up just past our home. Men and women of all ages were singing along to the radio, chatting with their passengers, and yelling at their kids in the backseat. They were wading their way through life with their biggest worry being late for lunch, or worse yet, for their husband to find smashed, dry cereal in the backseat of their eighty thousand dollar vehicle. And here I sat with a flyer on Cerulean Children to add to my growing repertoire of all things paranormal.

"Life isn't fair," I said and picked up the little gargoyle that guarded our front door and key and thought about how ugly and cute he was all at that same time. In that brief moment, I named him, too. Everything needed a name. "Bob," I thought. He looked like a "Bob," not very menacing, but trusted to do a job. I tried desperately to distract my brain with anything mundane. It wasn't working, and Kate was growing impatient for a resounding yes I couldn't muster.

"Maybe it is," she said and pointed to all the cars moving. "Or they're all just stuck in a boring routine without knowing why. You have way more life than any of them and maybe an awesome, divine gift, too."

"A gift—nice choice of words," I said, and patted Bob on the head and sat him back down to watch the traffic with us.

"What about Mom?" I questioned.

"One step ahead of you," she gloated. "Mason's buyer had some conflict next weekend and needed to postpone. I talked Lauren into going the same weekend we would go to Connecticut. This way, she'll be too busy managing Mason to bother us."

"All great, but did you tell her *why* we're going?" I asked.

"College visits," she stated simply.

My nervous reflex sent poor Bob nosediving off into the bushes. While I dug through the rough branches to free him out, I pondered why she would tell my mom such a ridiculous lie. Just a girls' weekend would have worked nicely.

"It would do you some good to research some schools anyway. Homework assignment due when we leave. We can review in the car and then provide your mom with a summary of our travels when we return." Kate stood in triumph while outlining her plan.

"Well played, well played," I said.

"So that's a yes then?" she asked with a large toothy grin.

"Yes," I sighed.

CHAPTER 10

ROAD TRIP

The subsequent four weeks passed by kind of fast, leading to my big day. Today would be the first time I ever stepped out of Ohio. I stood and stared into my full-length mirror and the mess of clothes on the floor that didn't make it into my new weekend bag. I packed like an excited kid heading off to a weekend away at an amusement park, thinking about everything I had done in September and everything I hoped to accomplish this weekend.

I had devoted most of my time at the store training Aggie. We never talked about the night at the 1816 Tavern. I chalked her offensive actions up to being the nervous, new girl in town. I was proud of myself for not abruptly blocking her from my life. She was turning out to be a good friend and a fun person to hang out with. Her weird quirks and strange comments had me questioning just what town or century she had ridden in from. Aggie struggled with everyday items like her phone or the computer; she wore odd clothes like a scarf wrapped up over her head when it rained. She used vocabulary like "dew dropper" and "egg" when she described people. But she was amazing at the store. Aggie had a genuine, working knowledge of antiques, which surprised me and made us money. Even my mom started letting her change price tags without asking first. In one month, we were selling more items for more money.

My phone dinged to announce that Kate would be here in five minutes.

I grabbed my full brown leather bag Kate had bought me as a gift, ripped the tag off of it, and carefully pulled the zipper closed. In my satchel, I placed my obsidian crystal stone, gold elephant, and wallet.

My phone dinged again, announcing a new ETA of just three minutes. My lack of response had Kate worried. I waited.

Ding. "Two minutes." I was aware of the conversation Kate was having with herself. She was sure I skipped out of here to hide. When she realized otherwise, she would yell at me for about thirty seconds until I handed over my homework she assigned to me. I did what she asked and researched some schools out east. It piqued my curiosity and sparked a bit of interest, but I wasn't planning on admitting it right away. I wanted to share some of it with my mom this morning, but she left with Mason without saying goodbye.

The sound of the front door opening and closing told me Kate had arrived. No one-minute warning, I thought. How dare she?

Grabbing my bag and purse, I took one last look around my room before stepping into the hall. My right hand slowly pulling the creaking door closed, I watched as the view of my furniture disappeared into fading light. Silence took over while I closed it and pulled it tightly shut.

"Abby," Kate yelled up the stairs.

Walking down the hall, I brushed my hands across my school pictures. My mom re-hung them in their frames, without the glass.

"Coming!" I yelled back down.

Rounding the top of the stairs, I noticed Kate standing at the bottom. She smiled widely, with nothing but lip liner and white teeth. She was dressed in her road trip leggings and an oversized pink sweatshirt with yet another pair of matching shades.

"Why didn't you respond to my texts?"

"I didn't know I needed to," I replied.

Kate gave me a harsh squint and grabbed my bag, which was bouncing off the handrail.

"Your mom home?" she asked.

"Nope! They left before I got up." Kate saw the disappointment in my face and offered her the best analysis of the situation.

"Probably better that way. The last thing anyone needed this morning was more questions or, worse yet, a fight between you and Mason," she said, pressing her lips together. She shifted her weight to manage my bag.

"You're right," I said. I handed my research on schools over to Kate, who was surprised by the level of detail I demonstrated.

"I did an impressive job, I must say," I said, tapping at each page as she struggled to thumb through the clear protective sleeves of copy paper and highlighted details of each school.

"You did all this? You sure it didn't jolt something you didn't know you had inside?" she peered up over the binder in a Mrs. Pickett kind of way.

"I've never been one to slack on my work, you know that," I said and grabbed the pages, closed them, and shoved it in my bag she was still holding. I zipped it, knocking her off balance.

She repositioned herself. "Proud of you."

"That's nice. Can we go now?" We shared a nod and a wink and headed out the front door to the humming sound of her fancy sports car.

I hopped into the front passenger seat and inadvertently kicked up a napkin that was on the floor. As it flipped over, I noticed writing in black ink.

"Thank you for Everything, Ryker," was written in small print in the center of the square cocktail napkin. *Hmm, never heard her mention him before.* I waved it in her periphery. She grabbed it, rolled it in a ball, and threw it over her shoulder.

"Don't ask," she said.

I turned sideways, resting my hands on the center console. "Do tell," I teased.

"Nope," she said, backing out and throwing her car in drive so fast the vehicle jerked forward.

"Why?" I whined.

"He was no one."

She wouldn't look at me. She had the same tell my mom had. I settled back into my seat and pulled the seatbelt over.

"You're allowed to date after a divorce—no reason to be embarrassed," I offered.

"I'm not. I just don't want to talk about the super cute gentleman who is too good to be true right now," Kate said and changed the conversation to the weather as she zipped away from the Creek. I let it go, comforted that she was healing. I would ask again later.

Two miles down the road, we came upon the pair of giant stone statues that flanked the bridge leading to the highway. The tall female figures with long flowing hair each wielded a dagger in one hand and a tall torch in the other. Two dog-like creatures sat at either side of their legs. I marveled at the intricate design best I could in the mere seconds it took for Kate to pass through and begin our trek out east.

Our journey through Pennsylvania moved ahead like a car commercial as Kate glided along the interstate. Forests soon blocked out the glaring rays from the rising sun. Red, orange, and yellow hues melted over the tops of trees, dripping color to the remaining green leaves below.

Engaging in idle chit-chat, we blew through matters on Aggie, Ben, Mason, high school, and the store. Kate understood how far to press me, and when to back off, so conversations never took a turn into a topic I was unprepared to discuss. I teetered on bringing Fabrizio back up, and the new mystery man, but hesitated to ruin the car's vibe. At times, when the conversation went silent, she would turn up the radio, and we would belt out the newest songs like a couple of old friends.

"Thank you," I said while continuing to sing and hum along to the radio.

"For what?" she asked.

"For giving me the road trip experience I've never had."

"Well, it's not a road trip until you have eaten an awful gas station hot dog," she said and mimicked a gag and dry heave.

"No, thanks. I'll take my trip minus a slimy dog," I returned.

While there really wasn't much along the Pennsylvania turnpike, we thankfully found a small country kitchen tucked off a highway exit somewhere in the eastern portion of Pennsylvania. It was a quaint little house that had been converted into a diner. We coasted from the smooth concrete of the exit ramp to the uneven, gravel drive leading to an open spot right off the front porch. The words "Frieda's Kitchen and Collectibles" were neatly etched in chalk on a black easel sign to the side of the front door. On the opposite side, another smaller easel stated, "Welcome All Travelers." Inside the window, several small groups of people sat hunched over, eating.

"Will this do?" Kate asked.

I leaned forward, squeezing my head between the dashboard and the front window. The modest wood-paneled house looked more like an old saloon with a front porch rail suitable for a horse.

"Better than a gas station," I said, relieved that I didn't have to actually eat any mystery meat today. Stepping out of the car, I arched my back and twisted to the left and then the right, creating a popping sound not typical for my age. Temporarily frozen, waiting for my last bone to crack, my eyes caught view of a medium-sized hawk circling above the diner's stone chimney. Then another glided in before they both flew off into the nearby woods.

Kate walked behind the car, shoving me toward the front door.

"Let's go on in," Kate said, strolling up past me onto the front steps, pushing her glasses up onto her head and opening the screen door for me.

The entryway had a similar bell to the one at the store, which announced our presence. At least one guest from each table looked up as we walked in. A couple of husbands took a bicep punch as their eyes stared a little too long at Kate. Thankfully, the hostess station had a "Seat Yourself" sign, which I did, in a corner, away from everyone else.

"The food smells decent," Kate offered, still standing, garnering more attention. We were definitely not in the Creek anymore. Everything looked dated, even the people. Wow, I thought to myself. Look at me being all judge-y. The Creek would be proud.

Kate finally sat, picking up the handwritten menu on notebook paper.

"Interesting; I guess we won't have to ask what the daily specials are," she said, holding back a smile while waving the paper. I grabbed it from her hands, hopeful there was something I would enjoy.

"Weird; there is no meat on the menu," I said though I was okay with it, just confused. The rustic diner in the middle of nowhere Pennsylvania didn't seem like a vegetarian establishment.

A short, chubby girl with a round face and big ginger hair stopped over to take our drink and food order all at the same time. She had on a bright green dress with a purple collar and purple trim around the short sleeves and on the bottom hem. A white apron stretched to its limits over her belly.

"I'm Ruby; you need anything, call out my name," she said, speaking in a nasal voice while tapping her white oval name tag with her pen. "And, no, we don't serve meat here; we love all our living creatures, and the food is fresh."

Kate and I requested some time before we ordered. Ruby acknowledged, wobbling away, singing a tune under her breath as she moved from table to table.

"Let's go check out what's for sale," Kate said. She was the girl who could never turn down a chance to shop or buy something, for that matter.

"Sure," I said and stood, directing my attention to the ceiling's vibrating lights above. Footsteps paraded across the second level, shaking the fixtures. The sound of feet slapping back-and-forth upstairs caught everyone's attention.

"Knock it off up there." I could hear a hoarse voice from an unseen woman and then two slams of a shutting door. The restaurant went silent for a moment, but the atmosphere was soon filled with forks and glasses, all clinking against each other.

I followed Kate as we walked in a slow circle around a few glass cases of trinkets and jewelry. Then we zig-zagged back to the perimeter of bookshelves containing oil lamps, frames, silver pieces, plates, and teacups, all tossed together haphazardly. Kate's body, on autopilot, returned to the jewelry case. An article caught her eye as she leaned over, pressing her hands into the glass.

The young girl removed a sterling silver ring with an oval-shaped amber stone at Kate's direction.

Kate held her hand up in front of her face. "Eye-catching and just the right size," she said. The warm brown-and-yellow tones danced in the light as she turned her hand and long dainty fingers.

"How much?" asked Kate.

"Thirty for the ring?" the girl replied.

"Is that a question?" Kate asked. The girl's head dropped forward, and she didn't respond.

"It's okay. I'm sorry. How about I give you fifty?" Kate pulled out cash from her purse and handed it to the young girl.

"Thank you," The girl said and raised her head slightly, just enough for us to see the beaming smile she tried to contain as she spoke.

"Why did you offer her more money than what she wanted?" I whispered.

"I bet the extra money would help this family, and she needed a confidence builder," Kate replied.

It was the one thing I always loved about Kate *and* Fabrizio. They shared their money in various increments with anyone they thought had a need. The thoughts made me question even more what had happened between them. He was considerate and gracious like her. What wore them down?

We took brief moments out of our shopping excursion to order some food. We worked our way around the rest of the store, taking in anything we could look at, and cracking jokes about some odd stuff for sale like a set of lamps with dancers in matching red outfits. Kate flipped the switch on which illuminated the bulbs and bellowed out a fancy merengue; it elicited Kate's hips to move in a way not meant for where we were.

I noticed the growing stares. "Just buy them and have fun back home," I said, but Kate stuck her tongue out at me and danced on. I moved away to a quieter section where the books were resting. All the hardbacks were warped with age. I opened one with a rough leather cover. The sweet smell of mature paper rushed up from the yellow pages. I shifted to the left when a hand reached up over my shoulder and pulled out a burgundy book with fading gold letters.

"Have you ever heard of numerology?" The same girl from behind the jewelry counter had moved on to the library area. She thumbed through the fragile pages that clearly had not been opened in a while. Dust fluttered into the air with each turn, tickling my nose. I sneezed then, placed my book back, and then spoke while trying to ward off another one coming.

"Yeah, isn't that like the way spirits can talk to you through numbers?" I sputtered. She disappeared and then returned with a tissue just in time for my second nasal shriek.

"Thank you," I offered.

"Kind of; all cultures view it differently, but there is an overall belief that numbers connect the mortal world with the divine," she said.

She was quiet but confident as her delicate fingers glided over the pages. The noise from the diner dissipated while she dug deeper into patterns and their meanings. But to me, it all seemed so complicated.

"What if someone doesn't need numbers to connect?" I raised my shoulders and pressed the tissue over my face. *Not another one.*

She stared down at the book, then closed the cover and slid it back into its place on the shelf. "Then that someone is one step ahead of the game; enjoy your lunch."

Ahead of what game? She moved away as Kate's voice called out my name, letting me know our food had arrived. I covered my face, subduing the next expulsion of air, and went back to our table.

Kate ate slowly and eloquently, picking apart her salad and toppings. I ate slower, not being able to get the girl out of my head. Her mannerisms, movements, and discussions stirred up a curiosity that I couldn't quite understand. Why did she seek me out to talk about numerology? Nothing about it felt random.

I ate about all I could of the rice and vegetable dish and excused myself to the lady's room. In the small two-toilet bathroom stood an older woman in oversized linen shirt with matching pants and sandals. She wore large multi-colored bangle bracelets that clanged together as she brushed her silver hair up into a French twist. I grinned at her before entering a stall, quickly minding to my business. When I walked out, she was still there, now drying her hands with a paper towel. While I washed mine, she sparked up a conversation.

"Traveling somewhere special this weekend?" she asked.

"Kind of. Meeting some new friends out east," I said, smashing my palm against the wall dispenser to get a dime-size amount of soap. She continued.

"Where east?"

"Connecticut," I replied.

"Beautiful state this time of year. Is it your first time?" she asked.

"Yes."

"You will love it. Good luck to you and have a pleasant day; always enjoy it." She crumpled up the paper towels and stomped on the small garbage can to open the lid. She dropped it in and walked around me to get out the door.

"I'm sorry; what did you say?" I asked, spinning to follow her as she moved away.

I received no answer as the door closed behind her. I yanked the paper towels from the dispenser, quickly dried my hands, and tossed them in the garbage. I pushed the door open. Looking both ways down the hall, I couldn't find her, but Kate appeared.

"Hey, I'm full, and I paid the bill already. Just going to pee and I'll be out."

She tossed the keys to me before rushing to the bathroom.

I stood still staring in each direction when something fluttered by my field of vision. I shook my head and waved my arms around like a kid who had just walked into a web. I inadvertently swatted my way down the hall away from the restaurant. Ahead of me was a screen door leading outback, to my sides, solid wood doors.

The sounds of pots and pans and voices stirred up on my right. To my left, a fluttering of tiny wings hovered in front of my eyes. Jumping back, my eyes rolled up and down then panned again out to focus. My heart rate picked up but then slowed at the sight of a hummingbird darting out of a small gap in the door to my left. Its body was various shades of gray, but its head and neck were an ombré of bright pink and green. Flying right up to the tip of my nose, it stopped, turned, and headed back in the open door, which closed after it entered. Looking back down the hall and over both shoulders, I reached for the knob. With an all-clear from my brain, I slowly turned the doorknob to the right. The telltale click of the spring latch echoed in the small hall as I pulled it open.

"Hi," said a teenage girl with wide-set eyes, full lips, and freckles across her nose. Her tousled blond bob highlighted with a light pink hue complimented her green eyes. The aromas of lavender and magnolia rushed in from behind her. Small wisps of hair danced in a slight breeze around her face.

Inhaling loudly, I jumped back, slapping my right hand against my chest.

She stepped back and covered her face with her hands. "Oh my. I'm sorry. Did I startle you?"

I withdrew and apologized, muttering about needing a bathroom. I was poking my nose into an area likely forbidden to guests and opted to lie instead of admitting to trespassing.

She pointed back down the hall. "No worries; you're just a few feet too far." Her eyes moved up and over my head, focusing on something behind me.

"Hi there, Nancy! Just redirecting a lost guest to the bathroom." She waved to her as fast as she spoke.

I turned to see the same old gal who spoke to me in the bathroom. I was busted and needed to retreat fast when Kate reappeared in the hall. We all stood awkwardly staring at one another.

Kate paid them no attention. "You ready?" she asked.

"Yep, I am. Let's go."

I rushed past the old woman with my head down and followed Kate out of the diner and back to the passenger side of her car. I fumbled around, digging for the keys in my pocket, and hit unlock. From the upstairs window, the girl who sold Kate the ring and the young miss with pink hair watched as we pulled out.

"You okay?" asked Kate.

But I couldn't take my eyes off either girl as we backed out. I offered Kate a quick "yes" before sitting back and putting my seatbelt on. Kate leaned over her wheel, looking up in the same direction, and then sat back and proceeded with the drive toward the highway entrance ramp.

"Neat place," Kate said before pressing her foot against the gas pedal. I slouched back, recalling what the old woman said while hearing Old Man Studdard repeat the same sentence. I replayed it over and over, but Kate kept talking, and the words got jumbled. I brushed it off to a mere coincidence. It had to be, right?

The drive continued with an occasional conversation break for whatever radio signal we could find. The conversations in between rolled along with every new turn through the mountains. Nothing too deep but sufficient to keep both our interests. The trees swept over the hills with colors that seemed to trickle from the top down. Old farms with large white or red barns popped against the blue tones and large white clouds. The winding roads were no match for Kate's car, either; we glided through as if on autopilot. Kate, her sunglasses and her smile, glanced at me occasionally. I wondered why I had never left the Creek. There was so much to see and feel outside Ohio, and this was only the beginning. This trip was such a release I questioned why I had not traveled sooner. And maybe Mason was right—that old jerk could be onto something about me leaving.

Pennsylvania's tranquility took a quick turn to disorder as we snaked through New Jersey and a short section of New York. Our lovely backdrop turned gray and ashen as cars merged in from all directions. I caught myself sitting upright and slamming my imaginary brakes every few feet.

This was a different way of moving through daily life. Everyone sped and yelled as cars blew past us. I was uncertain if this part of the trip was shorter or if the rapid speed in which we were moving helped, but it wasn't long before we entered Rhode Island. Kate veered off the highway, deciding to take more scenic back roads.

With each extra mile, the sun faded behind the low hanging clouds with hints of red, orange, and yellow. Every twenty minutes, Kate would glance over and give me a quick smile. My eyes wide and mouth slightly opened, I must have looked like a kid on Christmas. I was excited but also sad that at seventeen, all I knew was the Creek. Reclining back into my seat, I continued gazing at the incredible architecture lining the streets of Providence. Not realizing how relaxed I was, I dozed off, waking a few hours later to the car slowing. Our pace was less than half of what it was before as the car rolled into the seaside town known as Old Mystic.

"We're close," Kate said, holding up the navigation on her phone.

I pulled my purse up onto my lap and nervously opened and closed it. My arms tingled from my shoulders downward as my lungs fought to push off the heavy weight pressing down on them.

"You forget something?" Kate asked.

"No, I didn't," I said, sitting up straight. My excitement was replaced with paranoia. *Why would I think of sharing any of this with complete strangers? What if they were all frauds? What if this was some elaborate scam that we were walking into?* These were the life situations my mom warned me about. My inner alarm screamed as carrots, broccoli, and stomach acid moved back up my throat.

Kate rested her right hand on my shoulder and held it there for several seconds.

Her car slowed as we approached a bright green street sign on our right, Morse's Lane. She turned and slowly traveled down the private street. The gaps between homes offered quick glimpses of rounded ocean waves moving toward the shoreline. At the end of the cul-de-sac, she turned into a drive. The tires rolled across the white gravel driveway, announcing our arrival. We moved forward, slowing to a stop on the roundabout in front of the home.

My eyes widened at the sight of a large coastal home with an enormous, architectural front porch. The stark white siding popped against a dark-gray shingled roof. Windows distributed around both floors wrapped around toward the back, and an old screen door on the front blew open and shut with the wind. A mulch bed with medium-sized bushes and a few remaining flowers that had not yet succumbed to the cold added a variety of subtle colors. The smell of the ocean poured into the car's cracked windows and drew us out like toddlers on their first beach vacation.

"This was the right choice. I can feel it," Kate said as she walked up next to me, shoulder to shoulder, taking in the same deep breaths as me.

I only hoped she was right.

CHAPTER 11

CERULEAN SOULS

The front door swung open as a woman in her late forties stepped out. She had a thick, cream-colored cable knit sweater over a pair of brown leggings and knee-high mud boots. A huge smile showcasing large teeth and a welcome wave confirmed our presence at the correct residence.

"You must be Kate," she said as she approached, shaking Kate's hand, "And you must be the one I have heard so much about," she responded with an awkward squeeze. I politely backed away and offered the most authentic smile I could muster.

"Well it's nice to finally meet you both. I'm Nora Owens," she responded.

"Nice to meet you," I said, my voice cracking like a thirteen-year-old boy's.

"Let me help you with your bags," she offered.

"Thank you," said Kate. "Though we could manage or even grab them later if that's easier."

"No such thing, I'll bring them in now. You can get settled before dinner. She followed Kate to an opened trunk and stretched the bag straps over each shoulder one at a time. She grunted, struggling to stand straight.

I considered jumping back in the car, and leaving Kate to tell her about a wrong turn made about one-quarter of a mile back. If we left now, we would be home by tomorrow morning. But I didn't.

Nora winked and spun around, dragging the gravel beneath her shoes as she headed for the front door, leaning slightly to the right and stopping every few feet to catch her breath.

"This is our home," she boasted.

She was brushing back hair from her face with her elbow while still clinging onto our bags. The wood and metal from a nearby wind chime collided with one another with every gust of wind. Its soft lullaby was replaced with a thunderous melody that blended with the fierce waves crashing behind the house. Water droplets from an approaching storm danced across my face one tiny drop at a time with baby drops sitting on the tips of my eyelashes.

"This is a beautiful property," Kate said as she panned around, trying to take it all in.

"Thank you. It's a nice place to live when the weather is cooperating, but when the Great Mother gets angry, you'll be wanting to head inland. Speaking of, we should," she said and then motioned for us, as best she could with her right arm, to follow.

We trailed behind her and entered through the front screened door.

Our hostess for the weekend headed up the front stairs located to the left. Halfway up, the stairs turned a sharp 90 degrees before another small flight of stairs ended on the second level. A window seat with cushions framed a large window at the halfway point, offering a view of the storm clouds rolling in.

"I'll take these up and finish making your beds. Your room will be the first one on your right. You head straight back to the kitchen now," she said as she motioned with her neck. "My daughter, Chloe, is down there and expecting you. I'll be back there in a few." She forged ahead and up with Kate's bag, which was proving to be a mighty opponent. Her large feet, still stuck in rain boots, slammed hard on each step, and her lungs grew more winded as she approached the top.

"Wow, a lot of energy," I whispered.

"A lot of something," Kate said, walking over to a small foyer table with a shallow stone bowl filled with dry sage. A few of the leaves were smoldering a fine line of smoke up into the air. Using her hands, Kate fanned it upward and around herself.

Distant chatter from the back area of the house caught my ear. We ambled down a hallway with a walnut-colored wood floor. Small rooms flanked the hall with light coastal colors on the walls and white trim throughout. Whimsical furniture sat on area rugs that complimented the colors and the décor. Coffee tables sat adorned with small decorative bowls filled with a variety of stones. A foyer table extended down the right side wall with a little water fountain and a range of medium-sized, shallow pots. Kate picked up a handful of different crystals and turned them in her hands.

"They sure have a lot of these," she said and rolled multi-shaped rocks through her fingers, dropping them one by one back into the bowl beneath.

The hall opened up to the rest of the first floor. A large kitchen of white cabinets and a center island with a wood counter and breakfast bar created a divide between a sitting room, an informal eating area, and a great room with a wood-burning fireplace.

Two french doors sat open just past the dining room table. Outside I heard the broken voices of the others I was here to meet. My eyes tracked Kate's movements while I tugged at my clothes and cleared my throat. The peace I felt driving here was replaced with uneasiness. I took a step forward and then motioned for Kate to lead the way.

"It will be fine," she affirmed.

My heart rate intensified as the voices moved in on us from the outside. Three people rushed in through the back doors with the wind chasing them. The youngest and smallest was a girl who tripped over herself and fell in over the threshold. The other two shoved each other into the doorframe and then stepped over the young girl who was struggling to stand.

Kate and I stood, waiting for one of them to notice us. Kate caught me tiptoeing backward and, with a firm grip, stopped me from fully retreating.

Then, they noticed us, the smallest girl being the first to react.

"Hi," she said, waving and bouncing up as if the floor were a mini-trampoline.

Chloe Owens, the daughter of the host and all of twelve years old, skipped over with the same brown full hair as her mother with large eyes and olive skin. She was a miniature version of her mom. Chloe's hello ended with a giant hug for Kate.

"I am so glad you came," Chloe said, releasing Kate and then moving in my direction and giving me the same uncomfortable, welcome squeeze. "I'm so happy to meet you." Her fingers dug into my upper arms while the side of her head pressed against my rib cage. Pulling back slightly, I patted her on the back like a dog, causing Kate to shake her head at me.

"Sorry," she said. "I get so excited when I meet people like us."

She stood on her tiptoes and pulled her face close to mine gazing into my eyes. I crossed them out of nervousness. She laughed and gave me another hug.

She then started the introductions, pointing to a tall, thin boy who walked casually over to us. "This is Fitzgerald Bickley."

"Hi there, and you can call me Fitzly," he said as he reached out and shook both of our hands.

Fitzly had light brown skin, medium-length tight curls, and the same set of eyes that danced in various unnatural colors. I held his handshake a little longer than usual as I stared intently into them. It was hard not to study the eyes I had only seen in a mirror.

He chuckled a bit. "You really haven't ever met another one of us, have you?"

He tilted his head to one side and pulled out a soft curl from behind his ear, revealing his thick blue strands.

"Come on. It's just color." The words came from the other female turning to close the doors to the outside.

"Or a mutation not known to man?" Fitzly rebutted.

"You're the mutation," the girl said, snickering. They picked at each other like siblings, but with her mostly yellow hair and super pale skin, I doubted any relationship.

"Please join me in welcoming our group mean girl, Harper Blackmore," Fitzly said, while bowing and clapping in her direction.

She strolled over to the breakfast bar, unfolding the giant cuffs on her blue jeans and removing an oversized black hoodie to reveal a plain gray tee beneath it. Using a stainless steel pitcher, she checked her flawless pale skin. She primped and tugged at her medium-length, wavy hair before finishing off a loose diagonal braid in the back. She looked like a 1950s pin-up girl trapped in modern-day clothing.

"Come sit," Chloe said, blurting out her words with the excitement you would expect from a child. She guided us over to the sitting area and plopped down on a taupe sofa, slapping the seat cushion next to her with her hand. An additional loveseat and chair sat facing three expansive glass windows that showcased the ocean just beyond their backyard. Throw pillows in various shades of cream, taupe, and bright blue with decorative lobsters added hints of color to the neutral backdrop. Harper moved about in the kitchen, avoiding any interaction with us.

"Don't mind her," said Chloe. "She's always like that."

"Yea, high maintenance," said Fitzly, joining in while Harper ignored them both.

Nora walked back in from the hall with quick, heavy steps. She was bustling around, tidying up anything that was out of place. Her energy level matched that of Chloe's as they both fought to talk over one another. They were courteous and polite, extending the biggest welcome I had ever experienced. Nora's voice faded briefly as she walked back toward the front of the house, returning with a burning sage leaf over her right palm.

"It must have been a long trip for you. Are you tired?" asked Nora as she proceeded to smudge Kate before moving on to me.

"You're smudging me?" I understood what it meant, but I was feeling a little violated. My right eyebrow arched upward, and my wide, open mouth displayed what I was thinking.

"Yes, dear. Don't need you dragging anything in with you. No offense." She moved from our feet up to our heads and back down again in a rainbow-like shape. Kate and I stared at one another, bewildered and insulted all at the same time.

When she finished, she placed the leaf in a shallow shell on the coffee table nearest Chloe and Fitzly, eagerly waiting for us to sit. Kate and I stuck together and planted our butts on the loveseat. Fitzly and Chloe sat on the other one, legs bent at a 90-degree angle, feet flat on the ground, hands folded.

Nora retreated to the single chair, melting back and tucking herself between the arm panels. She had just settled in to speak when Harper blurted out her first words toward me.

"So are you haunted or just see ghosts, like ... what's your story?" She sat on a kitchen bar stool dangling and swaying her legs while she spoke and chomped on gum. I slouched, hoping no one heard her question, but all their color changing eyes focused on me and waited for my response.

"Give them a minute, will you?" said Nora as she turned and scolded Harper with her eyes.

Fitzly elbowed Chloe whose feet tapped non-stop against the wood floor.

"Don't," Chloe shoved him back.

"You're making them uncomfortable," Fitzly said, leaning in toward Chloe and speaking under his breath.

"I'm not; you are!" Chloe moved nose-to-nose with Fitzly, gritting her teeth.

"Would you two stop, please? They are not caged animals at a circus, and they can hear you." Nora shook her head and finger at them. The sound of another set of footsteps heading our way interrupted her, though. I braced, preparing for yet another Cerulean.

Nora sighed and rolled her eyes when this aged, petite woman appeared. White hair was slicked back off her face, stressing years of earned wrinkles. A cream-colored dress swooped in at her waist before popping back out below her knees. A dark brown apron covered in white flour wrapped her little frame.

She muttered under her breath while maneuvering through the rooms with a mop, complaining about the mud the kids tracked it from outback. Fitzly and Chloe glanced at the bottom of their shoes, apologized, and took their boots back to the door before returning. The old woman wasn't amused and didn't appreciate the apology.

"Has anyone offered you a drink?" she politely asked Kate and me.

We tried to decline, but she didn't hear us. She propped her mop and proceeded to pour two large mason jars of water with ice and lemon from a nearby brass beverage cart. She handed us the drinks, whether we wanted them or not.

"Thank you," we both offered.

"Dinner will be ready in an hour, nothing fancy tonight. See you in the hall at 7:30 p.m. For you new folks ... I am Anna, from

Dyersburg, Tennessee, so don't mind my accent. Anything you need here, food-related, give me a yell. Spirit-related, don't call me at all. We have a separate alley kitchen in the back where I do all my cooking. You want to cook, you cook in here." She disappeared back in the direction of the second kitchen, smacking her apron and dragging her mop behind her.

"That's my mom," whispered Nora, letting out another big sigh. "Been living with us for the last five years. She does most of the cooking around here. I don't make her. I think it's her way of earning her keep. It's in her blood to work. It keeps her busy and out of my hair."

"Oh, that's fine with us. We are not here to make anyone's life more difficult," offered Kate.

I took a small sip of water and used it as my reason not to speak, but Harper wasn't interested in silence. "Can you at least tell us why you drove all this way to meet us?" Harper dramatically slid off her chair, then leaned over the counter to play with the stones in one of the decorative bowls.

"I invited them, Harper," Nora glared at Harper, and then turned back towards us. "I swear they're not always this impolite. Let me tell you a little about us first?" Nora settled in to speak and proceeded to tell us about a blog she had started when Chloe was little. "I posted details about the experiences little Chloe was having. One day, I posted a close-up picture of Chloe showcasing her eyes and her thick strand of blue hair. Fitzly and Harper, who didn't know each other at the time, saw it. They reached out via email but, so did 100 more people claiming to have the same eye color and same experiences. I agreed to set up a meet-and-greet at a local park in the summer, but only these two showed up."

Harper walked around the perimeter of the room, fidgeting with anything her hands could touch. At the same time, Chloe and Fitzly sat patiently, waiting for their turn to speak.

"Your website is Ceruleanspirit.com, right?" asked Kate.

"Yes, can I ask how you came upon my site?" Nora was so relaxed with her legs crossed, and her right foot bobbing up and down. She reminded me of all of my past therapists.

"I found a printed copy of your homepage on the floor of our antique store. I went online and read some of your blogs and clicked on your contact info." Kate sat up straight as Harper's voice traveled loudly across the room.

"Ugh, an antique store. Seriously, do you know how much baggage you brought with you? We need to not just smudge them but let them air out on the back patio for a while."

"They're fine," said Fitzly, "and not the only people with baggage." He shook his head and waved her off with his left hand.

Nora chuckled. "Sorry, but sometimes I have to laugh about it all. Never in my life did I think I would have a child who could see the spirits of the dead, let alone have a handful of you sitting in my living room teasing each other about it."

"Could you tell us more about Chloe and what you were experiencing?" Kate asked, turning away from Harper to focus back on Nora and ignoring her attempt to make light of this.

She cleared her throat and continued.

"When Chloe was about two, we noticed her talking to things that weren't there. I chalked it up to an imaginary friend and never gave it too much thought. But Chloe quickly became afraid of her friends. She had a limited vocabulary, so it was tough for me to figure out what was going on. She talked about one in particular named Bessie."

"Yeah, her imaginary cow," retorted Harper. Chloe squeezed her eyes in her best attempt at a scowl, while Nora went on.

"She slept with me most nights after the fears set in. She wouldn't even go to the bathroom by herself. We took her to a couple of doctors, and they all said she had an overactive imagination. But then, weird things happened around the house. Lights would dim and turn off. Doors would open and close. Toys would roll off steps or across the floor," she went on.

It was almost cliché, but outside the wind whipped up, slamming into the glass and causing many creaks and cracks around the home. Dark clouds had moved in, covering the deep blue hue of the sky. Harper pulled out a tall lighter from the center island and walked around lighting jars of candles and several wall sconces.

Inside, I already knew the answer, but I wanted to hear someone else's experience without my own mixed in. "What happened next?"

"Chloe started seeing and hearing the voices of more spirits. Some she could see, some she only heard. Many of them turned nasty within moments of gaining her trust. I did research online. I was looking for anything that was not conventional medicine. All I found was a small group of parents who spoke about their Cerulean Children."

I tilted my glass toward my mouth and welcomed a few cubes of ice to chew on. The ice distracted my urge to panic and run. Thanks, Aggie, I thought to myself before moving on. "What exactly are Cerulean Children?" I asked.

"Ceruleans are born with a soul that allows them to connect with our world and the spirit world. The name itself is derived from Latin, meaning the heavens. Most outgrow their ability by the time they are five. An amnesiac effect takes over, and they don't even remember what they experienced as a child. Eventually, they and their families forget or simply remember their 'imaginary friends.' So I dealt with it best I could until she was five. I thought, like a switch, it would all shut off. But it didn't; it got worse. Then the headaches started."

Chloe was fidgeting and bouncing off the couch and spoke during her mom's next pause. "At random times during the day, I could hear voices. The closer the voices got, the more scared I became. Then, this pulsating headache would start at the top of my head and paralyze my entire body until I passed out. In my unconscious world, spirits would ascend on me with so many messages; I couldn't listen to them all."

"Her eyes would close, but I could see them moving quickly under her lids. I would shake her back to our spiritual plane," added Nora.

"Do you still have the headaches?" I asked. I wanted to stay quiet, but the story and familiarity with my own life had me craving for more information. My arms trembled as a chill took over my body. I was cold but not from the air.

"No. I don't fight it anymore," she replied.

"Fight what?" I asked.

A slight sound rolled off Fitzly's tongue, but Nora took back the discussion and squashed whatever he was about to say.

"I wanted answers for her. Fast forward to a summer trip out west in Arizona. Just like any other American family, we spent several days touring the Grand Canyon. But I had another plan. I had read about Native shamans, and I wanted their own opinion on Chloe. So we hiked to a place called Havasu Falls with a guide. He knew some of the Natives and thought it was our best chance to come across one on the path. Then on day two of the hike, Chloe collapsed from a migraine. It was the longest and worst headache she had ever had."

Nora stood and walked over to the back windows where water splattered across the panes from the approaching storm. Harper walked over, handing her a lit candle on a stainless holder. Nora nodded a thank you and went on with the story while she stared outside.

"We were roasting in the hot sun when a Native American man approached us from behind. He bent down on one side of Chloe and raised her head. He splashed cool, clear water over her forehead from a container he had in his leather satchel. Placing his hands over her eyes, he whispered in her ear. Then from his pouch, he pulled out pressed flowers in a variety of colors. He rubbed the tips of his thumb against his other fingers, and the tiny petals fell to her face, some clinging to the water droplets that had yet to evaporate. Looking at me, he spoke clearly and with intensity, I will never forget: 'She was born with energy unlike yours. She is a helper Spirit and must not fight it anymore. Her soul is cerulean and as pure as the color. She seeks peace and will learn to communicate with the other side. She only has to listen.'

"Chloe woke in his arms and whispered 'Thank you' as if his words had traveled to wherever her conscious mind lay sleeping. Chloe crawled into my arms, and he slipped away."

"I listened," said Chloe with eyes wide. "I went out to the campfire and wrote notes on tiny pieces of paper and tossed them in. I watched as each flame engulfed the message, curling it up into the atmosphere." Chloe gracefully lifted her hands up above her, fanning the smoke in her memory. "I had vivid, colorful dreams that night, and I wasn't afraid. In my dreams, the spirits answered."

111

CHAPTER 12

DARK STORM

Chloe's right leg was bent underneath her as she used her left leg to propel her up and down. Fitzly placed his hand on Chloe's arm, halting her movement but then stood to look outside.

"What was that noise?" he asked, motioning for Chloe to follow him to the window.

With the large dark clouds rolling in, the noise outside was likely thunder, but Fitzly was nervous as he moved up next to Nora with Chloe right behind. They pressed their faces against the window as flickers of light radiated across the sky.

"It's just rain?" I replied flatly.

Harper fixed her stare on me, which I returned. "If Fitzly is concerned, then it's not just rain. If you're actually one of us, you should have a sixth sense, too," she said.

I wasn't sure I wanted to be one of them or at least a group that included Harper. Still, I hated it when my mom doubted my intuitions, so I gave Fitzly the benefit of the doubt. I tapped Kate on the shoulders and walked over to join them. The winds and heavy rain mixed with the acoustic effect of thunder created a majestic atmosphere. I saw beauty in the turbulent and violent nature of the storm. Mother Nature might be angry, but there was something exquisite and pleasing about her rage.

Harper joined them. A blast of light lit up the sky, startling everyone. Harper threw on her hoodie and ran to the back door. Fitzly and Nora tried to stop her. They were all arguing over one another and tugging at each other's clothes.

"Are you going outside?" I asked, still hesitant to move in closer. "I think it's best to watch from here, don't you?"

Fitzly agreed with an immediate head nod and begged Harper to stay, but Harper, with a muffled voice, replied, "I saw something. I'm going, with or without you." Then, she stepped out into the storm.

Fitzly moaned but followed hesitantly, and so did Nora and Chloe. It was clear they all stuck together, no matter how poor the plan.

"When in Rome," I scowled. Kate and I walked through the glass doors and faced a blowing wind that knocked us both back.

Kate brushed the hair back from her face. "Why exactly are we going outside?" The stress in her voice grew with every step we took.

I shrugged.

Everyone else had already pushed ahead toward the coast, so I grabbed Kate's arm and put my head down. The short bursts of high-speed wind whirled around us. My cheeks and lips burned with every tiny punch from a million raindrops. I was soaked, cold, and shivering when my sixth sense kicked in, telling me to turn around, but I ignored it, and I followed them up over a wooden walkway toward the beach. The loud gusts and the sound of ocean waves violently slamming against the shore muted their voices. Kate pulled me closer.

"I can't see; I don't want to lose you," she said.

"Just hold on," I yelled.

I followed their movement, using my arm to shield my eyes from the water when I bumped straight into Fitzly. The others were already with him.

We formed a line where the waves of the ocean broke against the shore. The water rolled in toward our feet before retreating out into the angry ocean. Tall, fierce waves roared under an ominous sky.

"What are we looking for?" I screamed through the howling wind.

Fitzly leaned in, yelling equally as loud. "Something is out there."

"What?" I yelled back, but I couldn't hear his response.

Bolts of lightning struck down from the sky out in the horizon. One, two, three, four, five .... One after the other, large flashes of light slammed into the ocean followed by deafening thunder. Jumping into one another with each blast, we huddled into a small circle for protection. Screams from Chloe with each new unmerciful sound heightened the pace of my heart. Thunder echoed through the sky, carrying in the waves that collapsed like the end of a symphony.

"Look!" shouted Harper.

Out in the tide, sea life sprang out above the water, slamming into one another. Dolphins leaped into the air, contorting as various fish soared high above, battering their bodies. Pipefish shot up like fireworks as sea butterflies flew up and cascaded back down like parachutes. The saltwater scattered like rain in the wind, stinging my eyes. Hundreds of creatures were catapulted and then slammed back against the water.

"Something is coming; we should head back," repeated a nervous Fitzly, flinching with each roar of thunder.

Kate clutched onto me harder. "I agree, let's go."

But Fitzly suddenly froze and stared intensely into the sky. He lifted his arm up, slowly pointing out toward the horizon. He fought to speak and then stuttered.

"Do, you, you see?" he asked.

I wiped my face with my sleeves and then laced my fingers to form a shield over my brow.

"What, who?"

"Her!" Harper said, pointing out over the high seas.

A dark image of a woman rose up from the fog over the ocean. Giant black wings wrapped around from behind her, their tips resting in the harsh water below. Black lines streamed down her face and neck. As she grew taller, a cloak that covered her opened from below. One by one, narrow silhouettes shot out, high into the air. Demons with large black mangled wings and charred skin charged across the night sky. With every move, their burnt skin cracked, revealing a fierce fire from within. They gathered at the horizon, snarled and glared at us with their green and yellow eyes. The woman raised her arms, and suddenly the demons descended on us like famished hawks.

We were their prey. Kate clung on tight as the winds threatened to divide us.

"I don't see anything. Do you?" she asked, burying her head into my back.

I did, but I couldn't speak, paralyzed by the images, so clear despite the swirling wind and rain. The lightning flashes allowed for brief moments of clarity. They were coming, and they wanted all of us.

"We have to go, NOW," shouted Nora.

Fitzly yanked at my other arm, pulling Kate and me back toward the house with Nora, Chloe, and Harper falling into us as the energy from the wind slammed into our backs. The thunder roared, and with each new bolt, ten more figures appeared. The sounds of their giant flapping wings closed in on us. I fell to the ground, losing contact with Kate and Fitzly. The sand swirled up around me as I tried to crawl to their muffled screams. Water rolled up under me. My sense of direction confused, I panicked and rolled into a ball, begging for help.

I could hear their terror-stricken voices all around me but couldn't see them, couldn't touch them no matter how far I reached. I dug into the sand, squeezing the grit through my fingers when a pair of hands pressed down onto my shoulders. I rolled back and kicked, but an unfamiliar voice tried to calm me. I shielded my eyes when suddenly a face of a boy came into view. He reached out his hand. "Come, I'll get you back to the others."

I reached up, grabbing onto his forearm. He pulled me up and covered me with his jacket, but I stopped. They were still out there. They were close, and we were exposed. I looked back into the ocean toward the demons that were sure to find us. I could hear the grandeur of their wings, their cries, their howls. But their images were blanketed by thick fog. I trembled as he pulled me back toward the house. Over the threshold, everyone stood to wait for me, grateful that I was found. He pulled the jacket back from my head, and for the first time, I saw his golden-brown eyes mixed with specks of green and yellow. He wasn't one of us.

"Are you okay?" he asked.

I didn't have time to answer. He motioned to Nora to pull the french doors closed. As they slammed shut, he gathered us together and then moved us like sheep into the hearth room. He ripped off his wet button-down and pushed up the sleeves on his tight thermal. He filled the fireplace with logs. None of us spoke. We stood, shivering and dripping water onto the floor. The house was eerily silent other than a few pops from the fire. Chloe moved over to me, tugged at my sleeve, and pulled me down toward her. Nose to nose, she grimly whispered. "They're still here."

The shutters outside walloped against the siding as the wind howled. With another lightning strike, the house illuminated glaringly for a moment, and then darkness masked the rooms.

"Everyone, just stay put," yelled Nora. She grabbed a candle that Harper had lit earlier and rushed into the kitchen, digging out flashlights from under a cabinet. She returned, calling out our names to step forward and take one.

The area was too dark for me to risk moving around. The others rushed for the lights, tripping over chairs and end tables frantically, hoping to see what I wished not to. The beams of light cut through the darkness, casting shadows. Kate and I huddled together behind an armchair watching, waiting, and praying this would all end soon. Pain entered my right temple.

Suddenly, a strange noise broke the silence—the whipping sound a towel makes when quickly shaken out to dry—but this sound was intensified by a thousand decibels. The flashlights bounced off several dark silhouettes of large black winged creatures with wings fully extended. They darted forward toward each light and the person holding it. The flashlights dropped to the floor.

The sound of lamps, vases, and artwork from the walls crashed. Deafening screams filled the first floor, and the putrid smell of garbage and spoiled eggs wrapped around my face like a serpent suffocating its kill.

I pulled Kate down behind the arm of the chair. We sat with our knees pulled up to our chests. I held my breath.

"What's going on?" Kate's voice trembled as the harsh sounds grew behind us. I didn't answer. I found myself longing for the mornings after a nightmare, relinquishing the joy that being awake brought. I wished for the days where the shadows in corners were nothing more than an overactive imagination. Up until now, I could talk myself out of believing that any of this was real. But it was, and I knew I wasn't waking up from any of this. I wished that something in my life would've prepared me for what to do next. I was empty. Kate didn't press for an answer I didn't have. I placed my arm around her shoulder and offered whatever comfort I could.

Suddenly, a flash of orange and red lit up the corner of the wall. At that moment, a tall, male-like figure with the same charred skin and outstretched wings looked down at us, his human-like hands, long fingers, and sharp nails waved in front of our faces. Its muscles, tendons, and ligaments twisted around bones absent of skin. His eyes swirled with green and yellow streaks of color with the same black "X" in his right eye as the demon from my dreams.

My vocal cords strained as a terrifying scream released from my throat. I yanked a paralyzed Kate behind me, dragging her toward the kitchen area. The demons were all around us. They played with the lights, mocking us and laughing at each new shriek. They enjoyed the fear they were spreading and grew more obnoxious and terrifying with each second. They spoke to each other with a disembodied growl.

I couldn't see anyone else but heard the commands of the boy. He wanted me to hide; he didn't like that I was out in the open. I spun, trying to follow his voice. He called on the demons to leave. They grew restless and launched the flashlights hard against the walls. They shattered and fell to the ground. The room became darker with each loss of light. Only one remained.

In the center of the room, the shadow of the nameless boy returned. He stood tall and erect, shining his light up under his chin with unwavering courage. The demons flew in close, throwing handfuls of something onto the floor, and then backed off as if pulled away by an invisible force. Their sinister laughs echoed around the room when a glowing orange light surrounded the feet of the boy. He jumped to the side. A gust of wind blew up from the middle of the light. Soon, fire rose from the floor. One by one, each figure drew in their wings and retreated down through the portal. Their bones and wings fiercely slammed against the edges of the opening before descending into the flames.

"Sawyer!" cried out Harper from the darkness. The boy leaned away from the hot flames, shielding his face as each demon dropped into the floor. Then suddenly, the wings of one demon, slapped against the floor, propelling him back up. He hovered over the opening with the glowing light around him. He tossed something to the boy. He snarled and then hissed, "We don't need this; take it back!"

The lights flickered and flashed like a strobe light speeding up before coming to an abrupt halt. The house lights clicked backed on.

They were gone. It was silent.

Nora was huddled under the breakfast bar with Chloe, Fitzly was under the kitchen table, Harper was sitting on her knees in the hall, and Kate was buried into my back. The boy stood staring down at a black book he cradled in his hands. He raised his head slightly and focused on me. I didn't turn away. I was drawn to him, *but why?*

I pulled away from Kate and slowly walked toward him. I couldn't break my stare. Who was he, and what did the demon drop to him?

"Stop," he said, raising his hand, "don't step on it."

I took a step back, stopping when I noticed a diagram burned into the wood floorboards.

"It's a demon portal," he said.

I knelt down and noticed black sand following the burnt lines of a very detailed diagram on the floor. It was an elaborate pentagram surrounded by a circle of symbols.

The boy knelt down in front of me, wiped his hand across the diagram, and held it up for me to see. "It's sediment from the flames of hell. They can create a portal anywhere with this."

A small gust of wind swirled the sand, erasing the marks in the wood. I carefully placed my hand flat on the floor near his. It was still warm.

I stared at him intensely. How did he know all this, and what was he still clutching in his arm? Soon, everyone was hovering over us. Kate fell to her knees next to me. "I'm so sorry that your mom never believed you."

I rested my head on her shoulder and rubbed the warm grit left behind between my fingers, recalling each demon's charred-like skin and the flames they descended into. Touch now offered the most concrete evidence of their existence. It was left behind as a reminder and a warning. They're real, all around us, and coming back. I had proof that I wasn't crazy after all.

CHAPTER 13

SACRED SYMBOLS

Grandma Anna appeared, spinning in circles with her hands aggressively running up through her sparse white hair. "What in God's name did you all bring here?" she groaned.

The boy stood and walked away with Harper, his arm around her shoulder.

"Calm down, Ma," shrieked Nora.

"Calm down! Have you looked around? What the hell just happened, and oh Lord, what is that smell?"

She rushed and opened a few windows in the front rooms, but it only intensified the offensive scent. It was a combination of rotting fish and burnt skin. I covered my face.

Nora quickly responded. "I don't know what happened here, but the last thing we need is you yelling at everyone."

Anna turned her attention to Kate and me; we were still kneeling on the floor.

"What kind of voodoo hoodoo shit did you bring with you?" she asked.

"Mom!" Nora yelled, "Enough!"

Anna bit her lip and most of her upper chin before stomping down the back hall. She mumbled a series of different prayers while she groaned on about our presence. I no longer felt welcome and couldn't blame her either. *Did I bring this with me?*

"I'm sorry about that. Is everyone okay?" asked Nora, clutching Chloe in her arms. Her eyes welled with tears. "Everyone, please, watch for the broken glass on the floor."

"Don't worry; I'll clean up your mess," yelled Anna from down the hall.

I surveyed the damage around the room. It was not only a mess but also a huge loss. Many of their items were broken or destroyed. Guilt was growing within my gut. *Did they follow me here? Was it me they wanted?* But my need to understand what we all witnessed was outpacing anything else I was feeling.

The boy and Harper were having their own conversation within earshot of all of us. I approached them but only wanted him to answer.

"The demon, he threw something at you. Can we see it?" I asked him.

Harper glared at me. She blamed me too. But I didn't care. "Can we see it?" I asked again.

"Sure," he said. But as he was handing it over, Nora stepped in and ripped it away from my hands.

"This book came straight from the hands of evil; it won't be any of you who read it first," she said.

"Why?" demanded Harper. "If they wanted you to have it, they wouldn't have thrown it at Sawyer." Harper tried to snatch the black leather-bound book back, but Nora turned away and held it tight to her chest with her left hand. "I'm protecting all of you; I don't know what's in here. But I'll be the first to look."

Kate stood on wobbly legs. "Nora, please; we drove ten-plus hours to get here and have little time to stay. Could we all just view it together? Maybe there is something inside that could shed some light."

Nora wasn't able to decline Kate's polite request. Reluctantly, she moved to the kitchen table, ushering us all over with a quick wave. The chairs were tossed over on their sides, and one was snapped in half. We arranged them, and Nora sat at the head.

Three of the lights on the chandelier still glowed, illuminating everyone's features. Fitzly's light brown skin showcased freckles scattered across his nose and cheeks, and Harper's makeup had melted away, with mascara lines running down her face. Nora's premature wrinkles around her eyes and mouth detailed years of anxiety, and Kate, having gone through a human rinse cycle, was a hot mess. Chloe shivered with wide eyes that never stopped shifting, and the mysterious boy (who no one would introduce) paced.

Nora took a series of deep breaths, and then finally opened the book.

"What does it say?" asked an impatient Chloe.

Nora sat back. "Chloe, I just opened it. Give me a second."

Nora delicately turned through the thin pages while we all sat eagerly waiting for any response. The air soon filled with an abrupt aroma of flowers. Nora began coughing when Anna appeared from the back hall with a can of room spray. She held the trigger down as she walked around the table, the fine mist spreading everywhere.

"Ma! Stop; that's enough!" Nora yelled.

"Just getting rid of the smell. Sorry, you would rather breathe in sewage?"

Fitzly coughed. "We can't breathe at all." Then he pulled his shirt up over his nose and mouth.

Anna took the cue to leave but not before emptying out the can on the entire first floor. Harper retreated up front, opened the screen door, and propped some windows while all of us fought to clear our airways.

Nora buried her head back in the book, mumbling about her mother the entire time. She swore a few times, too, eliciting a slight chuckle from Chloe, then refocused. The minutes went by. Every three or four pages, something would catch her attention. She was far less delicate with each turn. We sat and waited until, finally, she broke the silence.

"There are at least one hundred some pages in here, and honestly, having y'all staring at me while I read is not helping."

It wasn't what we wanted to hear.

"Come on, give me something," Harper barked again.

"It's written in another language, I … I don't know." She spoke fast and was now skipping over pages at a swift pace. Harper slammed her hand on the book and slid it away from Nora. Nora didn't fight for it; instead, she let Harper take a turn. Harper glanced at Sawyer, and he moved in over her shoulder to see.

"What is it?" asked Fitzly.

She took a few moments then peered up at Sawyer, choking out her words, "I remember a bedtime story from my childhood about angels. They traveled back and forth between our world and theirs. They would guide and protect the weak and the vulnerable."

I watched as she tried deciphering the ancient book. Her dull eyes were struggling to focus as memories of her childhood flashed before her. I was careful and hesitant to respond, but Fitzly was antsy and leaned onto the table, resting his face into his hands, "And?"

She pushed the book over to Fitzly and then pointed out two pages. Fitzly viewed it close and then placed it in front of me. At the top of the left page was the word *Deliciae* written in script.

"What does *Deliciae* mean?" Fitlzy asked.

I recalled my honors classes from High School when the image appeared in front of my eyes, "It translates to *Charms,*" I shrugged, trying to make sense of it.

Harper and Fitzly questioned me with their expressions.

"I took three years of Latin in high school."

They continued their stares, Fitzly boldly asked, "So what does it signify?"

I rubbed my tired eyes, thinking of a polite response. If I had the answers, I would scream them out loud, "Sorry, I'm stumped like you."

On the second page, an angel held a tiny bird in her palm and at her a feet lay a sword. The word, *Viatoribus* engraved on the handle.

"Abby?" Fitzly said.

"I'm thinking!" then paused, "It translates to Traveler."

Fitzly flipped the pages forward and then back, "I still don't get it." Harper reached in and tapped her finger over the image. "I remember the Latin words rolling off the lips of my mother. I can't explain how but the beauty of the language resonates."

She struggled with each word. Her beaming arrogance replaced with vulnerability. I questioned the validity of each statement, but not the emotion behind them.

Harper was lost in a world she longed to return to, her voice trembled, "And the bird, I have one."

"You have a bird?" asked Chloe.

"Not a real one, a trinket, my mom left for me." Harper closed her eyes and rubbed the back of her neck. Sawyer delicately massaged her shoulder.

None of us were following. It was a stretch to believe any connection between this book and an old bedtime story. But I kept my mouth shut. It was the most she'd spoken since we arrived.

Harper begged Sawyer to finish, "You know the tale, please tell them."

Sawyer removed himself from the table, running his hand up through his hair. His back to us, we waited while he thought. Harper pushed him to speak. He sighed, bit the corner of his lip, and agreed.

"There are travelers, angels who walk the earth disguised as everyday people sent to protect us from evil because one day, there will be a war between heaven and hell."

Fitzly shook his head. "Sorry, but those demon-like beings were not angels."

I agreed. I spent a year in religion classes after my dad passed. My mom was trying to find a stronger foundation of faith for both of us. Each day, the depression chipped away at anything we were taught. Within a year, I became the church's first-ever elementary school dropout. I didn't learn much, but nothing I recalled covered anything about travelers or spirit walkers. No textbook ever depicted an angel with charred skin, red eyes, and blackened wings.

But Harper barked back. "He didn't say the demons were travelers. We have never read a book that even hinted at their existence until now. Maybe."

"Maybe what?" Fitzly grew more irritated.

"Look, I'm trying to piece this together. Isn't that what we all wanted here? Damn, Fitzly." She slammed her fist into the table. Nora tried to calm everyone.

I understood her bitterness. None of us wanted to be here. None of us asked for this. But I did want to know. "Maybe what, Harper?"

"Maybe the spirits we have all seen since childhood are the travelers. And maybe we are stuck between the wars they will have with the demons. It could all be outlined in this book."

"Yes, but why would a demon have a traveler's book and then give it back? They don't want to help us," Fitzly quipped.

Harper's glare burned a hole into Fitzly's forehead, we all felt.

Sawyer intervened and moved to the end of the table opposite Nora. He pressed his palms down onto the wood. "Maybe they stole it and don't need it anymore."

He spoke like a strong alpha male. His tone was low and dominant. It was Fitzly's warning to stop.

Kate was quiet, but the conversation was proving to be too much. She pushed her chair back. "I'm sorry; I need water or wine, maybe?"

Nora went to stand, but Kate quickly dismissed her desire to help. She wanted a minute alone.

Sawyer waited for Kate to enter the kitchen, helping herself to a bottle of red on the counter.

"Travelers float between the two worlds to protect, guide and prepare the Angel Army for the war that's coming. All of you can communicate with both sides, and it's not a coincidence you're here together. And it's not Abby's fault either. You can all sit here and fight about the details or use the open mind you were given to piece this together. It's all a sign of what's coming, and it's coming fast," affirmed Sawyer.

CHAPTER 14

MOOD RINGS

It was clear Sawyer and Harper had some sort of relationship. Maybe boyfriend, girlfriend? Maybe family? Whatever the status, he believed in her if nothing else. *I* just wasn't sure I believed in this whole brewing war concept.

Fitzly chewed on his lip, Harper picked at her nail polish, Chloe stared at Sawyer, Nora watched over Chloe, and I squirmed uncontrollably in my seat. My wet clothes were causing a severe itch I couldn't control any longer.

Nora reclaimed possession of the book and slapped it closed.

"We're all wet, distressed, and frustrated. It's time to retire to our rooms, get cleaned up, and regroup tomorrow. You all need a night's rest," she said assertively.

Fitzly scrunched his face. "Sleep? Who's getting any sleep tonight?"

I agreed. I wasn't sure any of us wanted to retreat to a dark room alone, especially with so many unanswered questions, but Nora was already up and planning her escape. I stopped her. "Wait, please. Just one last thing before you go up?" Nora looked back over her shoulder, and I shifted my attention to Chloe. "You said in your dreams that night the spirits answered; how … what did they say?"

Chloe turned to her mom for approval and then stepped toward me to answer.

"They showed me how to communicate. If I have a question, I write it on paper and then burn it. My words travel up into the atmosphere and over to the other side. Then, they answer. Sometimes it's a picture in a dream or a voice that sails in on a breeze. Their methods are always different, and the timing is never the same. It could take minutes or weeks, but eventually, they respond."

I walked over, knelt down, and held her hand. She was mature beyond her years, and despite the terrifying events in her short life, she spoke with an unwavering confidence that I was still trying to find in myself.

"You're so brave … braver than I've ever been. What have you learned?"

"There are plenty of good spirits who just need a friend, but there are more evil ones who want our lives, our souls," she said and moved in closer, and whispered, "They're getting stronger, and Sawyer's right; eventually, they will go to war with the heavens. I hope my friends will be okay."

Nora summoned Chloe, who said a quick goodnight to all us with a chilling bedtime request.

"Sleep tight and don't let the demons keep you up at night," she sang slowly, before following Nora down the hall and up the stairs.

Nora and Chloe disappeared with the book, leaving us to stare at one another. I wanted to go change my clothes, but I feared they would all leave. Instead, I moved to the other room, settling my butt and damp clothes on the hearth in front of the warm fire, waiting, and hoping someone would follow.

He appeared. Sawyer, the mysterious boy that everyone knew but us.

"You want to be alone?" he asked.

"No, not at all, actually," I replied.

He walked over and planted himself into one of the armchairs. His clothes were snug and outlined a strong but lean frame. His hair was slightly longer on top, brushed upward, tousled, and paired with a five o'clock shadow that embraced his strong jawline. He had a thin but well-defined upper lip. He was rugged and well put together at the same time.

"So do you think you're a Cerulean Child?" he asked.

"I don't know what I am, but I would be happy to be part of something that someone else understands," I told him.

"It should be more about being part of something you believe in," he offered.

"You think I know what to believe in?"

"Fair statement."

"Thanks," not that I needed his affirmation. "Before you try to guess anymore about my beliefs or lack thereof, how about you officially introduce yourself?"

He reached out and lightly shook my hand. "I'm Sawyer."

I reciprocated the shake. "Cool name, but I already figured that out."

"Ha! You want more dirt?" he asked.

"Yes, please," I replied.

"My mother was a writer."

"What?" I asked.

"You said my name was cool, and you wanted more dirt. My real mother was a writer who loved classic fiction. I was adopted as a young child, and that's pretty much all I know about her. At the very least, it makes a great story behind my name," he told me.

"So, your mom told impressive stories?" I didn't want to be rude, but his response was the perfect segue.

"Stop. I see where you're going. She loved fiction, but she didn't lie," he said.

"Sorry." And I was, a tiny bit. "I wasn't expecting such a personal response. Let me start over with something more basic. How about where are you from?"

"Massachusetts," Sawyer said.

"Just Massachusetts?"

"Kind of. My sister and I have lived in many places. So I guess we don't really have a home base."

"Sister?"

Like a stealthy spirit, Harper appeared behind Sawyer with a bag over her shoulder and one she dropped to the floor. She rested her hands on the back of the chair. "Yes, sister, as in me; try to contain your happiness."

Sawyer chuckled a little before confirming that he was indeed Harper's older brother. Harper didn't take her eyes off me. I felt her protection of him even when I turned away. His rugged good looks and the attention it brought must have become old for her. He was handsome, and I was mildly delighted they were only siblings. She picked up on it before I did.

"Where are you from?" he asked me.

"Allison Creek, Ohio."

"Ahh! Midwest girl," he returned.

"Can we be done here?" snapped Harper. She clapped her hands together in a rush to get him moving.

"It was nice meeting you," he offered, and slowly stood.

"Wait, are you leaving?"

"Yes," Harper was back into usual character. "Nora brought us here to meet another like us, you. And it didn't go so well. In fact, you brought along a slew of demons. I have no intention of staying for the encore."

"But you heard your brother; this isn't my fault. They want us together. There's a reason I'm here and you two clearly know more than all of us." I retorted.

"Wait, what?' Harper snapped back.

"Your little bedtime story you both shared. C'mon. You know more than you're letting on."

Harper straightened up like a python and peered low into my eyes, "It doesn't matter, I'm done."

"You can't leave," I demanded.

"Yes, I can," she said and handed the duffle on the floor over to Sawyer, which he tossed up over his shoulder.

"You really don't need to be so nasty," Sawyer said, nudging Harper toward the hall.

I trailed behind them. "Wait! They'll follow you. The demons showed themselves; they won't go away until they get what they want. Do you really want to face all of them alone?"

"Why do you know so much about demons, but you can't believe in travelers?" Harper squinted as she spoke. Was she suggesting I had summoned them? Her pace increased. I blew past Sawyer and grabbed onto her arm. I wanted her full attention.

"I'm trying to figure out what to believe. And, sorry, but most of my life, I have been haunted by dark beings. Do travelers exist? Maybe. But unfortunately, I haven't met one yet. One thing is certain. They showed themselves to all of us. They will be back, and wouldn't it be better to stick together?"

Harper yanked her arm away. "No, I have Sawyer, and he has protected me since I was a child. We'll be fine." Her hand reached for the doorknob.

I turned back to Sawyer. He was inches away when I moved in even closer and looked into his eyes. "Well, perhaps we could use some protection, too." It was desperate and needy, albeit, but I wanted him to stay. The only other man in the house was Fitzly, and he wasn't the guy you wanted by your side in a dark alley.

"Then find your own Sawyer," declared Harper.

I touched Sawyers arm, "Please," I mouthed.

Sawyer walked around me, then removed Harper's hand from the knob.

"She's right. It won't hurt to stay one more night. They're all scared. We should stay. Let's get some rest and head out early."

Harper glared at Sawyer and punched him in the chest. She didn't waste a dirty look on me. I had seen enough anyway. If I could survive a demon visit, I could handle Harper. Plus, it was getting late and the thought of what could happen in the long hours before the next sunrise weighed heavy on me. We did need Sawyer. Harper stomped upstairs and left him standing and staring at me. I offered a sincere 'thank you,' which he shrugged off. I was okay, though. He was staying.

"Headed back by the fire or up to change?" he asked.

I tugged at my clothes. The itch was awful, but I worried if I disappeared, even for a few minutes to change, he would too. He sensed my decision, smirked, and then held out his arms toward the living room.

"After you," he said.

I walked awkwardly back to the fireplace, desperately adjusting my clothes. I placed myself back in front of the fire and waited for him to sit. His strong physical presence caught my eye, but his acceptance of his sister touched a part of my soul that had lied dormant for years.

Harper was right to be protective. He had a strange way of commanding attention when he entered a space and likely a long list of girls wanting to be his significant other.

Fitzly appeared with Kate, wine glass in her hand.

"Can we join you?" she quietly asked.

"Of course," Sawyer responded.

Everyone shifted their attention to the sound of quick and light footsteps coming from the hall. It was Chloe in a floor-length, plaid flannel nightshirt.

"You're going to be in trouble if your mom finds you done here," said Fitzly.

"Oh, I don't get in trouble. How do you punish a kid who sees spirits and gets chased by demons?" she quipped.

"Good point," Fitzly patted the arm of one of the chairs, "Come, and sit then."

We all laughed. I twirled my blue strand of hair around my fingers, pulling it out in front of my face then let it naturally fall back onto my shoulders. Chloe pulled at hers, and Fitzly wrapped some strands around his long fingers. The dimming light from the fire didn't allow much detail about their eyes to shine through, so I asked Fitzly and Chloe.

"So, do your eyes change color often?"

"All the time," they both replied. Then Fitzly added some more flavor. "They're glass-like most mornings, but as the day goes on and I interact with beings, human or not, they change. What about you?"

"Yes and when I get mad, they turn all sorts of dark hues. They are my mood ring to my soul," I said.

"I love it," said Chloe, "my mood rings." She fluttered her tiny lashes.

Kate's wine had entered her bloodstream and relaxed her a bit. She rejoined the discussion. "What do you all make of the eyes and hair?" she asked.

Fitzly rubbed his lips and waited for someone else to answer but silence remained. He slowly spoke.

"Some believe that the meanings behind colors are divine in nature. The bright blue hue associated with Cerulean is thought to be symbolic of the ability to communicate with both sides. And our transparent eyes not only show the full view of our souls for those who can see but allow us to see what others cannot. Nora believes these are spiritual markings cast on our souls, and it's why they cannot be altered the way a person can change their physical appearance."

I suddenly had an image of Frieda's Kitchen and Collectibles. I remembered her sign out front, the hummingbird, and the numerology conversation. Angels, travelers, demons. None of it sounded deranged anymore. It sounded more like real life. A life only a few could see. We all reflected. Kate drank more wine.

"I know it's been a long night, but Mom will likely discover my absence soon," Chloe said to me. "We haven't learned much about you yet?" The hugging, squeezing, and bouncy Chloe was replaced with a more restrained version of herself as she delicately requested I share my story. I agreed.

Kate shuffled over to where I was sitting. "Only if you want to."

I wanted to hear more about Sawyer and Harper's mom. What else did she share? But I didn't want to divert the conversation and let Chloe down. For the first time in my life, I wasn't scared to speak, so with a deep breath and an eager audience, the words flowed.

"When I was five, my father died."

I had not said these words out loud in years and had to pause to not break down. The words rolling off of my tongue crushed my soul. I turned and stared at the flames wavering in the fireplace and swallowed the sadness that always crept in with thoughts of my dad. Chloe moved toward me and embraced me tightly around the waist, her head resting on the left side of my ribcage.

"My dad died too, when I was born," she said. I stroked her hair lightly. I was surprised by her statement but quickly understood yet again the world that this poor child had grown into. She didn't have a chance to make a memory of her dad. She needed the touch more than I did, so I didn't pull away.

"Are you sure you want me to go on?" I asked.

"Yes," Chloe replied.

I gathered my thoughts and continued. "My world crashed down around me. We were devastated. Never saw it coming. His funeral left memories of religious relics and symbols that suddenly had no meaning. The heaven that my parents spoke about when I was so young did not exist."

I closed my eyes sorting through the words in my head. How much should I share? Which pieces? I tugged on the strands of my hair listening to the ticking sound of the mantle clock. I was delicately nudged back to the conversation by the slightest exhale form Sawyer.

"I started having vivid dreams, traveling all over the world during sleep. I was a voyeur, observing how others lived. I was jealous. But then one day the dreams went dark. I was lost in the abyss, chased by evil. I was stalked and held hostage so I couldn't wake. I had to fight in each new nightmare, and every morning, I awoke after the vile beast brought me within seconds of death."

Fitzly eyes grew wide with each word then he stretched upwards to the sound of wheels rolling across the floor.

"You kids aren't having a séance in here, are you? I got a big enough mess to clean up. No more spirits!" It was Anna again in her shift and slippers dragging a vacuum behind her.

"No we're not, ma'am," Sawyer said politely. "Just good ole' conversation."

"'Good ole' conversation.'" She shook her head back and forth and then completed a 180-degree turn toward the back of the house. The extension tubing fell off the vacuum and bounced across the floor, leaving small attachments behind in a trail. We all shared a quick laugh as the humming sound of the vacuum, and the occasional crunch of broken glass beneath her shoes echoed through the air.

Their non-judgmental eyes fell upon me again. They were protecting me from the terror wanting to settle in, long enough so I could proceed. I relaxed back into my chair.

"It started with the dreams but then the spirits started showing themselves in my waking life. I would see them in corners of rooms, curled up on closet floors, watching me from a porch on my street. I hear them too. They speak with muffled voices and even whistle. I ignore them most days, hoping they will leave me alone. But they are always there. I can't tell the good from the bad anymore either. They all scare me now."

Fitzly fidgeted with a hand blower trying to get the fire on the left side ablaze again then he spoke, "We all have the same experiences, you're not alone anymore." He squeezed the bellow, forcing ash up and out of the fireplace. The flames grew large.

I grinned at Fitzly and I wanted to give him more time to speak, but the others were still focusing on me. I shared with them glimpses of my earlier life, the friends I lost, the doctors I saw, and the pills I took to ease the depression and anxiety. It all led here, to Connecticut with a "slew of demons" chasing us all.

Chloe fidgeted with the tassels on a nearby pillow, occasionally pulling out individual threads. "Why didn't your mom come with you?" At twelve, Chloe could ask the direct questions that an adult might tiptoe around. Fitzly did give her a fatherly scold with his eyes, but it didn't faze her. I understood her desire to know and answered.

"My mom doesn't understand what I deal with, and she has been through enough on her own. She can't comprehend a world where anything exists on the other side when I live in a world where I exist in both."

Kate squeezed my hand.

"It's okay. I need to finish this all in one night," I told her. The humming of the vacuum moved closer and became louder as Anna did her best to eavesdrop again. When one of us made eye contact, she would spin and head in a different direction. I kept going when the sound was far enough away that I didn't have to yell.

"I saw what it was doing to my mom, and it wasn't helping her. So I stopped talking about it. But not speaking about it and it not happening were two very different things. I collapsed one day in high school from a severe headache. Kate got the call at the store, and she came to the hospital. It was there in my hospital room that I told her everything and then I waited for the straight jacket."

Fitzly liked my joke by the looks of his grin. Sawyer launched a small pillow from his chair at him, which Fitzly quickly dodged and tossed back. I welcomed the light-natured reaction.

"But Kate didn't have me committed. She believed me and became a sounding board for all things supernatural. Most of the ghosts have come and gone. But one has stayed with me through all the years.

There is no rhyme or reason to when she visits. But she appears more frequently and is growing more aggressive. She was out there tonight, in the ocean," I told them.

"You have to be completely freaked out by all of this. How are you sitting here telling the story with no hint of fear?" asked Sawyer. And then, turning to Kate, he asked, "And what made you believe her?"

Pausing, I thought about what excellent, real questions these were, which deserved a genuine answer. Kate tapped at her lip. She wasn't ready, so I responded first.

"I am freaked out. I've spent most of my life wanting to believe I was clinically crazy. It's easier. I shrugged off much of the unexplainable as a diseased mind. But now, the authentic nature of these experiences is changing how I view both worlds. It's horrifying to think it's real. So I'm not fearless; I'm still processing."

Sawyer accepted my response with a soft, satisfied expression, and then turned to Kate, who sat mumbling under her breath. She twisted and rubbed the back of her neck.

"Lauren, Abby's mom, my sister, is a typical first-born, responsible, mature. She followed the rules and accepted everything, never questioning the status quo most of her life. As a result, I did." Kate spoke slowly, taking breaks to sip her wine. "After enough unsatisfying answers, I started to believe that more things were possible than what any of us were ever taught. I guess it was easy to believe Abby; I had no reason not to."

She took the last gulp of wine, tipping it back twice for any remaining drops. The alcohol opened a tiny window to the emotional side of her I rarely saw. Her personal feelings were never front and center. I waved off Sawyer, motioning she was done.

A shadow moved in from the front hall, catching all of our attention. It was Nora, back down from upstairs after checking on Chloe, absent from her bed.

"By some design, you were all brought here together, and you're all here for a purpose. Be glad you have one another. You're all always welcome here. This is a nonjudgmental space for you to seek truth and find comfort," said Nora.

No one spoke. The candles on the walls flickered while the flame from the fire settled to a soft glow. Kate's head rested on my lap. Nora pulled her bun down, scratched at her head, and then spoke directly to me.

"You've spent a lifetime trying to suppress what comes naturally to you. If you were not a true Cerulean, you would've lost your ability years ago. Your headaches are your conscious way of trying to suppress your abilities. You collapse from an internal tug of war between your physical body and your soul."

Nora stood quietly with her arms at her side and her head low, and then motioned for Chloe.

"It's time. Go to my room, Chloe, you can stay in there tonight."

Kate spoke up. "Why did I see them? I'm not Cerulean."

Nora replied, "Demons and Angels can show themselves to a human whenever they wish. Most of the time, they don't. Ceruleans can't shut it off. They see everything all the time."

Poor Kate didn't know whether to be relieved or scared. She repeatedly rubbed her face as her eyes flitted around the room.

Fitzly and an exhausted Kate followed Nora and Chloe up the stairs. I lagged behind to get my purse. Sawyer moved around, snuffing out any remaining lit candles. I watched but quickly turned when he noticed me looking. He wasn't a boy. He was a man, a man that stared down a demon and sent him back to hell.

The last hint of candlelight faded away. Only a few nightlights in the hall remained. Sawyer brushed against my arm as he passed by to trot upstairs. A tiny surge of energy flowed through my body, and I bit the inside of my cheek. I curled over. "Damn it."

He turned back, chuckling. "Your eyes are a beautiful shade of pink right now."

My shoulders sank as I watched him climb the stairs. The glass windows halfway up were blackened from the night sky. Standing, I watched the last bits of sage burn out in the bowl in the foyer, with the white noise of the vacuum fading off in the distance.

Ahead of me and at the top of the stairs, Sawyer stopped and looked down. I lifted up my hand to wave goodbye and goodnight. "It was nice meeting you and ... thanks for saving me."

"I was meant to, and you're welcome, goodnight," he replied.

CHAPTER 15

DANGEROUS BEGINNINGS

Saturday morning announced its presence with a golden light darting through the slats of white wooden blinds. The guest bedroom, like the rest of the home, had a nautical theme. Two off- white wooden frame beds sat divided by a matching nightstand with a large irregular shaped salt lamp that glowed all night while I tried to sleep. I was completely under a fluffy white comforter with large navy blue stripes, my head resting on two down pillows.

Despite Nora's attempt at a bed-and-breakfast type atmosphere, I awoke physically stiff after a night of little rest in an unfamiliar bed and an unsettling feeling. I should've taken a sleep aid, but instead, I watched the bedside clock flash 12:00 all night long. I tossed with every creak and crack of noise from the house. Thankfully, I squeezed in a quick shower before bed.

Kate snored in the twin bed just a few feet away, and my stomach rumbled as I pinched my side to stop the cramp. We never ate last night, and I hoped that Anna was whipping up some pancakes and eggs for everyone, though mine was sure to come in a to-go bag.

My phone battery chimed a low charge. I leaned over, dug through my purse hanging from the nightstand to find my charging cord, and noticed something under my bed. It was a small, oval stone with a symbol etched on one side. My phone chimed again, and Kate rolled over, opened her eyes, and stretched.

"Morning," she said, peeking out from under a tattered, yellow blanket she had since childhood.

"Morning," I replied, "What do you think my mom is doing right now?" I tossed the stone up into the air and watched it somersault several times before falling back into my hand.

"My guess, she's lying somewhere wondering what we're doing," Kate said, half-yawning, half mumbling.

"You're probably right," I tossed the stone up higher and with more force. It didn't spin; it dropped from the air and ricocheted off my pinkie finger onto the floor, bouncing a few more times before coming to a stop. Kate's long arm reached down, picked it up, and pulled it into her blanket cocoon.

"Where did you find this?" her muffled voice said, penetrating through her covers.

"On the floor, just now."

Kate rubbed her eyes, then emerged from the blanket. "Do you know what this is?" she asked, yawning for a second time.

"No." I didn't guess but I *was* curious.

She tossed her comforter down to the end of the bed and swung her long bare legs out to the side, holding the stone in her open palm.

"It's a Runestone. They were used for centuries in magic spells. They come in different shapes and colors and each has a specific design or carving."

"So you're telling me we have angels, travelers, demons, and now witches? We should invite a werewolf and a vampire to the party," I said.

Kate tried to stifle a laugh. "Lose their invite, please. I've seen enough."

"Ha! I've seen way more. But okay." I welcomed the idle chit-chat wanting a reason for a good hearty laugh. I needed it.

I rolled over and reached out, pressing my finger into the carving and traced the tiny, delicate curved lines with my finger. Kate's sudden knowledge of witchcraft was intriguing, but why Nora had one here was even more bizarre.

"How do you think it got here?" I asked.

Kate squeezed her hand closed over the stone. "You should ask Nora."

"Umm, I'll think about it and keep you posted." Kate's expression had me more curious, "How do you know so much about these stones and symbols?"

"We're in the business of all things old and odd. You pick it up along the way," she replied.

It was a very generic, smooth response, and she didn't offer any more details even after I attempted an inquisitive expression. I had been in the business too and witchcraft was never a topic whether I was hunting at an antique fair or working with a customer in the store. But I did have someone in mind who might know more.

"You know who can help us?" I asked.

"Manshaw," we both exclaimed, as I ripped the stone from her hand and placed it in my bag.

"Jinx," Kate shrieked, falling back into the bed.

"Don't say that," I threw my pillow over at her, slapping her in the face with a half a pound of duck feathers.

While Kate spat out a few feathers that snuck out from the pillow, the first voices of the day emerged from the hall as well. I walked over to the door and crouched down and listened through the small crack in the doorframe.

"What are you doing?" Kate asked loudly.

In my attempt to shush her, I lifted up my head, bumping it against the doorknob.

"Ouch, ugh, I am trying to listen; be quiet," I whispered back, rubbing the small bump growing on the top of my head.

"Listen to what?"

"I think its Sawyer." I couldn't hear details, just muffled jargon.

"I would say you're smitten. Be careful," Kate got up, emptied her duffle onto the bed, and laid out several outfits for the day.

"Not smitten, sunshine," I responded.

"You're rude and, may I point out, you're not over Ben. It's easy to find an abrupt replacement when you're suffering. It's even easier when the fellow is as sexy as Sawyer." Kate acknowledged, finally deciding on a camel-colored bell sleeve sweater and a pair of skinny jeans. She rolled everything else up in a ball and shoved it back into her bag.

"He is sexy, isn't he?" I wasn't proud of my new skill of stalking, and it was an inappropriate time for me to have interest in anyone. Still, I welcomed the distraction from all the darkness. Sawyer appealed to a part of me that had only ever belonged to Ben, and I wasn't sure what to do with the thoughts. Ben somehow seemed boring and outdated, while Sawyer's presence brought renewed energy and excitement. I didn't want him to become a giant human bandage over my broken heart, but my attraction to him was already starting to mend a few of the pieces.

"Puke," Kate grinned and gathered up her clothes and toiletry bags. She hovered over me, waiting for me to move so she could get ready. Then she curled over, slightly grabbing her stomach.

"Are you okay?" I asked.

Kate thought for a few seconds and then stepped backward, rubbing the lower part of her stomach. "Just hungry and in need of a shower, I think."

"I'm sorry I dragged you into this," I said.

"Dragged me? This was my dumb idea," Kate half-smiled before sliding me across the floor with her right leg. She squeezed out the door and wandered down to the guest bath in a quiet hallway, empty of any more voices.

After sitting alone in silence, I dragged myself to my feet and got dressed. In my fully packed bag, I found a pair of jeans and a long sleeve, jersey tee, and headed over to the vanity near the window. I layered on the eye makeup a little more than usual this morning. The dark black liner only accented my eyes, mostly amethyst today. I left my cheeks pale but grabbed a darker-than-usual burgundy lipstick from my Kate's purse. I was trying hard but didn't want to come across that way. It was a fine line between the two. And I didn't want to resemble Harper; I was showcasing a darker version of me. I pulled my long hair back into a loose braid that hung around to one side and left a few bangs out so my face didn't appear too thin. I didn't hide my blue streak.

On my way downstairs, I took a detour to the bathroom, brushed my teeth, and sprayed on some of Kate's favorite perfume. She was still in the middle of her shower, singing out the horror in some song stuck in her head. I swung back out of the bathroom and right into Sawyer.

My hands touched his chest as I braced myself from falling.

"Sorry," I said, pressing myself back into the door.

"No worries; she's really belting it out this morning." He motioned toward the bathroom behind me.

"Yeah, she's working out the kinks in her psyche," I replied. My face blushed with embarrassment for her.

"You look really nice this morning, too," he offered. Now I was blushing for another reason. His proximity made me giddy, nervous, excited, and scared. My body remained plastered against the door. He touched the blue streak in my hair and tucked it back into the braid.

"It was falling out," he said.

Think, Abby, think. He's just another human, relax, I told myself.

"Thank you," was all I managed to say.

"Not to change the subject, but ... Harper's gone."

Wait ... what? I *didn't* want him to change the subject. I hadn't been on the receiving end of a compliment in a while and wanted to bask in it a little longer. *Damn Harper*. But I couldn't be callous. "Where did she go?" I offered with as much concern as I could find.

Sawyer fidgeted, and then tucked his hands into the front pockets of his jeans.

"She took my car in the middle of the night and disappeared. And that's not the worst of it. She slipped into Nora's room and stole the book. Nora is pissed," he added.

My phone buzzed and vibrated, startling me. The phone made a loud thud as it hit the floor. Sawyer reached down to pick it up but not before glancing at the screen.

"Who's Ben?" he asked.

"Ben?" my voice quivered.

"Yeah, the Ben with two missed calls and a screen full of text messages," he replied.

I snatched it from his hands. *When did he call me? I didn't see this earlier!*

"Mind your business?" I said, turning back to head to my room.

"Did I hit a nerve?" he asked, his footsteps following behind.

My phone buzzed again.

"I bet that's Ben," he said, walking behind me and reaching for my hand. He grabbed my phone, hit answer, and handed it back to me.

"No reason to feel uneasy, just messing with you. I have to find Harper anyway," he winked and moved back down the hall.

The phone was in my grip, with my hand covering the speaker where Ben's voice tried to break through.

"Hold on," I held the phone at my waist. I didn't want to hear anything he had to say.

A few slow steps had me back in my room; I sank down the wall. I thought for a brief moment about letting the battery die but knew it would only result in a series of lengthy hateful voicemails. I crawled to my charger and plugged it into an outlet.

So many minutes of my life, I had waited and wanted him to call, and it had to be today.

"Hi," I said, trying to catch my breath and calm my heart.

"Abby. Are you okay?"

"Yea, fine. What's going on?"

"I stopped by the store this morning and saw that weird girl with purple hair, Aggie. She said you were out of town," he went on.

"Yes," I replied.

"Where?" he asked.

"Does it matter?" Background from people talking filled the air. He wasn't at home.

"Ben, what do you really want?" Part of me was happy to hear his voice. I wanted to share everything that had just happened, it was finally proof. Could I trust him now? Did I want to? I wanted to find Sawyer. Where did Harper go? I was emotionally stuck.

"I have to ask, Abby, and please be honest. Did Luke hit on you?"

I was immediately annoyed. "What? God, no," I smashed the top of my phone against my forehead three times before reluctantly placing my ear back in the path of his irrational thoughts. I didn't want to discuss a dead issue.

"You don't sound sure," his voice was loud with anger.

"Stop! He's your friend. He has been by your side through every-thing. No, he didn't hit on me," I spoke with a firm tone, infuriated by his paranoia. But he kept on spewing his garbage, forgetting that we were no longer together. I wasn't stuck now, I was angry.

"You like him, don't you?"

"You're legit crazy, Ben. No! That's flat-out stupid, and this is a dumb conversation. You're drinking again, and it's messing with your head. You're delusional and insecure," I replied.

I was trying so hard to be quiet, but Ben knew how to get me amped up. Pulling the phone away from my ear again, I let him go on without listening. When he finally stopped and paused long enough for me to speak, I asked a straightforward question.

"Did you call me to fight?" I dug my nails from my left hand into the floor.

"No, I just need to know if you like Luke," he replied.

"I don't, but even if I did, you don't have a say anymore. It's okay for you to date Riley, but I can't move on? You're even more selfish than I once thought."

"I'm selfish," he replied.

"Uh, yeah! Are you even listening to yourself?" I asked him.

"There is a guy friend code; you know that. You can move on. Just not with my friends," Ben was going on.

I sat quietly, suddenly wanting to cry. I was exhausted.

"Are you there ... Abby?" his voice came back on the phone.

My voice shook, "Ben, I'm done fighting with you. Please don't call me anymore."

I wasn't entirely convinced I meant it. Still, the logical part of me understood that everyone has first love, and it's rarely forever. In fact, it usually leaves a deep scar embedded with some life lesson. I was over the assignment.

I lay still, curled up on the floor, my head down as a few tears dripped off my nose. Regardless of my words, it was hard pushing away a boy I spent so much of my life loving. My thumb hovered over the red X on my phone, praying he would hang up first. I knew if I did, he would just obsessively call back.

But then, the bedroom door clicked and footsteps shuffled over.

Sawyer returned. "Are you okay?"

I didn't look up. I knew in that instant Ben heard his voice. I waited for the verbal assault to come.

"Abby, who is that? Who are you with? Is that Luke?" Ben screamed through the phone.

"Luke, who's Luke?" asked Sawyer, bending over with his hands on his hips, waiting for a response. "How many guys are you involved with?" he continued with a half-smile and a slight chuckle. I used my hand to muffle Ben's shouting. *Just hang up. Just hang up*, I told myself. My left hand covering my eyes in defeat, I listened to Ben scream, and Sawyer inquired about my insanely jacked-up life. "What's he so angry about? And really, who is Luke?" I peeked over my hand and watched Sawyer walk over to the dresser mirror, fixing his hair.

I shushed Sawyer with my pointer finger up by my pursed lips.

"Are you shushing me?" he whispered.

I hit the red X button. Ben would have clamored on for days if I let him. Still, I was also wondering why Sawyer was suddenly acting so intrusive. I didn't appreciate the fun he was having at my expense. Guys just suck. His handsome face was no longer appealing. Well, maybe a little. But still, I was mad, I think.

"Just stop talking," I assertively said, speaking through my teeth.

My phone buzzed, I hit Decline. Buzz … Decline. Buzz … Decline.

I buried my head in one hand.

"Did you need something?" I asked, looking in Sawyer's direction. My right thumb continued to send Ben to voicemail. It finally stopped until a loud chime announced a new voicemail.

I'll listen to that one later, I thought to myself and stood to face Sawyer.

Sawyer moved over close to me. He slid his hands onto my waist. I didn't move. I didn't want to. He was utterly violating my personal space as my heart raced, and my stomach turned. What was he doing, and why was I doing nothing?

"You should never settle on being anyone's second choice. There are enough souls on this earth to be loved fully by one. You might only have the first love once, but you can always be someone else's one and only." He backed away and changed his tune and the subject as if I had turned a dial. "Anyway, more important matters: Fitzly wants to go find Harper. Chloe is burning a note in the backyard. Nora isn't speaking, and I don't have my car."

His words were flying at me fast. I wasn't sure what to say, and he didn't give me much time to process any of it.

"Slow down, please."

"Well?" he asked, lifting his shoulders and arms into the air.

"Well, what exactly?" I asked.

"Do you think your aunt will let me take her car?"

Was he serious? I furrowed my brows. "Uh, no, not likely."

"Yeah, but what about you?" Sawyer stepped into the hallway to eavesdrop on the voices from downstairs, then jumped back into my room as Nora stomped up the stairs and into the hall.

"Sawyer, you better find her and that book," she said, waving her finger in Sawyer's face and then disappearing into her room.

I moved back farther into mine. "Oh, she's not happy."

"I have to find her. Will Kate let you drive?" he pressed.

"No way! Kate won't let me disappear with all of you, without her, and we would never fit in her car anyway." I glanced around, thinking, hoping for a solution. "Ask Nora to drive you?"

Nora overheard and responded as she moved past and back down the steps. "Nope, Sawyer can chase down his sister. I have enough on my plate."

I cowered. Perfect. Anna wants me gone; now I pissed off Nora too. Sawyer scrolled through his phone hurriedly and tapped at the screen, walking back out into the hall where Fitzly appeared. Sawyer bitched about Nora's unwillingness to help him when Fitzly quickly reminded him of the mess downstairs.

"Dude, it looks way worse during the day. Don't take it personally. She's rightfully upset," he said.

Sawyer was frantic and worried about Harper, but he was still capable of reason and abruptly ended his rant about Nora. We remembered the demons but forgot about the disorder downstairs. A hot breakfast wasn't on the schedule today.

"What about you, Fitzly?" Sawyer asked him.

"I already thought of it. I called my mom; she's coming. Get your stuff," he said.

Sawyer patted him on the shoulder. Kate then circled back into our room, oblivious to the commotion, still humming along to a tune in her head. Her wet hair flung water droplets in all directions like a dog shaking after a bath. I shielded myself.

"Enough with the water already!" I said, and then waited for her to notice my body language.

"What's wrong with you?" she snapped.

I caught her up on the morning events while Sawyer and Fitzly took turns adding small details. She affirmed I was not participating in a human scavenger hunt by switching from her role as a friend to her job as an aunt.

"No way. I would love to see more of the book, but chasing her down is irresponsible. Fitzly and Sawyer can go."

Sawyer and Fitzly agreed with Kate. It was best for the two of them to go alone. It just sucked they were leaving, and I wasn't sure when and if they were coming back. Kate's phone rang, and she excused herself by ushering all three of us out of her room.

"Good luck, boys. I'm sure we will see each other again," she said, winked at me, and then closed the door. The three of us stood crowded in the small hall. Fitzly excused himself to pack. He gave me a quick hug.

"It was nice meeting you," he said.

"Same here," I reciprocated.

Fitzly disappeared down the hall, leaving the two of us alone. Sawyer gently grabbed my hand and softly spoke. "I need to get my stuff together and go find Harper. We'll all catch back up. It really was a pleasure meeting you."

My heart sank. I needed my new group of friends. Funny how quick I forgot the irritating side of his personality he so blatantly showcased a few moments earlier. The truth was I needed all of them.

"You promise? You will catch back up with me," I said as I squeezed his left hand tightly, not letting go until he responded.

"Yes." Then he handed me a small piece of folded up paper, which I tucked in my back pocket. His left thumb glided over my cheek and slid down my hand before slipping away and out of my room.

CHAPTER 16

SURPRISE GUEST

Sawyer and Fitzly were gone within the hour, and Kate finally allowed me back in the room. Her concerned expression led to an update on my mom's current situation. My mom and Mason engaged in a heated debate in front of an antique dealer who was ready to sign a check for the lease and its contents. My mom couldn't accept it and made the decision to fly home alone, today.

I cracked a smile.

"It's a small win," Kate responded. "Not entirely sure what it all means yet, but good news, we still have the store."

The argument had to be intense for my mom to fly home without him. That was even better news, but Kate was right. It was a baby step and I couldn't count my chickens just yet. But a small win was still a victory.

Nora requested our presence downstairs. Kate and I descended the steps and then carefully stepped through the hall to assess the damage Fitzly had warned me about. The first floor was in complete disarray. Anything fragile was broken into pieces on the floor. Canvas wall prints were shredded, frames broken in half, and vases pulverized and smashed into the floor. Anna sat at the kitchen table in defeat with a broom, full dustpan and a large garbage can next to her. She didn't acknowledge us.

Nora was collapsed on one of the loveseats by the large window with Chloe curled up next to her. Nora rubbed her temples with one hand and stroked Chloe's hair with the other. The bright light from the outside showcased Nora's bags and dark black circles under her eyes. She forced a smile and a quick morning greeting when Chloe interrupted her.

"Can they come with us?"

Nora ignored her. I stood fidgeting with the sleeves on my shirt searching for an appropriate response to her greeting. But Nora gave up waiting on both of us and continued to speak. She never stopped rubbing the sides of her head.

"I realize you both drove a very long way to get here, but as you can see, my home is destroyed. I can't bear to watch my life being swept up into garbage cans. It's heartbreaking."

"Is there anything we can do to help?" I asked.

Anna scoffed. Her reaction was unsettling.

"I'm sorry." My stomach churned.

"It's okay, Abby; it's really not your fault. I don't think any of us could've been prepared for what happened." Nora shot a quick glance at Anna, who then removed herself from the conversation dragging her broom and can with her.

"I called a local cleaning company to come here and help my mom. I'm going to take Chloe to a hotel for the rest of the weekend. You're welcome to join us, but I understand if you wish to go home," she said.

Kate stepped forward and graciously thanked her for the invite and apologized again for the mess. She sympathized with Nora and tried to brainstorm ways to help. Nora clutched onto Chloe, grateful they had each other. Still, she was grieving the loss of so many personal items and belongings she had been collecting her entire life. Nora appreciated Kates's attempts, but in the end, Nora wanted to leave.

"It's okay, Abby and I will head back home today. It seems like a good time for us all to recover with family."

Chloe hopped up, ran over, hugged Kate first, and then me. She held me a little longer.

"Please come back," she pleaded.

I knelt down. "I have your mom's number. I will, and you can call me anytime." I pinched her cheek and then said goodbye to Nora. Nora didn't offer a farewell wish. She simply waved then answered her ringing phone.

Kate and I didn't waste any time packing. Within minutes, we were back downstairs by the front door. We debated for a moment on whether to go back and say a final goodbye, but we agreed it wasn't necessary. We opened the door, slipped outside, hopped in the car, and drove away.

In contrast to the ferocious weather pattern that blew in last night, today was tranquil. The sky was a deep blue hue with large white clouds that parted on occasion, letting the warm rays from high sun deliver warmth to the cool, crisp air. Kate and I stopped at a local diner to finally eat, but our eyes were bigger than our stomachs, and we ended up leaving half our plates behind.

Energized, we headed out to finish the eight-hour journey home, leaving the scenic route for another day. We zipped through New Jersey and New York and were in the middle of Pennsylvania by late afternoon, stopping on occasion to grab an iced latte or hot chocolate. The caffeine and conversation kept us moving even as the sun started to set.

I squirmed as something scratched along my lower back. Then I remembered the paper Sawyer handed me. I slid my hand into my back pocket and found the paper folded up in my pocket. Opening it slowly, it revealed a phone number and a name; "Sawyer" was written in small, distinct print. My blood warmed in relief. I had a lifeline. I twirled the paper between my forefingers and became lost in the aroma of male cologne drifting up and embracing me.

Kate glanced over. "Sawyer's number?"

"Yes," I replied, biting my lip to control a large smile. "I'm relieved to have new friends who are just like me."

She responded with a head nod and a pleasant smile, "Me too, Abby."

Headlights danced off the raised pavement markers with built-in reflectors, creating a strobe light effect. She kept her hands on the wheel and blinked a little more than usual. The highway lights curved as far as my eye could see, resembling a path cutting right through the stars ahead in the most transparent night sky. Kate slowed the car with the sight of orange flares glowing on the highway. The spinning red and blue lights of several police cars and two ambulances came into view. Kate merged over with the other traffic into one lane.

"Looks like a nasty accident. I hope everyone is okay." She sighed as the car slowed to a two-mile-per-hour pace, maneuvering around the pavement of broken glass and car parts.

I pointed at two white sheets covering bodies near the center median. An emergency medical technician kneeled over them and waved for the police to keep traffic moving. I turned my head away, catching a glimpse of a small bird flying next to my window over the front hood and back to the wreckage as we passed. The bird's body was dark with a magnificent rainbow of light shining through the tips of its wings and tail.

"Do you see that?" I asked Kate.

"See what? The wreck?" she asked.

The bird hovered and then pivoted before ascending and disappearing up into the dark sky. The colors faded into the blackness. "No, never mind," I offered.

"Well, you don't need to see anything else this weekend; turn away," Kate ordered, grabbing my lower chin and turning my head front and center as we passed by the wreckage to our right. I didn't speak any more about the bird. I wasn't even sure it was real.

Kate shifted in her seat with a visual chill that ran through her body. "I hate those awful images; they get stuck in my head," she said.

I crinkled my face.

She pressed on the gas pedal as soon as she was able. I watched out the back window as the debris disappeared into the horizon along with the souls of the departed. We sat silent until Kate's head started to bob from fatigue. I nudged her. We had to keep speaking, but we were both exhausted.

"Do you want me to drive?" I asked.

"It's okay," she replied. "I'll be fine; plus, we need to get our story straight about our trip and why we are heading home early. Your mom should be landing at the airport now. Let's review your college research."

I grabbed the binder out of the back seat where it hadn't moved since we'd left and flipped through the protective sheet covers. I wasn't sure it would keep either of us awake, but I honored her request.

"So I thought we could tell her we visited Yale?" I said, my tone came out higher pitched than usual, and I phrased it more like a question.

"Lofty goal … seems like you—you're super smart." Kate's head bobbed left to right as she thought about it.

"So they have a school of Medicine and a School of Art, and I could see myself doing either. I mean, I don't really know what I want to do, but …" I tapped at all the words I wrote on the page. New Haven, Ivy League, best of the best, rivalry, fourteen dorms, school of drama, a cultural center. In my best attempt at a fake road trip itinerary, I was a little sad that I didn't get to see the campus.

"Well, what about a school of business? It fits with wanting to own your own store." Kate bounced the tips of her fingers on the steering wheel as she thought.

"I considered that, which is why we can also tell her we went to Connecticut College. They have a great school of business and it's less tuition. I think it will show her I am realistic about this search." I circled the word Connecticut College a few times in my book as I continued convincing myself that lying to my mom was still the much better option.

"Awesome," Kate said. "Two is about all we could have fit in anyway. So this is good." We were both nodding like two giant bobbleheads before erupting into laughter. We were so overtired, and a delirious laugh emerged with every passing minute. We didn't stop until we were both crying, withering in pain from side cramps. Everything for those few moments seemed hilarious. We wiped our eyes, took deep breaths, and regained our composure until the next event set us off into a tailspin of shrieks and roaring banter.

"Homestretch," Kate said and moved to the farthest right lane after seeing the large green Allison Creek exit sign. I leaned forward, breaking away from the laughter, and curved my neck up to get another view of the statues upon our return to the Creek. Gaslight torches highlighted their flat expressions, and spotlights that lay at their bare feet cast a warm glow that extended upward into the night sky. Crowns rested upon their heads, and their cloaks flowed down to the pylons below. *Impressive*, I thought.

The hilarity ended as we crossed the bridge and approached home, both of us no doubt thinking about the events of the last two days and the lies we were getting ready to share.

"I don't think life will go back to normal, you know," Kate said, making the final left turn onto Oak.

"Has it ever been normal?" I said, looking over at a tired Kate shielding her eyes from any approaching headlights. She turned toward me but didn't answer as we pulled into the driveway and up behind a red pickup truck.

"Whose car is that?" asked Kate.

"Jack, I think?"

"Was he watching the house?" Kate slowed to a stop and placed the car in park, leaning back into her seat.

The house sat quiet, "Not sure," I responded.

Kate opened her door and the interior lamps turned on, "I guess we will soon find out."

We stood and stretched, welcoming the taste of the crisp, late-night air. Kate threw open the trunk and tossed me my weekender bag. The Creek was silent except for the symphony of crickets singing to one another.

"Welcome home," I said to Kate as I walked up the front steps, taking in the creepy view of our century-old home. In the day, our house was just another elegant but aged home but at night, it conjured up devious and ominous energy. It was far more noticeable now.

Kate tugged at the doorknob.

"Locked," I said, bending over to pick up the key that always sat under Bob. Just then, the screen door flung open and slapped me in the temple.

"What the hell!" I muttered.

"Oh, sorry, Abby." It was Jack. He nervously rubbed my head as if I were a puppy, apologized, and stepped back.

"Is Lauren here?" Kate stretched up onto her tiptoes to see over Jack's shoulder, forgetting it was our home, not his.

"Yes, she's in the kitchen, I think. I came to fix the toilet."

"The toilet? Now?" I dragged my hand over my face, sighing at the lie.

"Yeah, she came home and there was a large puddle around it. Not a pee puddle, more like a toilet water puddle. She didn't want it leaking all night and into the kitchen." Jack pulled the brim of his ball cap down, avoiding direct eye contact and attempting to hide the pink color emerging on his cheeks.

"Did you just say pee puddle?" Kate was on her way to her third delirious breakdown of the night as she roared in laughter. Jack stood silent, fidgeting.

"I'm sorry," I said. "It's been a long weekend and a lot of traveled miles. We're both exhausted."

"It's okay; have a good night. My work's done." Jack said, He pulled his hood over his cap, and maneuvered past both of us.

Kate held the screen open for him as he trotted down the front steps, "What about your tools?"

"They're in the truck already." He gave a quick wave and didn't look back in our direction until he realized he was trapped.

"I guess I need to move my car." Kate tossed her bag in the front hall and retreated back outside.

"Well, that was weird," I said out loud to myself, stepping over the threshold and switching the front room light to on.

"What's weird?" My mom's voice was unusually high and energetic for midnight, but the telltale smell of burgundy wine as she came closer brought the night full-circle.

"Why are you back today?" she mumbled.

"Didn't Kate tell you we were coming home early?"

Kate returned from moving her car with an "Oops, I totally forgot. Surprise! We're back!"

"Well, I'm tired and going to bed. I hope you both had a great trip," my mom said as she brushed past Kate and me and headed upstairs.

I hope you had a great trip? Was she serious? She didn't think to ask how it went and she never thought to explain Jack's presence at our home at midnight. I was insulted by everything she didn't do or ask.

I scowled in her direction. "Hope you had a nice trip, too," I yelled up the stairs. But it was too late; the bedroom door clicked shut.

Kate left me rattled in the front room as she went to check on my mom. I dropped myself down in the closest chair, tossed my purse into a corner, and flipped on the TV. For a few short moments, I lamented on how selfish my mom was. I was emotional, "that time of the month" sensitive. I wasn't sure whether I wanted to cry or smash something. But unfortunately, I was now wide awake. I flipped through each channel, desperate to find something to grab my attention; I landed on the late night news. The local station blared the alert for "Breaking News," as some anchor named Todd called out for his colleague Madeline over his microphone.

"Correspondent Madeline Hayes from our sister station in Milford, Connecticut, is here to tell us about a horrific storm that blew up from the Atlantic yesterday evening."

"Thanks, Todd. If you look around me, you can see the aftermath of an incredible thunderstorm that blasted the coast of Connecticut yesterday," Madeline reported on location in Connecticut in a navy-blue raincoat with matching rain boots.

"Tell us more?" asked Todd, sitting in a little box in the bottom right corner of the screen as the two reporters spoke to one another live.

"A fierce weather pattern blew in over the ocean yesterday. It blanketed the entire coastal region of Connecticut with a massive amount of thunder and lightning. Over 1,000 hits of lightning recorded over New Haven County alone. Here's some dramatic cell phone video."

Sitting straight up, I watched clips of several mobile videos of the storm moving toward land. Huge black clouds rolled up over the angry ocean. Rain fell fast as passionate videographers relished in the footage being captured. I held my breath waiting for the images of spirits to show themselves on national TV, but nothing, just clouds, wind, and an illustrious display of cloud-to-cloud lightning. I grabbed the remote, rewound, and watched the replay slower and slower, walking towards the TV until I stood nose-to-screen.

"What are you doing?" Kate's return startled me, giving me a moment to step back, rewind, and show her.

Kate stood, staring at the screen.

"What are you looking for?" she asked.

"I can't see the demons. Not one fish is jumping out of the water. Where are they?"

"Demons and angels can show themselves to whoever they want, remember?" she said.

"Any whenever they want," I quietly added.

The anchor and reporter shared a few more comments and annoying laughs before changing gears to update on sports.

Kate grabbed the remote, "How about turning something else on?"

She channel surfed from one lousy show to another when the screen blurred with vertical bands of color. A low humming sound emanated from the speakers.

"I don't like this," Kate's voice trembled and cracked as she spoke. The flashing colors on the screen reflected off her skin. The noise grew loud and she rushed towards the TV and ripped the cord out from the wall, "Remove the energy source and shut down all communication." She clapped her hands then stood with her palms on her hips, breathing heavy. The darkness and the silence brought me right back to Connecticut as I prayed for Sawyer to rush down the steps, flip on some lights, and hold both of us. This was why we should have stayed together.

Kate backed away slowly and then started to climb the stairs without speaking. "Wait; where are you going?" I demanded. I didn't want to be alone.

"I am so tired."

She abandoned me in the main level of a home where I no longer felt secure. I didn't know where I wanted to be, but I knew who I needed to be surrounded by. How would I find comfort until they returned? I was drawn back toward the television, where my reflection was cast back from the dark screen. My eyes glowed red.

Then, the speakers let out the most horrific screech. I dropped to my knees, cowering from the sound and fumbling for the remote. I pressed every button I could, but the signal wasn't connecting, the remote cracked.

A glare from outside the front window caught my eye, and the front door blew open, slamming against the front wall. The heat kicked on, and warm air blew up from the floor vents moving the sheers inward and outward around the window as if the room was inhaling and exhaling. I approached the window. Three men of equal height with dark black coats and matching hats stood out in the street. Was it the three men from the school picture? I hesitantly squinted for a sharper view. Suddenly, a bolt of light from a car highlighted their transparent bodies. The car sped through then hit the brakes. Their bodies whisked away into the night. The room went silent.

I choked from fear as the red lights from the car backed up in front of my house. A young man hopped out of his truck and began pacing in circles to assess the damage, but after looking in all directions, he jumped back into his car and sped off.

I stepped outside. The three men were gone. A light fog settled in over the tops of the nearby homes while the chirps of crickets rose from the adjacent landscaping. I walked carefully and slowly over my lawn toward the sidewalk. There, in the middle of the street, was a hat from one of the men. I gasped, backed away then turned to run back in. I was startled again by Cici standing in her front window with the curtain pulled back slightly. She shielded half of herself while she looked on, and then backed away when I noticed her. My chest rose and fell rapidly with each breath I took. I darted into my house and up to my room.

CHAPTER 17

PRECIOUS STONES

The sound of my overhead fan rattling the light chain woke me slowly. I lay with my eyes half open as the air from the spinning blades brushed strands of my hair across my cheeks. I shivered under my comforter, building up the energy to get up and shut it off. Flipping over onto my stomach, I was startled by Kate. She was sitting at my desk, her back turned to me. My loud gasp alerted her to my wakefulness.

"Good morning," she said, spinning herself on my chair in my direction. I jumped.

"Sorry to scare you, but I decided to check in and make sure you weren't suffocating in a sage haze again. But you were sleeping soundly," she said.

"So, you decided to stay and watch?" I inquired with a crooked smile.

"Ha! No. I have better things to do. I was merely resting for a mere second before starting my routine." Kate's eyes were wide, magnified through her thick, round plastic glasses. She had yet to change out of her matching pajamas, brush her hair, or even put her contacts in. "How did you sleep?" she asked.

I sat up and exhaled loudly, recalling images of the demon with bleeding eyes, the woman flipping coins, and the three men in suits. "Surprisingly well. It's weird. I haven't had a single nightmare for the last two nights. Images of the spirits I have seen flashed in my dreams like a camera taking a picture. They didn't move or speak. And in between those images was either darkness or light. I wasn't afraid," I told her.

Kate pulled her legs onto the chair and her knees into her chest. She thought for a minute before responding. "Maybe now that you're seeing them in this world, they don't have to insert themselves into your dreams. Maybe that's what Nora meant by letting them in."

I crossed my arms. "Is that supposed to be comforting?" I asked.

"No ... nope."

"How long are you staying here this time?" I joked.

"I think your mom would prefer I went home today," she said.

Kate stayed here a lot in the early years after her divorce, but after Mason moved in, she stayed only when he was out of town. Despite the difference in her and Mom's personality, the one constant thing was their mutual dislike of being alone. Kate stayed last night, believing we both needed her. I loved it, but my mom was changing her attitude toward Kate's presence.

"Why do you think that?" I asked.

"She doesn't want me inserting herself into her business right now. She doesn't want my opinion, so keeping me as far away as possible works in her favor."

I shook my head with disappointment. "She's selfish."

"Let me handle your mom. You handle your friends back east and let me know what you need. I'm going to the store today to work with Aggie. I'll get more information on what happened this weekend. Take a mental health day."

"Is that meant to be funny?"

"No, sorry. Just do whatever you need."

Kate shuffled her way to the door, then stopped.

"One more thing," she said as she dug deep into her pajama pockets. "I found this on the coffee table this morning. Is it yours?"

She opened her hand, revealing a vintage opal ring. I remembered Jack's smile as he held it in his hands weeks ago. I smiled inside but kept the secret to myself. It wasn't for me to share.

"No, it must be Mom's."

Kate was satisfied with the answer as she dropped it back in her pocket.

"Wait, let me give it back to her?" I asked.

Kate was surprised by my request but didn't argue. "Sure," she searched for it again, tossed it over, and closed my door behind her.

I wasted the next hour, taking my time getting ready, transitioning between glimpses of Jack's ring sitting on my dresser and the apartment outside and above our garage. Why was the apartment suddenly garnering my attention? Arrows of sunlight beamed down onto the roof through the last white cloud in a darkening sky. The ring glistened. Why did he bring the ring here? Why did he still have it? Droplets of rain splattered against my window. Thoughts swirled in my mind. I needed to go to the apartment. I didn't understand why, but I was listening. The reason behind the ring's presence would have to wait.

I threw on a zip-up hoodie, placed the ring in my back pocket, grabbed my purse, and started my journey out back. I jogged, dodging raindrops and puddles until I was back by the garage side door. Once inside, I searched for the light switch, manically swatting at spider webs. Our old SUV sat dusty after a summer of not being used and likely contributed to the smell of wet wood and gasoline. I walked up the middle part of the stairs that ran along the left side of the garage, avoiding live and dead bugs hanging out in every corner. At the top, I opened the door to space once used by my dad and his friends. I flipped the light on, displaying an area that had changed little in the last twelve years. A coat rack made from barn wood and repurposed door knobs hung on the wall next to the door, with two of my dad's favorite hoodies waiting for him to return. I swallowed the lump moving up my throat.

The black carpet, matching microfiber furniture, gray walls, and a large bar were the perfect cave for a man and his drinking buddies. Framed pictures of family and friends still hung on the walls, and antique tools sat layered in the dust on shelves. A neon bar light of a giant mug of beer hung on the wall. I pulled down on the rusted metal chain. The light hummed, flickered, and then faded.

I noticed a shadow over my shoulder, which sent goosebumps down my arm. Turning, I faced the bookshelf near the back of the space. A rhythmic knocking sound kicked up my heart rate as I approached the shelf, placing my ear close to it. A dim light penetrated a small gap that ran down along the left side when I remembered Jack talking about a few families in town with cool secret doors. I pulled back on the right side, my hands slipping off the dust-covered wood shelf. I yanked harder and inched open the door to a hidden room with a window and a broken shutter that slammed against the outside from the wind and rain. Hunting rifles and boxes of ammo surrounded a small safe that I couldn't open. On the floor was a cardboard box with an old pocket camera, film cartridges, and envelopes of pictures dating back to 1977. Everything was in chronological order, dating back to when my parents were born. The pockets in the back outlined their fun as young twenty-somethings, followed by shower and wedding pictures. I chuckled for a moment at the silliness and the reality of their lives before becoming parents. I flipped through the images of friends and families I would never get to meet.

A yellowed and wrinkled file folder was shoved down on the side. I opened it and found random pictures of rooms in our house. Then they took the same shots but with me in them. I was maybe three years old. I thumbed through the awkward pictures when I noticed small colored orbs in images where I was present. They were absent from the others. The interior back of the folder was also filled with dates and names "Hazel, Eleanor, Miles." The list went on, and as I read each word, memories flashed in front of my eyes. I fell backward. I thought the ghosts came after my dad died. They didn't. They have always been here.

I closed up the folder and sat in silence. There was one pack of large manila envelopes left to view, bound together by a rubber band. I slid the band off and found a stack of dark, blurry pictures. I paused. I wasn't sure I had the energy, but curiosity won as I hesitantly viewed each. Several pictures showcased a hand and a wrist with a silver bracelet and two charms, a bee and a daisy.

The pictures were slightly out of focus, but the small hand pointed towards a glowing light surrounded by darkness. A few more displayed walls of stone, black feathers, lit candles, and dirt-covered floors. Was it the tunnel system in my dad's blueprints? The peace of finding my parent's box of memories was now replaced with anxiety and dread. If my dad took these, then who was with him? Was this what I was meant to find?

Footsteps coming up behind me startled my heart. I shoved the pictures in my purse, pulling the shelf almost closed so I could peek back out into the main room. I saw her.

"Aggie?" I said faintly, stepping out and pulling the bookshelf closed.

"Wow! I never knew secret passages were a real thing," Aggie said. She stood and unzipped her dark purple raincoat, shaking off the water like a wet dog and revealing a black tee.

"Does that say *'A'* antique'?" I inquired. The upper right corner of the tee had a dark gold circle with gold A in the middle. Around it was a fancy scroll and the word antique in all caps below. Aggie pulled the shirt down, stretching it to make it easier to read, then turning to show me the back. Near the top, were the letters "Est." printed in the same gold color.

"The back is still a work in progress, but your mom agreed to brand the name." Aggie stood, pulling her hair up and waiting for her accolades, chomping on some hard candy. I liked it. It was more sophisticated than the baby blue and pink coloring we had always used.

"Wow! My mom agreed to the change?" My mom did her best to keep everything with the store the same. This was a big move down a path she never traveled.

"Yes; she really liked it." beamed Aggie.

"Well, I think it's a fantastic idea too. I am impressed with what you put together. It's a great start. Who made the design and the tee?"

Aggie was still spinning and showing off her shirt. "The kid next door—Colt."

"Colt Kennicot?" This was a big improvement. "How did you know he was making shirts?"

"I was over talking to Manshaw, and I asked him if there were any screen print shops in town, and Cici, his sister, was in the store and overheard. She told me her brother was starting a business, so I met with him. He actually came up with the design. This is the prototype. I just grabbed it this morning and thought I would stop by to show you," she rattled.

"Oh, thanks," I said. I turned back to check the bookshelf and made sure it was closed tight. "But how did you know we were home?"

"Kate called this morning and said you were back, and she would be coming in but didn't know about you. I really wanted you to see it. And there's more," she said, leaning to the right and noticing my usual flat bag now bulging with all the pictures inside. She shifted. "What do you have there?"

I quickly diverted her attention away from my bag. "Oh, nothing; just some old pictures of my dad, I wanted to move to my room. What else did you have to tell me?"

She accepted my response, swallowed what was left of the candy in her mouth, and then excitedly spoke.

"There are seventy-two unopened boxes of antiques sitting in the back room of the store. Seventy-two!" Aggie said and walked around the small space like she was leading a business meeting in a boardroom.

"Yes and …?" I replied. I was well aware of all the boxes and didn't need another lecture on clearing the clutter.

She pointed at me and then spread her arms and hands high into the air as if she was putting something significant on display. "You can't sell what people can't see. Let's turn the back room into an extension of the store. Unpack everything, unclutter the front by putting bigger pieces of furniture in the back, and use it to display the smaller stuff. We could hang a decorative scarf around the door leading to the back with a sign directing customers to another room." Aggie stood smiling confidently, waiting for my 'a-ha' moment.

I thought hard about her statement, and she was right. We had endless boxes of stuff to sell. I thought about the number of people who came in and bought nothing. Their "nothing" literally could be "something" and that "something" equaled more money, all packed in a box waiting to be purchased. It was simple but brilliant at the same time. Images of the back room scurried around in my head.

"We could totally handle this together," I responded with the beaming smile she was waiting for.

Aggie grabbed her coat and moved toward the door, saying,"Perfect! I'm so glad you're on board."

"Given my mom is open to your ideas, I'll let you talk to her. Just let me know what you need and when," I replied. Then I followed Aggie down the steps and headed out into the rain that had slowed to a sprinkle. As we were making our way down the drive, my mom pulled up in her white compact car.

"Aggie, I'll catch up with you later. I need to talk to my mom," I said, twisting my hand in a weak attempt at a wave, distracted by Mom's presence. We had not spoken but a few sentences to each other last night. Aggie acknowledged and waved bye, never slowing her pace, trotting down the drive around the car, jumping from the wet grass to any sliver of concrete she could before getting to the street. I approached my mom, wanting to know why she was back from the store and what had happened this weekend, but she ignored my request and switched the topic to me.

"I heard your school visit went well." The bags and dark circles under her eyes were more prominent than usual. Her skin was pale and her frizzy hair was worse than ever. I could sense her lack of excitement to see me, so I needed to be direct before she made a quick exit.

"Yes, but what happened with you?" I spoke slowly.

"Do we have to talk now?" she said and tried to move around me, but I stepped back into her path.

"Yes. Why are you avoiding me?"

She rubbed at her temples, annoyed by my presence. I stood firm with my arms crossed. I wanted something of substance. She wanted to run. "Mason found a buyer but I couldn't make myself sign the paperwork. You can imagine how upset he became. It was time for me to come home and put some space between him and me," she said.

I relaxed. "So is he gone? Moving out?" It seemed a long shot, but the mere fact she wanted to create any space between them meant the hold he had on her was crumbling.

"Abby, please. This is why I don't want to talk to you. I need my space from everyone right now. I'm tired of all the opinions and comments. I'm sorry your weekend was cut short, but hopefully, it wasn't because of me. I didn't ask you to come home," she said and abruptly walked past me toward the front steps.

"Wait," I demanded.

She turned, "What now?"

"Catch," I casually tossed the ring over to her, "You left it in the hearth room last night. Maybe you want to return it to Jack," I said.

I backed away slowly and watched her view the ring in her hand. She closed her fingers over it. Her expression was flat.

I yanked my hood up and simply stated, "Maybe if you actually talked to me, I wouldn't have to always corner you for answers or come up with my own."

CHAPTER 18

PEPPER

I left my mom standing in front of our home and approached the street where traffic began trickling into town. There was no sight of the hat. Did the three men come back for it overnight? Standing out in the open, I was a target. Were they lurking around still watching me? Thunder rolled in from the north, rattling the ground beneath my feet. Mother Nature was a temperamental force this morning, and I needed to get moving.

Small breaks in the rain only lasted a few minutes before starting back up and drenching anything in her path. Rounding onto Main, I froze, noticing movement at the corner space across the street. A soft light seeped out between the gaps in the newspaper that covered all the window space. One nosey passerby peaked through part of the window where the press had fallen, before being shoved away by an acquaintance. A shadow maneuvered behind the paper.

My clothes damp, I jumped under an awning. I found myself on the porch of the Creek's Village Store with three others, who were shaking off their umbrellas and chatting about some trucks blocking traffic. I wasn't interested and turned to face the street until a familiar voice spoke my name.

"Abby?"

I wanted to sprint away but couldn't in good conscience.

"Mrs. Pickett?" I said with a halfhearted smile. I swung around to see her in a melon-colored raincoat and matching plastic clogs. She wobbled her way between the other two women talking and pulled me into her waterproof armor.

She unknowingly brushed her sleeves off onto my sweatshirt. "Where are you going this morning?"

"The library," I said flatly.

"Oh, that just warms my soul. Hear that, ladies?" She looked over her shoulder. "This girl right here graduated a whole year early and is going to the library on a Sunday morning." Mrs. Pickett's cheeks glowed the same color as her coat as she went on and on about my accomplishments and how she helped guide me over the years. One petite elderly woman with spiky white hair and giant round black glasses bobbed her head like a puppet. Another older gal with a silver bob and heavy makeup sipped tea from a ceramic coffee mug with a gold rim. I guess a travel mug was too basic. They commiserated while impatiently waiting for the owner to unlock the door. Mrs. Pickett scooched in closer and spoke directly into my ear.

"I wish we had more kids like you in town; it seems we can't get rid of the bad ones." She motioned over to the chaos developing near the 1816 Tavern. Mrs. Pickett could tell by my expression that I didn't understand and she leaned in to share the gossip.

"Remember that student who used to draw on herself with black sharpies? She wore dark colors all time and didn't look anyone in the eye?" she asked me.

"Yes, Ellie Archer," I replied. I remembered her well. She kept to herself most days, but the constant bullying by girls who respected nothing different eventually got to her. She showed up for the first two months of school my sophomore year and then never came back. One teacher told me her parents sent her to live with her family, but the rumor was she ran off and joined a coven.

Mrs. Pickett leaned in further and whispered. "She goes by Nova now and is opening a fortune-telling studio up above the Tavern. The community was not happy, but you know her dad owns that building and is friends with the mayor." She shook her head up and down slowly while pressing her lips tightly together. I half-ignored her to see what was happening across the way while trying to block out the other two who continued on, complaining about the most mundane of topics.

I watched as two men unloaded boxes onto dollies at the direction of a girl with long black curls and loose, double buns. The rain didn't concern her as she helped unload boxes dressed in a black tee-shirt with tight leather pants and chunky black heeled boots. She stopped for moment and lifted her head and turned her palms to the sky allowing the water to pool in her hands. The men kept working, graciously following her orders.

I focused on her space and then pointed towards the corner glancing back at Mrs. Pickett.

"What's going in there?"

"Oh, I hate even talking about it;" she leaned in close, her eyes narrowed, "A friend of mine peeked in between the paper on the windows and saw animal skulls and knives."

"Skulls and knives?" I sneered.

Mrs. Pickett gaze darted back to the other side of the street, "I wouldn't lie."

Just, then the door swung open, knocking the woman with the cup back a few inches. Leah, the owner's teenage daughter, stepped out, ignoring the obnoxious sighs and dramatic facial expressions. She pushed the door wide to let them through, but not before responding to Mrs. Pickett.

"Leave Nova alone. You adults are worse than the kids sometimes," she said.

I agreed. Mrs. Pickett's tone and comments annoyed me, her open-minded nature replaced with snobbery. This wasn't the same bubbly, positive person I knew from school. She was like the rest. I struggled to swallow my agitation.

"Yeah, I can't imagine Nova will do well here," I said, glancing at Leah and then back to Mrs. Pickett and then her friends. "Really, who needs their fortune read in a town full of privilege and hypocrisy? Good seeing you, enjoy church today."

I moved out from under the porch, leaving Mrs. Pickett stunned with her friends who were still gasping from my comments. I was growing tired of the judgmental mindset too many shared.

Ellie, or Nova, was back. The question was, why now? Curious, I moved slowly, looking for any hint of what was in those boxes. A family trying to get around one of the parked moving vans on the narrow street blasted the horn from their car, startling an old man and his wife walking in front of me. The man tossed his umbrella up into the air as he grabbed his wife by the arm. I grabbed her other, stopping her knees just short of hitting the ground.

"Thank you," they both said to me as they gathered their things to move along.

The commotion caught the attention of everyone, including Nova, who now made direct eye contact with me. I walked along, watching her eyes follow my movement before dropping my head and turning into the library doorway.

Inside, the sweet smell of paper and the soft lighting calmed all of my senses. Tightly packed rows of bookshelves sat perched upon original wood floors that led to the back reference desk. My shoes squeaked along the floor announcing my presence to Mr. Vincent, the weekend librarian. He was a tall, older man with a short, graying afro and a matching beard. I never saw him in anything but a suit. He straightened his lapel on a dark grey jacket and welcomed me with a soft grin.

"Abby, you're up early this morning. How can I help you?"

"I was hoping to do some research in the archive room for a project?" I dropped my bag on the tall, ornate mahogany front desk while he straightened a purple paisley bow tie.

"What kind of project?" He was curious and polite.

"I'm writing an essay for a college application about where I grew up and wanted to review some history."

My newfound skill of lying impressed me, and I wondered if it was becoming a habit. Mr. Vincent didn't say a word but escorted me over to the stairs behind his desk.

"When you get to the top, go right past the tables and through the bookshelves. You will see the door straight ahead. Happy hunting," he said.

I walked up the stairs, glancing back at Mr. Vincent, now talking to someone who must have walked in behind me. I was upstairs, by myself, following his directions to double doors with elaborate carvings etched into the wood. I rubbed my hands over the design and then pushed down on two antique door levers, but the doors would not open. After trying for several more minutes, I retreated downstairs to request Mr. Vincent's help.

"Oh, those doors are so massive and can stick sometimes. I tried to get the city to replace them, but the townspeople went crazy because they are so old. I told them, 'You all come here and walk up and down these stairs every time they get stuck.' But no one listened." He ambled up the steps using the railing to propel him along. On the small landing, I stopped, noticing a piece of paper absent minutes ago. Kneeling down, I opened it. It was an 8?11 sheet of purple paper. In the center of the picture was the posterior side of a woman dressed in a long black dress. Her arms were up and curved around a large white circular object resembling the moon. Lines of ancient typescript ran horizontally across the page. I held my breath.

Mr. Vincent turned back. "You all right? Don't tell me you're more winded than this old man?" He wrinkled his brow and shook his head.

I swallowed the rock in my tightening throat. "Has anyone else been in here this morning?" I gave a fake smile and turned my attention back to the paper.

"Nope, just you," he responded.

I dropped my shoulders then glanced around. "Weren't you just talking to someone?"

He motioned for me to come up the stairs, and then he leaned in close.

"That was Pepper I was talking to."

"Pepper?" I surveyed the library's first floor, silent of anything and everything except for Mr. Vincent's words.

"Her real name is Mabel, but she likes Pepper better, and I'm just here to work and get a paycheck, not make a woman mad," he whispered.

"But you just said no one else was here." The tiny hairs on my arm stood tall.

"No one, but something, and it's Mabel … Pepper. This library sits on land that once belonged to her family. She was known for her excellent gardening skills. Guess what she grew?"

"Peppers," I quietly responded. Was it possible that some crazy, pepper-growing ghost left me these drawings? It seemed more like a spirit playing a joke. Maybe the town had more ties to another side than I had initially thought. Or perhaps this was just some strange coincidence.

Mr. Vincent's eyes were wide and rounded. "You got it!" He snapped his fingers to my response. "I don't tell many, but I've known you a long time, and you're not like the rest. If you see her, call her by her right name; don't say I didn't warn you if you don't."

Mr. Vincent moved to the archive room and returned before I was done scanning the library one last time.

He shook his fingers at me as he spoke, "Doors are open, and you can't look for her, she'll find you if she wants." I stood, slightly hesitant to spend any time alone in the archive room, but Old Man Studdard's advice rang in my ears. I stayed and made my way back to the room.

I wasn't sure what I expected, but the beauty of the library didn't transcend into this large, cold room lined with metal shelves. Boxes, binders, and poster tubes dated back to the seventeenth century. The sweet almond aroma of the library was replaced with an unpleasant, musty odor.

I browsed quickly, hoping something would immediately stand out, but nothing did. I dropped the paper on a rustic wood table with metal legs, which sat in the middle of the room, and tapped along the folding chairs that surrounded it. I strolled, trying to establish a connection with one of the boxes. I would be here weeks if I had to dig through everything, especially since I didn't entirely know what I was searching for.

The countless number of historical documents almost overwhelmed me. Suddenly, I noticed two small eyes peeking through a box labeled 2002. Inside the front panel sat a picture of Mayor Quartano. His eyes fit perfectly in the inset handle space. I thumbed through the stack of images that lay behind the photo. It appeared to be a celebratory event outside of the city hall. The last picture showed him shaking another man's hand in his ostentatious office, fitting for a fellow of his nature. Then, as if it floated up from the picture, a metal piece shaped like a sector of a circle sat propped behind a glass shelf behind him. I took a picture of it with my phone, which allowed me to zoom in. My jaw dropped. Some of the symbols matched parts of my puzzle pieces. Why would Quartano have this on display in his office?

My body temperature rose while my feet tapped on the floor. Suddenly, the quick sound of a match lighting emerged behind me. I swallowed my spit and cautiously turned my head and peeked over my shoulder, preparing to come face to face with Pepper. I fell backward and braced myself against one of the shelves as the paper I left on the desk erupted into flames. I froze and watched in horror as the paper disintegrated in front of my eyes. In seconds, it was gone. I crept over to the table and rubbed my hands where it once laid. No ash or smoke or even the presence of heat remained. The heavy doors began to waver.

If Pepper was present, I wasn't sticking around to meet her. I tucked the one picture of Quartano into my bag, shoved the others back in the box, and slithered out of the moving doors. They sluggishly closed as I crossed back over into the other room. I trotted down the steps and gave Mr. Vincent a quick goodbye, which he acknowledged with a slight wave.

Almost outside, but still, in the doorway, I stopped to catch my breath when I was shoved from behind. I fell to the sidewalk. I turned myself up with my arms and turned to see the faint image of a figure being sucked back inside. My heart stopped for a second as the door slammed shut. "Nice meeting you, Pepper."

CHAPTER 19

CROSSING OVER

After taking a few deep breaths, I opened my eyes to the sight of chunky black boots. I followed the clean lines of tight leather pants up toward the girl's pale face with the double buns. It was Ellie.

She offered her hand. Layers of beaded bracelets slid down both wrists as she pulled me up from the ground. Her nape was covered in necklaces adorned with charms. I offered a thank you and wiped myself off.

Suddenly, the man with the long brown hair and his wife appeared.

"Are you alright?" he politely inquired.

"I'm fine; thank you," I returned.

He noticed Ellie then glanced at his wife, who hid under the scarf she always wore. Ellie backed away, but the strange man grabbed her forearm and pulled her close to his face. His eyes penetrated hers as she squirmed to break his grip.

I stepped in, "Please, stop, you're hurting her," I begged, but he didn't let up. The veins in his arm bulged as he squeezed even harder. I reached for him. His skin was like ice and it burned my hand with the most intense chill that traveled up my arm. He let go of Ellie and tuned to me, "I'm sorry, I didn't mean.." His wife tugged at his sleeve and the mysterious couple moved past quickly without saying another word. Not one person on the sidewalk noticed the encounter. Everyone was tending to themselves. I spun in dismay while the two disappeared into the crowd. Ellie retreated to the other side of the street before I could ask any questions.

Frustrated and confused, I brushed myself off and took jolts from a passerby while considering my options. I couldn't shake the couple from my head. *Why was he so angry? Why was he so cold and who were these people?*

I noticed Aggie stepping out of our store with Kate as they both talked and pointed toward the front window. Just then, I was shoved again by a young woman out with her mommy walking group. She didn't appreciate my existence in the middle of the sidewalk. I didn't appreciate her loud sigh. *What was the deal with everyone this morning?*

"Sorry to encroach on your public space," I offered loudly. A couple of the moms snickered over their shoulders but turned away before I could express any more gratitude.

I let out an incredibly loud groan and refocused on my next move. I didn't really feel the need to visit the store, but with Aggie and Kate both outside, I decided I didn't have a good enough reason not to. Plus, a mental health day was moot at this point, so I approached and waved at them. Aggie stood deep in thought with her fingers tapping on her chin.

"What are you both up to?" I asked.

Aggie proceeded to tell the remaining details she hadn't shared this morning, which included a newly painted storefront. The more Aggie spoke, the more visibly excited Kate became. Aggie wanted to show me some drawings inside, which I agreed to after stopping to chat with Kate first.

"Hey, my mom came back home this morning. Do you know why?" I asked.

"She wasn't feeling well, pale as ever. Maybe a stomach bug," said Kate, who was still marveling over the store and holding up her hands like photographers do when they are thinking of taking a snapshot. "What was she like when you saw her?" she asked.

"She wasn't in a great mood. I was hoping for a long rant about what a miserable prick Mason is, but no such luck," I told her.

"Well, don't start packing his bags just yet; their relationship is a tad strained right now, but I'm not sure it's over," Kate replied.

I wondered if it was, though. But Kate didn't know the ring she found last night belonged to Jack. It had to mean something, and after so many years of mutual friendship, maybe my mom meant way more to Jack than she realized. The question was whether or not my mom reciprocated the feelings.

"It's a lot for her to deal with. Aggie and I will keep working on the changes here, then we pray for the best," Kate continued.

Design was not my forte, and I didn't need one more thing on my to-do list. I trusted Kate, and I admired Aggie's creativity, so I happily let them take over. While Kate looked on, still visualizing the design board in her head, I started digging in my bag, eager to show Kate what I'd found. However, Manshaw, who could be a nosey fellow, appeared, inquisitive about what Kate and Aggie were planning. Already having my fill of idle chit-chat for the day, I smiled and retreated inside to wait for a better and more private moment.

The bell above the door rang, announcing my entrance to Aggie. To my surprise, the store was bustling with people, happily pricing treasures for their homes. In my haste, I bumped into one of our customers, Tober Blair.

"Sorry," I blurted. Tober always made me uneasy. She moved here one year ago and frequented our shop and Manshaw's weekly. She was our youngest regular. Tober hid behind her long strawberry locks, spoke faintly and rarely made eye contact. And when she came in, she took her time, touching everything before making a choice. She didn't respond to my apology but circled me in an unsettling manner before turning toward a shelf of old wooden jewelry boxes.

I sidestepped and approached Aggie, who sat at the back counter, drawing eagerly with charcoal and cutting up paper. She was oblivious. And while I wasn't thrilled to see Tober, I was fascinated by all the other customers. "Where did these people come from?" I asked.

Aggie didn't look up. "We're advertising more and starting the store facelift; it seems to be working."

"Wow, this is awesome, Aggie. Thank you," I said as I leaned in to see more of her drawing, "If this works, I hope to repay you someday."

"You're already paying me," Aggie said. She continued cutting paper letters to spell "Anderson" and then placed them onto her drawn picture of the storefront.

"Yes, but you are going above and beyond," I responded.

"No, actually, I'm just a valued employee. You and your family have always settled for mediocrity. Don't anymore, with all due respect," she returned.

Aggie was better off ignoring me while I hovered over her work, because in that instant, she broke her concentration. Her eyes went wide as the swooshing sound of the large metal blades cut her hand. Aggie dropped them to the ground and jumped out of the way as they bounced up, threatening to also stab her in the foot. She crouched over, tucking her hand up under her armpit, and ran to the backroom.

Running around the counter, I grabbed a roll of paper towels. I followed Aggie, unraveling a wad, and then shoved them toward her. She grabbed them with her other hand but then barked back, "I'm fine. It's fine. Just go."

"I can't leave you. You need to go to the hospital. I saw the blades slice your palm," I retorted.

"I'm fine," Aggie reaffirmed, brushing past me, the store of customers and out the front door.

"What happened?" Kate spun around in the chaos and blocked me from chasing Aggie.

"She cut her hand; can you watch the store?"

Kate motioned for me to leave, "Of course, go!"

The rain had finally passed for the day, but the high sun created a glare, making it difficult to see in which direction Aggie ran. Manshaw still stared at his own store from the curb, his wide body worsening my view.

"Mr. Wu, did you see Aggie?"

He pointed toward Oak. I rushed past him, and he shoved the paper towels into my arms.

"I don't need these, but thanks," he mumbled.

Half-running and half-skipping down the street, I juggled the paper towels, grossed out by the thought of the blood and tissue likely stuck in them. I stopped at the crosswalk wondering why she would toss them at Manshaw. I held the paper up in front of my eyes and shook them out. No hand guts, no blood, not a drop! How was it possible?

The pedestrian light chimed and lit up white in one direction and red in another. I caught a glimpse of Aggie heading west and dodged some light traffic as I crossed to go after her.

I was weaving in and around pedestrians as I struggled to see Aggie when suddenly Ben appeared and stopped me in my tracks.

"You can't ignore me now like you have my calls," he said and grabbed me by the sides of my arms. Standing on my tiptoes, I tried looking around Ben's shoulders. But he anticipated my every step and was undoubtedly not letting me go anywhere until I acknowledged his questions.

I stopped. "What do you want?" Then I noticed his long bangs covering his right eye. I pushed it back behind his ear. "Oh, Ben, what happened?"

While I didn't have time for this, I couldn't help but notice the fragile skin under his right eye was puffy and bruised.

He dropped his head, shielding the right side of his face. "It's nothing," He grabbed my wrist and pushed it away.

It was something. It meant another night of heavy drinking and an outburst that led to a fight with a stranger. He was troubled and not changing. I sighed in frustration.

"Stop staring at me like that," he demanded, "and tell me why you are running into the Valley."

The Village sat east of Hunting Valley. It was a flourishing community four decades ago. Today, it sat abandoned and nobody, except a few high school kids on Halloween, ever ventured in, and especially never on foot. To my left sat the fire station. To my right sprawled the large Creek parking lot that ran parallel to Main, neither of which I would routinely visit. I shifted my sight back toward Ben.

"I'm stopping at the fire station."

"To see who?" he questioned.

Thankfully, I noticed Jack chatting it up with some firemen outside. "I need to see him," I said, pointing in Jack's direction, "about help my mom needs, so unless you want a scene with six firemen, I recommend you move along."

I couldn't comprehend his motivation. He was still dating Riley but incredibly consumed with me. And what was he doing out meandering through town on an early Sunday morning? Was he following me? Had he even gone home? He wouldn't let me heal.

"Fine," said Ben. "I'll stick around here until you meet Jack. I'm not leaving you alone, though, this close to the Valley."

I chewed on my upper lip, angry. Where was his protection months ago?

"Fine," I said and quickly glanced in both directions before darting across the street.

Unfortunately, Jack now noticed me, and I had no choice but to act like he was part of my original plan. He met me at the end of the station driveway.

"Abby, hey! What brings you around?" Jack wore an olive green hat with an imprint of a black eagle spanning across the brim.

Thinking about what to say, I stalled and traded glances with Ben while wondering where the hell Aggie went and why. I decided on a hint of honesty.

"Look, I bumped into Ben, and I don't want to talk to him. I told him I was coming here to speak with you. Can we pretend long enough for him to go away?"

"Of course," Jack raised his brow up to view Ben and lifted his chest.

"I don't need you to fight him; I just want him to leave," I affirmed with a tiny smile.

Jack blushed and relaxed as we chatted about absolutely nothing for what felt like an hour.

"He's moving. But don't turn around. He keeps looking back at us," Jack waved his hand, signaling for Ben to keep walking. I waited.

"He's gone," Jack said.

I was in the middle of a 'thank you' when the fire alarm cut short our fake conversation.

"Glad to help, but we need to get out of the way, and I need to get back to the shop. Are you okay now?" he asked waiting for his fist bump.

"Yes; thank you," I said, my knuckles touched his, and then backed out of the way.

Two of the three glass garage doors opened in the old stone and brick firehouse. A group of men and one woman threw on all their gear and split up between two trucks. Ducking to the other side of the building, I watched as they pulled out and made a left into the Valley in the same direction as Aggie ran.

Are you kidding me, of all days?

I didn't have to follow the fading siren; I could turn and go home. I spun in small circles, talking myself in and out of it. My gut won. I had to find Aggie; it was the right thing to do. I started jogging toward a town they write scary movies about. Hanging close to the tree line, I focused on my breathing. I concentrated even harder on not turning toward any shadow or movement in the brush. I started at the pavement, but at full speed, I tripped over a chain that once ran across the roadway. Tumbling to the ground, I tucked and rolled in a less than graceful fashion. My clothes and hands wet with mud, I pulled at the chain, flinging it back and almost hitting myself in the head, with the small metal sign that read "KEEP OUT, TRESPASSERS WILL BE PROSECUTED".

Wiping my hands on my pants, I stood viewing the road that curved up over a small hill ahead. Trees with thick, bare branches twisted up to the sky, filtering the sun's rays so much that it was day in the Falls but evening in the Valley. The ground was blanketed with wet, decaying leaves that covered any hint of a path that existed at one time. It was silent. No chirps emanating from a bird's nest, no rustling from a squirrel or a fox. I exhaled.

Then, on the opposite side of the street, a figure of a young girl appeared barefoot in a white gown. Her light hair was partially pinned up. Long, loose strands covered her eyes. She kept her head low and peered at me. I crouched down and stared back at her. My heart raced. The firemen didn't see her. I was sure no one else would either. I couldn't sense her intentions. She stepped back into the woods, her body melting away into the tree line. The wind picked up and swirled the haunting laughter of a child around me. I blinked, and she was gone.

I didn't know if I was being summoned or warned, but proceeded forward cautiously, for Aggie's sake. I climbed up the cement half-wall that lined each side of the street and tucked myself in the trees, stomping forward until I was over the hill and in view of the large roundabout in the center of town. I approached, staying close to the tree line until reaching the side of an old brick building. The town's main storefronts sat abandoned along the perimeter of a large roundabout. In the center, on an island of grass, sat a small, condemned white church where the firemen were circling. Connected to the church stood a tall tower made from stone with stained glass windows high above. It stood proudly over the rotting wooden church.

Boom!

I jumped. Smoke billowed up from deep in the woods. I ducked between two garbage cans, clutching my chest as additional sirens roared up behind me. Local police joined the effort and headed south down one street, their cars kicking up stones and dust, throwing them my way like shrapnel. I covered my face with my arms then ran through the thick, dense haze to the opposite side of the roadway to get a better view. Suddenly, I heard screeching breaks heading right for me. I braced. A car stopped inches from me as a male voice yelled for me to move.

My pulse rate exploded as I wiped my face with the backs of my hands, trying to remove the dust burning my eyes while recognizing the voice screaming at me.

"Sawyer?" The blurry vision of Sawyer behind the wheel of an aged black muscle car slowly came into focus.

"Abby? Get in!"

CHAPTER 20

HELLTOWN

Fitzly, sitting in the passenger seat, opened the door and yanked his seat forward so I could slide in the back. His door was half-shut when Sawyer hit the gas, launching us backward on the rough leather seats. He turned down Old Mill Road. The wheels spun in the broken-up asphalt before moving, kicking up earth and pebbles as we headed north, deeper into a town full of tragic secrets. I sat with my head between the two front seats, taking in the view of a town I had never seen.

Fitzly stared at me. "How did you get here? I can't believe we found you!"

"How did *you* get here?" I returned.

Fitzly held up a piece of white copy paper with a drawing, but laid it back on his lap too fast for me to make anything of it. "Chloe got us here. But it was Harper we thought we would find."

"Harper's here? Where's Chloe?" I asked.

"We *think* Harper is here, and Nora wouldn't let Chloe come," Fitzly answered.

The questions were flying at a furious pace. We were all stunned by each other's presence.

"Is there a place we can stop and talk?" asked Sawyer.

"You want to stop in here?" I responded.

"Why not, where are we?" he inquired.

I simply stated, "Hunting Valley, nothing but empty century homes surrounded by acres of overgrown farmland." I gulped. I was nervous the police would find us, and I had no intention of going in

179

this far. I wanted to find Aggie, but we were trespassing on dangerous land. They couldn't see my concerned expression and instead shared a glance with one another. Sawyer responded.

"Let's find a place in here, away from the police. Fitzly is sure Harper is in the vicinity," he said.

Fitzly held up the paper again. "Have you ever seen a home that looks like this?" He pointed to a small drawing of a box-shaped house with some trees around it.

"Really, that could be anywhere," I said.

He tapped at it again. "Yeah, but this one has an entryway with a gate, with small, dark-colored birds sitting atop the stone columns."

I didn't want to burst his bubble, but his added detail could be anywhere in Ohio. Fitzly quickly reminded me that the piece of paper guided him and Sawyer here, where they found me. He didn't understand why I was pushing back.

"Sorry, I guess I'm still trying to get used to this anything-is-possible viewpoint. I don't know where it is, but I'll help look," I replied.

The winding road cut through the rolling pastures. A white, three-rail fence ran along the route on both sides, worn and broken. Large, dilapidated farm homes sat back away from the road.

Fitzly braced himself on the dashboard as Sawyer's car bounced over an obstacle course of potholes.

"What the heck is up with the mailboxes?" asked Sawyer. Fitzly rolled down his window as Sawyer inched along the pavement. In the bottom corner of each black mailbox were tiny white crosses painted on an angle.

Fitzly rolled the window up slowly while I slouched back into the seat.

"Maybe this really is Helltown," I muttered.

"Helltown?" Fitzly rebutted.

I leaned over the front seat, "The people who lived here disappeared in the late 1970s. One day they were here, the next day, gone, and the town's been abandoned ever since. Urban legend is that the devil himself rose from below and stole their souls. You mix that with stories of ghosts and witchcraft from a few generations of teenagers and you get a name like Helltown."

"Perfect," replied Fitzly, who turned his attention back to the paper in his lap.

"You asked," I mumbled.

Sawyer used the rearview mirror to glance at me as he spoke, "No one ever tried to move back in?"

I sneered at him through the mirror. "Would you live here?"

"Nope," replied Fitzly.

"Likely not," said Sawyer.

I saw it. "There." I pointed. On the right side of the street just past the tree line sat an aged wrought iron gate propped open between two deteriorating columns. Sawyer pulled in and slowed the car to get a view of the medium-sized black stone birds that rested on opposite sides of the gate.

"Ravens," he remarked, "The Keepers of Secrets."

"Odd choice for a family farm," responded Fitzly.

"Maybe not a family farm located in Helltown," Sawyer said with a cautious smile.

"Wait, what's the significance?" I asked Sawyer as he moved in past the gate.

"Ravens are messengers between two worlds."

"So, like a traveler?" I quipped.

"Yes, but used mostly by practitioners of magic," he went on.

"You mean witches," I retorted.

Sawyer didn't respond.

Fitzly peered back over his shoulder. "I don't think I want to know any more until we are out of Helltown." The car went silent.

Sawyer's tires rolled over the gravel driveway that curved back along a murky tree line. American elms stood tall, lining the path with their remaining yellow-toothed leaves and gray, vase-shaped trunks. The stones and pebbles crunched under the car's tires until the path opened and ended with the view of a large wood-framed colonial with gable roofing. It was similar to Fitzly's picture. The once-white wood siding was now faded and broken. A small front entry sat crooked, sinking into the earth below. A large stone chimney rose from the center of a roof that was caving in around it.

Fitzly pointed. "The driveway continues around back."

181

We slowed to a crawling pace as we past an old storm cellar with a missing door and parked at the edge of a large field of overgrown brush and grasses.

Sawyer hopped out, his boots sinking into the wet earth. Fitzly groaned, "Looks like we're getting out."

We both slid out of the passenger side when Fitzly officially greeted me with a 'hello' hug. Sawyer followed his lead but then stepped back, pointing to my muddy clothes. "What happened to you?" I refrained from describing my recent acrobatics and shrugged it off with a crooked smile and changed the subject.

"Now what?" I asked, taking in the view of an undoubtedly haunted house in the middle of a ghostly town. Suddenly being arrested seemed more comforting.

Sawyer snickered at my lack of response then stared intently at the abandoned home. Fitzly and I both knew where his mind was wandering off to.

"You're not thinking about breaking and entering?" asked Fitzly.

"It's already broken so entering is not a problem," Sawyer responded half-smiling. "And if Chloe's picture is right, Harper could be inside."

"It's still trespassing," Fitzly murmured, hesitantly following Sawyer, who was inching closer to the home.

"We will trespass a little, only on the first floor. I'll call for her once inside, and if Harper is not here, we'll leave or at least hide out in the car for a while," Sawyer assured us.

Fitzly wasn't satisfied with Sawyer's plan. "Oh, okay! Yes, officer, according to my wise friend, we're only trespassing a little."

The rustling of leaves from the brush along the tree line seemed to change Fitzly's mind.

Sawyer noted the change in Fitzly's demeanor, "You coming?" Sawyer asked then walked ahead, waving for us both to join him.

I strolled, switching my viewpoint between the cellar and the eerie woods until I was within arm's reach of Sawyer. "Why and how did you get here?" I asked again, still confused about the picture Fitzly was holding.

"To find Harper," he repeated.

"Why is she here?" I asked.

"Do you remember how Chloe mentioned she speaks with the spirits?" asked Sawyer.

"Sure," I said, remembering how Chloe wrote things on paper then burned them.

"Last night Chloe called Fitzly and then emailed him a picture of this. She found it in a flower box outside of her bedroom window." Fitzly handed it over to me.

On one side was the word "Harper." I flipped it over. The other side was a drawing of the house we were now standing in front of with other pictures drawn around the perimeter.

"Look closer up in the corner," Fitzly pointed. "Do you recognize the tall tower with the glass windows above? Any recollection?"

I squinted.

Fitzly got impatient. "It's the Danwer Memorial Glass." He grabbed the paper vigorously away from me, tapping at the tower in the picture then pointing back toward the road. "It's the tower down the street with the four stained glass windows. The windows are called the Danwer Memorial Glass," Fitzly said confidently.

"You can tell all that from this picture?" I asked in disbelief.

Fitzly pointed out small sketches of symbols in the glass; alpha and omega, a sun cross, a dove, and a phoenix. He spoke slowly, "They collectively represent the beginning, the end, the earth, the soul, and the ability to overcome darkness. When I researched the four terms together online, an image of The Danwer Memorial Tower was displayed. When the sun shines through the glass, it casts shadows of these sacred symbols along property's four sides. The stained glass was a gift to the founding pastor, Mr. Danwer, as a gift of protection for the church," he explained.

"Protection from what?" I asked.

"I don't know, but when I clicked on the map online to show me its location, it zoomed in down the street. We used GPS to get us here," he said.

"Can we go in now?" remarked an impatient Sawyer.

Fitzly and I hesitantly agreed and followed Sawyer. At the same time, Fitzly continued to give me a brief history of the symbols and their meanings. We got so caught up in the conversation we both tripped into Sawyer.

"Would you two pay attention, please? We need to figure out the easiest way to get in," Sawyer said.

One small door sat in the middle of the back wall of the home. Multiple size windows with muntin bars lined the two levels. The windows were not symmetrical to the rest of the house, and the sizes did not match. Its haphazard layout only added to its aged beauty.

"Are you sure it's safe?" Fitzly asked.

"No, I'm not," Sawyer cautioned, stomping the overgrown brush deep into the ground to create an alternative path for us to enter.

Fitzly stood, shaking his head behind him while trying to passively coax Sawyer into changing his mind. "An old house that could be blown over with one gust of wind in what she deemed as Helltown. Great plan—one of your best. Can't we just stay in the car?"

He walked up behind Sawyer and then turned to offer his hand to me. The wind howled softly as the late fall breeze had cooled down to an uncomfortable temperature. I was shivering. Sawyer stepped gingerly on some wood planks just outside the door, each piece cracking and popping under his weight. At the backdoor, he pried open the screen. The knob on the main entrance was latched.

"Who takes the time to lock up when they leave for good?" he said before asking Fitzly for his shirt.

"What? Why? You have one," he said.

Sawyer tugged at Fitzly's sleeve, saying, "I'll give it back. You have two layers on."

Fitzly brushed Sawyer off, mumbling under his breath, then took off his button-down flannel and handed it over. He was shaking in his white tank top, his scrawny arms clutched one another. Sawyer wrapped the flannel tightly around his fist, and with one fast punch, rammed his hand through the glass window on the door.

"Seriously," said Fitzly between his teeth. "That's a decent piece of clothing."

"And it still is," Sawyer said as he unbundled the cloth and handed it back over to him. With the glass cleared, he reached in and unlocked the door while Fitzly obsessively shook out his shirt before putting it back on.

"If I get cut, dude," Fitzly was saying, but Sawyer ignored him.

"Ladies first," he said as Sawyer motioned Fitzly to move ahead.

"Neanderthals last," Fitzly muttered while he fixed his collar. With his long legs, he stepped into the home, making a very lame attempt to shove Sawyer, whose frame wasn't the least bit rocked. Sawyer pinched Fitzly behind the arm, which only aggravated him more.

"You know it's all fun and games until someone gets eaten by a demon!" snarled Fitzly.

"Oh, you two are a couple of toddlers," I said as I pushed forward, leaving them to fight. I walked through the narrow entryway. The walls were covered with aged and peeling navy blue paper with tiny pink and white flowers and gold leaves.

"Do you believe the stories about Helltown?" Fitzly stumbled up from behind. The floor beneath his feet bowed as he jumped and swatted at anything that tickled his skin. I glanced back every few seconds, pushing him off of me.

He didn't calm down, so I stopped and answered. "I believe it's a place I don't want to be after dark."

"Then why are you here?" asked Sawyer pushing Fitzly through the remaining part of the hall until we all were standing in the kitchen.

I covered my nose from a strong, musty smell hovering in the air and spoke through my hoodie. "I stopped in at our store this morning when our new girl cut her hand with scissors. She freaked and ran in this direction. She's new to town, and I didn't want her in here alone."

"So you live one town over?" asked Fitzly. "How did the tower not look familiar?" He didn't wait for a response. "Wait, I wonder if the paper was meant to lead us to Abby and not Harper," Fitzly pointed out to Sawyer, but Sawyer's attention was drawn outside. He pulled back a faded curtain that opened to a rotting deck out back.

"No. Chloe was sure Harper was here," Sawyer finally remarked.

Fitzly turned his attention back to me, pointing at the tower again.

I rolled my eyes, "Like I said, the town has been abandoned for decades. What I know is the rumor. This is my first time actually stepping foot in the Valley."

Fitzly huffed, "Maybe Harper is here, then?"

I flipped the light switch out of habit, noting Sawyer's coy smirk. "I guess the natural light will have to do." I was too curious to stand still. It was like antiquing but better. Everything was still chillingly in its place. A small table with four wooden chairs painted black sat against one wall. To the right was a large brick, wood-burning fireplace with pots still sitting on the hearth and smaller utensils hanging across the mantle. A pile of wood for burning sat rotting in the large patina container, and a sink full of moldy dinnerware overflowed onto a small counter. The one remaining wall was lined with wooden shelves holding various jars of herbs.

Fitzly pulled out one chair, testing it for stability before sitting down and studying the picture.

I moved carefully through a solid wood door frame, regaining my footing as the old planks slanted toward the edges of the next room. It was an impressive area, with oak beams lining the ceiling. Old furniture rubbed up against the peeling wallpaper and another wood-burning fireplace sat flush to floor, surrounded by a hearth of red brick.

A large opening led to a dining room with a built-in mahogany hutch that took up an entire wall. A beautifully aged brass candelabra with burned out and blackened bulbs hung over a long table. Eight chairs with leather seats and brass rivets sat around the perimeter of the table. Heavy dust and cobwebs covered the furniture, windows, shelving, and décor.

A series of cold chills circulated through my body and down my spine. My hands lightly touched framed paintings hanging from the walls. I was careful with each step, not wanting to disrupt all the history and memories left behind. Sawyer was less restrained.

"Harper!" Sawyer called out several times, his voice echoing off the walls as he walked in behind me. There was no response, just the popping and cracking sound of old wood. He rushed around the different rooms opening and slamming doors shut. I walked up to him, my heart racing from his sudden burst of intensity.

"We'll find her," I said, catching my breath and lightly touching his arm. I started to walk away when he pulled me back into him.

"Thank you," he whispered into my ear, his stubble lightly brushed against my cheek. Tiny little hairs on my arms stood upright as I searched for something to say, but Fitzly returned.

I glanced down, embarrassed like a teenager caught holding a boy's hand for the first time. Sawyer backed away, frustrated, pulling out a bench seat to an old player piano near a fireplace. His brown hair fell forward while he scrolled through his phone, his elbow inadvertently hitting a few piano keys. The movement jarred something awake as the spool turned the music roll. The melody rang out like a wind-up music box, its volume and speed varying into an array of disturbing notes.

I covered my ears as Sawyer yanked open the upper drawer, exposing the spool box. Sawyer carefully reached in. The noise reverberated throughout the house until the spool finally ripped. The music ended but the sound of torn paper slapping around the metal spool continued briefly before slowing to a halt.

"I can't even hear myself think," Fitzly complained.

"Maybe that's the point," I said. I suddenly didn't feel welcome. Howls from the wind squeezed through cracks in the windows and then I heard the whistling of not one but two, maybe three people.

CHAPTER 21

GATEWAYS

The high-pitched but slow melody drifted in and around us. I froze, waiting for Sawyer and Fitzly's reaction.

"I'm going to check upstairs, and then we'll go!" Sawyer yelled. "Watch Abby!" he barked at Fitzly.

"Wait; you said the first floor only!" Fitzly yelled back.

Sawyer ran fast past both of us to an opened door leading to a steep, narrow stairway. I moved, but Fitzy grabbed my arm.

"Sawyer wants me to watch you," he said.

"Well, then watch me run upstairs," I remarked as I broke free from his grip. I followed Sawyer up the narrow steps to a sketchy low wooden railing that swayed in both directions. Fitzly joined, angry we were all upstairs. He stepped in front of me with his arm out, stopping me from moving down the hall. I scowled at him, but he stood like a proud soldier after taking direction from his general.

Sawyer moved though, running in and out of four different rooms, trying to find the whistle's source while it continued to grow louder. I peered up over Fitzly, anxiously waiting for Sawyer to find Harper, or worse yet, the three men.

"In here," he ordered. I shoved Fitzly out of the way and followed his voice to a bedroom at the end of the hall with two twin beds and brass headboards. The white quilts with large pink roses were drawn back as if the kids had rolled out of bed this morning. One dresser and an armoire sat dusty with drawers half opened, and a small cradle with a porcelain faced baby doll rested in the corner near the window Sawyer faced. I tripped over an area rug bunched up on the floor, falling into Sawyer.

"Be careful," he said, grabbing my hands and stopping me before I fell onto the sill lined with sharp glass pieces from an old broken window. Carefully leaning over and outside, I noticed the larger glass pieces lying below on the wooden porch outside. My attention was drawn to the back field, where the whistling continued. Every gust of wind parted the tall grass and brush enough for me to see the three men from the night before. Off in the distance, they stood upon giant rocks that surrounded a large tree with branches that twisted and contorted up to the sky. There was not another tree in sight.

"It's them. They're here," I whispered. Their suits and matching hats were dark, and their skin transparent.

Sawyer ripped the old pink curtain to get a better view of the backyard.

The world was suddenly closing in on me as if I were being squeezed into a box. The surrounding air was scarce as I struggled to inhale, and my heart pounded against my ribs. I reached for Sawyer's hand with my quivering arms while my legs fought to keep me upright.

I stumbled to the dresser. My eyes fixated on a small oval frame with a black and white picture of a little girl in a white gown with long blond hair. My limbs went numb, and my throat tightened. It was her.

Sawyer embraced me and yelled at Fitzly. "Grab her other arm."

Fitzly and Sawyer guided me to one of the nearby beds to sit. I closed my eyes and focused on my breathing, telling myself I would be okay. Sawyer knelt before me, rubbing the sides of my arms and calmly spoke to me.

"It's okay, Abby. Just breathe. You're safe with me," Sawyer said.

His light touch soothed my soul, now collapsing in terror. Fitzly moved to the side of the window, slowly moving his head around the frame to peek outback. He took a few quick glimpses before retreating and plastering his body against the wall.

"Who are they?" Fitzly grimaced as he summoned Sawyer to look for himself.

I shrugged.

"I'll find them and ask," Sawyer said and darted past me and back down the hall, leaving Fitzly and me staring at one another in shock and disbelief. I screamed out all sorts of curse words in my head. I couldn't follow him if I couldn't move. I yelled at Fitzly to stop squirming. I gritted my teeth and focused on slowing my heart. Fitzly sat next to me with his head down. He stood in for Sawyer as best he could, rubbing my shoulders.

"Thank you," I said, still trembling.

"Are you okay?" Fitzly asked.

"I think so; just help me stand. We have to go get Sawyer. No one should be running around here alone."

The sound of a loud crash from the first floor jolted me out of my thoughts. A surge of adrenaline shot through my veins. I jumped up and sprinted down the hall and then slid down the steepest of steps, screaming for Sawyer. I followed his groans until I was pulled backward by Fitzly grabbing onto my jacket, yanking me, and saving me from a twelve-foot drop to the basement. I let out a loud exhale before crawling over and looking over the edge of a giant hole. Sawyer had fallen through the kitchen floor and now lay below on a pile of broken flooring.

"This way," Fitzly said as he helped me up and carefully guided me around and back outside where the half-open cellar door sat.

"Oh no," I mouthed. Something dreadful hid out down there. Its presence suffocated me the closer I moved to the opening. I was now the fearful one, watching as Fitzly turned on his light, holding out his hand, waiting for me to join him. I swallowed hard and closed my eyes as I let Fitzly guide me down the steps.

Fitzly left me at the bottom of the stairs as he rushed over to Sawyer, who was trying to stand. I stood hunched over, opening one eye at a time, waiting for what would come. The atmosphere crushed me. Fitzly rattled off a series of questions to Sawyer. I cautiously stepped toward them until I was finally by Sawyer's side.

"Are you okay?" I kept my voice low. Anything louder eerily echoed through the small space. I brushed off Sawyer's clothes and checked him over, expecting to see a broken bone or blood, but there was nothing. Instead, he stood arching his back and rubbing his left shoulder. I stared dumbfounded. He wasn't injured.

"I'm good. A little sore but better than the alternative," he replied.

"I'll say!" I exclaimed.

I shined my light up onto his face, wiping the dirt from his cheeks. I was startled by what I saw behind him. A dark, arched doorway appeared. I traced the outline of the stone opening with my phone light. Dry, red paint dripped down the wall from the ceiling as if the stone sat injured and bleeding. Above, the following words were written in black color:

"Leave your soul behind as it is no longer yours to keep."

Fitzly and Sawyer stood behind me. Sawyer snatched my phone and walked closer, shining the light inside. I grabbed his arm just before his foot crossed over the threshold.

"Do you believe it?" he asked, turning back at me.

"I don't think I want to find out. Do you?" I took my phone back and shined the light slowly around the room. To my horror, it illuminated a painted scene of wolf-like creatures with large fangs and horns dancing around fires. Thousands of small symbols painted in black adorned the ceiling, while sticks in the shapes of pentagrams swayed from vines that were tied to ceiling beams.

"Some of these symbols match what I have found," I said.

"What?" quipped Fitzly.

"Look," I pointed upward. "They match." I sidestepped, then tripped over Fitzly and fell near the stone opening, a sharp pain shooting up my arm. Drawing my hand back to my chest, I clutched my wrist, opened my fingers, and pulled a small piece of wood out of my palm. I let out a loud, garbled sigh. Sawyer dropped to his knees to look at my hand.

"You all right?" he asked.

"Yeah, it just stings a little," I replied. The pain quickly dissipated to a dull throb, and with its small size, I opted not to make a bigger deal out of it. Sawyer had fallen twelve feet into the basement, and here I was complaining about a paper cut. I clamped my jaw down and shrugged off the achiness.

Sawyer sifted through the dirt, pulling up the small piece that had penetrated my skin. He spun it around in his light, noting varying shades of cream and brown colors, and then he tapped at it, creating a hollow-like sound. "It's part of an animal horn," he said.

Fitzly knelt down to get a better view. "Where's the animal it came from?" he stuttered. I pondered for a second, viewing the wild horned creatures on the walls and the abyss only inches away from us. We unanimously agreed it was time to flee. Fitzly squeezed his fingers into my arm, gathering our attention. He then placed his pointer finger up by his mouth. "Shh."

The slight sound of small, quick steps emanated from the tunnel, followed by a tapping sound. Tap, tap, tap, silence. The three of us kneeled, huddled together, and then a disembodied growl bellowed towards us. Sawyer grabbed my right hand, clutched it tightly, and motioned for the steps. "You; then Fitzly. Go! Go now!"

I ran faster than I ever had in my life. I glided over the uneven gravel and through the grass to the car. I yanked at the handle and slid into the front with enough space for Fitzly. I wasn't wasting time diving into the back. Within seconds, they were both in, their force sandwiching me in the middle. With the doors slammed shut and the ignition on, Sawyer peeled around and out. Glancing over at the open cellar door, I saw that two pairs of glowing golden eyes hovered in the darkness. I looked away and then back. They were gone, but Fitzly turned to me, and his expression confirmed he had seen them too.

"Maybe just raccoons," he uttered, looking back and pressing his nose into the passenger glass.

Sawyer swerved down the driveway, "Too tall for raccoons," he said and yanked the steering wheel to the left and avoided a full-on crash with a tree. I braced myself against the dashboard. The powerful hum of the engine roared as Sawyer's tires spun and then swerved, scraping the side of the car on one of the gates. I shielded my face and ducked as the metal on metal sound reverberated throughout the car. After clearing the drive, Sawyer made a sharp turn back toward town.

A nervous Fitzly dug his feet into the imaginary brake pedal on the floorboard. "How are we going to find Harper?" he asked.

Next thing I knew, my chest slammed against the dashboard as Sawyer hit his brakes. "I think she found us."

CHAPTER 22

SECRET AGENDAS

I peeled myself off the dashboard and rubbed my aching chest. What little cushion I had failed to prevent my ribcage from the impact. With a slow and painful deep breath, I swore out loud as the man I hoped to be my protector hopped out to tend to Harper, now standing with her hands on the hood of the car. Annoyed, I sat in the middle of the street, with Sawyer stuck between yelling at Harper and wanting to embrace her. His hand then motioned over and pointed directly at me in the car. Harper leaned in for a better view. She wasn't just shocked to see me, she was annoyed.

"She's back," I said, low and under my breath, which didn't matter because Fitzly left me too. His door was open, and the sound of them both clamoring on about how we all found each other met my ears. They were all pointing in different directions and talking over one another when Sawyer raised his voice, stopping both of them.

"Can we please just leave?" Sawyer said as he walked Harper over to the driver's side and helped her in the back. She tucked herself against the window and pulled her hoodie up over her head. Fitzly kindly slid back with her rather than squash me in again. I gave Harper a quick hello with a nod, which she didn't return. Sawyer threw the car in drive, slowing near the roundabout. I rolled my window down a few inches and took in the faint smell of smoke still present in the air. The red and blue lights of both fire and police bounced through the nearly bare branches of the wooded forest south of town. At the same time, the church's perimeter sat aged and broken now, roped off with bright yellow caution tape. There they were the stained glass windows of the Memorial Tower. Sawyer slowed, waiting for my direction, but I was consumed with the image Chloe drew and the old tower next to my hometown. It was breathtaking and gut-wrenching at the same time.

"Abby!" Sawyer snatched my attention back, "Which way?"

"We have to go back into the Creek," I motioned for him to turn back down the same straightway that brought us all here. He rolled slowly over the pavement, then placed his hand on my knee.

"Where next?" he asked again.

I couldn't take them to the store or even back to my house, and taking them out in public only increased my odds of running into Ben. We had one option.

"My Aunt Kate's; we can go there," I said.

"Are you sure?"

"Yeah, she is staying with us right now to help my mom. I know where she keeps her key."

I always had an open invitation to Kate's. She understood my need for space from my home, especially after Mason moved in. She was at the store and likely heading back to my house with Lauren for the evening. My mom wanted her out, but Kate wouldn't give in that easy. I used my hand to motion to Sawyer, occasionally noting the burn of Harper's eyes into the back of my head. I was not on her favorite person list.

Sawyer broke the initial awkward silence, demanding the location of his car while using his rearview mirror to send scolding facial expressions her way.

"Whose car are we in?" I asked, forgetting Harper stole his from Connecticut.

Fitzly leaned over the front seat, saying, "It's mine ... well, my dad's car. My mom picked us up yesterday morning and took us back to my house. That's when Chloe called. Sawyer convinced my mom to let us borrow it. She won't be happy about the scrapes and dents upfront." His eyes spun over toward Sawyer then he punched him in the shoulder.

"Don't snap your cap, Fitzly. I'll fix it," Sawyer returned.

My eyebrows squished together, and my mouth dangled open. These east coasters sure had a rich vocabulary. Snap your cap? Really, it was right up there with many of Aggie's zingers.

I dismissed it. It wasn't the time for a vocabulary discussion. But I was curious why Fitzly wasn't driving and inquired about it.

Fitzly slouched back into his seat, and with his head low, he responded, "Can't drive a stick."

It didn't surprise me. Sawyer's rough masculinity fit the profile for a muscle car driver. Fitzly, not so much. My giggling and his embarrassment ended quickly with Sawyer still demanding answers from Harper, who finally barked back at him.

"It's in the parking lot behind the bank. You passed it not that long ago," she said.

"How did you get to the church, then?" he asked.

"Duh! I walked. I saw the no trespassing sign, turned back, parked it, and walked to the church." Harper crossed her arms over her chest and pulled her hood down lower.

"Why didn't you say something? We could have grabbed it," he added.

"I would have, but you were too busy yelling at me," she replied.

Sawyer smacked the steering wheel with closed fists and teeth clenched. I wanted more information about the church and why she was there, but I wasn't asking. I nudged Sawyer's forearm, glanced back at Harper, and whispered "tower" several times. He finally caught on.

"Why were you at the Tower?" Sawyer peered at Harper through the rearview mirror.

"I didn't intend on leaving before dawn. But I had a dream about it. I was lying in bed researching it on my phone when I found it. I couldn't sleep, and this voice just kept telling me to go, so I left. Anyway, how did you end up here?"

Fitzly tossed the paper over to her from Chloe.

"No shit," she said.

"What did you find?" Fitzly asked.

"Just another girl," Harper mumbled.

I turned back toward Harper, "A young girl in a gown or an older girl with black and purple hair?"

She hesitated, then answered. "I didn't get that close. But it was a girl and she moved around town darting in and out of alleys before walking to the church. I tried to follow but was startled by the cryptic sounds of a choir. We both were. She circled it slowly several times then disappeared into the woods."

"What do you mean, disappeared?" I peered over the headrest at her.

Harper sighed. "One minute she was hovering by the tree line, and the next minute she was gone. I waited a few minutes and then went over to explore the church tower and the eerie sounds below. It was creepy, let me tell you. Next thing, there was a loud explosion, and I ran and hid in the trees."

"Did you see anything else?" I still wondered if it was Aggie or the young apparition. But Harper was growing more irritated with my questions.

"Just the police, oh, and you all. I saw the back of Fitzly's car head down that road, so I worked my way in your direction, staying hidden in the brush," she added.

"Why didn't you call me?" demanded Sawyer.

Harper held up her phone and waved it in the mirror. "No signal," she said.

Fitzly nervously nudged Harper's arm. "Can you go back to the choir singing? What was it?"

Harper turned to Fitzly and grabbed his arm, "It was like cathedral music but dark, no words, more like chants or humming. It shook my core."

Fitzly gulped and pulled his hand back. "Thanks."

Sawyer tapped on my thigh as we approached a light and asked, "Which way?"

"Straight," I said rubbing my hands on the vinyl seat watching the buildings disappear as we approached the last residential streets in town. Out of questions, the car was silent as we all mulled over Harper's terrifying responses. I worried about Aggie, and I cringed at the thought of a demonic choir. I picked at the dry skin on my lips, anxious to get to Kate's.

Kate lived on the northern edge of town, up a hill, and down a winding side road just past a graveyard that horror movies were written about. I shuddered. Roughly thirty mini-headstones dating back to the early 1800s sat scattered behind a wrought iron fence. An arched double-gated entryway sat closed with the words "Resting Place" carved out of metal and painted black, hanging and swaying in the wind.

"Sad," said Fitzly, leaning toward me and speaking over my shoulder. "No flowers."

There were never any flowers, only a small rusted wagon with a ball that somehow made its way around within the fence. "They're not lonely," I assured him. I hated this stretch of road. It was dark, no matter the time of day. If I stared long enough, the women with long curls in exquisitely decorated bonnets and gloves would arrive. Their significant others joined them as well, in tailcoats, conical hats, and knee-high boots. Fitzly sunk back.

"I'm not going to ask," he said.

"Sounds good," I responded.

Kate's home emerged after the bend in the road. I directed Sawyer to the narrow drive. "There on the left, the mint green home."

The car slowed to a halt. Without hesitation, I opened the door and stepped onto the manicured lawn. We stood and stretched under the late fall sun. Sawyer gave Harper a momentary break in questioning while they took in the view of Kate's home. Kate's house had a storybook quality that garnered awe from whoever stopped. It wasn't massive but detailed and ornate. Harper walked up to the cream-colored front porch, sliding her hand along the rails. Then, she sat in the evergreen porch swing. "Wow, it's beautiful."

It was the kindest thing ever to roll out of Harper's mouth and my one chance to find familiar, common ground with her. "It's a Queen Anne, built in the late 1800s," I said, approaching the steps. "Kate bought it after getting divorced and fixed it up. The inside is even better."

I located Kate's key in the same hiding spot we use at home and let everyone in. They all followed close behind, each of them oohing over the magnificent woodwork and a grand staircase with a deep red and gold carpet running up the center. I let them view the lower floor without me tripping over them. We all needed some space and a moment to collect. There was enough here to distract all of us. While they walked around, I made myself comfortable on the floor in the front room, across from an old fireplace with a cast iron cover. A large wood coffee table sat in the middle of the space, where I dumped my purse contents, then started the daunting task of separating everything from importance. I heard Harper's footsteps nearing the front door and stopped her.

"The upstairs isn't remodeled yet. Not much to look at it," I said.

"Oh, I was hoping to see the inside of the tower with the windows," she replied.

I didn't want to disappoint her, so I gave her the okay to move up. From the outside, the tower and turret rose from the house in distinct style; however, inside, it was a tiny, empty room at the top of a very narrow stairwell. Harper bolted up the steps.

Sawyer returned and settled into one of the brown leather chairs that flanked the fireplace, his appeal worthy of a magazine cover. He sat in his worn-out blue jeans, short leather boots, and a cream-colored thermal that embraced his chest. "Thanks for letting us hang out here, it's the first time I can breathe since losing Harper," he said.

I separated my belongings on the table and took small breaks to peek at Sawyer. I acknowledged his conversation with the occasional head nod, so he didn't feel ignored.

"What do you have there?" he inquired, kneeling down on the opposite of me. He rummaged through the pictures.

"Odds and ends that somehow go together. I just haven't figured it out how yet," I replied.

"Then let's all help you," he said and called out for Fitzly and yelled up the stairwell to Harper. But Harper didn't respond.

"I'll go get her," I offered and walked up the steps to the second level, down the hall to another set of stairs that led up to the turret. I hated the steps and smallness of the space as I curved up into the little room surrounded by windows. Harper was kneeling over something on the floor.

"Harper, are you okay?" I whispered.

Harper turned back, pulling the hoodie down off her head, revealing a messy do, little makeup, and bloodshot eyes. But it was her blue strands of hair that stuck out most. She noticed my stare.

"What?" she snapped.

"You have so much blue, I never noticed."

She pulled her hair back up into a pony and then a bun, hiding any hint of the color we all shared, "I've learned how to conceal it."

"Mine looks odd, yours is trendy. You could totally pull this off as intentional," I told her.

Harper relaxed some and offered a quick 'thank you' with a nod, then leaned to the side and revealed a medium-sized wood box with intricate carvings. I kneeled down next to her.

"What is it?" I asked as I touched the rough dark surface of a small chest, with an engraved star and elaborate design. I didn't remember ever seeing it.

"It's a spell box," she said, pushing my hand out of the way and opening it. I turned my head away from the smell of black licorice and rotting vinegar. Harper picked up a small jar with no lid and a few droplets of clear liquid. "Here's the culprit," she said and placed it on the carpet hiding her face in her sweatshirt while we rifled through its contents.

Inside were trinkets and tools, and a variety of small glass jars with faded labels and cork toppers. A small knife with a white handle, crystals, and candles were covered in herbs and seeds. Harper dug through and found several old keys, holding them up in front of my face.

"Spell boxes keep a witch's most cherished belongings safe. Every-thing a witch needs to conduct her magic would be kept in here. Why does your aunt have one?" she inquired.

I raised my eyebrows and shrugged my shoulders, and then gave the response Kate would offer. "She's been in the antique business for years. She probably picked it up somewhere and will sell it."

However, I wondered why it was tucked away up here and not at the store. By Harper's flat expression, she wasn't buying it either, but I didn't want to sit and debate it. I grabbed the empty jar and the keys from her hands and tossed them back in. The keys clanged then bounced off of something hidden in the corner of the box. Its bright yellow color drew my attention. I reached in and pulled out a small charm of a bee. My heart sank as I clutched it in my palm. Could it be the same charm from the old photo? Why would Kate have it? I swallowed the rock in my throat. Harper noticed my concern.

"What is it?" she asked.

I dropped it back in the box and closed it. "Nothing, we should head down," I suggested.

Harper was frustrated by my lie and my desire to leave, but I slowed to change direction. "You saw the young girl in the woods, didn't you?"

Harper's shoulders dropped. She avoided any direct eye contact initially. I waited until she spoke.

"The girl in the gown with the light blonde hair?" she asked.

I acknowledged her with a nod, "Harper, we're the same. We have to work as a team, or it's just going to make all this harder for everyone."

"Okay, then tell me why that charm has you so rattled?"

I bit my lip, what would I tell her? She was judgmental and critical of everyone, and she wouldn't trust Kate if I gave her any reason not to. But I was starting to wonder if I should, either. I had to lie, "The charm reminded me of something my dad gave me as a young girl. Just brought back a bitter memory."

Harper's intuition was on target, and she was in the middle of a harsh response when Sawyer yelled up for both of us. I didn't let her finish and retreated back to the foyer.

"What were you both doing?" Sawyer asked.

"Nothing," I said and turned to make sure Harper was behind me. "Just checking out the view of the Creek."

I touched Sawyer's arm and guided him back to the living room. Fitzly was already rummaging through the contents on the table. I grabbed his wrist. "Let me show you," I said.

Harper hesitantly found a place on the floor near us. Once I had all of their attention, I started with the first piece of paper I found and moved in chronological order regarding my experiences. I spoke about the pictures at the school, the blueprints, Santos, the stones, the three men, and the newspaper print of Mayor Quartano's office. With each detail, I handed them whatever object or picture I had to back it up.

Harper gravitated to the four pieces of paper, quickly placing them together.

Fitzly sat deep in thought before he picked one thing to focus on.

"You mentioned the blueprints of the tunnel system. Did it run under the farm home we were just at? Do you think the opening we saw was part of it?" he asked.

"It's possible, but some of the pages were missing, so I can't be sure. And someone wrote on the blueprints, 'To Find the Witch is to Find the Way.' Strange, given what we saw in that basement."

"What?" Harper asked.

Forgetting that she wasn't with us, Sawyer had to bring her up to speed, ending with the ominous warning painted in the cellar. I then explained what I knew about the symbols on my puzzle pieces and shared information about the sabbats. I glanced at Fitzly and pointed. "In that basement, the markings on the wall matched these papers I found on the street in the Creek. That's what I meant."

Fitzly sat quiet, his eyes were full and bright, I could almost see what he was thinking.

"I hate to conjure up any more details about witchcraft, but we are definitely dealing with someone who practices magic, maybe even an entire coven," I declared.

Harper viewed the puzzle pieces again then sat up straight, requesting tape. I quickly got her some from Kate's office as we watched her perfectly line the pieces and place them together.

She pointed, "Guys, look." We leaned in and watched eyes wide as words, symbols, and intricate designs appeared filling in all the remaining white space between the original markings. The simple drawing replaced with the most elaborate diagram. The words, "Life, Death, Rebirth, Earth, Air, Body, Water and Fire" were printed in script within a giant 8-pointed star.

Magic was occurring in front of us. But why now? Why couldn't we see it before? We stared at one another.

Fitzly spoke first, his voice trembling, "I'm afraid to ask, but does anyone know what this is?"

Sawyer answered, "It's a wheel of ancient Pagan symbols."

"Or armor?" replied Harper. Harper pulled out her bag and then a book.

"Is that the one you stole from Nora?" asked Fitzly.

"It wasn't stealing; it wasn't hers to keep," she retorted.

Fitzly shook his head at her and Sawyer. They both had a skewed way of justifying all their actions, and I could only assume it was how they'd survived growing up. Regardless, I was eager to see what she'd found. She flipped to the latter half and revealed another circular design. She tapped on the aged, yellowed paper while looking around at each of us. The Latin words morphed to English.

"Read it before it disappears," Fitlzy insisted.

"It's a century's old shield, known as La Nalina. It was a gift given to the Black Magic Queen from her mentor, the most powerful Black Magic Goddess known to walk between the two worlds." Harper stood and paced while reading directly from the magical book.

"The Black Magic Queen will one day rise and fight for control of her kingdom with the protection provided by La Nalina. La Nalina has two sides, one of heavy iron for protection, and the other a crystal core that holds the most dangerous spells ever written."

I nudged Fitzly over and found the image of Mayor Quartano in his office with the metal décor propped on a stand. I held it up in front of Harper's eyes.

Harper ripped the picture from my hand, "They all match, exactly!"

Sawyer grabbed the newspaper print next and viewed everything up close.

I pulled down hard on the strands of my hair. "Why would a black magic shield be found in a book that might belong to a traveler?"

Sawyer responded. "Well, if I were a traveler, I would want to know what I am up against, right?"

Fitzly pulled his shirt up over his mouth and mumbled, "If the mayor has part of her shield, then where are the remaining pieces?"

None of us knew. And the more we thought, the more flustered and distressed we became.

"Can I get a drink?" Fitzly stuttered nervously.

"Of course, and take Harper with you." I knew she likely needed something too, and we certainly were not going to figure anything out in the next five minutes. I needed the space to think. Fitzly walked Harper back to the kitchen for a much-needed break.

I moved closer to Sawyer. "This gets more deranged by the minute. I'm not sure how much more I can handle."

"You can handle more than you know," he replied.

I wasn't so sure but appreciated his words of encouragement. I took the book and slouched in an armchair, taking turns between flipping pages and rubbing my eyes. After a short time, Sawyer asked to see it, and I handed it over. He stroked the leather-bound book and then paged through it slowly.

"What is it?" I inquired.

"Just tired, like all of you." He closed it back up after a few more minutes and held it tight to his chest, closing his eyes. I took the moment of peace to watch him rest. It took me time to entrust Ben with my demons, and in his defense, he did what he could to help me, for a while. But it was tough. I guess it would be on anyone who didn't understand it or maybe even believe it. But here was Sawyer, handsome, secure, and along for the ride without any worry he would leave.

His body jerked him awake, tossing the book up into the air after only minutes of sleep. Harper caught it on the way down with her one hand, juggling a can of ice tea with her other. Fitzly returned with three cheese sticks and a can of sparkling flavored water. He juggled everything while he clumsily sat back down on the floor.

We assumed our places at the table and waited for Sawyer to join us. Harper sat the book down and flipped back through to another page. "I wanted to show you this, too," she said.

The pages weren't numbered, so it took her a minute to find a picture of a star pentagram. The wings of an angel wrapped round the star splattered with shades of yellow, pink, green, and blue hues. I spun it back so I could see it right side up.

"Do you think this is a satanic ritual manual of some sort?" I asked.

Sawyer sat up straight. "No, not Satan!"

We all stared at him. He went from barely conscious to angry at the very sound of the words. I held my hand up to Fitzly and Harper so they wouldn't speak, and gave Sawyer a chance to clarify.

"The media has made the five-pointed star a symbol of Satanism. Most people don't understand that the direction in which the star is turned determines its meaning. When the star has one point facing up, then it's actually a sign of faith. The colors and points represent the five senses and the five earth elements. The circle around it represents the universe and nature. If the star points down," he said and spun the book slightly, "then it becomes symbolic of a goat's head, its horns, and evil. It has many more positive associations than negative, though."

He didn't take a breath, and I wondered whether this was another crazy story his mom shared with them. I was curious to his change in demeanor but Harper and Fitzly quietly sat and let him finish. Harper shifted the focus back on her and pulled the book center and pointed. "It also has this."

Her index finger hovered over the center of a bluish-purple dot. Under it, she revealed the words "Caeruleus Crystal" written in cursive around the perimeter.

"I don't know about you three, but I have never heard the term Cerulean until Nora spoke about it, and now it's in some weird ancient handwritten book?"

I agreed with a slight shake of my head. Its very presence in a book dropped by something not mortal brought about a wave of more questions. Fitzly used his phone to look up the crystal. He scrolled through multiple lists, but not one identified as Caeruleus. Sawyer sat back with his fist resting over his mouth.

"Is it anywhere else in the book?" I asked.

Harper shrugged her shoulders and then handed it back over to me. The delicate pages were filled with drawings and symbols, but nothing else alluding to this crystal. Out of frustration, I closed it but not before noticing the inside back cover. An image was pressed into the leather. It was a large circle made up of repeating and overlapping circles. The initials *TC* were embossed in the lower right corner and in the bottom left was *Deliciae*. My fingers lightly traced the smooth geometric pattern when Harper leaned in.

"All of these symbols? Maybe we should get back in touch with Nora. I don't know who else can help us?"

Remembering my brief encounter with Ellie, I realized I was long overdue for a reading. "There might be someone in town I could ask."

I walked out the front door to relieve a heaviness that had settled onto my chest, my mind flooded with images of ancient symbols and spirits of the dead. I stood watching the traffic go by. In an odd show of concern, Harper joined me.

"Are you okay?" she asked.

I had to laugh, as she did too, over her terrible question. How could I respond? I took a minute and used it to illustrate a sneak peek into my life and build some trust.

"At age six, I took the bus to school. It was a short drive that looped around the side streets. I saw right into the front room of every lit home in the dark morning hours of winter. The lights from their TVs reflected back on families immersed in their morning routines. And there I was, this outsider looking in, crushed by life at such a young age. I remember thinking, *why, why do all these people get to live an ordinary life? What did I do to deserve all the pain?*

Harper stepped up next to me as close as she could be without touching and said, "We all have pain. Some are just better at hiding it. Be grateful for all things you do have, as crazy as it may all seem. At least you have a family."

"You have a family?"

"I have Sawyer. My parents left when I was a toddler. We spent years moving through the system."

The weight of her words fell upon my shoulders. The pain of her loss mixed with mine and knotted in my stomach. Her eyes were colorless and transparent, then flickered and faded into a swirl of greys and blues.

"I'm sorry, I didn't realize."

She picked at her dark blue, nail polish, "It's ok, not like we going around introducing ourselves as foster kids. You think you've been running from your demons, imagine what we endured? This town is a little jacked up, but it's still a home," she winked.

She was right. I have a small family, an old love, a store, and a set of new friends. I still had enough to fight for in this life, even if it meant a battle in a world I had yet to understand. And maybe, if Harper would let me in, I could be part of the family she never had.

We shared a tiny smile over our first real exchange of raw emotion, but I had to ask, "Are you staying this time?"

"What do you mean?" she retorted.

"Are you going to run off alone, or are we all in this together?"

Harper paused and began pulling little pieces of flaking paint off the rail, peeling off a long strip, and hanging it in front of my eyes. I crinkled my face, grabbed it, and dropped it into a bush, hoping Kate wouldn't notice.

"Sorry," she said exhaling. "We're all in this together until we are told otherwise. But I do need to get back and see Chloe. Maybe more spirits have answered her, and hell, given they guided Sawyer and Fitzly here, we should listen."

"Or learn to listen on our own," I winked.

The front screen door squealed open as Sawyer and Fitzly rejoined our conversation. Sawyer rested his hands on our shoulders.

"You two bonding?" he asked.

"Nope," Harper snapped back.

"Nada," I affirmed.

"Well, since you two aren't friends yet, I assume we are all headed in different directions, then?" he went on.

I half agreed. Harper wants to go back east and pick Chloe's brain for more answers, and I have someone here in town that might be able to help. What do you and Fitzly want to do?"

I was crossing my fingers behind my back, hoping Sawyer would want to stay, but it was selfish and unlikely he would send Harper back alone.

"We have two cars here. I say the three of us go east and come back in one car," Sawyer answered, pointing at Fitzly and Harper. "Your mom will likely want her car back, and you can't drive it anyway."

We agreed that our separate journeys brought us all together in the Creek, and it was here we all needed to be. But each of us had to settle our business at home, first. Either way, they were coming back, which made me appreciate the part of my life that had been stagnant for some time.

"We can all stay here tonight and split up tomorrow," I asserted.

With four mutual nods, we walked back to settle in for a long night of more theorizing and, hopefully, a few hours of restful sleep.

CHAPTER 23

ALLISON'S INVITATION

Sawyer dropped me off in front of the 1816 Tavern, per my request. I waved goodbye and watched them drive off after promising to call in a few days with a plan for their return. We spent most of the evening combing through the mysterious book, sharing spooky stories from our past and hopes for a future we wanted to exist in. Harper cornered me again about the bee charm, but I didn't tell her about the picture I had found at home. I couldn't drag Kate any further into this mess until I had more facts. I stuck with the story about my dad and even conjured up a few tears to make it more believable.

Eventually, the three of them melted away to sleep on whatever piece of furniture they fell upon. I texted Kate late to let her know I was staying at her home and updated her on the surprise houseguests. In her usual fashion, she was okay with everything, though stunned that the three were here in the Creek. I agreed to catch up with her during the day.

With the car out of sight, I turned my attention to the Tavern's large glass window. The bustling energy of a full house from the night before was now replaced with silence and calm. The shadows of a barkeep moved around, mopping the floors and setting up the chairs for today's lunch crowd. I wasn't here to eat—I was here to satisfy another craving.

Every building in town had the same entry to a set of stairs that led to an upper unit. I side-stepped over to a full glass door with a rounded decal: "Around the Sun, In the Stars, Of the Forest." The words arced over a bright yellow artistic sun with an orange crescent moon, a star, and a tall skinny evergreen.

The waiter from my first dinner with Aggie arrived for work at the Tavern and stood knocking on the front door, waiting for the only other person inside to let him in. He saw me despite my best attempts to hide my face.

"Hey, I remember you. You have that friend with the whimsical taste in drinks?" he said.

"Yes, that would be me. How are you?" I responded. He shivered in his white long-sleeve button-down, black pants, and tightly wrapped waist apron. His beard was a little longer and fuller.

"I'm good; thanks. If you're looking for Nova, she's upstairs. She worked all night getting her place ready. I hope she does well," he said.

"Yeah, me too," though I wasn't sure I meant it. If she had a true gift, then I was all for it, but if she were fake, then that crossed a line for those of us with so much to spiritually handle. Either way, I would find an ally or a foe.

The barkeep pushed the front door open, knocking the waiter off his feet and into an umbrella stand. While toppling over, he formally introduced himself, half-laughing, half-embarrassed.

"I'm Charlie. I hope to see you and your friend, uh, what's her name?" he said.

"Aggie," I offered.

"Yes, Aggie. You should both come back around some time," he added.

"I'll see what I can do."

He tripped his way over the threshold and inside while I took the slow walk up the wooden stairs to Nova's place. At the top of the stairs, long, multicolored beaded strings hung from the top of the doorway. I walked through to the sitting area. Brightly colored tapestries with complicated circular designs hung from the walls and the ceiling. A large wrought iron and crystal chandelier hung down from the center. Three dark blue velvet love seats sat around a rectangular coffee table with brass candleholders and recently lit cream-colored taper candles. The smell of patchouli and lemongrass hovered in the air from two burning incense sticks, each with long ash dangling over its wooden cradle. The sound of a wood wind chime emanated from behind a large curtain.

On the opposite wall, a door sat half-opened. A bright blue light radiated outward. I reached for the door. "Ellie, Nova?"

"Abby?" The girl's coarse and mysterious yet familiar voice arose from behind the fabric panel where the wind chimes sang. She stepped out from behind the curtain.

Her slender body, hugged by a light green satin corset and a short black jacket with butterfly sleeves, moved toward me. A floor-length black skirt partially covered her bare feet as she inched toward me.

"Sorry," I mumbled, "is it too early?"

We made eye contact. "No, your timing is fine," she said. A single strand of black gemstones sat upon her long-dark locks like a crown. Her curls cascaded over her diamond shaped face, light colored eyes, and full lips. She reached out and softly grabbed my hands.

"Ellie?" I inquired again.

"It's Nova now," she replied.

She let go of my hands and dropped her arms to her sides, removing the jacket and showcasing long black tattoos that started up near her shoulder and ended on the backsides of her hands. As she walked past me toward a closed window, I noticed that the tattoos continued over her shoulders and down her back, disappearing beneath the tightly bound fabric.

"It's good to see you, Nova. What brings you back to town?"

She pulled open the dark blue curtain that covered a large pane of glass that overlooked the Creek.

"Allison was calling me back."

"Who's Allison?"

Her gaze fixated on something outside.

"Allison is Michael and Grace's daughter, the founding family of the Creek. He named it after her," she said.

I chewed on my lower lip and cringed slightly as my skin split. In under a minute, she intrigued me with the beginning of an eerie tale, but I wasn't sold on its truth.

"You know Allison personally?" I questioned.

She didn't appreciate the hint of sarcasm. Nova raised an eyebrow and drew her hands up to her hips, and then she walked over to a small bookshelf. She handed me a red book with an aged and faded beige spine displaying the title in gold print, "Allison Creek."

"You can borrow this. It's an interesting read about our history," she said.

I opened the yellowing pages and flipped through some of the pictures dated back centuries. Tucked in the back I found a piece of wrinkled ivory paper. I unfolded a 5x7 painting of a woman in a white dress staring out a window. Her right hand rested on her cheek as she gazed out into a blue sky. A long red scar wrapped around her forearm. I was interested, "Thank you, are you sure?" I asked.

"Of course, now what brings you by?"

I thought about bringing up the encounter on the street but decided against it. I didn't know how much time she would allow me to stay or what she would be willing to share. I was going to keep it cordial and neutral as long as I was able. "Just stopping in to see an old friend," I said casually.

She cut me off. "Friend?" She laughed and walked past me, brushing against my shoulder. "I don't remember us being friends."

"Sure, we didn't hang out, but you weren't exactly social," I quipped.

She sauntered around, lighting a few more candle sconces on the walls and several tapers on the coffee table. "And you were?" she challenged.

My plan wasn't working. "No, but I wasn't mean to you either. Look, can we just start over? I didn't come to pick a fight."

She paused but ultimately agreed, walked me over to the couch, offered me a seat, and then sat on the other. Her hands rested in her lap while I fidgeted with my bag. "Sure, let's start over. What do you need from me?" she said flatly.

"Rumor is you're here as the new town fortune teller?"

"You're here about a rumor?"

"No, but it would help to confirm what you do before I ask you anything," I told her.

She stared at me for a moment and then replied, "Okay, I prefer a spiritual guide. I hope to enlighten and help those who need it, and if it looks like fortune-telling, then so be it. Everyone's experience will be different."

It was a vague response, and I guess I expected it, so rather than waste any more time, I decided to jump right into why I came. I opened my bag and spread out the stones, the pictures, and the taped-together shield on her table. "Do you know what any of this is?"

She moved over to my couch and scooched me to the side with her hips. She picked up a stone. "These are Runestones." She held it up toward the chandelier light above us. "The symbols on them etched in by their creator's hand have their own meanings and powers. They have a long magical history, dating back thousands of years."

Kate was right, but I wanted more specifics. "Used by witches?" I asked.

"Mostly," she said, glancing over with the side of her eyes. "Often, they are used to predict the future, but others use them to conjure a spell."

I picked up a stone and focused my attention on the symbol. "Does it mean anything?"

"There are 24 to a set, each with their own significance. You can find a chart online with definitions of the most commonly used however, anyone who practices magic can create their own alphabet," Nova explained.

I raised my eyebrows. "Why would someone do that?"

"To invoke specific powers from the universe," She tossed it into the air, watching it flip around before catching it in her palm. She swiftly released it from her grip watching it bounce on the table to its final resting place. "And it typically, it's from someone with great power and an abundance of experience with the craft."

I remembered the picture from the school of the woman flipping the coin and the Mayor flipping what was in his hand as he walked down the street. "Why did you do that?"

She was surprised by my question. "Why did I flip it?" she clarified.

"Yes, why?" I insisted.

"Those who carry the stones often flip them to invoke their spell. Then they hold it tightly in their hand and visualize what it is they want. I flipped, hoping to get a sense of this one's meaning. I watched how it twisted and fell, but the radiating heat its generating in my palm is too hot to hold onto," she explained.

"What is it then?"

She shook her head, "Something sinister."

I clenched my teeth as a cold wave shrouded me. She's creating more questions than answers. I dropped back into the loveseat and rubbed my tired eyes, watching her transition from the stones and the photos. She held each item in front of her face to study the details. She paid extra attention to the shield but didn't speak about it.

So far, I was more impressed with her style than her talent. It was then I remembered the book. I let Harper take it back with her but not before snapping a few pics with my phone. I sat up, opened my phone, and handed it to her.

"I forgot this; scroll through. Tell me if there is anything that stands out," I said.

She sat hunched over, scrolling and zooming. The ash of the incense stick finally fell as the smoke dissipated into the air carrying its scent away. I didn't care much for the smell of patchouli. I grabbed it, stirred the ash, and lightly blew the remaining smoke away.

Her demeanor changed. "Are these pages from a book? Where did you find it?" She dropped the phone onto the couch and got up to pace.

I didn't want to tell her how or where. "It's a long story, but yes, it's from a book."

"I'll be," she muttered under her breath.

"What?" I asked.

"I think you found the Travelers Creed," she said, displaying a hint of disbelief. I was initially at a loss for words. Did she just refer to a traveler? Did it carry the same meaning it did for Harper and Sawyer?

Her hands moved as she spoke. Her calm demeanor was replaced with a sense of excitement.

"No one, as far as I know, has ever seen the book. Travelers are spirit guides born from the souls of the departed. They're sent back to earth to watch over humans and gently guide and protect them. They move back and forth between heaven and earth. They have a creed they follow, their rules displayed in a leather-bound book," Nova went on. "Toss it back to me."

I did, and she continued to scroll back and forth at a swift pace, then stopped and focused. She flipped it, displaying the picture with concentric circles. "This," she tapped her finger on my screen, "is the Flower of Life. It's the symbol of creation and the hallmark sign of a traveler. Do you have the book?"

"I don't. I left it with a friend."

She sighed with disappointment, "I would love to see it if you ever gain it back in your possession. It's believed to not only outline their rules but provides guidance on how to defeat the wicked. In the wrong hands, it could be disastrous for all beings."

"Sure," I said. I wasn't truthful. I would never give it to anyone. Protecting its value was paramount, at least long enough for us to find its rightful owner. I took a long deep breath remembering the TC initials etched in the leather. They weren't initials after all; it was the title. There was still the burning question of how this rule book got in the hands of demons, but it was not a question I would ask now. I didn't trust Nova enough.

She dropped my phone again on the couch and began separating the pictures on the table. She covered her mouth with her hand and rubbed her lips with the tips of her fingers.

"You have items symbolic of dark powers and of light. You didn't get any of these by accident. You are in the thick of whatever is coming, and you're in danger. Come with me," Nova said.

She stood and walked back through the curtains to the side I had yet to see. I followed, leaving my stuff behind. My heart raced. Slowly, I pulled back the fabric. Multicolored giant square pillow seats covered the floor, with one row left open to the front window. Nova stood staring at a large wood altar in the corner. On it were multiple large crystals sitting upon bases that varied from robust and straightforward to ornate and delicate. She raised her hand next to her face to request my silence. I stood and waited until she summoned me forward.

"Crystal balls?" I asked, scrunching my face in disbelief of the cliché.

Clearing her throat, she responded, "Sort of. Crystal balls don't occur naturally. They're shaped by human hand and therefore altered by mortals. These crystal gems are in their natural state, unaltered by man. They contain the purest of energies."

After a pause, she looked at me and added, "It's okay, you can touch them."

Suddenly, the smell of smoke broke my concentration and jolted my attention back to the other room. I darted over with Nova right behind me. A taper candle fell over and lit my pictures on fire.

I scrambled. Nova grabbed a metal lid from a small trash can and stifled the flames. Falling to my knees, I quickly assessed the damage and carefully placed everything back in my bag.

"I think that's my cue to leave." I grabbed a twenty out of my wallet, handed it to Nova. Her hand rested over mine with a searing burn. I gasped and pulled away. The sight of glowing embers rose above a blinding fire. Flashes of women dancing and howling as the small pieces of fiery leaves burned their flesh. I rubbed my eyes and threw my purse strap over my head, clutching the bag tightly in my right hand.

"It's unnecessary," she responded, attempting to give the money back.

I waved her off and grabbed the red book as well. "Thank you again. I'll see you around." A sharp pain stabbed at my right temple and traveled across my forehead before settling into my left side. I tried shaking it off.

She grabbed my forearm. "Be careful," she stressed.

I parted the beaded doorway before walking through, catching my breath at the top of the stairs. As I turned, I was startled—two elderly women and one middle-aged man stood on the right side of the stairway. Their heads hung low as they waited in line. I moved down past each of them, the wood steps creaking underneath me. The last gentleman peeked up from under his grey cap and twisted his pepper-colored mustache. I trotted faster down the steps and back to fresh air, blue sky, sun, and a few fluffy white clouds. Sidestepping over, I braced myself against the stone exterior. At the same time, I allowed my headache to melt away.

The air from my breath was now visible as the temperature outside continued to cool. I was still breathing faster than usual when a man dressed as a jester skipped down through the street, handing out flyers. He giggled and laughed, then pressed the 8?11 piece of paper onto my chest before skipping away. I pulled the teal and gold embellished paper away from my chest, and on it, in a fancy scroll, the words read:

Allison Creek Hallow's Eve Masquerade Ball
October 31st
7:00 p.m.
As the town prepares for the witches' return,
Hide your identity and hide it well,
Or the witches will find you and send you to hell.

A purple masquerade mask sat upon a bed of flowers near the bottom of the paper. Above it was the directions on where to buy the tickets. It was a social faux pas to miss the event, so buying in advance was a "must." The affluent Creek afforded residents the most exquisite and most elaborate costumes ever seen. The finely dressed celebrated Hallow's Eve in dramatic flair, until the early hours of the morning at the Civic Theater in town. Kate was adamant about us all going together this year. My stomach was queasy.

I tucked it into the inside cover of the book then turned and looked back through the doorway. The people were gone.

I started my walk home rather briskly when I spotted Aggie outside of our store. I darted across the street and in front of an angry driver who was not skittish with his horn.

"Sorry," I mouthed, lightly tapping on the front of his car as I jumped forward, out of the way and toward Aggie.

"Hey! Are you okay?" I asked.

"Me? Are you okay?" She glanced over at the car and the man displaying his anger with his left hand out the window. Then, she stepped back with a small camera in her one hand, her other bandaged.

"Sorry, I got spooked yesterday. I have a fear of doctors and needles. It's fine, though, I took care of it," she said.

The door opened again, and Kate walked out. "Did you get the picture?"

"Working on it," said Aggie, waiting for a break in traffic to get a picture of the whole storefront from the street.

Kate noticed the book and pulled it out enough to read the title. "Interesting," she smirked.

"That's what Nova said," I muttered.

"Who?"

"Never mind; fill you in later," I responded.

The flyer fell out of the book, and Kate caught it midair. "Oh, the pesky little jester found you too this morning?"

"Yes, he did," I said and turned my attention back to Aggie and her wrapped hand with so many other questions spinning in my head, but with Kate present, I didn't know where to begin.

"I'm buying tickets for you and Aggie," Kate said.

"What?" I asked.

"Tickets to the ball. Your mom is coming too," she said eagerly.

I thought about Sawyer. "Can you get three more tickets? I'll pay you."

Kate's head tilted. "For your friends? Are they still here?"

"No," I said as I spun away from Aggie, "They went back east this morning. The ball would be a fun time for them to come back, and it would give me enough time to get things done around here while doing more research."

A prying Aggie caught half of the conversation. "Enough time for what?"

I looked at Aggie and back at Kate. "Enough time for me to prepare for the big night, of course."

CHAPTER 24

THE CUTLER

I spent much of the last two-and-a-half weeks researching what I could at the library and online, taking breaks to manage the store while Kate and Aggie worked on remodel plans. I taped my research and any notes to the inside wall of my closet and tried to salvage what I could of the burned pictures. Thankfully the damage was not extensive. Every inch of wall space behind my clothes was covered with clues.

At night, I sat in my closet. I stared at it all: the Black Magic Priestess Shield, pictures of the Travelers Creed, and memories of the demons out over the shore of Connecticut. Images of the demoness with bleeding eyes haunted me in my dreams while snapshots of the young girl with the black ponytail flipping runes played out in my head. Could it be that demons, witches, and Travelers were preparing for war? Were they all near? And why were a few choice humans stuck in the center of it all?

I spent an entire rainy Sunday reading "Allison Creek." It outlined the story of several Massachusetts families who were deeply entangled in witchcraft during the 19th century. The trouble, I couldn't determine if it was fiction or not. Nova specifically said, "To learn our history," but it read more like a dark fairy tale and ended with a terrible curse that resulted in the whole town burning down. If it was true, then the land on which Allison Creek sits was founded by one of the witches that fled persecution. Worse yet, Allison and her family were central to it all. I called Nova the next day to drop it off. I had so many questions, but when I arrived, all I found was a two-sided note.

"Sorry I missed you. Just leave the book on the shelf. I hope you enjoyed it."

On the other side, she wrote, "On Hallow's Eve, don't let the costumes fool you. The veil will be thin, and those who hide will now be front and center. Follow and find the answers you seek." *Was this just some light-hearted Halloween riddle, or was there more to it?* I added it to my growing repertoire of madness.

I was physically and mentally exhausted. While my nightmares subsided, my wakefulness brought an increase of run-ins with all sorts of spirits, including the three unknown men. Their eerie whistling traveled in on the backs of a breeze, choking me with coldness and pure terror. I couldn't get away from any of it. I phoned Sawyer and Fitzly on the worst of days. Sawyer would talk me through, but Fitzly was feeling the weight too. We needed each other's comfort and security. Being alone became distressing, and unfortunately, I had one more afternoon of mostly solitude.

Kate was meeting me at the store to deliver my costume for the evening. I chose to hide in the second level, where many of my dad's personal items were hidden in boxes away from Mason. Mason traveled so much now; he was always gone, and Mom wouldn't confirm or deny their current relationship status.

I sat across from the open window that overlooked Main, snuggled in a large soft grey hoodie. The scent of late-blooming fall flowers that lined every inch of town soon replaced the cardboard box smell of my sweatshirt.

A few people were out, still placing their lanterns with lighted cream-colored candles by their storefronts. They would remain lit outside every door, front porch, or stoop until tomorrow morning. It was part of an old belief that the light protected the buildings from any vile deity that may try to enter on Hallow's Eve. I wasn't sure everyone believed the superstition. Still, most were too fearful not to, especially after the disappearance of everyone in the Valley.

The store, like all the others, would stay closed today. Halloween was historically the worst sales day of the year. Everyone was too busy preparing for the parade and the ball. I sat breathing in the air that was bringing with it change.

The sound of two quick knocks, the door opening, and the voice of Kate nudged me from my thoughts.

"Hey there! You hiding?" The loud creeks of the floorboards muffled Kate's soft voice.

"Sort of," I replied.

Kate walked in with a large dress bag over her one arm. She meandered through the path of boxes, dressed in sweats with her hair up in a big messy bun sitting high on her head.

"I have your costume," she shrieked with excitement. I left her in charge of finding me something. I didn't have the time or even the ability to pick out a getup that would meet Creek standards. I trusted her decision and smiled wide in appreciation.

"Should I look now?" I asked, reaching and taking it off her hands. I couldn't see the costume underneath the tissue paper in the clear bag.

"No, take it home. Don't unwrap it in this dusty old space."

I agreed and turned back toward the window.

"What's wrong?" she asked, resting her hand on my right shoulder.

I still had questions about the witch's box and the bee charm at her home, but I struggled with what to ask. This was the one person who always had my back; I wasn't ready to face any more disappointment about a loved one so I kept my response general. "I'm worried about tonight. Something is going to happen."

Kate's fingers tapped across my shoulder blades as she spun around in front of me, perching herself on the ledge under the window.

"Yeah, or maybe it's your gut telling you that the Masquerade is a big deal, and it will be an awesome fun night you desperately deserve."

"Have you forgotten about Connecticut?" I clutched the dress bag and peered at her, begging for honesty. The more I shared with her over the weeks about the stones, the tunnels, and the pictures in my dad's garage, the more Kate dodged. *What was she hiding?*

Kate pressed her lips together, exhaled, and dropped her shoulders. "No, I haven't forgotten. But honestly, I've been working with Aggie so much on the rebranding and the remodel. We all want to save the store, and it's the best use of my time. Your friends are your best bet for all things supernatural," she added.

I pulled the hoodie up over my mouth and rubbed the soft cotton along my lips and cheek. Kate hopped off the ledge and kneeled before me, resting her hands and head on my lap. Her love was wrapped in guilt. I pondered why as I played with her hair.

"When will the crew be here?" she asked, lying on my lap and twisting the plastic knot at the bottom of the bag.

"Later; it's a long drive, so maybe at nine o'clock."

"Do you like him?" She looked up at me, in no rush to be anywhere but here.

Sawyer's image haunted me in the most fantastic way. It was difficult controlling a grin, "Maybe. I'm letting Ben go, but I'm afraid of who I might be without him. Sawyer gives me hope, but my heart is confused and vulnerable."

"It's okay. You'll figure it all out in time," she reassured.

"Time is a funny thing, though," I said.

Kate leaned back and curled up in a fetal position. "Jeez, Abs, you're so deep in your thoughts today. You've always been the philosophical one in the family," she said, winking then punching me in my arm.

"Thanks, but I really need to be strong," I replied.

Kate stood, hugged me hard, and kissed me on the head. "You're both. Now get out of here, go home, shower, and get ready."

A disturbance was escalating outside. The sounds of people on the street grew loud. I shimmied my chair over to the window. I leaned out over the edge, following the lines of people moving until I noticed a gap where everyone parted. A young man dressed in jeans and a brown leather jacket walked north up Main. He casually chewed his jacket's collar while gliding a small knife across a chunk of wood. The splinters fell as he repeatedly shaved off pieces.

Kate walked up behind me. "Who is that, and why is he whittling down the street?"

I smirked, "Whittling, really?"

"That's what he's doing, isn't he?"

He was, but her choice of words made me chuckle.

He glanced up toward our window and brushed his dark shaggy hair away from his eyes with the back of his hand. "New kid," I mumbled, still watching, intrigued by his mannerisms.

Kate leaned in front of me. "New kid, obviously unaware that people here don't brandish weapons even if it is for artistic purposes."

With a smug grin, he slid his knife into an interior jacket pocket and then turned away. With short, quick strides, he crossed the street and disappeared down the walkway toward the falls.

She patted me on the head. "Seems like we're getting a lot of newbies these days with odd hobbies." She chose her path toward the back door and walked away, yelling out one last piece of advice. "Remember, tonight, you get to be whoever you want. You can be strong, or smart or normal, whatever that may be, and you can hide it all behind a beautiful mask."

CHAPTER 25

TRANSFORMATION

I made my way home after stopping at the local drug store for some blonde and blue hair dye. I had been thinking about a bold change for weeks, and tonight brought an opportunity for such a metamorphosis. In the mirror, I gazed one last time at the tired, fragile girl I had become.

I bleached it first, blow-dried it, and then carefully separated sections for the bright blue color that would match what I already had. Using a brush, I swept the color from the middle of my strands down to the ends. The bitter smell of dye that burned my nose and eyes was worth the exhilarating feeling slowly creeping in.

I rinsed the gook out, towel-dried my hair and swung my head up in front of the mirror. Cool white strands melted into bright blue ends. I blow-dried it for the second time with great excitement. My natural blue streak remained untouched by the chemical process. It blended in with the blonde and blue ombré coloring I had desired. I blinked. My eyes transitioned from a golden brown to a fierce blue and purple hue that swirled around my pupil. I was mesmerized with the dominant being I embodied.

Eager and elated to get ready, I devoted more time than usual on my routine. Then, I turned my attention to the costume, still lying on my bed housed in a zippered dress bag. Pulling back the zipper, the fabric, while delicate, came layered with a sense of new confidence, and I was curious about what Kate had chosen for me. The smell of a new outfit rushed out of the bag as I held it up by the hanger.

"Yes, Kate, you did not disappoint!" I shrieked.

It was sexy and edgy but still me, and I rushed to put it on with the excitement of a five-year-old headed out for trick or treat. I stood primping and posing in my mirror, taking in the attire's awesomeness. A sleeveless black and dark blue velvet shirt sat under a floor-length cloak, held together at the neck by a black stone choker. Long bell sleeves flowed over my hands that I placed on the hips of my black leather shorts. Sheer black hose and tall lace-up black boots that I already owned covered my pale legs. The final touches, a tall black hat with a matching dark blue silk band, and a delicate black half mask with blue crystals and beading around the edges. Kate was all about the details, and it shined through in this costume. I became the most animated version of myself and spoke out loud in an obnoxious yet dynamic manner.

"Abby, you are killing it right now and your hair is perfect! Look out, Riley!" My heart wasn't tripping over Ben anymore, but my rage toward Riley had not lessened. Pride, I guess. I wanted my moment.

A cold chill sent random shivers through my limbs. I shook and shed the timid layer that had defined me for years, leaving it behind like a snake's skin. I had thirty minutes left to get to town and meet Kate and my mom. It was just enough time to look through my closet—not at my clothes, at the collection of my life's darkest secrets and fears boxed up, taped up, and hidden away from the mortal world. Photos from my dad's man cave, faded pictures of random strangers and a few partially burned images of Ben hung haphazardly behind a row of hanging shirts. I touched each one before thumbing through my dream journal, the images coming together like a scary picture book. My sleep and wake world dancing along to the sounds of the eerie whistling I struggled to forget.

My phone dinged with a message from Sawyer, jarring me back to the present. I fumbled to view it from behind the mask.

"ETA is roughly 10 p.m. We'll meet you inside. Text you when walking in; be safe," the message read.

After typing different replies, I decided on a simple "Okay" before sending it. I ripped what was left of Ben's charred pictures off of my wall, crumpled them up, and tossed them on the floor. I closed the closet door behind me.

223

I stepped out onto my front porch, expecting some rock anthem to ring out from the universe. Instead, the air was filled with the giddy laughter of couples engaging in their masquerade roleplay and the banter of young twenty-somethings making their way to town, already intoxicated by the day's events. I settled for a series of my own self-serving compliments, hoping the brawn this shielded identify provided would also be bold enough to protect me from the other side. For now, I just needed to dodge the sidewalk traffic.

Old Man Studdard was out on his porch this evening. The crowds ushering in and out of town made for the best people-watching event of the year. But as I looked up at the porch, I noticed that instead of sitting and rocking, the old man was standing dressed in a perfectly tailored silver suit with a black vest. A hat sat tall on his head and, a shiny black cane with a pearl handle replaced his usual walking stick. I inched closer to get a better view.

"Mr. Studdard, are you heading to the party?" I asked, surprised, and impressed with all the details, including a gold amulet that hung low around his neck. He twisted it when I noticed, then shoved it into his shirt.

"Party? Oh, this is not just a party. No, no, this is a monumental celebration. It must be your first," he replied.

"Yes sir, it is," I said, wondering if he knew it was me he was talking to.

The old man did his best strut down the steps tapping his cane right up to my place on the sidewalk. A hummingbird flew down past him then landed on a bold orange, red-colored flower pinned to his label. I jumped back, alarmed by its sudden presence. He lifted his right hand and lightly touched it, prompting it to fly away.

"Trumpet Creeper," he remarked.

"What?"

"Trumpet Creeper flowers attract hummingbirds," he said, "and you have to be gentle with them to avoid breaking a wing."

Another tiny, colorful bird hovered in front of eyes then pivoted and flew off into a bush but the old man ignored it and quickly shifted the topic back to the party, leaning in and whispering over my shoulder.

"It's my first too," he said with a cheeky smile, "But I've seen pictures and heard the stories. This will be an incredible experience for both of us. You need a walking buddy?"

"You know it's me, Abby, right?"

Old Man Studdard spoke to everyone in town and with my blond and blue hues and covered face, I wanted to make sure he knew exactly whom he was walking with.

"Of course, I know it's you. I recognized the eyes. Your hair is impressive, too," he replied.

"Thanks," I said, beaming. He may be old, but I was happy to accept my first compliment of the evening.

Studdard straightened his lapel. "How do I look?" he inquired.

"Striking," I said.

He reveled in his compliment as well, then stuck out his right arm, "You ready?"

"Sure. Why not?" Dressed as a young carnival gypsy, I walked with a man three times my age, dressed like a pimp. It beat arriving alone.

The closer we got to the center of town, the louder and more crowded the streets became. The old man skipped with every step to the bass roaring from the direction of the theater. His demeanor and smiling face, which moved to the beat of the music, slowly turned to the sky as three hawks glided and swooped down over us and back up over the building on Oak.

"They must want to take part in the festivities, too," he joked, still dancing his way to town. I held on to his arm, astounded how well he moved for a man who never left his front step. "Wait," he said suddenly, pulling me to stop.

He reached into his inside coat pocket and pulled out a black and silver mask with a long bird nose. He shook it out, plumped it up from being pressed inside, and then placed it over his face, adjusting it until he was comfortable. The cackling of hundreds of townspeople dressed in the most dramatic and elegant costumes engulfed us as we turned onto Main. Like a herd of finely dressed cattle, we all moved in the same direction, passing handmade floats now used as giant decorations for the late-night events. We stepped over the pumpkin guts still splattered on the road from the Pumpkin Crawl the night before.

"Always wanted to participate but never invited," Studdard remarked.

Every year, kids from the Creek stole pumpkins from unsuspecting homes. They would take the pumpkins up the big hill near the perimeter of the town, smash them on the road, and then slide down on sleds. Remnants would remain for days or at least until a heavy rain came through.

I shrugged. "Never participated either."

"Ha, life goals then!" he responded.

He knocked some seeds off his shoes with his cane, then like me, turned his attention back to all the floats. Grand mummies, snakes, dragons, jack-o-lanterns, and witches bordered the parade route, each illuminated by the string of lights that hung from streetlamp to streetlamp. Adults dressed as zombies dragged themselves through town, scaring unsuspecting guests like a giant outdoor haunted house.

"This is exciting, dear Abby, very exciting."

I nodded and spun, viewing a completely transformed town in the most elegant and haunting way. A low-hanging moon glowed orange in a clear night sky. The wind was crisp with the smell of winter coming on every gust winding its way through town. My heart rate picked up the pace and skipped a few beats. I was hidden, but so was everyone and everything else.

"You know what I love best about dressing up?" asked the old man, adjusting his mask so he could move his upper lip as he spoke.

"No, what?" I asked.

"It gives the soul the chance to be free, to try out something new," he replied.

There would be an "aha" moment to his statement, but it was too early in the conversation to understand what that was. I played along as always and asked for clarification. "How so?"

"We're born and given this life, and from an early age, we're taught who we are, and we grow up believing that we always have to be that way. Sure, we change interests and even grow in our opinions. Still, we get comfortable in our shells, and that blocks out new opportunities."

We were still meandering along, though I slowed the pace, wanting to get to his point before reaching the theater.

"What new opportunities?"

"You're protected behind the mask tonight. Be the opposite of whatever you believe yourself to be. Take in the view and get comfortable being something other than Abby, the gal who finished high school a year early. You have way more purpose on this earth," he said.

"I do?" If I had a purpose, I had no clue what it was.

"We all do," he said with his big toothy smile.

Today's dose of enlightenment was fitting. I felt my transformation slowly evolving. I was leaving the old, fearful part of me behind, moving forward into a life where I wanted control. But still, I wondered, what was my divine objective?

"Abby?" My name echoed through the sea of masks when a hand with a gold band and a giant ruby ring grabbed my arm. The touch jolted me away from my thoughts.

"Is that you?" Aunt Kate lifted her red mask.

I raised my mask to acknowledge her.

Her eyes widened. "Your hair! Is it permanent?"

"I dyed it. I guess it's permanent until I change it again," I said with a twisted smile.

"Wow," Kate pulled her mask back down and twirled her fingers through my locks.

"Good thing I knew what you're wearing. I would've never guessed it was you," she said.

"Perfect, just the way I wanted it."

Kate wore the most fantastic blood-red strapless dress, tight at the top and flaring at the bottom with ruffles down to the floor. It was like Satan meets the southern belle. She'd pulled her hair back into a loose bun with a matching red and black mask sitting snugly over it.

"You look fabulous," I remarked. "And I love my costume."

"Glad you approve. You need to feed your inner wild child every now and again. It's good for your soul, though, with the color change, you figured that out for yourself."

I smiled and held my chin and B boobs up high like a woman and less like a child.

"Who's your date?" she giggled.

I turned back to Mr. Studdard. "Enjoy your evening," he said. "I am heading in for a good seat and a drink. See you later, maybe. And thanks for accompanying me." Then he disappeared into the crowd.

"That, believe it or not, was Old Man Studdard," I told Kate.

"Really?" she asked. "He dresses up nice." Kate turned my face over my shoulder, placing my mom in my field of vision. "You all do."

"Isn't she beautiful?" said Kate, squeezing my jawline, but my mom didn't recognize me.

She walked closer, showcasing her black strapless short dress with an intricate peacock design wrapped around her right ribcage and faded down to just below the hip bone. She sauntered over to Kate, taking quick glimpses at me. I enjoyed the moment of anonymity. She stretched upward and whispered to Kate, still inches shorter than her, even in the highest heels. She adjusted her eloquent embroidered mask. The beading and magnificent blues and browns were sophisticated and alluring at the same time. Matching feathers rounded up to the left with an arched eyebrow of tiny rhinestones. It had me wondering just who she was trying to impress. Suddenly, she realized who was standing before her.

"Please tell me that's a wig!" The shocked facial expression was covered by the mask, but her tone was clear and direct.

"It's not a big deal. Please, for the love of something, don't make this an issue. I love it. Let it go," I said and gritted my teeth and clenched my fists. To my surprise, she did what I asked. She wasn't one to make a scene in front of all these people. I used it in my favor and turned away, distracted by all the activity around us.

The lampposts around town flickered, which garnered my attention. Kate shrugged it off as a power issue due to all the energy being drawn. I wasn't so sure but moved up the stairs with the crowd, toward the giant stone lions flanking the doorman.

My phone dinged, alerting me to another message from Sawyer.

"One hour. How do I find you?"

Kate pulled me upfront and handed our tickets over to the tall and wide doorman.

"Will leave tickets with doorman then find you inside," I texted back, which was dumb because I had no clue what he was wearing. But I was slowing the line, aggravating the big dude in front of me and all the people behind me.

"ID?" the man asked one more time in a low voice with an annoyed tone.

"I'm under 21," I said.

"Then hand ..." I was stamped and ushered in by an overly excited Kate and nervous and fidgety mom. But I turned back to hand the envelope with Sawyers name and the tickets to the doorman. He lowered his brow at me. I walked away, smiling before he could toss it back.

Once inside, we walked down a narrow black carpet with a maroon roped hallway. On both sides of the ropes stood male bongo players dressed up in suits with the sleeves ripped off, beating on drums with their hands. Their faces and arms were covered in black makeup in a variety of linear type designs, mimicking tattoos. They swayed to the music's pulse dramatically, energizing the lines of people moving through. My mom leaned over me.

"It only gets crazier," she yelled, her voice barely breaking through the noise.

They made eye contact with every passerby as strobe lights flashed at a rapid speed. A slight ache developed in my temple as the sound of disembodied voices blended with the rhythmic dialogue of the bongos. I remembered what Nora explained about not fighting it. I walked slow, staring at each of the drummers. I wanted to hear what they had to say. I noticed the pain dissipating, and the voices became more lucid. I listened to the whisper.

"Follow her," I turned in disbelief and then shoved my way through the line. I couldn't find the source of the voice. Kate caught up with me.

"Why the rush? Are you okay?"

I ripped my mask off and took a deep breath to calm my heart. Heavy bass vibrated off the walls and ceilings. I took Nora's advice, let it in, and received my message. I couldn't believe how easy it was to just listen. I wanted to hear more and shrugged off Kate.

"I'm fine; it was a little too loud," I said.

"I need a drink; you want to come?" Kate was yelling.

Part of me wanted to stay glued to her hip like a child, but I couldn't; I needed to forge ahead alone.

"No, go ahead; I'll be fine. Catch up with you later. I have my phone." I opened my jacket and showed her the cell tucked away neatly in an interior pocket.

I used a made-up version of sign language to communicate anything she didn't hear then turned away before she questioned anything else.

I pulled my mask back down, entered the expansive theater and listened. But my sense of hearing was overwhelmed by my sight of the most glorious Halloween Ball I had only heard stories about. All of the seating was removed and replaced with a click-together fake wood floor. Tall drink tables sat covered in deep red velvet table covers with thick gold piping. The covers cascaded down to the wood floor and stayed in place by gold star-shaped plates housing lit candles in a variety of sizes and deep hues. Fog machines blasted out smoke that hovered low to the floor. Up in the balconies, guests mingled in a grand affair, sipping fancy drinks from oversized glasses and mugs. Impressive mahogany wood bars lined the outside walls with bartenders and maids serving up colorful, fizzing alcoholic beverages.

Guests laughed loudly while they waited in line, dancing to the music that blared from the center stage. A DJ dressed in a black suit, white shirt, and a full black-and-cream Venetian mask entertained guests with an interpretive dance, embedded in a thick fog and flashing lights. Large speakers sat in front of an open floor where only a few couples ventured out to gyrate. And a magician on stilts meandered through the crowd, mixing a combination of dance with magic and a little fire for added flare.

A tall, man, or woman standing alone in a corner caught my attention. A cream-colored swallowtail jacket hugged the slender frame of the motionless stranger hidden beneath a full goat mask with tall horns, pointed ears and, a long face. Its stare paralyzing me until the sound of my name broke the spell.

"Abby?"

I sighed; it was Ben's voice, and for a moment, I thought, "No, sorry, someone else." But I didn't. I nodded yes when I should've run.

"You look … great. I saw you lift your mask when you were talking to Kate," he said as he ran his hand up through my hair and pulled the blue streak out forward. "You don't have to hide it tonight."

I gave a quick thank you and desperately searched for a compliment to return. In typical Ben fashion, he showed up in a black mask, black shirt, black jeans, and black tennis shoes. It was a new low threshold for minimal effort.

He then licked the palm of his hand and rubbed the stamp off mine.

"Really?" I said, wiping my hand across my shorts. But he didn't hear me. He had turned and grabbed two foaming drinks off the tray of a waitress, spun, and handed one to me.

"Non-alcoholic?" I questioned.

He nodded, and I drank the bubbling punch with a bite of alcohol and yet another one of his white lies. I went with it. What harm would one drink do? We acted silly together with every sip, but Ben was drinking faster and getting more emotional. The spiked drink had me lost in time but not in the past. His closeness had limits for my comfort level, though it was clear he was pushing for the removal of boundaries.

Suddenly, my face was out in the open. My mask ripped from behind with such force that my neck snapped backward. A sharp pain traveled down my spine to my hip. I turned, blond hair, tight green dress—it could only be one.

"What the hell is wrong with you?" Ben screamed directly in her face.

Riley launched my mask back at me then did a double-take.

"Abby?" she turned back to Ben. "It was bad enough I thought you were with another girl, but really, you're rolling with the trash again. Nice color, hooker." Riley's hands rested on her hips as she waited for an answer.

I pushed past Ben and shoved her as hard as I could. She flew back into her girls and bounced up like a punching bag coming straight at me. Ben intervened, stopping her, but then the sound of another loud, low voice hit my ears. He grabbed at Riley's arm and yanked her back, excusing him and her. It was her dad, in full costume with his mask pushed up onto his head, his face contorted into a snarl. Ben didn't like the way he was pulling at her. He glanced at me but then followed her with her bitches tagging along behind.

I backed up slowly, trying to separate myself from the pandemonium and the attention we had drawn to ourselves, bumping right into another partygoer.

"Who was that?" the familiar voice brought an instant smile.

I spun. "Sawyer?" I asked.

A simple form-fitting black and navy blue jacquard jacket sat snug over his frame. His hair cascaded over the front of his matching half-mask. His three o'clock shadow gone, he ran his hand up through his hair, pushing it back, and leaning in for a quick hug. Fitzly moved in for a squeeze in an impressive black and silver ensemble and a head full of bright blue highlights streaming from his hair.

"Embracing the blue too?" I acknowledged.

"Temporary?" he retorted with a playful smile.

"Permanent," I boasted, twisting at a chunk of my strands.

Harper initiated a subtle wave, flustered by the attention her tight black mini dress, cleavage and elaborate mask with feathers, and rhinestones brought her.

"You going to answer?" Sawyer scoffed again. "Who was that?"

"An old flame; no one," I retorted.

"You sure?" he asked.

"One hundred percent," I returned.

I meant it, too. Sawyer's immediate concern and a hint of jealousy were flattering. He stood, insanely handsome, inches away. I struggled to articulate anything of great substance. Harper and Fitzly were quick to grab a few drinks and disappeared into the masses, joking and elbowing each other along the way. They didn't want to dive into all the mess yet; for once, they just wanted to enjoy what life was offering. I was living in the moment as well and walked around casually with Sawyer.

"How is Chloe?" I asked, sipping another colorful drink.

His face, expressionless, gave me immediate concern. "She's not good."

"Why?"

"Nora is even more protective than usual. She is pissed at Harper for taking the book and refused to sit and talk about it. She wouldn't let Chloe be alone with us, either."

"So, now what?" I tilted my head and lifted back my hat that was growing heavy on my head.

His expression remained neutral. "Nothing; we keep moving forward."

"Did Fitzly try Chloe on her phone?" I took another sip of my cocktail.

"Yes, but Nora monitors it, too, now. Chloe couldn't speak." He muffled his concern under the mask, but his tone spoke of frustration, "After we round up those two, we can head somewhere more private and talk, so ease back on the alcohol." His forehead bounced off the brim of my hat, and then he smiled.

"It's holiday punch," I said as I choked on my drink, cleared my throat, and sat the glass down on the nearest table. I didn't need it. Plus, I wanted to remember all this in the morning.

We found a tall unoccupied table and stood opposite one another. I fidgeted and peeled the black label off a jar candle while he spoke.

"I really love your hair. Your whole costume. It suits you well," he said.

Elated by his compliments, I longed for more.

"You sure it's not too much?" I asked.

His teeth shined with his giant smile. "No, it's pretty great."

At that moment, Ben and Riley walked by hand in hand. She didn't even try to look in my direction or bark off a nasty remark. She was still upset, and Ben was right there to coddle her. Again, I didn't want his attention, not with Sawyer near, so I turned my back to them.

Sawyer was quick to notice, "What is it with that dude?"

"That's Ben," I remarked.

"Ben from your phone?" Sawyer followed them with his eyes until they blended in with the crowd.

"Yes, and that's his girlfriend. She hates me. I dislike her for hating me." I didn't want to talk about them, but Sawyer wouldn't let up.

"You don't dislike her for her crush on Ben?" he questioned, already not believing my words.

I took my hat and mask off and placed them on the table. I couldn't have this conversation tucked away behind fabric and plastic.

"I did, initially. But we both needed to move on. It was high school love, my first that I thought I needed to keep forever. I don't anymore. I'm not the same person. He might be. But I've changed. I had to, and I'm not only okay with it, but also welcome it." I was firm and short with my comments. He brushed the hair back from my face and over my ear.

"I got it," he said. He placed my mask and hat back on. I was grateful for immediate acceptance, but I also wanted to know more about him.

"What about you? What are you passionate about? What gets under your skin? Tell me anything, there's so much I don't know," I asked.

He thought for a second and gave me an effortless response. "I drove nine hundred and fifty miles and put together my first Halloween costume in years. I want to enjoy my night, with you, of course. Now let's go find our kiddos and see what's up."

CHAPTER 26

THE GATHERING

Sawyer avoided most topics about himself, leaving me frustrated again. Still, as I turned to meander around the room, he dropped his arm to his side then moved it back behind himself. Wiggling his fingers was my cue to grab on.

"Damn it," I said under my breath.

I clutched his fingertips in my hand and followed him through the mass of people. I was mad at myself for diving in too quickly, but his light touch sent waves of energy through my body.

"I don't see them," he yelled over his shoulder.

I didn't respond; he wouldn't have heard me anyway, and I wasn't surprised. We weren't going to find anyone in here, not now. But we did bump into Old Man Studdard walking and dancing his way through the crowd. Sawyer quickly released my hand and apologized.

A loud gong rang out twelve times, announcing that midnight had arrived. Mayor Quartano appeared on stage with his stout frame squeezed into a costume and a mask struggling to conceal his face. His deep, low voice boomed through a microphone, announcing the night's festivities had only just begun. Women dressed as beautiful witches paraded from behind the stage and into the crowd, dancing and throwing confetti and glitter on a now full dance floor. They screamed like banshees and spun and twirled; some swallowed swords of fire while they navigated through herds of people. The guests roared and danced to the sounds of the bongo drums playing alongside the music. Men dressed like modern-day devils rushed in from the front of the theater, swooping up the witches and carrying them onto the stage before disappearing into the fog. Loud screams collided with a cheering audience, welcoming yet another magician to the stage.

With all the movement, Mayor Quartano lost his footing, tumbling to the ground. Small, shiny objects dropped from his coat pocket and bounced in different directions.

"Wait here." I let go of Sawyer and snuck through the crowd in his direction.

Quartano frantically tried to pick up the pieces between the dancing feet of the attendees. I spotted one and crawled over to it when he was facing the other way. I jumped up, and the man with the goat mask appeared. He didn't move, and I couldn't see his eyes. I gulped, mumbled, "Excuse me," and bolted back toward Sawyer.

I heard my name being yelled but didn't dare turn around. I kept moving, falling into Sawyer with Fitzly and Harper tripping over me.

"Didn't you hear me?" said Fitzly, lifting his mask.

"Yeah. I was ignoring you," I spoke through my teeth.

"Why?"

I held the shiny stone up to Fitzly's face. "Because I needed to see what the mayor is so damn protective of."

He stepped back, saying, "Oh, sorry."

Harper fanned herself with a napkin, sweat beading on her neck. "All these open flames should be a hazard; honestly, I'm ready to go if you all are."

Fitzly nudged us and pointed up. In each balcony stood men in long black hooded shirts and skull makeup. Their eyes glowed yellow and green, and they snarled down on the crowd with their sharpened teeth.

"Yeah, let's go," I said.

Sawyer led the way. I slithered out, holding tightly to his hand. The bouncer navigated us to a side exit, which dumped us into the alley.

Harper ripped off her bracelets and a choker necklace, tossing them to the ground. Fitzly fixed his clothes and threw his mask down. My grip on Sawyer tightened. He removed my hat and mask with his free hand, tossing it on the ever-growing pile of costume accessories.

A sudden jolt separated our bodies. Knuckles bounced off the side of Sawyer's face, knocking his mask off. He flew back. Ben rushed at him, but Sawyer lunged forward, hitting him in the jaw. Screaming, I tried to tear them apart, but Riley and her friends clawed at me.

Ben spit blood. "Is this the guy from the phone?"

Riley beat on Ben with her bony arms flying, her bangle bracelets smacking against one another. He grabbed her wrists together and pushed her back.

"Stop for one minute; stop!" The spit flew off his lips while he yelled, Riley cried.

Sawyer stepped toward him again. "You don't shove a girl," he yelled.

I placed my hand on Sawyer's chest to calm him. Ben would take more punches to the face before he would ever stop. I didn't want to watch, "Please Ben, just go home," I pleaded.

Sawyer stepped in front of me like a protective pit bull.

"Do you want to be with him?" Ben yelled.

I didn't know how to answer the question. It was way too soon for me to air my desires to the world when I was still trying to figure it all out myself, but Ben would not leave without an answer.

I stepped out from behind the protective shield of Sawyer and lightly touched his arm to signal I would be okay. I walked over to Ben and rubbed his face, still red from getting hit. Avery and Casey huddled around Riley. Ben calmed down for a moment as I spoke softly.

"I loved you once, and I won't forget any of it. But you left, and my eyes opened to something new. I don't know what the future holds, but I get to navigate it my way," I told him.

"You need me, not him or anyone else," he said, and his eyes welled up with tears as he tried to draw me in.

All this time, I couldn't figure out why he was always so confused, but his alcohol and drug use created a double life, one with extreme highs and hopes for new opportunities and one with devastating lows layered in guilt and remorse.

I backed away. "That's just it, Ben. This whole time I thought you were keeping me together, and in reality, it was me keeping you whole," I told him. I had to let go.

With a growl, Ben lunged at Sawyer again. They rolled around in the grass, thumping at one another. Suddenly, Luke sprinted into the alleyway. He dove down to pull them apart. Riley was back swinging at me but was ripped backward.

"Aggie?" I yelled, regaining my footing.

Aggie tossed Riley onto the ground behind her. "Grow up and get the hell out of here," Aggie yelled over her. "Go home now."

Riley sniffled, wiping away tears from her reddened face. Her friends collected their accessories that had flown off during the scuffle bitching as they headed back toward the street. I glared at Fitzly, who was just standing and watching Luke pull everyone apart.

"Go, help!" I fumed.

Fitzly bounced on his feet and then went in, trying to pull Luke and Ben back so Sawyer could break free. He was sloppy and uncoordinated but able to put enough of himself in the mix that Luke could control Ben.

"You want to go whore around, have at it." Ben tripped over himself, flinging nasty comments in my direction as Luke tried to restrain him.

Sawyer went in for more blows, but Luke stepped in front of Ben, willing to take a hit for his old friend. Harper inserted herself and yanked Sawyer away from the chaos. Luke dragged Ben up toward the street.

I waited and watched Ben and Luke move away. I couldn't help Ben anymore. He had to help himself first. His problems only compounded mine. With all the realizations, my shattered heart still ached to be healed. But could it?

Sawyer startled me with the slightest touch around my waist. He buried his head in the side of my neck, his breath pulsating against my skin.

I closed my eyes, thankful he was here with me. I would need his armor tonight. But I needed to move slowly. My attraction to him was mostly physical, but it gave me hope that I would one day experience genuine love again. I buckled slightly with images of Mason and Jack. Had I been too rough on my mom? I struggled with heartbreak for months. My mom had been dealing with it for years. Maybe she longed for hope too.

Aggie was suddenly standing in front of Sawyer and me; arms crossed, nervously tapping her foot, dressed in a short beaded and fringed flapper dress with a matching headband. I squinted.

"Why are you dressed circa 1920?"

She pressed her hands firmly onto her hips. "I thought you said it was a roaring 20's party," she barked back.

I shook my head in amazement, "I said no such thing. And anyway, where have you been?" I returned.

She twiddled on the beads of her dress. "I've been here for a few hours."

"Where? You don't even have a mask. I would've seen you."

"Maybe you were too caught up with Sawyer," she spoke to me like a child. I was aware from experience that conversations never ended well when she started crossing the line over and into my personal life.

I scowled at her while I thought of something to say, but then my phone chimed with a text from Kate. She was leaving. Her texts were usually short, but this time there was so much to scroll through. I turned away to read all of it.

"Oh God," I said out loud.

"What is it?" asked Sawyer.

Within seconds, all of them circled me.

"My mom collapsed inside."

"Is she okay?" Aggie's tone changed to one of genuine concern.

"I don't know." Kate rambled on in her text. I was motionless.

The sound from an ambulance siren soared loudly.

"I need to go," I said, dashing up the alley toward the street.

Partygoers emerged from the exit in hordes. They all followed, rushing with me toward the front steps. I reached up onto my tiptoes when the crowd out front parted. A man dressed in a red velvet suit coat carried my mom out of the theater and down its grand steps.

"Who's the guy?" asked Sawyer.

I didn't know. I pushed to get through, but the crowd was so thick, I never made it to my mom or the ambulance. I saw Kate hop in with them, but not before glancing out at the staring mob.

Then, the man in the red mask lifted it and off his head as he leaned in to console my mother before they placed her in the ambulance. He said a few words, caressed her hand, and then moved through the crowd and away from the theater.

SPENCER K. PRESCOTT

"It's Jack," I stuttered.

"Who?" asked Sawyer.

My stomach knotted, "A friend of my mom's."

I braced my temples in my hands. The people, music, and lights were all closing in on me. Sawyer drew back. High-pitched laughter pierced my ears and my heart. I breathed through pursed lips as Aggie and Sawyer began fighting again. Harper brushed them both aside.

"Seriously, not the time for you two to squabble," she said.

The crowds scattered their way back indoors, and Harper led me back down to the quiet alley. "Don't let the panic set in; you got this. Just breathe," she said.

I handed her my phone. "Ask Kate if I should come?"

Harper took over texting for me. A few quick dings and Harper responded, "Kate wants you to stay with your friends. She doesn't think it's serious. She'll call you."

The grip around my lungs released. I remembered what Kate told me this morning and wondered if she was right. Maybe the change tonight was merely a long-awaited night out for a new me, new friends, a crush, and an overdue, solid goodbye to Ben.

CHAPTER 27

WITCHES' WALKWAY

I placed my phone back in my pocket, but it clanged against the stone the mayor had been scrambling for. I showed it to Harper. She held it up under the spotlight that shone down through the alley, revealing a tiny symbol similar to the letter *F*. Back by the street, Aggie and Sawyer argued. Fitzly did his best to intervene.

"What are they arguing about?" I asked Harper, without taking my eyes off Aggie reprimanding Sawyer.

"You, I guess," she smiled.

I didn't agree with her. They fought like old acquaintances still hashing out an unresolved conflict. But how could they know each other?

Harper released the small, flat gold stone into the air towards my open palm when another hand in a gold-laced glove reached in and ripped it from me. Harper and I moved only our eyes. It was the masked goat stepping backward, a stone clutched in its grip. It shook one finger at us, and then slowly retreated back into the exit door.

Harper leaned in, "Who or what the hell was that?" she whispered. We didn't take our eyes off the mysterious drifter who disappeared back inside.

The door slammed shut. "I saw that person earlier tonight, watching me. The goat apparently wanted that stone as much as the mayor," I replied.

We turned toward each other. Harper's sweat was replaced with a cold shiver. Rain slowly fell down upon us. I thought it was mascara running down her face as I reached up to wipe her cheek. It wasn't, it was sand, the same black grit from the portal in Connecticut.

"They're here," Harper mouthed.

The warm mix of sand and rain fell upon us, our hair, and down our clothes. Sawyer, Aggie, and Fitzly looked up and trotted first toward Main and then back down by us.

"It's everywhere," Fitzly said with a sense of urgency as he held his palm up to the sky, collecting it in his hand.

Sawyer nodded. "The partygoers out front are dancing in it. They think it's part of the festivities—a trick of some sort."

"One hell of a trick," I uttered. "And seriously, is this whole town becoming a portal? There wasn't this much in Connecticut!"

Lighting shot through the sky. Thunder bellowed.

"Maybe it is," stuttered Fitzly.

This was it; this was how this night would change us all. I closed my eyes and scrolled through every memory I had in a matter of seconds. My life flashed before me, I took a deep breath and then welcomed and accepted my new reality.

Harper yelled. "There!"

My eyes snapped open. Without explaining, Harper pointed down the alley and then sprinted and disappeared into the darkness. We followed her to an overlook deck and a set of stairs descending into the woods surrounding the river.

"Where are we?" asked Sawyer as we stood atop the observation deck with Harper nowhere in sight.

The only light radiated from a restaurant on the opposite side overlooking the water. Fierce swooshes of rushing water crashing on rocks replaced the fading sirens. Broken and splintered wooden boards that once blocked the stairs now lay at our feet.

I was yelling back over my shoulder to the others while trying to spot Harper.

"Down here," Harper yelled up. The warm sand falling into the cold water created a thick rising fog from below. I paused and then trotted down the slick steps to warn her.

"Harper, stop! Wait for the others," I pleaded, out of breath, holding onto her arm, and then using it to prop myself upright.

The other three joined us, sliding down the steps together.

Sawyer held out his hand in a stopping motion, in Harper's face. "Don't move until Abby tells us where we're headed."

I paused, carefully choosing my words. I was worried but needed to be honest. "The path along the river dead-ends into a tunnel. The tunnel connects the Falls with Hunting Valley," I said.

"So?" said Harper.

"The river flows through the tunnel known as Witches' Walkway. In the early 1800s, witches inhabited the Creek. The town tried to hunt them down to burn them at the stake, but on All Hallow's Eve night, the coven gathered up their belongings, ran through town, down the steps, and disappeared into the tunnel. They cast a spell to dry up the water, long enough to make it through to the other side. Once in and over, the tunnel filled again. The townspeople never went in after them, fearful of what might be on the other side."

Lighting shot across the sky. With every glance, I could see the hint of a wing or the fierce glow of red eyes.

I yelled loud over the crashing roar of the falls.

"The story didn't end there," I went on. "The witches set up a colony beyond the safety of the tunnel that lies ahead. Those that walked through transformed and pledged their souls to the coven. It was the beginning of the Valley, and those witches were the founding mothers. The city council boarded up the steps years ago to stop anyone from coming down here."

Fitzly stepped over and tossed his hands up at Harper, "Why did you run down here?"

"An apparition drifted down this path," Harper replied.

"Okay, since when do we chase apparitions?" he shouted, but no one answered.

The rushing water and falling rain continued to drown out our voices. I was barely listening to any more of their remarks. All I could see was Nova's note, "On Hallow's Eve, don't let the costumes fool you. The ones who hide will now be front and center. Follow and find the answers you seek." And all I could hear was the sound of the voice I heard inside, "Follow her."

She was front and center. I made a quick decision to support Harper, "If we continue on this path, it will lead us to the tunnel. We all need to make a choice on how far we will go," I said.

I motioned toward the deep black cloud and light show above. "And they're coming too! We can't just stand here and debate. We have to make a move."

"Oh, this is it for me," Fitzly asserted.

"Then, why did you come?" Harper snarled at him, taking steps along the overgrown path, deeper into the woods. But he didn't give a response. "We didn't meet each other by coincidence. Something brought us together and is guiding us in a direction … this direction." Harper pointed forcefully into the darkness. "I'm tired of the dreams, the voices, and the headaches. I want to be free from whomever or whatever has their grips on all of us. If you want to go back and be a prisoner to this thing, then go. If not, then please just stop talking," she yelled.

Harper's demeanor had changed since our visit out to Connecticut. She couldn't run anymore, and she was finally willing to face whatever it was haunting all of us, and so was I.

"I'm with Harper," I announced.

Aggie stepped forward, glancing at Sawyer and then at me. "What is Harper talking about? Who has a clutch on you?" she asked.

At that moment, I forgot that Aggie was not aware of anything that recently happened, and I wasn't interested in suddenly sharing. While we waited for Fitzly to decide, I had an idea.

"Fitzly, maybe you don't want to take this path, but I could still use your help," I said.

"What is it?" he asked cautiously. He wouldn't like my idea, but it was better than him sneaking around in a dark forest.

I pulled him over to the side away from Aggie and spoke quietly and quickly. "I need you to go to the library. Upstairs is an archive room with the historical records of Allison Creek *and* Hunting Valley. Once the Valley was abandoned, the mayor had all the documents transferred over here. Find out who used to own the land and who owns it now."

He tilted his head back, covered his face with hands, and mumbled incoherently.

"You said you want to learn more about the Danwer Tower. It will all be in that room. Look, it's either there," I pointed back up towards the light in the alley, "or the woods."

He thought for a minute and walked a few feet back toward town. I clapped my hands for an answer following behind. He stopped.

"What about Aggie?" he asked, rolling his eyes over to her impatiently rubbing her hands.

"She doesn't know what's going on. I'll make up something. Just follow my lead and lose her when you're in the library."

I stepped back from Fitzly and gave Harper a wink.

"Take Fitzly and head to the town library," I said to Aggie. "Harper left her bag inside, and she needs it back before Mr. Vincent finds it in the morning."

Aggie groaned. "What? Why me?"

I walked close to her.

"Harper is under a lot of pressure. She's a little manic right now because she left her purse with special personal belongings in the library. She doesn't need Mr. Vincent to find it and I can't sneak her in there. She's too loud and agitated right now. You know the layout of the town and the library better than Fitzly, and I would rather you go in pairs."

"And how should we get in?" she snapped sarcastically.

"Go down the back alley behind it. The backdoor has a lockbox on it. The code is 1212."

"Why do you have the code to the library?" asked Aggie.

"The old librarian used to be my mom's teacher when she was in middle school. My mom volunteered there when she was older, and sometimes I would go with her. It was how we entered the building and how we locked it up," I explained.

"You don't think it's been changed?"

"No. How many people sneak into libraries?" I barked. We were running out of time.

Aggie wasn't happy, but I needed to get rid of her, and I was sure there were items I missed in the archives. Fitzly had a knack for detail, and he was better off in an old building than tripping over us out here.

"Send Sawyer with him," Aggie urged.

Sawyer snapped back. "What? No way. And leave two girls here in the woods? Nope; sorry, Aggie, you go."

Aggie crossed her arms tight across her chest, "And what are you three going to do other than lurk around in the dark?"

Everyone stared at me for the answer.

"Umm," I cleared my throat, "Harper thought she saw something, and she needs to see for herself that it was nothing. We will stay with her, and as soon as she is convinced, we will come back. Right, Harper?"

I glanced over at Harper, who stood casually nodding in agreement.

With that, Sawyer took a few steps with Fitzly, his hand over his shoulder, whispering in his ear. He patted him on the back and motioned for Aggie to go with him.

"And watch out for Pepper?" I included, which Fitzly didn't appreciate by the look on his face.

"Not even going to ask," he said. "Come on, Aggie."

They hesitantly turned away and faded into the darkness; Aggie nagging him until they disappeared into the fog.

"Thanks," said Harper, grinning. "Which way now?"

I pointed toward an overgrown path that ran along the bank of the river. "We follow it, I guess, to the tunnel. Never been there, so I don't know how long it will take," I replied.

"I'm going first," said Sawyer, who moved up ahead with Harper. I followed behind.

The trees stretched high as we moved ahead, forming a canopy that protected us from the rain. Tiny droplets of water trickled off the dying leaves. Thunder rumbled after every flash of light from above.

Every few feet, Sawyer yelled back a question.

"What else do you know?" he asked.

"The tunnel leads so deep in the woods that no human has ever entered and lived to talk about the other side," I yelled, while navigating through the maze of tree branches, sticks and mud.

"What happened when the witches moved from the Creek to the Valley?" he asked next.

"The witches came out only at night for supplies. The Creekers locked up and never left their homes after dark," I yelled.

Harper chimed in. "Where did the witches disappear to?"

"Who said they disappeared?" I added.

We slowed. The narrow river we followed opened toward an expansive tunnel, much broader and darker than I had imagined.

"I'm out of shape," Harper gasped. She narrowed her eyes at me. "How do you know all this?"

I was winded too, clutching the cramp in my side, and I was cold from the early winter chill and wet clothes. It was after midnight, and our only light source was the moon and our fading phone batteries. I was also tired of being the resource manual but did my best to answer what I could.

"I literally just read a book about the haunting history of the Creek and the Valley. It was full of macabre stories and eyewitness encounters with evil. I don't know if it's true, but with each step I take, I am finding it frighteningly credible," I said.

"Perfect," Harper and Sawyer responded in unison. They were, for the moment, out of questions.

Harper moved forward, holding up the flashlight from her phone. It illuminated a giant stone tunnel with vines snaked over it. Rotted pieces of wood were stacked haphazardly across the opening, with two large signs preventing anyone from entering.

DANGER
KEEP OUT

The water from the Creek flowed fast after the rain. It moved through the tunnel, splashing water and crashing onto the broken boards. Giant natural sandstone steps lined the edge of the Creek, creating a platform for us to safely stand on for the moment.

Graffiti in various colors covered the exposed stone over the archway of the tunnel. Pentagrams and "666" in bold red paint protruded in a 3D-like effect. The sight chilled my bones. I understood why only witches walked through. Pure souls were stolen here.

A faint laugh echoed through the tunnel. Harper yanked on the planks, peeling the wood off like stickers from a book. Sawyer pitched in to help, trying not to lose his footing on the slippery rock. Something fluttered by my face. I waved madly and fell into Sawyer.

The laugh grew louder and wrapped around us before escaping up and into the trees. My skin stung from the cold water that splashed up from the river. My senses were overwhelmed as the voices of Harper and Sawyer became garbled and distant. I swallowed the rock that sat in my throat. A long silhouette of a female appeared deep in the tunnel. With her hand up, she used her pointer finger and motioned for us to come. Slowly, she moved it back and forth like a parent summoning her child. The water dried up around her.

Harper jumped down to the bed where the water once flowed.

"It's unholy," yelled Sawyer. He tightened his grip around me and then whispered. "You said earlier we all needed to know how far we would go. You don't have to do this," he urged.

I released myself from Sawyer's grasp and then placed my hands on his cheeks. I was going to kiss him but didn't. Instead, I held his cold face in my hands. My heart dropped into my stomach. I couldn't. I didn't want to.

"This is the beginning," I said, pulled away, jumped down into the dry bed, and ran toward Harper. We entered the tunnel and turned to look at Sawyer. Sawyer was miles away from us.

Harper grabbed my hand. "We have to go alone."

I squeezed her hand harder. "We have each other."

CHAPTER 28

LUCA

My lip quivered as we stood at the base of the tunnel without Sawyer. I watched the outline of his silhouette fade into the atmosphere, fearing why the boy who spent his life protecting Harper would not step foot onto this ground. Why did he not do more to stop us? Was this being on the other side affecting him, controlling him? My core shook from the inside with absolute dread.

Harper and I shared another glance and a firm squeeze of our hands. A tiny part of me felt secure, the other, questioned why I followed. She drew herself in, close to my face.

"The way I see it, we can either run through fast and get out on the other side or take our time and drag this out." There was no correct answer, but I was immediately aware of her decision.

She bolted forward first, pulling me behind until I conjured the speed and courage to catch up. An invisible force was slowing us down. I shined the light from my phone low. I didn't want to see too far ahead, but Harper shone her light on the walls. Various sized letters in different colors of dark paints spelled out the name "ALLISON" on every exposed inch of stone. It was on the walls, on the ceiling, and down to the rock bed. I choked on my spit as the lurid letters bled downward.

Harper's pace slowed as she spun and walked at the same time. "Who's Allison?"

I stared intently at the name, remembering Nova's comments. I whispered them out loud.

"Allison called me back?"

"What?" snapped Harper.

I turned to her and mouthed the short version of Nova's reason for returning to the Creek.

"You're joking?" she asked.

"No," I whispered.

Harper's light blinded my eyes as she swung her phone around frantically.

"Stop," I said, trying to refocus. Harper placed her finger up by her mouth, begging me to be quiet. She placed her hand by her ear. A soft swishing sound was coming from behind us. Water splashed against my boots. We lowered our lights to the riverbed. "Water!" I screamed.

"It's coming back, run." Harper emphasized "run" with a growl in her voice. The sound of our screams echoed off the walls.

Harper and I darted through the winding tunnel with the rushing of the river closing in on us. Its fierce energy threatened to suck us under to our deaths. Harper made it out first, leaping up to a rock and pulling me with her. The water roared past us like rapids. We fell upon the flat rocks gasping for air. Trembling, I wondered if we had just entered the colony of witches who founded the Valley and if Allison was waiting for us somewhere in the darkness. I shuddered to think whether we would ever make it back or had we just given up our souls for a life of craft. Harper pointed up.

The sky glowed in various shades of red, with black clouds moving fast over the trees. An orange and yellow moon cast light down, allowing us some visual of the realm we entered. We crawled along, careful not to slip into the river. We followed the bed until it opened up into a giant, calm lake with a light haze hovering over the water. In the middle sat a little cabin with smoke billowing out from a chimney on the roof. Behind it was a dense forest of weeping trees and hanging moss that stroked the earth with every gust of wind.

My phone dinged as if I had a message. But it was empty, just a green bubble with no words. Harper's did too as she held it up for me to see.

"Call Sawyer," I nervously requested.

Harper fumbled some more with her phone. "Can't; no signal. My phone is frozen," she said.

We were too stuck without any idea of the next steps, aware the female spirit was watching, laughing, and waiting.

"You see a boat anywhere?" I joked. It wasn't the time, but my nervous energy was desperate to feel anything but fear.

Harper glowered at my comment. She stood and walked on the rocks that created a large perimeter around the lake. Her mask and feathers were still propped up on her head. Despite how well our costumes fit in with the backdrop, she noticed my stare and promptly tore it off her head and launched it into the water.

"Where are you going?" I voiced, but she didn't answer; I followed.

We walked roughly one hundred yards when the cabin came into full view. There, in the front door, a woman stood waving us over.

"Does she think we can walk on water?" Harper moaned.

"Maybe we can," I reasoned.

Harper rolled her eyes, thinking it was another bad joke, but it wasn't.

I bent over, watching the rippling reflection of myself. Past my worried eyes lay nothing but a bed of pebbles. I stepped down carefully into several inches of water then smiled back up at Harper. I ambled toward the cabin. With each step, the clear water never raised higher than mid-boot. Halfway there, Harper joined me and we walked onto the island together.

The cries of two hawks gliding overhead and around the lake caught my attention before they flew off, disappearing into the clouds. Wings fluttered around me. I swung and then noticed several solid onyx butterflies maneuvering in an erratic pattern before settling on a wrought iron fence with black finials. A porch swing wavered in the wind, while the front door sat wide open. A light smoke meandered out the half-open windows with the smell of sage and mint leaping off each droplet.

A voiced drifted in on a soft breeze.

"You found your way. What took you so long?" she asked.

I expected a harsh greeting, but it was welcoming, with the slightest hint of an English accent.

"I'm Luca; come in." I guess it wasn't Allison after all, but her name came with little relief.

In the doorway, a young woman appeared. She was not a ghost. Her skin porcelain white with platinum blonde hair pulled up into a tight, pointy tail that broke out into narrowly pointed dreadlocks in the back. Black gemstones glistened above her brows, and star-shaped stones adorned the skin under her eyes and above her cheeks. A thick onyx tattoo ran from her left shoulder down into a black form-fitting tank top and a flowing full-length black skirt. Two knives with cream-colored handles hung from a leather waist belt that sat low on her hips.

"Come in. I won't bite, but one request," she said, pointing at both of us. Her arms, adorned with silver bracelets in the shape of skeleton hands, swayed as she moved. "No screaming, or you will scare my birds."

She retreated inside. Her movements and mannerisms smooth but chilling.

Her words did little to reassure me. Maybe she wouldn't bite, but stabbing us was fair game. Harper and I walked in, barely fitting through the narrow entry.

We entered one large, rustic, and eerie room lit by hundreds of candles. Intricately carved cow and ram skulls painted black, red, or silver hung on the walls. I shuddered and turned my view away from the hollowed-out eyes that tracked our movements.

A deep purple area rug covered much of the floor. To the right was a stone fireplace with a blazing fire. Copper bowls in various sizes hung from iron hooks lodged deep into the mantle. A red velvet couch trimmed in dark wood sat close to a desk near the back wall with a large matching velvet chair behind it. Along the walls hung a tiered sword, knife, and ax rack with a variety of colored and elaborately designed handles. Eccentric gold birdcages housing one blackbird each sat in the corners, their caws more like human shrieks.

"Quiet," she snapped, slapping her veined hands together. Her giant rings of creatures with ruby red eyes clanged as she clapped at them a second time. The birds went silent.

"Do you like my home?" she enunciated as she spoke, then walked to one of the cages and placed her slender fingers in to lightly rub the top of one of the birds. We nervously watched each of the birds take notice of us with their deep black eyes while she talked to them like children.

We elbowed each other, fighting over who would speak when Harper offered, "Comforting," trying to control the tone of her voice.

Luca was unimpressed with her answer but then turned her attention on our dress. "You Creekers," she laughed, "you spend all year being good little humans; then, one night, you all dress up and pretend to be dark and powerful."

Her comments didn't make sense to me. I understood enough about the holiday that dressing up was intended to hide among the evil that walked on earth, not to share in it. But Luca disagreed.

"Please, Halloween gives you the chance to taste what it's like to be dark, dabble in it, and then energies like me sort you out and pick the good ones, or bad ones, I guess. You could be a bad one, Abby. It's in you."

"No, thank you," I politely offered.

A second figure appeared from the shadows near a set of stairs. My heartbeat pulsated in my throat. He was slender and tall with olive skin and deep black eyes, short, dark spiky hair, and silver disks in his lobes. An intricate solid black tattoo wrapped around his neck and spread to his bare chest, disappearing under a pair of tight black shorts before running down his legs to his bare feet. Any un-tattooed skin was covered in black soot. He glared at us and swayed over to a tall wooden chair the female sank into beside the roaring fireplace. He rubbed her back, played with her hair, and kissed her neck passionately. We stood, watching, sharing uncomfortable glances until the female had enough of his constant touching.

"Stop," she said as she pushed him back slightly, and then rubbed his head down to his neck, leaving her left hand resting on his shoulder. "Look at them. What do you see?" she asked him.

He lightly bit her left ear before whispering softly into it. Her response to him was an exaggerated laugh.

"You're both so brave coming here without protection," she declared.

"Who would protect us from you?" Harper quipped.

"Well, the boy and the girl, right?" Luca sat with her right elbow up on the chair. Her thumb rubbed the tips of each of her fingers as she spoke.

Was she referring to Sawyer? Who was the girl? Was this just part of her game? Harper and I stood still with flat expressions. I couldn't speak when I was still struggling to understand where we were.

"Oh, you don't know; that's cute. Well, let's move on then, shall we? I can't make everything easy for you," she said, her accent growing thicker. *Easy?* I thought. She enjoyed this game.

It was evident she was running the conversation, but Harper and I had questions that needed answers. I had to choose wisely, though. She wouldn't give us an endless amount of tries. Thoughts scurried around in my head and then I finally asked. "Why did you follow me to Connecticut, and who are you?"

"Wow, you cut right to the chase. I grow more impressed with you each minute. A straight question deserves a straight answer," she said.

Her posture was rigid, while her left hand stroked the shoulders of the man kneeling next to her. His eyes half-closed, he welcomed the touch. His body moved back and forth, resembling a cat rubbing against the legs of its owner.

"I didn't follow you to Connecticut. That was someone else. But I have kept my eye on you. You all have something that belongs to me," she said.

"We don't have anything of yours," I responded politely, gulping down my spit and all the alcohol and fruit juice rising up from my stomach.

"Your families do," she said nodding.

"Our families ... I don't have family," scoffed Harper, but Luca ignored her and kept her attention on me.

"Oh, come on, girls. I've left you enough clues. Abby, be the smart, cunning Anderson you were born to be," she went on.

The sound of my last name so delicately leaving her lips caused me to step backward. I crossed my arms over my stomach and clutched the fabric of my costume in my hands. Images of the four pieces of paper and the shield from the book flashed before my eyes. The identity of its creator was revealed.

"The papers. That was you?"

"Ding, ding, ding. You didn't like my game?" she asked. "I know it was simple, but I didn't want this taking forever. We're all on borrowed time."

Her horrifying houseboy caressed her skin while she squirmed, "Follow me, children," The flames from the fireplace grew large. I wiped my brow.

"Just tell us," Harper stated assertively, "what makes you think I want to follow you?"

I cringed and closed my eyes, waiting for Luca's response to Harper's disobedience.

"No," she barked back. "I make the rules. If you want to know why you are here, then follow me or leave." At that moment, the fresh screams and the haunting laughter of women entered from all of the open windows. Images of witches running through the forest clouded my head and brought more terror. In Connecticut, we were surrounded by demons; here it was witches, and soon we would learn why we were stuck in between.

Luca quickly rose. Her bare feet moved to the back of the cabin with her man in tow. We followed her outside to a covered patio, steps tentative. I begged Harper, quietly, not to piss her off again.

Luca pointed to the back yard. "Kensey," she said, looking at the man who stood to wait for her direction, "shine the light."

Kensey grabbed an oil lamp off a tattered wooden table, turning the knob and illuminating the glass. He walked out into the darkness and cast his light on three small wooden staffs that curved upward into a hook. From the hook hung antlers and rib bones, clanking together like a grotesque animal-made wind chime.

"Are those graves?" I whispered.

"Yes," said Harper, "and I hope they're not for us."

As Luca stared out over the graves, she paced back and forth, not once looking at us while she spoke.

"There lie the bodies of three Ackerly babies, all sadly stillborn. The end result of a curse placed on their family hundreds of years ago. Haddie Ackerly, was a preacher's daughter living in a small community in Massachusetts in the mid-1600s. Their family neighbored another family that had three young girls. The youngest, a little girl named Lilianna, had a mental ailment so severe that she was deemed a witch by Haddie. But Haddie had other motives. See, Lilianna had a brother Michael who was deeply in love with Haddie's sister, Grace. Grace returned his love, not knowing that Haddie hoped to marry him one day herself. Her jealousy of her sister and her hate toward Michael led to this horrific accusation and revenge that ended with Lilianna, a young, innocent child, burning at the stake," said Luca.

She spoke sharply, taking little breaks to chuckle at inappropriate times. Goosebumps spread down my cold arms. Her brief history lesson matched one from Nova's book. I hid my shock in my shaking core. The hawks returned. Their caws mixed with the slight howl from an unknown animal. The noise emanated from deep in the woods. Luca paced dramatically, sharing the most haunting pieces of her story while I focused my gaze on the three graves.

"Haddie wanted to run the family out of town so that her sister and Michael could no longer see each other. It was the worst plan that got an innocent, beloved child murdered," Luca said and dropped her head and went silent. Kensey fell to her feet, embracing her leg, burying his head into her thigh.

"I still don't understand what this has to do with us," Harper inquired.

"Of course not; you should listen more than speak." She picked up a stick, snapped it in half, and tossed it out into the field.

I punched Harper in the side. "Knock it off," I pleaded.

Luca took a brief kiss from Kensey before proceeding.

"Lillianna had a sister named Clare who left the Village and traveled west deep into the woods. There, Clare learned a true form of witchcraft from a black magic priestess, Goddess Seraphine," Luca went on.

Her hands flew into the air as flames drew up from the ground illuminating the gravesites below. The heat from the fire warmed our damp skin, the light providing a visual of the evil that surrounded us. We remained frozen like scared children listening to a ghost story around a campfire.

"Clare returned to her home village on the first anniversary and set a curse in motion that ended with the deaths of three tiny souls that once belonged to Haddie."

"So those are the bodies of Haddie's babies?" I stuttered.

"Yes," she simply stated.

"How did they end up here?" I asked.

Luca walked and stood over the graves. "Haddie was pregnant at the time of the curse and fled into the woods by herself and delivered her first stillborn here. Two more pregnancies ended the same. Talk about imposing on someone's property, right?" she said with a sarcastic laugh.

"In the end, Haddie lost her entire family and her sanity before dying herself. She made a pact with the devil that day. She wants revenge and the curse broken so she can rule by the devil's side with her three boys," Luca continued.

I stepped forward, still stuttering, "Please. What does this have to do with us?"

She turned back towards us and slowly walked over while speaking. "Oh, dear, that's so much more polite. Thank you," her words and movements layered in incredible sarcasm, but the end result was finally a response to our question. "She wants to destroy us all."

The words settled deep in my soul. We weren't just being haunted, we were being hunted.

Harper's voice broke. "Why?"

"I have her babies, of course, and a power that she wants and needs to be Hell's Queen. I don't need the devil; I can run my own Kingdom. They both want me gone, but I need my shield to protect my coven and myself. And the curious little cats in your families took it," she said as she stomped her leg like a child whose toy had been stolen.

But this was no toddler's game. I was still confused.

"Are you the Black Magic Priestess?" I immediately worried my question would offend her. I braced myself and squeezed Harper's arm as we waited for her response. The cackles of thousands of witches surrounded us. Her jaw was tight.

"I'm something to be feared. I fight for my followers, but I need my shield," she said, speaking slower and enunciating every syllable.

"Why should we help you?" asked Harper, stepping back from the growing sounds in the woods and the piercing stares from Kensey.

Luca's neck snapped in our direction as she walked over to the porch. Kensey moved ahead of her and shined the light up into our eyes, waving it back and forth before like a pendulum so she could get a good look at our eyes as she spoke.

"If Haddie destroys me, she will destroy your beloved earth as well. You must help, or the ground you walk on every day will turn to dust, and not even a heaven will exist for you to retreat to when you die. The hope you all believe in will be dead," Luca said firmly.

The man leaped up onto the porch, scurried over to us, smelling us from our hair down to our wrists. Luca swayed herself back over and grabbed two leather wraps attached to a metal chain that hung on the back wall of the house. She handed the one end to Kensey then yanked him closer to her. "I need the girls," she let go of the chains, "retrieve the boys."

She summoned us back into the cabin with a few hand gestures, away from the woods' horrific sounds.

Kensey hissed over his shoulder, prompting us to slow. The birds cawed and thrashed about in their cages, intensifying our fear.

Luca pointed out the front door. "You should go now, find my shield and leave it at the entrance to the tunnel. You're running out of time."

Harper and I slithered past Kensey, who sat on all fours like an animal glaring at our every move. He lunged forward, causing me to fall back into a closet door. A sharp, burning pain radiated through my palm, and I let out a high-itched cry, startling the birds. Their wail reverberated through my bones. I pulled out a sewing needle that pierced my skin and tossed it into the closet as the door was slowly opening. Gritting my teeth in pain, I tried to stand with Harper's help. Luca pulled back Kensey, reprimanding him to sit and stay. I paused, noticing something in the closet.

Darkness penetrated my soul with images from Ben's phone whirling inside. "Oh my God!" I said under my breath.

I grabbed the candle from a nearby shelf and held it up. A large white doll with long blond hair hung on the wall. I cautiously reached forward, running my fingers through the coarse, dry strands. Luca snickered, "It's real."

I yanked my hand away, and stepped back. The light from the wick swayed and grew large, revealing a spiral stone staircase leading under the cabin. How would I explain this to Ben? I turned toward Luca, who stood proud in the shadows of the candlelight. A low, dull chant echoed up from below. The floor shook; Luca stood smug then moved in closer, invading my personal space, but I spoke first. "It was you? Why?"

"I'm sorry, I didn't mean for you to be blamed, but the Creek and its surrounding land was mine before it was anyone else's. It's amazing what humans will sacrifice for money and power. Unfortunately, Mayor Quartano needed a reminder of who is in charge. I told you, Abby, humans can't resist what evil sometimes offers."

She reached over to a small rickety wood table, digging through a bowl of stones and shiny round objects. She separated them until she found one she wanted. Then she held it up and flipped it over to me with her thumb. It spun in the air before landing in the palm of my bleeding hand.

"The rune of good fortune?" she enunciated, rolling the R's off her tongue. "Would you like to keep it? The mayor already has a few."

Her dark, almond-shaped eyes with specks of burgundy, red, and orange penetrated mine. I fixated on the tiny gemstones that highlighted her face and glistened in the candlelight. She closed my fingers over the stone with hers. The stone seared my small wound with a hot flash. A mix of energy and intense emotion traveled up my arm. Hate, passion, anger, lust, greed, anguish shot through my limbs, tearing at my insides. Luca squeezed hard, "You're connecting, and your roots are tangled but spreading. You crave a strong foundation, and I can give that to you."

I suffered through and then slowly turned my hand over hers, dropping it back into her palm. I swallowed the burn then noticed a scar wrapping around her forearm. I remembered the book and the photo. Heat surged through my body.

"Abby, your eyes are so red. Go with it," she whispered.

I exhaled slowly, steadying my soul. "No," I hesitantly replied.

She shook her head. "The pain will change you, too."

Harper grabbed my arm, pulling me away from Luca, but I struggled to take my eyes off her as we approached the door. The birds were screeching, and the wolf-like creatures howled as she pushed it open to the outside.

"Wait," I shoved Harper off. I stepped back over the threshold into Luca's space. I stood tall and spoke without fear. "How does Haddie break the curse?"

259

Luca ordered Kensey back to his feet and then she disappeared through two wooden doors near the back of the room. He brandished a short, shiny knife that sat strapped to his shorts and spun it in the light, staring intensely into his reflection. With a malicious voice and a creepy giggle, he screeched, "By spilling the blood of a baby."

"A descendant's baby," Luca clarified, returning with a large headdress of feathers resting upon her head. Her dreadlock ponytail sat high, blending in with the long black feathers that flowed down to her shoulders. Two ram horns sat low and curved down over her ears. She adjusted it. "It was Haddie and her army of demons that followed you to Connecticut. She is waiting for the baby! Go! I've told you enough."

As she moved toward us, I caught a glimpse of what was behind the two open doors. Above a substantial altar full of various jars, plants, and candles hung a sizable dark piece of fabric with a moon in the center and scripted writing displayed beneath. It was the same picture I found in the library. It wasn't just a moon; it was where her shield once hung. Luca moved over to it and held up her arms as if she was her holding the shield above her head. She glanced over her shoulder and reminded us one last time, "I want it back."

Harper dragged me outside under a darker blood-red sky. The wind roared, slamming the cabin door behind us and creating small waves in the shallow lake. The howl we heard from the back now approached from the sides, where two tall wolf-like creatures stood. Their coats were reddish-brown like a fox, with long legs and a black mane. Their large ears turned with the slightest movement by Harper or me. The one tapped its front foot hard into the brush.

"It's time we go," Harper urged.

There was only one direction.

"I agree," I said and pointed ever so slightly out into the woods, not wanting to turn my back. Harper squinted.

"What?"

Witches dressed in black cloaks with hoods were layered along the tree line. They clung to the trees under each veil of moss. Their lower bodies contorted and blended in with the peeling bark of each trunk. Pale faces and dark circles for eyes watched us intensely. Then the young girl I saw in the Valley emerged from the trees. She giggled and danced under the canopy of leaves and twirled around a network of vines. My heart sank as the name "Allison" traveled through the air. It was Luca's voice calling for her.

Harper grabbed my hand. "We must go now!"

We drifted to the edge of the land, keeping the creatures in view while the onlookers slipped away into the darkness. Allison's spine-chilling belly laugh faded into the forest. The wolf-like animals moved next to one another and then ushered us toward the lake. They stopped at the edge. One growled low, and the other let out a high-pitched whine. I was taught not to run away from a predator, but they were closing in faster the slower we moved. We changed our pace and darted through the water, which was growing more violent with every step. I didn't turn around; I prayed that I wouldn't soon feel the searing pain of one of their jaws clamping down on my leg. A loud whistle called them back. We leaped up and onto the rock bed, safe for the moment. The view of the cabin and fierce creatures disappeared in a blanket of thick fog. The water in the lake rose and rushed toward us and through the tunnel leading back to the Creek.

"Now what?" I asked, winded and cold, my pulse out of control.

Harper covered her mouth and rubbed her face while she thought. She crouched and stretched, trying to view another way out. Stone and blackness surrounded us. I stepped over to a large piece of sandstone and turned to face Harper. I was taking charge.

"The current is heading back to town. We jump in and let it carry us through," I said, shouting over the rushing water's sound.

Harper was quick to respond. "Are you insane? We'll drown! The current's way too strong."

I understood her fear and her reasoning, but reassured her best I could. "Luca needs us; she brought us here, and she'll get us to the other side."

I didn't have time for her to talk me out of it. Without another word, I stood, held my arms into the air, took in as much breath as my lungs could hold, and fell backward into the cold, rushing water of the Creek.

CHAPTER 29

ENTANGLED SOULS

My body dropped at a rapid pace into the river. The current pummeled me. I thrashed my arms and legs as the powerful water pushed me through the tunnel until I fell to a depth where the water calmed. I opened my eyes to glimpses of light, making their way through the murky water. I dropped and arched as my muscles craved oxygen. Had I just sent us both to our deaths? Luca wouldn't let us die, she couldn't. A force from below pushed my body vigorously upward until my face broke through the rippling stream.

The current slammed my body up onto the rock. Sawyer yanked at my forearm and pulled me up on the ground. Spitting out water, I pointed toward the tunnel where I was hopeful Harper would emerge. Her head bobbed in the water. Sawyer reached in and yanked her out next to me. I turned on all fours, forcing the water from my airway and wiping the hair back from my eyes. With my breath louder than the wind, I collapsed back onto the sandstone.

Harper dragged herself over to me with Sawyer's help. I rolled to my back and noticed the blue sky and sun peeking through the trees. It was morning.

"What time is it?" I muttered.

Sawyer tended to Harper, patting her back as she forcefully coughed water from her lungs. "It's 8 a.m., I thought you both were dead!" he shouted.

How were we gone that long? It seemed like an hour, tops. "It couldn't be 8 a.m.," I said and sat up, tucking my head between my knees and hiding behind my wet, matted hair.

"You were, and I've been here the whole time, waiting. I sent you both texts." Sawyer's voice faded in and out as he moved between us. I recalled the empty green text bubbles on the phone now swimming in water in my jacket. I pulled it out and dropped it and its black screen to the ground.

Harper stretched up, waving her arms at us. "Be quiet, listen," she demanded.

The November wind whipped down over the water, carrying hundreds of chanting voices. The tone was low, and the pace slow as its volume grew. Sawyer spun around. I crawled toward Harper and gripped her sleeve.

"Is that what you heard at the church?" I lowered my voice to a whisper.

"Yes," Harper squirmed, and we both shivered in our cold, wet clothes.

"Let's go," commanded Sawyer. He helped us both up. We moved in a pack down the path and back up to the very spot this all started hours earlier. The haunting melody dissipated into the breeze. We shook and cowered.

"Where can we go?" asked Sawyer.

I pointed in a vague direction toward town. "To my store. It's across the street, down to the right," I said, stopping to catch my breath and take a view of the town that somehow didn't seem all that picturesque. Its history blanketed in dark secrets begged the question: who other than Quartano was manipulated by Luca?

The town sat empty of people. It was a far cry from the visual splendor offered the night before. Parade floats sat torn and wet on the ground. The bright-colored confetti now clung to the curb on each side of the street, piled up and dirty, waiting for the street cleaning crew to whisk it away. Even the magnificent theater seemed drab and not all that grand. Feathers, garlands, and streamers picked up by the wind jostled in front of our faces before falling to ground. I buckled at the smell of rain, alcohol, and puke, noticing the piles of black sand that surrounded storefronts.

We arrived at the store when I noticed someone inside. I was relieved to see Aggie and Fitzly as I remembered not having a key, but the low, full sound of a wind chime emanated from behind us. I directed my gaze across the street then froze in horror. I tugged on Harpers dress. Above the 1816 Tavern, a figure in a goat mask appeared in an open window. It fixated on us, before slowly drawing the curtain closed.

Alarmed, Harper shielded her face with her hair, "Why is the goat still in costume?"

I didn't hide despite the cold chill coursing through my body. It was Nova's space. Was it her and why?

Aggie yanked open the door, Harper and I tripped backward while the sound of the bell announced our arrival. It garnered immediate concern from both of them as we stumbled in like castaways, finally making our way home. I assured Aggie we were merely wet from a night out in the rain, lost in the woods. Aggie didn't question my story and disappeared to the back room, returning with clothes she found in a box. They were smelly and ugly but dry. Harper and I took turns changing in the bathroom.

I collapsed in an office chair in the backroom in my orange corduroy pants and cream sweater with yellow-striped sleeves. An ornate mirror leaning against the sidewall showcased my ridiculous ensemble. My smoky eye makeup ran into streams of dark color down my cheeks and my eyes glowed in a variety of hues. I was a mess, pulling up my hair it into pony and twisting the pieces into mock dreads. I had lost my bravado from the night before.

"What are you doing?" Harper asked with her face and nose all wrinkled upward.

I dropped the hair from my hands and spun around to Harper, standing in high-waisted jeans and a black-and-white checkered print shirt.

I pursed my lips. "Nothing," I said. Harper just stared at me with her brows arched high, then pulled up a chair at a folding table. Sawyer and Fitzly followed her lead, blocking out any room for Aggie.

I turned my chair toward her. "Aggie, can you run and get us some coffee?" She wasn't fond of the idea but finally agreed, noting on the way out that they never found Harper's bag. She'd caught on to the goose chase.

The bell-ringing upon her exit was our cue as I propelled myself forward, scraping the wheels of my chair along the floor. Harper and I began telling them our story, taking turns filling in the details. We spoke fast but whispered, worried about Aggie's return. Sawyer didn't sit still. He paced, chomping on gum, asking a million questions about Luca and the story she told. Fitzly was far more concerned with the shield. We didn't have all the answers, and the more we spoke, the angrier I became with myself. There was so much more I should've asked. We were frustrated and tired.

Fitzly fidgeted through a brown paper bag, taking breaks to sigh when he put his hand up and motioned for us to stop talking over one another.

He dumped out its contents.

"Nice bag," remarked Harper.

"I didn't have anything else. Next time, you can break into a library and maneuver around in the dark with a nasty farm maiden named Pepper. Now shut it," he said.

Harper closed her mouth and gave Fitzly the floor. He deserved it.

"I know you both have been through a lot by the looks of you." He tried hard not to giggle at me in my 1980s cartoon ensemble. "But I found some interesting stuff last night, other than a feisty ghost; thanks for that." His head tilted toward me with his one brow raised. I shrugged my shoulders and then requested he share what he found other than her. He shoved a piece of paper toward the middle of the table.

"This is the deed to the Hunting Valley. And guess who owns it?" He peered at all of us as if one of us might guess.

"Just tell us; we don't have a lot of time," I said sarcastically, but with a witty smile. I couldn't be mean to him.

"Mayor Quartano. He owns all of it. And that's not all. Guess who he bought it from?" He leaned back, crossing his arms tight across his grey hoodie and navy jacket that he likely retrieved from their car overnight.

He pushed the paper over to me. "James Anderson," he stated softly.

My heart sank. Images of my dad whirled in my head. It didn't make ...

"That has to be a mistake," I said and pulled the document closer, running my fingers over the words. There in black ink, it read:

James Anderson: Transferee
Rhodes Quartano: Transferor
Amount: $600,000.00
Date May 17, 1997

"Who's James Anderson?" asked Harper, leaning forward and resting her elbows onto her knees.

I held the aged, yellow paper in my hand, rubbing the raised edges of the notary stamp between my fingers. I thought back to all the debt and the struggle and wondered where the money went. Why did my mom never speak of the land or their business relationship with Quartano?

I responded hesitantly, "My father." Aggie saw the document and had already informed Fitzly. Harper and Sawyer stood speechless while I processed.

Fitzly paused then asked, "How much does Aggie know? She caught me reading the deed, and pushed for the truth on why we were there. I was vague with my responses, but she wasn't buying it. She's going to corner you today."

"She doesn't know anything, or at least I don't think so. But the timing of her arrival in the Creek has me second-guessing myself. I don't trust her," I confessed.

"I'm sorry," Fitzly said, "she caught on when I kept disappearing, and it sunk in when the bag never appeared. I told her Mr. Vincent must have already grabbed it."

I was proud of Fitzly even though I was stunned by the news. He followed through and handled Aggie for us. But he wasn't done. He rubbed the back of his neck and then pulled aside two more 8x11 documents. He slid them over to me.

"There were also city permit applications tucked into the same folder."

"I don't understand," I asked.

"It's a permit request for work on the Danwer Memorial Church that James, your dad, requested. But it was denied by the City Council and signed off on by the mayor," Fitzly said.

I combed over the permit, chewing on my upper lip.

Fitzly pointed to another sheet of paper. "The second permit was a request by a man named Santos Quartano, the same man from your father's blueprints. The denial paperwork, also signed by the mayor, is in the folder, but the full detailed request is missing. There's also a note." He proceeded to unfold a lined piece of notebook paper.

"Santos penned a letter to his older brother, Rhodes. By the sentiment in this letter, he was not happy with Rhodes' decision to decline either permit. And Abby, he mentions your dad in this letter. They knew each other and together had plans for that land, which never came to fruition. Three months after these denials, your dad sold the property to the mayor."

I fell back into my chair. "And a month after that, my dad died in a horrific car crash just past the outskirts of town." The words choked my throat.

No one spoke, but then a familiar but fragile voice broke the silence. "Abby, what did your friend just say?"

The voice did not belong to one of my friends. Why was she here?

"Mom?" I stretched up to see the doorway that my mom walked through. Kate was a few steps behind her. Their costumes had been replaced with oversized sweatshirts and leggings.

"What are you doing here? You should be resting in the hospital," I said.

My mom stood pale and fragile next to Kate. The mascara on Kate's fake lashes bled onto the skin around her bloodshot eyes. "The spare key is missing under Bob. I have to grab your other one, and then I'm taking your mom back home." Kate's one eyebrow rose at the sight of my outfit.

"Don't ask," I begged.

Kate didn't and strolled into the back office, loudly fumbling through the desk drawers while my mom took a quick look at my new friends before turning her attention back to me.

"I was discharged from the ER. There wasn't much they could do," she said.

"What do you mean? What's wrong with you?" Every awful thought imaginable traveled through my mind.

"Abby, I'm okay. Can we talk about it later, though?"

I didn't want to; I wanted to know now, but with a room full of strangers, I agreed only for the sake of her privacy. My stomach churned over the unthinkable. My awkward movements increased as I fought through terrible thoughts. I was hoping she would walk over to me, but instead, she walked to Fitzly.

"Fitzgerald Bickley, is that you?" she said.

The muscles in Fitzly's face dropped. His mouth opened slightly, but nothing came out. My mom lifted his chin gently with her hand before turning to Harper.

"Harper … baby girl Harper. I don't believe it. How is this possible?" My mom looked at me as stunned as I was of her.

"How do you know Fitzly and Harper?" I asked.

"I was going to ask you the same question," she said.

My mom sat down opposite of Fitzly and next to me. The sight of them overwhelmed her as her hands trembled. She rubbed her forehead, eventually moving down the right side of her face and down toward her chin, her eyes showing the same level of concern and confusion as mine.

"I'm not sure why or how you are all here," my mom said. She stopped, but I motioned for her to continue. We were all fidgeting.

"James, my late husband, was friends with both of your dads. They met on a job site in Pennsylvania in the early 1990s. They were hired as subcontractors to build new schools. James and your fathers traveled out there every week for work and quickly became buddies. Harper, you were born first, then Fitzly, and then Abby. You were all at our home together, when you were babies."

Harper stepped forward and cleared her throat.

"You know my dad? My real dad and my mom?" She fixated on my mom's eyes, trying to read the validity of my mom's statements, but it was intrusive.

My mom posture slumped forward, "I'm sorry. What do you mean 'real dad'?" she asked.

I stepped over and placed my hand tightly on Harper's arms, whose fists were clenched and whose face was turning from pink to red.

"Don't touch me!" she yelled back, breaking away and moving closer to my mom.

"Harper, stop!" I demanded, but she didn't.

"How dare you sit there and talk about my parents. What about him? Do you remember Sawyer?" She pointed over towards him, leaning against the wall with his head low, chewing and popping gum. My mom looked over at Sawyer but quickly shook her head no.

"I only knew about you. We lost touch after the accidents. I never knew about a boy," she said, but her voice shook, pleading with Harper to listen.

"What accidents? Sawyer is older than I am. You would remember him, too. You're a liar!" Manic, Harper fired off questions and accusations.

My mom sat distraught over her comments but couldn't summon a response.

"Why don't you take a break, Harper?" said Sawyer. "Maybe go outside and get some air."

Harper moved past all of them, even lightly shoving Sawyer out of the doorway. I turned my attention back to my mom, sitting bewildered by the strange events of this morning. I offered some backstory to bring some clarity to Harper's manic emotional state.

"Mom, Harper and her older brother Sawyer spent most of their life in the foster system. Did you really know her biological parents?"

"Yes, her father's name was Aaron, and he was engaged to Harper's mom, Molly. I knew they struggled financially, but when Aaron died, Molly fell apart, and we lost touch. She must have given up Harper after. They both adored her. I don't know anything else," she said, fighting back plenty of tears that quickly evolved into a steady stream.

"Molly would have never given her up unless she felt helpless. We couldn't reach her, though. She just disappeared, and I'm sorry," she said, looking over at Sawyer. "I never knew she had another child."

Harper didn't mention her dad passing. I worried they didn't know and wondered if the emotionless Sawyer was merely protecting Harper again. Still, it wasn't adding up.

"And your dad," my mom said, looking over at Fitzly." You're the image of him, and I guess you have the same loving, witty personality he had, with a laugh that could light up a room."

"I miss him," he said.

"Miss him? Where is he?" I demanded. We had all spent time together, trying to figure out our futures. He never offered any information about his past, outside of anything supernatural.

"He died when I was six," he said.

"Wait, you mean to tell me we all lost our dads, who were once friends and colleagues? Why didn't you say something earlier? How did your dad die?" I should've been more empathic given the nature of the discussion. Still, I was mad at myself for not asking more personal questions sooner, and I couldn't understand why he never thought to mention it.

"A boating accident; they hit a column under a bridge, and I guess my dad was tossed into the water. My mom said he died on impact. I don't like talking about it," Fitzly responded.

"And your dad?" I asked, looking at a nervous Sawyer. It was callous, but I had to question him. My mom answered when Sawyer chose not to.

"He fell off a set of scaffolding at a construction site and was gone before he made it to the hospital. And that wasn't the worst of it. They had another friend, Oliver. He died too, a couple of years later."

Fitzly straightened up, "Wait, Oliver, as in Oliver Owens? Chloe's dad?"

My stomach churned.

"I don't know Chloe, but his wife's name was Nora," my mom said as she slumped back into the chair and rubbed her temples. "You know Nora, too?" her voice wavered.

I pressed my lips together and nodded. Tears welled in my eyes. We were all family, and through her game of puzzle pieces and papers, Luca had guided my journey to Connecticut. Of all the questions we sought answers for, there was now one more. Who murdered our dads?

I dropped back and scrunched myself up into a chair, recalling the pictures hanging in my closet. There was one with the dads and the kids. It was them, a tiny Fitzly, a bold, little Harper, and me, with no sign of Sawyer. I filled my cheeks up with air and slowly blew it out, observing Sawyer standing in the doorway with his legs crossed at the ankles and his arms crossed at the chest. Kate appeared in the office doorway with her key ring in hand, and her mouth slightly opened but silent. I wanted to throw up.

My mom pressed on, albeit in a very polite manner. "Fitzly, I overheard you when I came in. You spoke about the land that my husband sold. Can you tell me more?"

Fitzly told my mom the same information he had shared with us just moments earlier. His hands trembled, and his eyes strained at my mom's very sight and the details she shared about his dad.

"I never knew we owned any land. And we certainly never received money from the sale of it," she said, but she struggled to find the right words when she spoke. Her expression was as flat as her tone.

Kate walked over and kneeled down next to her and placed her hand on my mom's back. Her dull eyes bounced between my mom and me as she viewed the documents one by one. Lauren turned to her sister for comfort Kate couldn't offer.

"Could this be real? Could James have owned and sold something without telling me? And why would he hide the money? I swear I never saw a dime," my mom said and sobbed, first turning toward Kate than to me. She was hoping someone could shed more light. But we couldn't. We had been living in the dark for years.

"I believe you, Mom," I said, and I did. I witnessed our struggle growing up without him. That money would have made the life we were left with more comfortable. She didn't have it. And if he did, he would have left it for us. Tears flowed in streams down her pale face.

Fitzly chewed at his lips. He wanted to cry too, but he wiped any hint of water before it fell from his eyes. He craved more for more information about his dad but treaded lightly with his questions.

"There was another permit request, by Santos Quartano. Did my dad know him?" Fitzly asked.

Mom gulped down the rock in her throat and wiped at the tears dripping from her nose. "Absolutely; he was the architect for the construction company they worked for in Pennsylvania. They had plans to start their own company one day, together," she said.

My mom continued with details on everything, from their grand ideas for work to their thoughts about family and kids. But she couldn't remember any conversations that dealt with the Valley.

My mom took a deep breath and stretched upward. "I want to know how you all met, and how you ended up here in the Creek. But, honestly, I'm not feeling well. This is a lot, but maybe you all could come over soon to catch up?" She patiently waited for one of us to respond.

"Sure, Mrs. Anderson," said Fitzly and then glancing over at me, he said, "I'm going to head up front and look for Aggie. Coffee sounds really appealing right now." Fitzly stuck his hands in his jean pockets, dropped his head, and ambled to the front.

"I should check on Harper while you two talk," remarked Sawyer, absent of any facial expression. He exited quickly.

We had our privacy and space, which we wasted being silent. I couldn't form a sentence; I struggled to think of individual words. The English language was a literary puzzle I couldn't piece together.

The sound of our front doorbell ringing broke the awkward moment. It was likely Aggie returning, but I used it as an excuse to walk away. I needed a few seconds away from everyone. I wasn't ready to process any more details. I was numb.

CHAPTER 30

REVELATION

"Let me check that out; I'll be right back," I said, touching my mom's forearm, reassuring her of my return.

I wandered up front and saw Jack heading toward me with a steaming coffee mug in his hand.

"Hey, Abby," he said, "Aggie mentioned your mom was back here. Just checking in on her. She didn't tell me you were here?"

I was surprised to see Jack so early but I moved out of his way and allowed him through. She would be delighted to see him and based on the mutual hug that followed, I was right. I let the door close behind me. Kate soon followed and offered to take Harper for a walk after a heated discussion with Sawyer. The store and its heaviness were weighing on us all.

Aggie arrived a minute after Jack with cup holders of coffee. I grabbed one, dumping a handful of sugar packets into the liquid, blowing the hot steam away from my lips, and then sipped it slowly. It wasn't great, but my bloodstream graciously welcomed the flow of caffeine as it surged through my body. Sawyer chatted with Aggie behind me. I ignored them both. I wanted to run home.

Fitzly approached and rested his hand over mine on the register table. "I believe your mom," he offered, "I never thought though that someone might deliberately hurt my father. We're connected in so many paralyzing ways."

I appreciated his trust in her, "There is so much to decipher but where do we even begin?" I chose my words carefully. We were all fragile. Harper was bitter from a lifetime of parental abandonment, and Sawyer was curiously devoid of any reaction or emotions. I needed Fitzly to be my foundation right now.

He half-grinned and grabbed his own cup from the drink holder, gulping it down black. His face contorted, "bitter," he remarked.

"And hot! How's the burn?" I knocked into him, searching for anything playful to say.

"I'm fine, needed a jolt," he replied, though he stuck out his tongue and curved it in the air, trying to fan it from the scalding liquid. I let out a much-needed laugh while he tried speaking.

"What do you make of all this?" he gurgled.

I was okay with sharing what little I pieced together. I hushed my voice.

"Our dads must have found the shield in the Valley." I moved closer to him. Aggie and Sawyer were still near. "I don't know what they were planning or why the mayor has a piece, but he's the only one still alive. He hides the secrets. Maybe you can all stay at Kate's for a while until we figure this out. Let me talk to her."

Fitzly agreed and pinched my arm in a brotherly way, taking another gulp.

"It's numb now," he joked and then retreated outside to a bench.

Aggie joined Fitzly and Sawyer stepped over to me. He rubbed my arm, and commented on the sweater's course texture. I didn't want his small talk.

"You okay?" he asked.

"What do you think?" I was growing angrier. He had secrets too, and there was no time for a cat and mouse game I didn't want to play.

"You're mad, I can see it in your eyes." His brows drew close, and his face scrunched.

"At you, maybe," I said. The benches outside suddenly seemed like a much-needed vacation. I took two steps in that direction when he circled around me, with his back now to the front door. I didn't give him another chance to ask any more questions. It was he who needed to provide answers.

"Does Harper know her dad is dead?" I was specific with my choice of words.

His head fell forward, his eyes shifted up, "We were told that early on, but she never wanted to believe it, hopeful she would find them both."

"But you knew? Who are you?" I fixed my stare on him.

He inched closer, and I allowed it only to whisper under my breath as assertively as possible without making a scene.

"I have a picture in my closet with Fitzly, Harper and their parents. You're not in it. Why? Did they leave you behind with a sitter? And how do you know Aggie? Why do you know Aggie, but Harper doesn't?"

Sawyer erased the distance between us. The smell of cinnamon rolled off his lips onto mine.

"I have a right to know who you are," I demanded.

He stepped back, scratching the base of his neck. I tried to leave, but he stopped me. He started unbuttoning his shirt. I felt uncomfortable and embarrassed.

"Sawyer!" I said, reminding him of all the people hanging around, but he put his hand up and wouldn't let me finish my sentence. I nervously watched over my shoulder, praying my mom wouldn't walk out, and then shifted forward to view the front window, hoping no one would walk in. I couldn't comprehend why he had to do this shirtless.

He pulled the last button free. His black dress shirt lay partially open, revealing his smooth skin and a gold necklace with an amulet. I tried not to look and worked even harder not to blush. He hesitated at first and then lifted his left hand and pulled the shirt back. On his chest, there was a geometrically shaped tattoo with multiple overlapping circles arranged like a flower. I held my breath and placed my right hand on his skin, gently outlining the black and grey lines. An electric wave danced across my fingertips. I closed my eyes, recalling every moment with him since we'd met. Images of him clutching the black book with TC initials embedded in the leather, spun in a web of intricate flowers.

"The Travelers Creed," rolled off my tongue. He placed his hands over mine and pressed them deep into his skin.

This, I was not expecting. I buried my head into his chest, hesitating to look at him. Spirits of the dead, demons and witches surrounded me in this town full of secrets and deadly lies. He was sent here to protect us but my comfort was replaced with vulnerability. I already knew the answer to the question, but I needed to hear it from him.

I lifted my head, and with wide eyes, I muttered, "You're a traveler … does Harper …?"

He squeezed my wrist, resting on his chest as he spoke. He was assertive with his message. "No, and she can't. Not yet," he said.

"Why?" I asked, my legs wanting to buckle beneath me.

"I'm the only family she has. It will devastate her, and she won't be safe." His chilling words slipped darkness into my veins.

"Why wouldn't she be safe?"

"Evil beings smell desperation, and they feed off it. It gives them power. You're all Cerulean; as it is, you're already open. They'll pounce, take her soul when she is at her weakest and use it against us. It's happened before," he explained.

Images of Sawyer standing on the rocks as Harper and I descended into the tunnel last night and the words he spoke rang through my head.

"You *couldn't* walk through the tunnel?" I asked him.

"No, Luca wouldn't let me," he said, and his firm grip lessened and changed to a series of soft touches, lightly brushing my arms and sending waves of energy through my bones.

"Why didn't you just tell us?"

"It's not how this works. Humans struggle to understand anything outside of their day-to-day reality. You had to experience it, or your fear would have tricked you. I would've been the evil one," he said.

I squinted. "Evil?"

"Humans label ideas they don't understand as sinister, malevolent. The four of you had to be prepared slowly to build trust. You have to believe in something one hundred percent before you can genuinely fight for it," he went on.

I moved my hands down his chest to the area right above his pant line, my arms trembled uncontrollably.

He pleaded with me. "Abby, I know what you're thinking. While you didn't know *who* I was, my intentions are pure. I still feel."

His words did little to counter the betrayal swirling inside of me. I tuned out his voice and swallowed what truth I understood. My life had officially changed. I was no longer just Abby Anderson. I was a Cerulean tasked with fighting and surviving evil before my life would ever settle into normal. And … I was deceived by a boy I thought would mend my tattered heart. One day, he would leave, and I would be left broken again. My gut stopped me from kissing him the night before. My guard back up, I began pushing away. I longed for the loyalty he could no longer provide.

I closed his shirt, staggered around him, and waved him off.

Was this another horrible nightmare? Lightheaded, I steadied myself against the front doorframe, allowing the crisp air to enter my lungs and cool the wave of heat that followed my increased heart rate.

Fitzly and Aggie glanced over at me. Aggie stood, but Fitzly grabbed her hand and pulled her back to the bench. Tears welled in my eyes. With every minute that ticked away, I felt more powerless, confused, and angry. I was in the middle of my fourth deep breath when the door pushed open, knocking me to the side as the bell rang.

It was Jack.

Jack's ball cap was replaced with a winter beanie with a half-black skull patch on the front. He pulled it down close to his eyebrows. "Winter air is definitely settling in?" he said.

I kept the small talk going. I didn't want to alarm him as the world spun rapidly around me. I buried the hysteria into my core and sputtered out a few words. "You taking the day off?" I asked.

"I am." He stretched up and rocked back and forth on his feet. He fought back a tiny smile that he tried covering by playing with his goatee. I noticed him peering over my shoulder and toward a shadow that was entering from my right. It was Old Man Studdard dressed in a tracksuit that was way too young for his age. He didn't have his cane or the walking stick either.

"Good morning, Abby. Good morning, Jack. Everyone enjoy the party last night?"

We both nodded.

"How about you?" I asked.

Studdard hummed as he spoke, tapping his feet as if the music still bellowed out from the theater. "Best ever. I love when my expectations are far exceeded."

"Yeah, me too," offered Jack.

Sawyer stepped out from the doorway toward us and acknowledged the old man's presence with a slight hand wave. I stepped to the side to say goodbye to Jack.

"Make sure your mom gets enough rest," Jack expressed, leaning in toward me. "She needs to take care of herself and the baby."

The air drained from lungs. I braced myself on Jack's forearm, noticing Kate and Harper walking across the street. Jack glanced over to Kate then me.

"Oh my God, you didn't know. I thought Kate told you," he said, his hands covering his face. Then, he rotated for a quick escape. I took a few steps to follow him but let him leave. This was too much. I viewed Studdard over my shoulder.

He straightened up; his posture was suddenly tense and rigid. "A descendant baby," he said, directly to Sawyer.

I dropped my cup onto the pavement, hot coffee splashing onto my bare feet, "What did you say?"

Aggie jumped up, interrupting her conversation with Fitzly. I stumbled backward, losing my footing, but the old man approached, gently grabbing both of my hands. A hummingbird flew in and hovered over our palms. The slightest wind and the softest touch from its wings brushed against our skin before flying up and joining a group of other brightly colored hummingbirds.

"It's a charm," the old man responded, welcoming the birds that fluttered in.

"What?" I was weak and losing my balance.

He offered me assistance while Aggie interjected, "A charm is a group of hummingbirds," she remarked flatly.

"*Deliciae*, charms," I let out a nervous laugh, "*Viatroibus*, travelers," my voiced strained.

Sawyer, Aggie, and Old Man Studdard surrounded me, suddenly divulging their best-kept secrets. I begged the old man to say more with my eyes.

"Abby, I know Sawyer has already spoken to you, even though it wasn't his responsibility," he said and lowered his brow toward Sawyer. "We've been watching Haddie and Luca for centuries and are preparing for what's brewing."

I stood motionless and raised my head toward the red sky and dark black clouds that fell upon the Creek like a curtain. It engulfed the town. I gulped and swallowed. The old man placed his hand on my shoulder.

"There are a chosen few who can see what others cannot. Not everything is meant to be seen by everyone. Your shell is human, but your soul is Cerulean spirit, born from an angel, and you will learn how to use it because humanity and the heavens are counting on it."

Sawyer's hand touched the lower part of my back as I bent over, forcing down the coffee that was making its way up my throat.

My voice cracked, "What makes us Cerulean? Why?"

"Do you remember our conversation of the butterflies?"

I thought hard. I saw the words, but it took a minute to arrange them. It was coming together. The muscles in my face dropped. I spoke slowly.

"The mortal body is a shell that protects our soul. Our soul is forever." The world around me stopped. Everyone but the four of us was blurry and out of focus. Studdard continued.

"Your Cerulean soul is protecting you from what's below and in between, from up above."

I shook my head. This wasn't real. How could he speak so elegantly about a topic shrouded in so much ambiguity?

"It's hard for you to believe right now, but you will each embrace it. Luca and Haddie will go to war, and whoever wins will go to war with us," he said.

I winced, "I don't understand, just because we can see and hear what others can't doesn't make us warriors. I can't fight my own shadow let alone a demon?"

Studdard gave Sawyer approval to speak next. My head fell upon his shoulder. He gently twirled the strands of my hair around his fingers, "You have unique powers buried beneath your human skin you will learn how to use," Sawyer assured.

I nervously gasped, "What are they fighting over?"

Studdard swallowed hard and then spoke.

"Souls," he said. "Haddie snatches them after death and turns them into demons with blackened wings and charred bodies. Luca steals and transforms them long before humans take their last breath. Luca is initiating more into her growing coven, angering both Haddie and the devil himself. Haddie's armies of dark angels are much smaller because of it."

We all paused; then, Studdard went on.

"We knew what was coming but we never thought we would need Cerulean help until now. You, Harper, Fitzly, and Chloe have a bloodline that makes you more powerful than you know."

Sawyer braced my sides and then leaned in. "You specifically, *also* happen to be a descendant of Clare."

My eyes opened wide in disbelief. Was he joking? I clawed at my arms, covered my ears and closed my eyes. *I'm related to the witch that cursed Haddie, the demoness chasing us all?* Luca's words from the night before replayed over and over in my head, each one stabbing at my ribcage. I muttered a fear worse than I had imagined.

"My mom's baby is in danger?"

"Yes," Studdard firmly stated.

The words punched my gut. I folded over.

"Your sibling's body contains the blood needed for Haddie to break the curse. If she does, she will transform and join the First Hierarchy of Lady Demons, ruling by the Devils side with her sons. Together, they will seek to destroy all of their enemies on earth, in the heavens, and between. Luca needs her shield and her spells to protect herself, her coven, and the kingdom she has built.

A sensation of heat overwhelmed me, my voice cracked, "How are we going to help?"

Old Man Studdard paced but spoke with confidence, "There are more of you we must find. We'll teach you, and together we will defeat both Haddie and Luca. We need a full army to win or life as we all know it won't exist. But we have to get the shield back to Luca first."

I wished my soul to be free of the constraints this world had placed around me. I wanted out of the box of normalcy, and I longed to be proud of it. But this? I tried to straighten my thoughts.

"But, won't Luca use her shield against us?"

Studdard bit his lower lip. "Maybe; she has never been a threat to us before, and we don't understand all of her motives," Studdard paused,

"Luca doesn't want Haddie spilling your sibling's blood either. She recognizes that Haddie would become the most powerful demoness any of us have ever battled. Luca and her followers are a wicked force and can weaken Haddie's army in volume and strength. We get her shield back and let her and her coven fight Haddie first, while we prepare."

I closed my eyes. I now faced not one but two ungraspable battles for humanity, our souls, and the heavens. I braced myself against Sawyers frame than half-stepped away, letting go of his protection. Studdard pushed his right sleeve up and placed his palm in my hand, exposing a complicated yet beautiful tattoo with concentric circles on his forearm. It matched Sawyer's.

My mind raced with thoughts and memories, all twisted together until it came to a crashing halt. I glanced at Aggie. It was time for her to reveal herself too.

"You're one of them?"

She gave me the slightest nod, "Yes, we're *Charms*."

I dropped my face into my hands and then ambled to the curb's edge and fixated my stare west, over the buildings, deep into the trees that grew on the sacred land of a fierce coven. I survived the journey into and out of its grip. I was meant to. The other side was all around us. I was numb until Fitzly mumbled my name.

I turned my attention north toward the theater, following Fitzly's troubled gaze. I craned my neck to see around him. The boy with the shaggy black hair I saw yesterday was casually leaning against the wood fence that overlooked the falls. He chewed on a silver medallion that hung from a chain around his neck. He watched us all.

Suddenly, a small group with black feather crowns appeared on the opposite side of the street, turning onto Main from Oak. The women wore long, dark cloaks that opened in the front outlining their exposed, tattooed, and slender frames. The skulls that hung in Luca's cabin now sat on the heads of men. Feather capelets draped over their bare chests and tight black shorts. Exposed skin showcased intricate inked designs that wrapped around their pale bodies like vines.

They ambled, chanting, in front of our view and toward the boy still leaning on the wooden fence. The female headdresses of various lengths of thick black feathers dripped blood onto the pavement.

Sawyer approached, placing his hand on my lower back, and whispered. "The witches rip the feathers from every fallen demon they defeat and display them on their bodies. You can tell their hierarchy by the lavishness and fullness of each crown or capelet.

Multiple bolts of lightning rocketed across the sky. One of the women turned back, her movement stopping the others in their tracks. Aggie stepped forward and turned her attention towards the young man with long hair and the lady with the scarf who suddenly appeared. They walked towards the coven. The little girl in the woods of the Valley skipped up from the path overlooking the falls. She stopped in the middle of the street giggling, singing a soft but eerie nursery rhyme, and then turned and ran back down the alley. The man with the long hair darted toward the group, crying out, "Allison!"

My heart stopped.

Explosive thunder roared, and dark clouds rolled violently into town. The woman in the scarf fell to her knees and sobbed into her hands.

The coven of witches disappeared into a fog down the alley before the man could reach them. He desperately clawed at the thick mist, grabbing at nothingness, and then turned to the boy. They shared a deadly stare with one another but never spoke a word. I watched on as the boy followed the faint laughter of Luca and Allison. The man stood distraught and defeated with his hands clenched at his sides before returning to his weeping wife in the street. My eyes burned.

In the store, my mom sat, carrying my sibling, both of whom I would have to protect. In front of me, the witches watched and waited for my help while angels soared in on the wings of tiny, magical birds. My father's soul stuck somewhere in the madness. I wanted to embrace the beauty, the hope, the colors of our future, but I was scarred and broken from life.

I glanced toward Old Man Studdard. His face dropped in concern. "What is it?" I asked.

"You're irises, they're turning a deep shade of burgundy."

I remembered Luca's last remark about them. I wasn't just Cerulean; I was a descendent of a witch, and perhaps the little girl ghost who haunts the Valley. They all needed me. Like the Emerald Swallowtail, I had two sides. I stood for the first time without trembling, witness to a world so many can't see. I always believed the veil that separated us from evil, from the dead, would be a blurry threshold, like barricade tape with a warning. But it wasn't, when Allison Creek awakes this morning, they will mingle and dance, unknowingly with the souls of the departed, the good, the evil, and the wicked.

Luca's voice traveled in on an aggressive burst of wind. My hair whisked across my face sending a harsh chill down my spine. "Abby, your roots are starving."

My soul might be forever, but it would adapt and evolve to survive. The two opposing sides of my lineage fought for control of my spirit. My ancestry was not equally divided. One side would always be stronger than the other.

Sawyer stepped next to me and clutched my hand tightly at his side, "Abby, once the wing of an angel is damaged or broken, it's very, very difficult to mend."

Rain fell from the sky and cascaded down my face. The white noise of the steady shower masked the madness circling me. Cool water and warm black sand collected in my palms. I blinked, "Then I hope that whatever changes lie ahead will be for the better."

Made in the USA
Columbia, SC
04 October 2020